Colin Falconer is the author of thirteen novels, which have been translated into sixteen languages around the world. A former journalist, he was born in London and now lives in Western Australia.

ALSO BY COLIN FALCONER

ANASTASIA

COLIN FALCONER

BANTAM BOOKS
SYDNEY • AUCKLAND • TORONTO • NEW YORK • LONDON

ANASTASIA
A BANTAM BOOK

First published in Australia and New Zealand in 2003 by Bantam
This edition published in 2004

National Library of Australia
Cataloguing-in-Publication Entry

Falconer, Colin, 1953– .
Anastasia.

ISBN 1 86325 467 6.

1. Anastasiia Nikolaevna, Grand Duchess, daughter of Nicholas II, Emperor of Russia, 1901–1918 – Fiction. 2. Nineteen twenties – Fiction. I. Title.

A823.3

Transworld Publishers,
a division of Random House Australia Pty Ltd
20 Alfred Street, Milsons Point, NSW 2061
http://www.randomhouse.com.au

Random House New Zealand Limited
18 Poland Road, Glenfield, Auckland

Transworld Publishers,
a division of The Random House Group Ltd
61-63 Uxbridge Road, London W5 5SA

Random House Inc
1745 Broadway, New York, New York 10036

Cover and internal design: Ignition Brands
Cover photographs: Getty Images
Typeset by Midland Typesetters, Maryborough, Victoria
Printed and bound by Griffin Press, Netley, South Australia

10 9 8 7 6 5 4 3 2 1

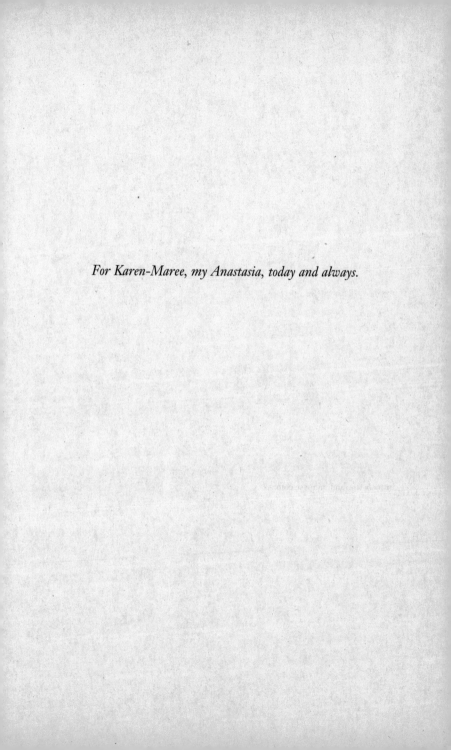

For Karen-Maree, my Anastasia, today and always.

Acknowledgements

With heartfelt thanks to Tim Curnow, who unwittingly set this book in motion, and is the best agent and friend a guy could have. Thank you to Kim Swivel, my wonderful editor, for her enthusiasm and incisive work on the manuscript. Thanks to Elana McCauley, Zoe Walton and Emma Rusher at Random House, and to Fiona Henderson for her unswerving support for my work.

PART ONE

THE HOUSE OF SPECIAL PURPOSE

Ekaterinburg, Russia, April 1918

'Anastasia? Oh, she had her virtues, I'll give her that. God had given her a gift for languages and a good ear, and what did she do with it? She used it to make fun of others. There was a Duke who would sometimes join us on board the royal yacht Standart, *the poor man had a lisp and how many times I heard her mocking him behind his back.'*

The train carrying the past and the future of the Russian Empire moved slowly across a landscape of drab pines. The Urals in the spring, patches of ice that glistened in the sun, a vast and dismal emptiness; a few horses grazing, a smudge of smoke drifting from the chimney of a fall-down cottage.

Nothing remarkable about this train for the casual observer: no bunting, no wreath across the engine, the carriages not especially luxurious. The trail of white steam hung in the air, heavy and still. After it had dissipated, there was nothing to take its place.

Anastasia, dozing at the window, blinked open her eyes as the train began to slow. It rounded a bend and she saw another sad little town, a desert of cold blue sky and dark pine forest. 'Well, here we are,' she said. 'Beetroot Country.'

Their nanny, Sophie Karlova, shot her a hard look, as if Anastasia had broken wind at some boring ceremony – a feat she had managed more than once. No-one else took any notice. Jemmy hopped on her lap and she petted him. Jemmy was Tatiana's, but he had attached himself to Anastasia as a dog will to anyone who pays it endless attention and feeds it a limitless supply of sweets.

Her relief that the endless journey was over gave way to a niggle of fear. She didn't understand the politics, though her father had once tried to explain it to her. All she knew was that she was never going to dance with the handsome officers on the *Standart* ever again, and that every day, every mile, took her further away from Tsarskoe Selo, the only home she had known.

'You mustn't say things like that,' Sophie said.

'Why not? No-one's going to hear me.'

'It will only make it worse for us.'

'How can it get worse?'

She looked out of the window. The station was crowded with Revolutionary guards, peasants and factory workers in Bolshevik uniforms, so puffed up with their own importance yet none of them looked like they owned a razor. She was still not accustomed to seeing such pompous looks on the faces of men who couldn't write their own names. They tried to appear unimpressed with their royal captives while they jostled each other for a place in the front row.

'We should be all right for potatoes,' Anastasia announced to the others.

Her three older sisters ignored her. Even though she was almost seventeen they treated her like a child. 'Because you behave like one,' Sophie liked to tell her.

Jemmy was nuzzling her leg. She reached into a pocket and found a small piece of chocolate and felt his eager wet tongue lick it out of her fingers. She held it down by her knee so that no-one could see her, but Tatiana's quick grey eyes were on her instantly.

'You have chocolate?' she said.

'It's for Jemmy.'

'Oh, you little minx.'

There had been no treats of any kind since they left Tobolsk and they were all hungry. Anastasia felt her cheeks grow hot with shame.

'Where did you get it, Stushi?'

'It's mine.'

Anastasia stared in awe as a fat teardrop rolled down her sister's cheek. She had never seen Tatiana cry, not ever. Olga put a hand on Tatiana's arm. 'Oh, leave it, Tati. It doesn't matter,' she said, but then gave Anastasia a look of such reproach that she had to look away. She began to plot her redemption in the usual way: she would make them forgive her by making them all laugh.

The train stopped with a hiss of steam, and one of the Bolsheviks climbed aboard the carriage carrying a rifle, bulky in a thick woollen coat and tall hat. All the sisters sat a little straighter, and Anastasia sensed their fear.

'Look at him,' she said to Tatiana, in a voice loud enough for him to hear, 'his forehead's so big, it must be like living under a balcony.'

The man stared at her. He was huge, and his coat smelled like a goat that had stood too long in the rain. A face like a rotten potato, and huge eyes, black and malevolent, that were supposed to scare her to silence.

'Where are we?' she said to him.

'That is of no c-c-concern of yours, c-c-comrade.'

Anastasia returned her attention to the small black dog on her lap. 'Don't be f-f-frightened, Jemmy, I won't let the b-b-bad man hurt you.'

Olga and Tatiana gave her a look. Still the proper and demure young princesses even now. Well, Anastasia was having none of it. The man was plainly a clod and she wouldn't let him bully her.

She knew he wouldn't hurt her. Revolution or not, she was still a princess and he was just a country turnip answerable to a people's committee or whatever nonsense it was they talked about.

'What is going to happen?' Marie whispered to Tatiana.

'We are going to see Mother and Father very soon,' Tatiana said, and stroked her sister's hair.

'They'll probably make us dig potatoes,' Anastasia said, and Marie turned pale.

'Hush, Stushi!' Tatiana said.

'Or clean lavatories,' she added, and was delighted with Marie's reaction.

Another man stepped aboard, strutting like he was a colonel in the Household Guard. He wore a tall astrakhan hat, his jacket cuffs were frayed and there was mud on his boots. 'I am Comrade Sokolov, General Secretary of the Ekaterinburg Workers Committee. You are all prisoners of the Ekaterinburg Soviet. You will now disembark the train and follow orders.'

This man's eyes did frighten her. They had no luminescence, were as dull as a fish that had lain for several hours in a fisherman's basket. A lot of them were like that, she had noticed. The only time their faces came to life was when they spoke about their beloved Revolution and their economic theories and Marxist propaganda. They were inspired only by their own banalities.

'Where are we?' Tatiana asked.

'Potatoesburg,' Anastasia said.

'It does not matter where we are,' Sokolov said. 'We are

a long way from the White Palace. Is that answer enough for you?'

'He doesn't know,' Anastasia said, in a deliberately loud whisper. 'He can't read the station sign.'

'I read well enough to know what Comrade Marx would have done with the likes of you.'

The way he said it, he might as well have dashed a glass of cold water in their faces. He meant what he said, no doubt of it.

Anastasia eventually poked out her tongue at him but he had already turned around and was gone.

Sophie put a gloved hand to her mouth. 'You little fool!'

I don't care, she thought. Tomorrow these peasants can shoot me if they want. But they won't see me cry.

Soldiers in drab brown uniforms stared at them as they got off the train. Once she would have had the captain of the Guard box the ears of anyone who looked at her like that. There was no pity there, only the rough and brutal faces of men who had spent all their lives in potato fields and in factories.

Anastasia set Jemmy down and let him scamper around. A real spring day, frost on the ground, a sky of palest blue, a cold wind burning her cheeks. There was no platform and there were icy puddles everywhere, the frosty ground turning slowly to mud.

She watched the men climb down from the other carriage: Gilliard, their tutor, shaking with fright; then Klementy Nagorny, the sailor assigned as bodyguard to her baby brother Alexei, carrying the boy in his arms. The great Czarevitch Alexei, heir to all Russia; even getting out of bed threatened his life. He had suffered from birth from something the doctors called haemophilia, a deceptively benign word that did not even begin to define the boundaries of his suffering.

He looked so pale, like a large porcelain doll in Klementy's arms. He held them all in his thrall, this boy, all of them enraptured with his sickness and his gender and his sweetness. Hard not to hate him.

'At least it's fine today,' Anastasia said, 'there're no raindrops to bruise Baby and make him bleed.'

Olga shook her head, a gesture of despair.

Their suitcases were unloaded from the train and deliberately hurled into the nearest icy puddle. When it was done

Sokolov pointed to them and said, 'The prisoners will carry their own luggage.'

They all stared at him as if he had spoken to them in a foreign language.

'We have to do what?' Olga said.

The soldier with the rifle stepped forward. 'You will c-c-carry your own s-s-suitcases.'

'I never c-c-carry my own anything, c-c-comrade,' Anastasia said.

The look he gave her was poisonous. Sophie gaped at her. Am I brave or just boundlessly stupid? Anastasia wondered. Even when she was terrified, as she was now, she could not, would not, back down and keep quiet. Her mother had once said to her that even if someone cut out her tongue she'd grow another one, like a spider growing more legs.

'There are no more servants in the new Russia,' Sokolov said. 'If you don't carry your own cases, we will leave them here in the mud.'

He marched away, his hands behind his back. Anastasia mimicked him, exaggerating his tiny, self-important movements so that even the soldiers sniggered. Marie closed her eyes and whispered a prayer to the saints to save her little sister from a terrible fate at the hands of these brutes.

Anastasia finished her pantomime. When she turned around, she saw Olga walk to the pile of luggage, pick up two of the heaviest cases and start to heft them through the puddles. Tatiana and Marie followed her lead.

Jemmy was running in circles now, barking at the soldiers. Anastasia scooped him up in one hand, and with the other she picked up a suitcase and started to drag it through the freezing slush.

When she reached the gate she heard a commotion behind her. Some soldiers had surrounded Sophie and Gilliard to prevent them leaving. Sophie held an embroidered handkerchief to her eyes, and she was crying, with shame or relief or distress, impossible to know.

'I cannot come with you,' she shouted. 'These men say they are sending us back to Saint Petersburg.'

The older sisters, of course, dissolved into tears at this. They ran back and hugged Sophie, weeping and saying nothing much that was sensible, as far as Anastasia could tell. Gilliard watched and bit his lip.

Then it was Anastasia's turn.

Sophie held her while she said goodbye. Anastasia kept her arms rigid at her sides.

'Please be careful,' Sophie whispered, dabbing at her eyes with the perfumed handkerchief. 'You must promise to be good for me.'

Well, what is the use? Anastasia thought. Sophie was the best friend they had ever had and now she was abandoning them, too. She took a step back. Just go, she thought. Like all the others. It was as if there was a stone in her throat.

She saw Tatiana's accusing stare. Well, I'm sorry, I can't be like you and weep over everything.

She trudged through the mud outside the station to the waiting cars, under the gaze of the guards. Jemmy trotted beside her. The suitcase she had with her was heavy and several times she dropped it in the mud. One of the men laughed. She felt her cheeks burning with anger.

'Where are you taking us?' she shouted at them.

This made the soldiers laugh all the more. Then Sokolov called to one of the drivers: 'The House of Special Purpose.' She realised that was where they were going and she wondered what that special purpose might be.

'I remember every sunset on the Standart *the captain would fire the cannon in royal salute. We all stood and watched, such a fine sight, with the sun sinking over the sea, but little Anastasia would spoil it all, she would run around the deck with her fingers in her ears, her eyes rolling in her head, making out they were firing the cannon at her. And her father would think her comical!'*

They were herded into the back of a covered army truck. Anastasia found a tear in the tarpaulin and peered through it to see what was going on outside. They drove through a large square, and she had a brief glimpse of an imposing cathedral.

The truck rumbled down through the gears. It was with her face pressed against the tarpaulin she first saw the house. It had two storeys, and was built of stone, a palace in a backwoods such as this. She could not see the lower part of the house because a timber palisade had been built right the way around. Two Red Guards hurried to unlock the wooden gates and then their truck lurched through into the courtyard.

The soldier with the stutter threw back the canvas and let down the backboard. He held his rifle at port as if he was expecting trouble from four unarmed girls and a sailor holding a crippled thirteen-year-old boy. Another hero of the Revolution.

'Out,' he said.

Anastasia stared at him. 'Do we still have to c-c-carry our c-c-cases?'

'Don't make trouble,' Olga hissed at her, as if the daughters of the Czar Nicholas could somehow avoid it.

'Perhaps we are going to meet Mother and Father,' Tatiana said, and that lifted their spirits.

They followed the guards inside, Klementy leading the way with Alexei, the rest of them hefting the cases up the stairs. Like common servants.

A door was thrown open and over the heads of her sisters Anastasia saw her mother and father.

Oh.

They had grown so old. Alexandra, pale and wasted in her wheelchair, and Nicholas, beside her, handsome yet somehow faded, as if he had stepped out of an ancient photograph. How bowed Mama looked now, Anastasia thought. And Papa, so much grey in his beard and in his hair. Wrinkles criss-crossed his skin in a spider web. They were standing with their backs to a casement window, but the glass had been painted over, making the room gloomy even at this time of the afternoon. The opaque glass was the colour of milk.

Anastasia looked around. How pathetic we all must look.

But then Papa's face split into a grin of absolute delight and that transformed everything. Olga and Tatiana and Marie rushed towards him, while Klementy went to Mama, Baby in his arms. The Czarina cried and held out her arms, still in her wheelchair. It was hard for her to stand on those arthritic knees these days.

Her father embraced them all, great bear hugs that made even the sturdy Olga squeal. Anastasia buried her face against the rough wool of his uniform jacket, listened to her mother's delighted cries, and finally she allowed herself to weep also, into the folds of his tunic where no-one could see her. Everything would be all right now.

The house, Nicholas told them later, belonged to a retired engineer and industrialist called Nikolai Ipatiev. It was a mansion compared to what they had expected. There was hot running water and electric light, for Ipatiev had been a man of some means. There were even indoor lavatories.

'I didn't know anyone in Beetroot Country knew what a lavatory was,' Anastasia said, so that the guards could hear her.

The house had been built in the Russian Gothic style; the doorways and windows decorated with arches and scrollwork. But although the house was comfortable enough, there was no attempt to imitate Ipatiev's pre-Revolutionary kitchen. Their supper that night was black bread and tea, served in a dining room with no windows and smelling strongly of mould. But it might as well have been a banquet in the Alexander Palace; they were all talking and laughing at once, happy and excited to at last be together again. Two months since they had seen each other; two months since Mama and Papa had been forced to travel ahead without Baby, not knowing if they would all see each other again. This might be yet another, more distant prison, but at least they were together again.

There were not enough beds that first night and Anastasia and her sisters instead threw cloaks and cushions on the wooden floorboards. Alexei snuggled up to Mama in her bed.

But none of them slept. Alexei was constantly crying out in pain from his swollen knee. Anastasia heard Mama murmuring to him, trying to gentle him. Her doctor, Botkin, slept in an adjoining room, and he came in several times; Anastasia heard him pleading with the guards in the corridor outside for cold compresses. They kept saying nothing could be done. They didn't care, they wanted him to suffer.

The dining room would have been grand once; the carved chairs were inlaid with latticework, there were gilt mirrors around the walls, and a filigree chandelier hung from the ceiling. Neglect had overtaken it; there was a thin film of dust on every flat surface, and the framed pictures of complete strangers on the mantel above the hearth only added a deeper sense of melancholy. She guessed Ipatiev had been forced to leave in such a hurry there had been no time to salvage personal treasures.

The room's formality was at odds with the poor fare provided for their breakfast; there was no tablecloth and though a few tarnished silver spoons had been turned out, they were hardly of use to them, for once again the meal consisted of an urn of black tea and stale black bread. One of the soldiers brought soup left over from the guardroom, but Olga had seen him spit in it on his way up the stairs and none of them would touch it.

Anastasia chewed at a piece of hard bread, her eyes on her father. He was staring at the table, his face dark with anger. He was a mild man and it was rare to see a display of temper from him; such occasions merited lowered eyes and hushed voices.

Finally, Papa got to his feet and addressed the guard sitting in the corner of the room: 'Tell Avdeyev I want to see him.'

The man shuffled his feet and stared sullenly at the floor. Nicholas advanced on him. 'Now!'

Perhaps it was because Comrade Romanov was once the Czar; perhaps it was the shock of seeing their mild prisoner in such a rage: the guard turned and retreated down the stairs to find their warden.

This was the first time Anastasia and her siblings had seen Avdeyev. He marched into the room with his chest puffed out, as arrogant and pot-bellied as a Prussian ambassador. It was plain that he had been woken from a drunken sleep, for he smelled strongly of sweat and vodka. Some of last night's supper had dried in tiny, oily specks on the front of his uniform. Father said he had been foreman at the local smelt works once; now he was foreman of the Czar and Czarina of Russia and the responsibility had quite gone to his head.

'What is it, Citizen Romanov?'

'Are you trying to starve us to death?'

Avdeyev threw a contemptuous look at the table. 'This is what ordinary people had to eat while you were gorging yourselves on sturgeon roe.'

Stupid little man, Anastasia thought. Caviar was reserved especially for banquets. If he had dined with us at Tsarskoe Selo he would have been bitterly disappointed. But Papa let it pass.

Instead he said: 'You mean there are no chickens and cows in the Urals? Even the humblest farmer has a little milk and some fresh eggs, surely?'

'You are not allowed eggs or milk.'

'By whose order?'

Avdeyev chewed viciously on his lower lip. 'To hell with you!' he said and stormed out of the room.

Papa glowered after him. Mama reached across the table and took his hand. She patted it gently. 'It will be all right, Nicki.'

'I don't understand what we have done to deserve this.'

'He is just a stupid little man.'

'There are many stupid little men just like him, and our lives are in their hands.'

Last night's atmosphere of celebration had quite evaporated. Anastasia stared at Marie across the table; her eyes were filling with tears.

'It will be all right,' Papa said to her. He tore at a piece of black bread and washed it down with a gulp of tea. The clock on the mantel chimed the hour. Ten o'clock. A long day stretched ahead.

'Oh, Anastasia! Olga and Tatiana, now, they were so serene, so responsible. Tall and stately, they would have made fine princesses. And Marie, a gentle and happy child, she was always smiling. And then there was Anastasia. What a wicked little child. And so unlike her sisters! She was always a little dumpy but she went completely to fat in her teenage years. And such an embarrassment to the rest of us!'

In the days that followed they were expertly tortured by way of boredom.

As Nicholas had told them, the house had once belonged to a businessman called Nikolai Ipatiev. Prior to the Czar's arrival, the local Bolshevik Workers Committee had given him twenty-four hours to leave and then commandeered the house for their own designs, renaming it, using the dense yet sinister vocabulary that had become their hallmark, the 'House of Special Purpose'.

The family were confined to the upper floor, the guard-room directly below. Nicholas and his wife had been given the front corner bedroom; there were two beds, a couch, a bookcase, and a single armoire to contain the wardrobes of the richest Emperor and Empress in the world.

After that first night on the floor, camp beds were brought in and Anastasia and her sisters were given a room adjoining their parents, which they shared with Alexei. Alexandra's maid, Anna Demidova, was given a small room towards the back of the house, Doctor Botkin the salon, while a butler, Alexei Krupp, and a cook by the name of Kharitonov slept on cots in the hallway. There were several guards present at all times.

The overcrowding bothered them less than that there was simply nothing to do. They rose each morning around nine o'clock, and at ten they shared their breakfast, which never varied: black bread and unsweetened black tea. They said their prayers and then Alexandra would read from the Gospels. Afterwards they would be permitted half an hour to walk in the garden and then they would be sent back inside to amuse themselves with cards or to read until lunch, which was at one o'clock. They might be allowed another half an hour in the sunshine during the afternoon. Dinner was at five, tea at seven. Then Nicholas would read to them, again from the Bible; his favourite passages were from the Book of Job. They would have a light supper at nine, and then retire.

Each day followed this same exasperating routine.

Two days after the children arrived, they had the last snow of winter, but summer followed quickly without the pleasant whispers of spring. One afternoon a thunderstorm sent lightning arcing across the sky, rain quickly filled the gutters and fell in sheets from the eaves. The next day the air was like warm treacle, and within a week an oppressive heat settled on the town.

In Siberia you baked or you froze.

The stone house heated quickly and, since Avdeyev would not allow a window to be opened, the rooms became unbearably hot. The smells coming from the kitchen, where Kharitonov had decided to bake their own bread, hung in the air, and the extra heat from the oven added further to their discomfort. They each longed for the brief respite they were allowed in the garden, though even there it was uncomfortably hot, and instead of exercising, Anastasia and her sisters sat in the shade of the bushes, drained of energy and spirit.

Nicholas tried to overturn Avdeyev's decree about the windows. Once one of the most powerful men in the world, he now had to campaign for over two weeks to open a window in his own bedroom. Finally, six cadres from the local soviet presented themselves at the house one morning to inspect the room and make a decision on which window might be opened. Apparently these men were not able to make this momentous decision alone, and in the ensuing days more officials came, singly or in pairs, to silently examine the bedroom, studying the windows as if they were a curious architectural puzzle.

Finally, three weeks into June, two soldiers entered unannounced and removed one of the windows. The whole family crowded around, breathing in the fresh air. The slightest zephyr was greeted with the exclamations due the arrival of a visiting prince.

Once her father had commanded armies of a million men but Anastasia wondered if he had ever had a victory as sweet as this.

The lavatory was down the hall.

An armed soldier sat outside with a rifle across his knees. It was the soldier from the train, the one Anastasia had taunted because of his stutter. He had grown a boil on the end of his nose since the last time she had seen him and it was difficult not to stare at it, to wonder when this purulent and purple growth would burst. It hovered above his egg-yolk yellow moustache with sinister intent.

He leered at her as she approached. 'Where are you going, c-c-comrade?' he said.

Anastasia stared at the toilet; the door had been removed. 'I am not your c-c-comrade,' she said, her cheeks burning hot. 'My name is Anastasia Nicolaevna Romanov and I would like some p-p-privacy.'

The soldier controlled his temper and instead gave her an expression of theatrical surprise. 'Why, what are you going to do in there, c-c-comrade?'

Anastasia looked again at the lavatory and then back to the guard. She fought an impulse to kick the brute in the shins. She wondered if she might be able to contain her bladder until the change of watch later that evening and decided she could not. The man wanted to pay her back for her taunts or perhaps this harassment was another of Avdeyev's petty tyrannies.

'What's the matter, c-c-comrade?'

Oh, look at him, grinning at me. She shrugged, as if this latest humiliation was of no consequence. She went into the lavatory.

Someone had scratched a pornographic sketch on the wall; it was of her mother, wearing the diamond tiara of the Czarina, legs apart and with Rasputin lying between them, his penis engorged. She gasped and covered her mouth with her hand.

She looked over her shoulder, saw the guard winking at her, enjoying himself hugely.

Nothing in her life had prepared her for this. She had been a prisoner in Tobolsk and at Tsarskoe Selo, but there, at least, they had been treated with respect. Here they were helpless, at the mercy of men who behaved like animals. She had never felt so afraid.

How can they do this to us?

The guard was still watching her.

She would not look at him, would try to pretend he was not there. She lifted her skirts as modestly as she could, lowered her undergarments without allowing this pig, this animal, one glimpse of her flesh. Then she sat down on the seat and waited for the stream to come.

'What's the matter, c-c-comrade? A wooden seat not as nice as the g-g-gold one you are accustomed to, I suppose.'

She wanted so badly to pee. Why could she not do it, when her bladder felt as if it would burst?

The guard cocked his head. 'Maybe a princess doesn't p-p-piss like everyone else,' he said.

'Would you kindly turn your head, please,' Anastasia said.

'Why? You're not d-d-doing anything.'

She just could not do it while he was staring at her. She heard him chuckle, deep in his throat. He had won.

Finally, she heard her water hiss into the bowl. When she was done she realised she could not wipe herself without him seeing under her skirts. So she rushed out of the lavatory and past him, still dirty, and heard him jeering her all the way down the corridor.

The guard's name, she learned, was Grishkin. He wasn't a soldier at all, he was a factory worker, like most of Avdeyev's men. In the blackhead plant, Anastasia supposed, if his face were any guide to his talents. He had now made it his duty, when he was on watch, to take up sentry post outside the lavatory. The girls tried to avoid using the lavatory during the daylight watch, when they knew Grishkin would be there. Nicholas complained to Avdeyev who responded in his usual way, as if this request for basic dignities was akin to requesting grilled lobster for breakfast.

Only Anastasia chose not to avoid him. That would be an admission of defeat, she decided, a submission of the spirit. She would not succumb to his petty bullying. She used the lavatory as often as she wished, and after that first occasion did not even give him the satisfaction of a single glance in his direction.

One day a drawing appeared on the wall in the corridor. Anastasia saw some of the guards gathered around it, laughing aloud. Grishkin lumbered up, peered over the heads of the others with a lop-sided grin on his face. No doubt he thought it was another of their disgusting cartoons, Rasputin degrading another of her family.

But then his expression changed.

For it was a caricature of Grishkin himself, his nose the size of his bloated body, and covered in suppurating boils. He was standing guard outside the lavatory, with flies swarming in thick clouds around his head.

Underneath was a caption: 'We have found a way to keep the flies out of the toilet in summer, c-c-comrade.'

Grishkin's face twisted. He turned around and saw Anastasia, knew at once who had made the drawing, and how it had come to be there.

Later that day when she made her way to the lavatory Grishkin was there, waiting.

She ignored him and went in. Almost immediately she took a step back and came out again. Excrement had been smeared on the walls and on the seat. And a new sketch had been added to the obscene tapestry, depicting her father, bent over a table, Rasputin mastering him from the rear.

She felt tears welling in her eyes. I cannot stand this any more. I won't.

She stamped her foot and rounded on Grishkin. 'You're a pig!'

He seemed hugely gratified by this display of petulance. 'What's the matter, c-c-comrade? Never seen shit before?'

'I have to look at it every day, when I pass you in the corridor!'

He stopped smiling and his eyes were hard. 'Poor little princess,' he said. 'Where are the f-f-flies going to buzz now?'

'Little Anastasia. Her hands were always moving, twisting the edge of her handkerchief into knots, sitting well forward, one foot behind the other, never relaxed, her restless mind always at work, anxious lest someone else should steal away the attention that was hers by thinking of some joke or prank before she did. She was not beautiful in the classic sense, as Tatiana was, but her luminous blue eyes and restless personality lent her a magnetic quality.'

Nine o'clock and they had finished another supper of tea and black bread and were sitting together in the Yellow Room, which was how they referred to their parents' bedroom. Tatiana and Alexandra read to them from the Bible, the prophet Amos. Tatiana had to raise her voice over the sound of the guards' drunken singing from downstairs.

Anastasia recognised the song: 'You Fell a Victim to the Struggle'. It was accompanied by someone playing the piano in the parlour, and very badly.

She was bored to the point of feeling physically numb. Olga and Marie seemed intent on the scriptures. She tried to be as devout as her sisters, but her mind always wandered away from the devil's designs and she found herself thinking of other things.

Downstairs they had moved on to 'Let's Forget the Old Regime' and she started humming along under her breath.

Before long, she heard the drunken party making its way up the stairs. Tatiana persisted with the Book of Amos, though she knew interruption was imminent. Anastasia was the only one who looked around expectantly towards the door.

Avdeyev burst in. He was drunk, of course, and he had brought some of his friends with him, from the factory. Like Avdeyev, they all reeked of cheap vodka.

'Here he is,' Avdeyev crowed. 'Bloody Nicholas!'

The others crowded in the doorway and gawped at them like they were exhibits in the zoo.

Nicholas got to his feet, eyes blazing. 'What is the meaning of this?'

'My friends were curious to meet you, Citizen Romanov. You can sit down now.' He spoke to him as if he was a common servant: no doubt, for the benefit of his friends.

Nicholas, his hands clasped regally behind his back, advanced on him. At the last moment he veered away and

19

took hold of one of the unshaven peasants in the doorway. 'What's this?' he said, fingering the man's shirt.

The man was dressed in the most astonishing fashion Anastasia had ever seen: peasant trousers held up with a battered leather belt, and one of her father's monogrammed dress shirts. The effect was utterly ridiculous but the man was too drunk or too stupid to know it.

'This is one of mine,' Nicholas said. He turned to another of the mob, a man in a heavy greatcoat. 'So is this.' He patted the man down as if searching for weapons. He put a hand in the coat pocket and took out a bottle of perfume: By Royal Appointment. He held it under Avdeyev's nose. 'You've been pilfering from us.'

'Lenin has done away with personal possessions. Everything belongs to the people now.'

'Wonderful. Then perhaps we might be allowed some of Russia's eggs for breakfast. They belong to everyone, after all.'

Avdeyev realised Nicholas had turned the tables on him in front of his cronies. He puffed out his chest. 'You can't tell me what to do. I'm in charge here.'

'As you never cease to remind me. So do you take full responsibility for giving away Russia's possessions to your personal friends?'

When Avdeyev didn't answer, Nicholas turned his back on him. 'I shall be making a full report to your superiors. Now, perhaps you might like to leave us in peace. The hour is late.'

Avdeyev swayed on his feet. 'Ah, to hell with you!' he said and left, slamming the door behind him.

Baby has had a hard time of it, Anastasia thought. His bed had now been moved into the Yellow Room. She could not imagine lying there all day, with only Mama and Sednev, the kitchen boy, for company. Bad enough being a prisoner in this house. Little Alexei had spent most of his life this way.

The bleeding sickness meant that the merest bruise on his knee or elbow would cause him excruciating pain, which would grow more terrible over days, even weeks. Doctor

Botkin had tried to explain it to her; he said that because the bleeding did not stop, it collected inside the joint and the pressure would slowly wrench it apart.

Sometimes the original injury would be so minor that Baby could not even remember it. They would just wake one morning and Baby would call out: 'Mama, I cannot walk today.' Anastasia had learned to dread those words, for they signalled the start of another episode that would end in horrifying shrieks of pain. She could not count the times she had heard him crying from his bedroom: 'Mama, Mama, help me! Do something, please!' But there was nothing Doctor Botkin or anyone could do, except apply ice packs and pray to a merciful God who showed Baby no mercy at all.

It was the strain of Alexei's illness that had sent Mother's hair grey, Papa said. She looked like an old woman already, Anastasia thought, so much older than Nicholas.

But no-one was more tired of the endless wheel of suffering than Baby. He spoke often of his wish to be like other boys. The Czarevitch would have rather been born Sednev the kitchen boy, if it meant he could play in the snow. In the last year he had become reckless, as if inviting his illness to do its worst, instead of shrinking from it. Just before they left Tobolsk he had ridden a homemade sled down the stairs.

It had, of course, left him crippled ever since, a terrible episode from which he had only now begun to recover.

Mama stayed up at nights to nurse him if the pains were strong. Here, as in Tsarskoe Selo, her conversation was solely about Baby. In the morning, as they trooped in for breakfast, she might smile and say, 'Baby had a good night,' and the day would appear at least a measure brighter. But there were other times when their breakfast conversation consisted only of how often Baby had been able to sleep, and how much he had suffered. The days of his life were measured off in degrees of pain and the circumference of his swollen joints. Sometimes he would be taken out into the garden in his wheelchair but most often he lay in bed, his knee encased in the plaster of Paris casts Botkin had made for him.

Anastasia felt sorry for Baby, of course, but her compassion was exhausted by the never ending round of small victories and agonied defeats; she could not dedicate herself to him, as Tatiana and Olga did. During the day they would sit with him, read him stories, play cards with him. Saints in the making, of course; one day, she thought bitterly, they would be painted as icons.

But they were not there, none of them were, the day Baby got Klementy killed. Everyone was in the garden, escaping the heat indoors. Alexei sat on his bed, propped up with pillows, staring at Voronin, one of the guards. Voronin sat on a stool in the corridor, morose and twitchy. He would occasionally lift his eyes in the direction of the Czarevitch as if he were some other man's sheep he would like to slaughter for his dinner.

Alexei had his toys spread on a tray in front of him, and was gloomily flicking through a deck of playing cards. His eyes were dull from boredom and he caught Voronin's eyes and stared. Voronin stared back.

Alexei picked up a crust of black bread from his lunch plate and hurled it in his direction.

'You,' Alexei said.

The muscles in Voronin's jaw rippled.

'I want some chocolate.'

Voronin jumped up, his stool clattering onto the floor. Klementy, who had been dozing in the corner, woke with a start and also stood up, alarmed and bewildered.

'Didn't you hear me?' Alexei was saying to Voronin. 'Don't stand there gawping at me like an ox.'

'You can't talk to me like that anymore,' Voronin said.

'Don't you know who you're talking to?'

'We're all comrades now,' Voronin said. 'You want chocolate, you have to fetch it yourself.'

Klementy went to Alexei's bedside. 'What is wrong, Highness?'

The boy pointed a pale finger at Voronin. 'He insulted me.'

Klementy rounded on the guard. 'Get out of here.'

'That little cripple can't talk to me like that.'

Klementy moved towards him and Voronin fingered the safety on his rifle. 'Get out,' Klementy said.

Voronin didn't see how this crowd could order him around

anymore. But the only way he could stop the bodyguard was to shoot him and he didn't want any trouble for himself. Besides, he had never shot anyone before and he didn't known how he felt about doing it now.

'I shall report this to Comrade Avdeyev,' Voronin shouted as he retreated down the stairs.

'You do that, you fat peasant,' Klementy said.

Alexei laughed.

The next day Comrade Voronin was back at his post outside the Yellow Room. Klementy Nagorny was taken away by four of Avdeyev's Red Guards. They never heard from him again.

'The thing I remember most about her is her laugh. If there was mischief going on, you could lay your last rouble it would be Anastasia who started it. She had the loveliest blue eyes but she would never look at you directly, she would say something and glance at you from the corner of her eye, some calumny about one of her aunts or one of the servants, and then she would laugh. You couldn't help but join in, but sometimes her fun was just wicked. She would even trip up the servants if she was bored and no-one would scold her for it, not in the last years.'

Nicholas sat on the edge of the bed, staring at Baby. A look of such bitter fondness on his face. After four daughters, God finally gave him his longed-for son, but it was poisoned fruit. A cruel God, a kind man.

'How are you feeling today?' he said.

Baby managed a smile. His skin so pale, you could make out the tiny blue spider web of blood vessels at his temples and on the backs of his hands.

'Better,' Alexei said.

Nicholas put a hand on his. 'That's good.'

'Papa, when are we going to go home?'

Nicholas managed a smile. 'Soon.'

The lie fell easily into the room, like so many others Baby had heard. 'Is something going to happen to us?' he said.

Anastasia held her breath, wondering what Papa would say. 'Let us give thanks we are all together again.'

'But is it?'

Nicholas laughed. 'You think the King of England would stand by and let his own family come to harm? We are cousins, he and I.'

There was hope then, Anastasia thought. But if the King is such a friend of ours, why has he already let us suffer so long?

Anastasia noticed one morning that one of her shoes had a hole in the sole. She had been allowed just one pair from the luggage they had brought with them from Tobolsk and she had worn this same pair since their arrival.

When Avdeyev made his usual casual and arbitrary inspection of their rooms just before lunchtime, Anastasia positioned herself in the doorway, blocking his exit. He stank as usual and he had not shaved. The new face of Russia.

'What is it, Citizen Romanov?' he said to her.

'I need a new pair of shoes. From my luggage.'

He stared at her, bleary eyed, and she thought she saw both irritation and guilt on his face. She knew what that look meant; everything had been pilfered.

'To hell with you!' he said and pushed past her.

She saw Grishkin standing there, triumphant. 'Don't worry about your shoes,' he said, 'the ones you have will last you a lifetime.'

At once the fine summer morning grew unnaturally cold.

But she had her revenge on Grishkin, finally. As she had promised herself.

Sometimes, when the sisters were walking in the gardens, the guards would leave them unattended to cadge cigarettes from the guardroom or take a sly swill from a bottle of vodka. But one day Avdeyev roused himself sufficiently from his afternoon stupor to make a snap inspection. He found Anastasia sitting on a bench against the wall of the house, reading Tolstoy, Olga and Tatiana beside her, and not a guard in sight. He went into a rage.

'Grishkin!' Avdeyev roared. Anastasia heard Grishkin's bleats of alarm as he stumbled up the passageway from the guardroom.

As he reached the threshold she stuck out a foot and sent him flying headlong over the step. He fell on his face and his rifle, which he had neglected to put onto safety, discharged. The deafening explosion was followed by a dramatic silence as both Avdeyev and Grishkin waited for a scream of pain or alarm that must surely follow. But the bullet had fired harmlessly into the air.

Avdeyev had fallen instinctively into a crouch, eyes wide with terror, and he looked so comical, hunched over like that, that Anastasia started to laugh.

Meanwhile, Grishkin stumbled back to his feet, too drunk to realise what Anastasia had done. Avdeyev was furious. He aimed a kick at Grishkin, slapped him hard around the head with the flat of his hand, aimed another kick at his shins. Grishkin stood there, like the sack of hometown beetroot that he was, and took it all.

Anastasia experienced a glow of satisfaction. It was one of the few happy days she remembered.

There were consequences, however. Anastasia did not think anyone had seen what she had done, but she was wrong. Nicholas had seen everything. Later that evening he took her aside in the Yellow Room, sat her down, and gazed at her for a long time, and the sad blue eyes seemed to say: When will you ever learn?

She could never look directly into those eyes, they saw straight into her. It would have been better if he sometimes got angry with her, but when she was wicked all she saw was disappointment, and it hurt her more than her mother's sharp words or her tutor's scolding.

'I know what happened out there today with Grishkin,' he said, finally.

'He deserved it.'

Nicholas shook his head.

'He did,' she insisted.

'Is that why you did it?'

'He's a pig.'

'It's true some men do not behave as well as others,' he said.

Oh Papa, she thought. Is that all you can say of them? After everything they have done to you, that they have done to us?

'You cannot trip up the whole world, Anastasia.'

'I can try.'

He sighed. 'One day you will learn.'

She felt her temper rise. She wished she could dam it up but, as always, it carried her along with it, like debris in a flood. 'What will I learn, Papa?'

'You will learn to be gracious.'

'Is that what it is when you let them tramp their boots all over us, when you give up the empire without a fight? Is that what you are, Papa? Gracious?'

Oh, there. It was said. The thing she was never meant to say, or even to think. I might as well have spat on the Holy Cross. What made me say such a thing?

The hurt in his eyes was unbearable; hurt not, she supposed, by what was said, but because one of his beloved daughters had said it. She knew in that moment that not even the imprisonments and humiliations of the last months had touched him, until now. His face crumpled.

'Haven't I always been a good father to you?' he said, and his heart sounded as if it would break. She realised with blinding clarity that this was how he measured himself. Never mind that he was the richest man in the world, and ruler of one of the great empires. He gauged his worth by the good opinion of his family.

She wanted to tell him how sorry she was for what she had said, but the words would not come. Pride, of course. Besides, she knew it was too late. You cannot take back a knife after it has been thrown, especially when it is hurled with such force, and such deadly accuracy.

'I do not understand you,' he said. 'One day, I hope you will recall this moment with regret.' He got up and turned his back to her, lit a cigarette. Her sisters were staring at her from the other side of the room as if she was the devil incarnate.

But even the guilt did not quite banish her rage. She hated this taciturn man for his lack of spite and fire; as much as she hated herself for those same qualities, which, it seemed, she possessed in abundance.

The next afternoon they sat in the garden, all of the girls together, Anastasia between Olga and Tatiana, Marie on the end of the bench. Anastasia listened to the drone of the insects, finding luxury in the simple pleasure of sitting in the open air, staring at a perfect blue sky. She could hear the everyday sounds of the town beyond the garden's high walls, donkey hooves on the cobblestones, the cries of street vendors.

Anastasia found herself wondering what life would be like if by some miracle she could transport herself beyond the walls, where no-one would recognise her as a princess. She had always been inside some kind of prison, she supposed, the palaces at Saint Petersburg or Tsarskoe Selo were only different kinds of confinement.

But at least in Tsarskoe Selo, there was always something to do.

She watched her father chatting to one of the guards, old Voronin. Papa offered him one of his cigarettes and started to discuss the weather. It was her father's way to talk lightly with servants, not like her mother at all.

Voronin was wearing one of her father's monogrammed shirts. She wondered if her father knew he was talking to a thief. How could he not notice one of his own shirts? She supposed he had just given in, as he always did.

Papa was dressed in customary fashion, a khaki soldier's shirt with an officer's belt, battered black leather boots. He was so unlike the Czar the people, especially his enemies, imagined. She had always been in awe of him, not for his greatness, but for how ordinary he was. She knew she could never be so simple in spirit. He could talk easily with anyone, Prussian ambassadors or grooms, pompous British attachés or gruff Cossack cavalrymen. And now he even conversed with the very peasants who thieved from him.

He left Voronin, and walked over to the girls. He stood there for a while, smoking a cigarette, staring at the sky, exhaling pale blue smoke through his nostrils. They all knew he had something important to say and they waited until he was ready to speak; big, serious Olga, Tatiana so serene, her hand resting on Marie's. And Anastasia, wanting to pull a face, make a joke. But for once she couldn't think of anything.

'We none of us know what may happen to us tomorrow,' he said, finally.

'Papa?' Olga said.

'There is something you girls should know.' He drew again on the cigarette, his manner casual, as if commenting on an inclement change in the weather. 'Should the situation demand, there is money put aside for you in the Bank of

England in London. Five million roubles each. If you find yourself in need of funds, you should find a gentleman there by the name of Bardenov. Tell him you wish access to these accounts. He will ask you for the code for these deposits. The code is Otma.'

Otma: Olga, Tatiana, Marie, Anastasia.

This speech was made without looking directly at any of them, and there was no inflection in his voice at all.

Then he said: 'I think the breeze is a little cooler today.'

Marie lowered her head and looked as if she was about to cry.

'We will not let them part us again,' Olga said.

'Things sometimes happen over which we have no control,' he said. 'Whatever tomorrow brings, you must always remember who you are, and that there is Romanov blood in your veins.'

They were all silent. He reached out and placed a hand on Marie's shoulder. He continued to smoke, gazing up at the washed-blue sky.

'It may be warmer tomorrow, I think,' he said.

'*When you think about it, I suppose she had no choice. There was Olga, the heiress; then Tatiana, the pretty one; and Marie, the bright, clever one. She must have decided from the moment she could walk that she would have to be the bad one. There was no other way to compete. She could not impress with her manners, her beauty or her brain, so she would shock people.*'

Voronin watched from the doorway.

Anastasia was wearing one of her brother's khaki military shirts, and holding an empty bottle of vodka she had found in the garden. Her three sisters sat on the bed, watching her, Marie giggling behind her hand.

Anastasia affected a stagger, clutching at a table for support. 'The People's sub-committee of the Workers sub-sub-committee of the Supreme Soviet of the Urals has consulted the manifesto of Comrade Lenin and now gives you, Citizen Tatiana Romanov, permission to put sugar in your tea!'

Tatiana gave a polite curtsey.

'I want the window open!' Marie shouted.

'You think you can oppress the workers with open windows and fresh air!' Anastasia took a swig from the empty bottle and staggered back. 'Oh, to hell with them!'

The girls laughed at this biting impersonation. But then Anastasia turned around and they all saw Voronin.

No-one spoke.

Voronin straightened his shoulders and turned away. 'Oh, to hell with them!' he muttered under his breath and tried to keep from laughing.

After a while you lost your hate, Voronin decided. Like a coin that dropped through a hole in your pocket. One day you went looking for it and it just wasn't there. It was easy to hate someone you did not know. It had been easy to hate the Czar, before he met him. That was the hell of it.

But how did you hate a man and his family, when you saw them every day close up like this, witnessed their helplessness? How did you hate Bloody Nicholas, the Monster of

Saint Petersburg, when he remarked to you every day on the weather and carried his crippled son in his arms to sit in the garden and enjoy the sun? What did he have to fear from this bedridden old woman they claimed was the Empress of Russia?

It was hard, impossible really, not to pity them as human beings. Easier, in fact, to despise Avdeyev. After all, tyranny seemed to sit easier on his shoulders than on theirs. Who was it that denied helpless young women and a crippled little boy a few eggs and a little milk for their breakfast, when there was plenty to be had in the town? What sort of man would make others beg for an open window on such stinking days?

And what does this make of me? Voronin thought. I might be a simple man, just a worker in a factory all my life, but it seems to me that tormenting this family does not right any wrong that has been done to us by Russia in the past.

I feel soiled by this.

He thought of his own three daughters. They would be ashamed if they saw me now.

Is this the family they taught us to hate and to fear? They seem to go about their daily business much as the rest of us; they drink black tea and eat black bread for breakfast, nurse each other when they are sick, they squabble and they fuss.

I think Avdeyev is the monster in all this.

In fact, it wouldn't worry me if they escaped. I wish they would. If I saw them running for that gate right now, and Avdeyev ordered me to shoot them in the back, I wonder what I would do? Well, I think I know what I would do.

I'd shoot Avdeyev.

Anastasia sat in the shade of a lilac bush, breathing in the fragrance of the honeysuckle that climbed the wall. She was alone, for a moment; Tatiana and Marie were strolling with Papa, Olga was inside with Baby and Mama, who were both too sick to come out today. Olga was such a saint, giving up her time in the garden to read to them. These precious few minutes in the garden slipped past so quickly; the thought of having to go back inside that furnace of a house was unendurable.

A shadow fell across the sun. She looked up. It was the old guard, Voronin, the one who had caught her making fun of Avdeyev.

There was a cigarette stuck to his bottom lip and it wiggled as he talked. A strange man, with huge, sad eyes and a big grey moustache that made him look like a walrus.

'A hot day, Citizen Anastasia,' he said.

She ignored him. She was not about to start conversing with factory workers, even if they did have rifles. She was still a princess of the Russias, and she hadn't forgotten it, even if he had.

He looked around, and now there was something furtive about him. He reached into his pocket and held something out to her, clutched in his fist. 'Hurry,' he said. 'Take them.'

She held out her hands. Three eggs. She stared at them in wonder, then wondered at herself. She thought of the trinkets Fabergé had designed for her mother, golden eggs encrusted with jewels. What this Voronin had given her impressed her more than anything the royal jeweller had presented to Mama. What had happened to her that she now treasured something so commonplace as an ordinary egg?

'Don't stare at them like that!' Voronin hissed at her. 'Put them away! Hide them in your dress! Avdeyev will have me shot if he sees you.'

Anastasia did as she was told. She looked up at Voronin, but the sun was behind his head and she could not make out his features clearly. 'Thank you,' she said. These two strange words caught in her throat.

'You'll have to share them,' he said, needlessly, and then walked away.

The mournful ticking of a clock on the mantel.

The hours dragged towards dusk. Tatiana was reading to Baby; Botkin and Olga were playing bridge with Mama and Papa. Anastasia tried to concentrate on the book in her hands but she could smell the warm air through the window and longed, so longed, to be outside.

'Will we ever get away from here, Papa?' she said.

'Our allies are not far away, *malenkaya*,' he said. *Malenkaya*: little one. A long time since he had called her that. 'We cannot know what will happen tomorrow.'

And that was the worst thing: not knowing. They were completely isolated from the outside world, did not know if the war went well or badly for them. One day they had heard a demonstration in the town square, there were gunshots followed by shouts and screams. Avdeyev had told them it was an uprising of local anarchists and that they should be ready for evacuation at a moment's notice. But nothing came of it.

'Will no-one come to rescue us?' Olga asked.

She saw Doctor Botkin glance at her father. Some signal must have passed between them, for the Doctor suddenly said: 'Did Shura say anything to you before she got off the train?' Shura; the family's pet name for Sophie Karlova, their nanny.

Anastasia wondered why he would ask such a question. Olga glanced at the rest of them for confirmation, then shook her head.

'There was a plan,' Botkin said. 'Once Shura was freed she was to alert the Whites to our whereabouts. But we have been here over two months now and no-one has contacted us. It is possible they have murdered her.'

'Or she has betrayed us,' Alexandra said.

There was a long silence.

'She would never do that,' Tatiana said.

No-one else spoke.

'Not Shura,' Tatiana repeated.

'Anastasia had blonde hair with a reddish lustre to it, long and wavy and soft. And these wonderful blue eyes, like her father. They were ice blue. I would have given anything to have eyes like that. And her eyebrows. Fine and fair, they almost met in the middle. But no, not beautiful. You couldn't think of her that way. She was so fat, you see. A real little pudding.'

It was a perfect summer morning, the air clear and cool, not too hot. Perhaps today they would not bake.

There was no warning that anything had changed; instead of a bleary-eyed Avdeyev stinking of drink, a dark man in a black leather jacket presented himself in their quarters, accompanied by a squad of Cheka. Nicholas rose to his feet and eyed them with the wariness of a man who has lived a long time in death's corridor, and suspects every departure from routine as dangerous.

'Citizen Romanov,' the stranger said, 'Doctor Jacov Yurovsky. I am taking over command here.'

He had a dark moustache and black goatee beard. The men with him wore the uniforms of the Bolshevik secret police.

'Where is Avdeyev?' he asked.

'Comrade Avdeyev has been replaced.'

'I see.'

Anastasia saw Papa hold out his hand. Yurovsky looked at it with distaste, kept his own hands in the pockets of his black leather jacket.

'I do not wish to shake hands with you,' he said.

They stared at each other, in mutual incomprehension.

Yurovsky said: 'There have been reports of drunkenness and lewd behaviour here. It will not be tolerated by the Urals Soviet.'

'It seems to have been tolerated well enough till now.'

Yurovsky ignored this. He looked around the room. Anastasia felt his eyes pass over her, and the effect was chilling. His eyes were quite blank; nothing there at all.

'There have also been reports of theft,' he said.

'Most of our possessions were taken from us at the station and have never been returned,' her father agreed.

'This situation will be rectified,' Yurovsky said. 'A search will be made of these apartments so an inventory can be made. Then there can be no further discrepancy.'

A look passed between her father and mother. 'That is

what your drunkard of a predecessor said, before he stole my perfumes and my husband's clothes,' Alexandra said.

Papa was more conciliatory. 'We will, of course, co-operate in every way we can.'

Yurovsky clicked the heels of his black leather boots together and swept from the room.

After he had gone there was silence. They all looked at Nicholas.

'He's looking for the medicines,' he said.

The medicines: their code word for the fortune in jewels they had brought with them from Tsarskoe Selo.

Alexandra clasped her Bible to her bosom. 'God will give us strength to see us through our trials.'

'I hope so,' Nicholas said. 'For this latest specimen I like least of all.'

Yurovsky's arrival brought small improvements in their situation. Their new guards were Latvians, Letts they called themselves, more solemn than the local militia but better disciplined and not as disposed to drunkenness. The petty harassment on the way to the lavatory ceased with Grishkin's departure.

Otherwise their days continued with the same relentless monotony. They found variety and interest only in their illnesses and the caprices of the weather. Anastasia's seventeenth birthday passed without fanfare.

From czar to cook they had merged, in their circumstances, into an extended family. Doctor Botkin would sit with her father and mother after supper to talk and play cards, and during the day he would entertain Alexandra and Baby while the others took their walks in the garden. Krupp shared the task of carrying Baby outdoors, and Kharitonov showed the girls how to make dough and bake bread in the kitchen. From Demidova they learned how to darn socks and linen. When the doctor became violently ill with colic, it was Alexandra who sat by his bed for five days and watched over him.

But the spectre of Yurovsky hung over all of them.

Mama was lying on her bed. Except for Botkin's illness she had hardly left the Yellow Room since the four girls arrived at the end of April. Every day she lay there with her head propped on her pillow, her eyes closed against the persistent migraine headaches, while Tatiana or Olga read to her from the Bible or *The Life of Saint Serafin*.

She looked so like an old woman now, the milky light from the windows emphasised each wrinkle in her face. Her hair was almost completely white, yet she was the same age as Papa.

She had been sick for as long as Anastasia could remember, either with her nerves or heart palpitations. She and Baby were united in their misery.

But today Mama announced: 'I think I shall go out into the garden for a while this morning.'

Anastasia bit her lip and wondered how this dramatic decision might affect her.

'I want you to sit with Sunbeam while I am outside.'

Sunbeam: her latest term of endearment for Alexei. So that was it: she was being asked to forfeit her time in the garden.

'Why can't Olga or Tatiana do it?' she said. 'They enjoy it.'

A peevish expression crossed her mother's face. She lowered her voice so that Alexei could not hear. 'And when was the last time you sat with Baby?'

Anastasia knew her mother was right. She spent hardly any time with him. But Alexei had attention enough, she thought. Perhaps if I had the bleeding sickness they would pay more attention to me.

No doubt Mama wanted to punish her for not being a pious and dutiful sister like Tatiana and Olga. She sat in sullen silence as Papa and Doctor Botkin helped Alexandra out of bed and down the corridor.

Anastasia looked at the little square of blue sky, the fragments of rooftops, their only view of the outside world.

She returned her attention to Alexei. Yesterday he had had his first bath since Tobolsk. He had got in and out of the bath unaided, Mama had said, as proud as if he had led a cavalry charge.

He was dressed as usual in peasant trousers and collarless military shirt, the same as Papa wore. They were alone; no Mama, no Tatiana or Olga. Baby had a tray in front of him, a set of playing cards, and some toy soldiers set out on it. He opened a little tin, spilled out the contents; some oddments of string and coins and nails and bottle tops he liked to treasure.

I should feel sorry for him, she thought. After all, he is trapped in here every day. But all she could think of was the sunshine and the garden and how she had been robbed of her brief respite.

'I wish I were dead,' he said.

His attention was concentrated on the oddments from the tin, and there was nothing on his face or in his manner to suggest that he had spoken at all.

She sat on the chair by his bed, and watched him as he sorted some nails into a pile, then replaced them in the tin, one by one.

'I should like to be dead now,' he said. 'Only it would make Mama so unhappy.'

'You mustn't talk that way.'

He looked up at her, and for a moment he had the eyes of an old man. 'Easy for you to say, Stushi. You don't bleed.'

She did not know what to say to him.

'What would you do,' he said, 'if you could do just anything you wanted?'

She shrugged her shoulders, uncomfortable with this black mood.

He looked away from her, at the little patch of sky framed in the one open window. 'I would have liked to have been a soldier,' he said.

Baby. A soldier.

'I like being a princess,' she said. 'I don't want to be anything else.'

But he wasn't listening. His eyes were fixed on the window. They were pale and empty, like the sky.

Tatiana woke in the middle of the night and slipped silently out of bed and down the corridor towards the lavatory. Two of the Letts were sitting on chairs at the end of the hall. She felt their eyes on her but she tried to ignore them.

A shadow slipped behind her, unseen, unheard, and a hand clamped across her mouth. The guards jumped off their chairs and strong hands clamped around her arms as they carried her, struggling, to the bedroom at the other side of the house. A rag was stuffed in her mouth, and the three men held her to the floor.

They then helped themselves to a grand duchess. Well, it was an opportunity too good to miss; a man only had so many chances in his lifetime to fuck royalty.

'I remember this about her: I remember I hated her. When I heard they'd slaughtered them all, I felt sorry about Nicholas, such a gentle soul, and Marie, of course, and the boy, who never harmed anyone. But her. I thought: I hope she suffered. Yes, I know, it's a terrible thing to say. But you didn't know her like I did.'

Anastasia did not immediately understand what had happened. When she woke next morning Tatiana was not in her bed. She heard weeping from the Yellow Room and thought it must be Baby, another bad night. She put on her dressing gown and slipped through the half open door.

Tatiana lay on the sofa, still in her nightdress. Doctor Botkin was with her. Nicholas stood by the window, his back turned. Her mother's face: a death's head. Even Baby's little cries were forgotten this morning.

Nicholas turned around. He was shaking with anger. But there was something else she had never really seen on his face before: fear.

'Go back to your room, *malenkaya*,' he said.

And she did.

The rest of the day was spent in silence. They ate their meals without speaking; it was as if there had been a death in the family. The guards were strangely subdued also, speaking to each other in whispers as they patrolled the hallways.

A line had been crossed. Anastasia guessed what had happened long before Doctor Botkin finally whispered to her the truth.

That night, the local priest, Father Storozhev, was allowed to come and read vespers, just the second time it had been allowed. He was a solemn young man, dressed all in black, much like Yurovsky. Priests of a different cloth, Anastasia supposed, but both invested with darker powers.

They all filed down the stairs to a drawing room off the courtyard, Anastasia holding on to Olga and Marie, all of them silent but for Tatiana, sobbing as she clutched at her father. Mama had put on her best lilac dress and Doctor Botkin helped her down the stairs and into her wheelchair.

When the service began Nicholas fell to his knees. Is it an act of humility or an act of surrender? Anastasia wondered. We are truly desperate now.

Then they sang the Mass together, and prayed to the Holy Mother for their salvation, if not in this world, then the next.

'Anastasia was a little devil. No-one ever disciplined her. That mother of hers spent all her time praying and sitting with her "Baby", which is what she called Alexei, and closeted with that madman priest. The children just ran wild, did as they pleased. Anastasia was a bully, if she didn't get her own way she kicked and scratched and pulled your hair. There wasn't a kind bone in her body. In my opinion, the world's better off without her.'

They heard a brass band in the town square, the sound of marching feet, probably a detachment of Red Army volunteers on their way to the front. All that week they had heard the crump of distant artillery fire, knew the Whites were battling their way closer to the town.

The morning began grey and sultry, but later the sun broke through and their spirits rose, too. The sound of gunfire meant that rescue was only a few miles distant.

They had all gone out for a walk in the garden that morning, except Baby and Mother, as usual. Afterwards, on Alexandra's instructions, all the girls arranged their 'medicines' in anticipation of a hurried departure.

After tea, Mama read from the Bible; Tatiana curled up on the bed next to her mother, as she had done when she was a little girl. That's what Tatiana looked like now; a little girl. All she did was sleep and cry.

Only Baby seemed brighter. He ate the boiled eggs that Yurovsky had brought him; an act of inexplicable kindness from their unsmiling warden.

Just before supper, Sednev the kitchen boy got a message from his uncle at the Popov house. He was needed there urgently. Anastasia wondered if they would ever see the boy again; so like the Bolsheviks to make someone disappear, without warning or explanation. Like Klementy.

That night, unable to sleep, she lay awake listening to her mother and father playing bezique in the other room.

She wondered if there would ever again come a time when she could lie in bed and think peacefully of the future.

Yurovsky stopped for a moment outside the doctor's room to adjust his uniform and collect his thoughts. The late arrival of the truck had made him nervous and now, to his dismay, he had discovered a tremor in his fingers.

Until this moment, he had been sure he would be remembered as one of the great men of Russian history. Now, too late, he wondered if perhaps he had not rushed things. Well, there was no time for wondering any more. The Whites would be in Ekaterinburg in a few days and he would have to be far away by then.

One of the guards was watching him. He told himself to be calm. When future generations spoke of tonight it was important that his coolness and precision was remarked on by history's witnesses.

He pushed open Botkin's door.

The doctor was snoring.

Yurovsky turned on the light and went over to the bed. Botkin blinked awake. He was not wearing his false teeth and he looked much older without them.

'What is it?' Botkin mumbled.

'There is unrest in the town. It is unsafe. Wake the others. Tell them to dress and be prepared to leave within the hour.'

Yurovsky walked out and returned to the guardroom downstairs. He threw a nervous glance at the clock on the wall. The truck should have been here by now. Already his careful plans were starting to unravel.

Anastasia washed her face in cold water from the jug by the bed and dressed quickly, remembering the medicines. The family were already gathered in the hall, and she received a cross look from her mother for being the last to be ready. Her head ached from lack of sleep, she fumbled around in the fog of half-remembered dreams.

Her father was dressed in military shirt and trousers, with leather boots and forage cap. He held Baby in his arms. Mama was limping on her cane, Olga supporting her. Tatiana had Jemmy in her arms and when Anastasia reached for the little dog she refused to give her up. Her punishment for being late, she supposed. The doctor and Demidova were carrying pillows for Baby.

Too late, Anastasia realised she had forgotten her hat and her wrap.

Yurovsky was there, the horrid little man, dressed in black as usual. He led the way downstairs. She wondered where the Bolsheviks intended to send them now. Papa said the Bolsheviks wanted to evacuate them before the Whites surrounded the town. Still, it was exciting. A change from the terrible monotony of the last few months.

They went out into the courtyard. It was a clear night, stars scattered like a handful of diamond chips across black velvet. Anastasia shivered, took a deep lungful of cold air to try to revive herself.

They followed Yurovsky through the basement door leading to the guardroom. There was a disused room at the end of the passage and they all filed in. It had no chairs, no furniture of any kind; there was a single, arched window on one wall, barred by a heavy iron grille. There was a door on the other side of the room and Yurovsky checked that it was locked.

He started to arrange them around the room, as if he was posing them for a portrait. 'You, Citizen,' he said, addressing Nicholas, 'you will stand here. You,' he said, pointing to Alexandra, 'you here.'

They were too exhausted to remonstrate with him. Anastasia wondered what this was about. Yurovsky finally stood back, apparently satisfied.

'What now?' Nicholas asked him.

'You will wait here.'

'For how long?' Nicholas grumbled. 'Don't you have any chairs? Can't we at least sit down?'

Yurovsky looked as if even this simple request was too great an imposition to be borne. But he barked out an order for chairs anyway and then left the room.

Two guards came in with chairs for the Czarina and the Czarevitch.

What on earth is going on? Anastasia wondered.

43

Yurovsky couldn't believe the Czar and his family did not know what was happening. And the peasant militia all had such looks on their faces, you would think they were the ones about to be shot. It disgusted him how sentimental these brutes were. They swaggered around, boasting their allegiance to Lenin and the Bolshevik cause but, when it came to it, they baulked at the chance to be a part of Russian history because they would have to shoot a few women. As if sex made any difference. They all professed to have given up the old stupid moralities, but scratch the skin of any peasant and you found a priest's lapdog.

At least his Latvians had no compunctions.

Perhaps. When he entered the guardroom the air was thick with cigarette smoke and vodka fumes. Some of the Letts were fiddling with the safety catches on their revolvers. Even they seemed nervous. What was wrong with these people? Didn't they want their freedom?

'Aim for their hearts,' he said. 'It will kill them quickly and there will be less mess to clear up afterwards.'

Their chairs scraped on the concrete floor as they got to their feet. Some of them couldn't meet Yurovsky's eyes. He knew that when the Whites came, half of these men would be lighting tapers in the cathedral and giving thanks to the priests for deliverance.

The family were sitting there, exactly as he had placed them. So complacent, without the wits to be frightened. They have not known fear as we have, Yurovsky thought, they haven't lived their whole lives with the terror of the secret police, haven't endured exile and torture in the camps. They cannot imagine what it is like to die.

Well, that will change.

Eleven in the firing squad, one for each of the party. He satisfied himself that everyone was in place. The Letts were crowding into the doorway behind him, other members of the guard squeezed in behind, wanting to watch. There was even some jostling among them, as those at the back tried for a better view.

Look at them.

The Czar and Czarevitch were wearing those military shirts; an old man who had never been in a battle and a boy who had never fired a gun. They made him sick.

One last check.

The Czarina was seated beneath the window by the wall, the fat princess standing beside her. Botkin was standing behind the boy's chair, his hands protectively clasped on the back of it. The other princesses were ranged along the wall, the maid to one side, their butler and cook on the other.

They all heard the truck backing up to the doors. Nicholas got to his feet ready to leave. He looked at the others, gave a slight shrug as if to say: Well, here we go again.

The boy put on his forage cap and Krupp reached for the pillow on the Czar's chair, no doubt thinking to cushion the royal rump on the bruising truck ride.

The driver was racing the engine right outside the basement door and the noise was deafening. Nicholas turned to Yurovsky. 'Hasn't your fellow learned to drive?'

Anastasia wondered what was going on. You could sense something was about to happen; even Yurovsky looked scared.

He stepped up to Nicholas and took a piece of paper out of his pocket. Anastasia could hardly hear him over the roar of the truck engine: 'Nicolai Aleksandrovitch, your relatives have tried to save you and they have failed. The Supreme Soviet of the Urals has sentenced you and your family to death for your crimes against the Russian people. We are now obliged to shoot you all.'

Nicholas either couldn't hear him over the noise of the truck, or couldn't believe what he was hearing. 'What?' he said. 'What?'

There was wailing around the room, Mama made the sign of the Cross. Anastasia felt a hot stream of urine run down her legs. She looked over Yurovsky's shoulder at the men clustered in the doorway, perhaps a dozen of them, jostling each other as they raised their guns.

She heard her father's voice again. 'What?'

Yurovsky took the Colt revolver from its holster on his

belt. He aimed it at Nicholas' chest and fired. It sounded like a cannon shot.

Papa fell to the floor.

Now everyone was screaming.

Another of the Cheka stepped into the room and fired his Mauser into Mama's mouth. Hot blood splattered over Anastasia's face. She screamed.

Doctor Botkin threw up his hands and turned his face away. The Cheka officer fired again and she saw the bullet strike Botkin's neck. The doctor clawed at his throat, blood spurting through his fingers like tiny red worms. Two more bullets hit the doctor in the stomach and as he doubled over she saw another bullet make a sudden, dark hole in the top of his bald head, and he collapsed onto the floor.

The soldiers were firing their guns wildly, bullets ricocheted around the room, they sounded like hailstones. Anastasia put her fingers to her ears and willed herself to die, quickly. She saw her papa lying on his back on the basement floor, his head in a pool of black blood, the gentle blue eyes already glassy in death.

Yurovsky winced at the noise. There were revolvers firing by his shoulder and he panicked, realised he might take a shot to the head himself. He felt a sting of pain as a bullet actually grazed his cheek.

He kept firing but the princesses would not die. The bullets seemed to be bouncing off them. That damned maid was crouched down by the wall, hiding behind two pillows. Feathers flew into the air as the bullets thumped into them but still she crouched there, as if sheltering behind an iron barricade.

The Letts were cursing aloud now, the room was filling with smoke and it was difficult to make out their targets.

Why wouldn't they die?

How long did it go on for? A lifetime.

Marie screamed, clutching at her thigh, her face twisted in pain; she seemed to be saying: Help me.

Anastasia felt something hit her hard in the chest. She gasped at the pain. Then Olga fell on her and knocked her to the ground.

But she could still see the men with the guns, could still smell the blood. She wondered if she was dead, was watching this now only as spirit; she saw Jemmy scampering and barking, heard Yurovsky shouting orders. Her mother lay beside her with a ghastly, bloody hole in the middle of her face; poor Demidova was still shrieking somewhere in the smoke.

Baby was writhing on the floor.

She squeezed her eyes shut, willing it just to be over, seeking the sanctuary of oblivion.

Yurovsky was panting hard. One by one the soldiers behind him stopped firing, out of ammunition. He shouted an order, but could not hear his own voice; the noise had deafened him. The room was thick with smoke, you could hardly see anything, the single light bulb like a lamp in a foggy street. Incredibly, the maid was still moving and he could hear moans from some of the others. Even the dog was still barking. How many bullets did it take to kill eleven people?

There was an acrid stench of gunpowder in the room, and the coppery smell of blood. The floor was awash with it. Two of the women were crouched against the wall, sobbing. He couldn't make out who they were.

He was breathing too fast. Several of the guards behind him had become hysterical.

Someone ran in from outside. 'Comrade Yurovsky, there're people gathering in the street. Everyone can hear the shooting!'

'Get out your bayonets!' he shouted. The men clustered in the doorway rushed back into the guardroom to get them.

One by one they ran back into the room and began frantically clubbing and stabbing at anything that moved.

The Czarevitch was still twisting on the floor. His face was contorted with pain, and he was clutching at his father's shirt. 'Papa,' he was moaning. 'Papa!' One of the guards kicked him in the head with his boot, it made a noise like someone stamping on a cabbage. The boy's neck snapped back and he lay still. Yurovsky raised his Colt but then remembered it was empty. He took the Mauser from his pocket and shot the Czarevitch twice in the head.

That damned maid wouldn't die. The guards were stabbing at her with their bayonets as she ran back and forth along the wall, shrieking like a cat. One of the Letts started laughing. She was holding up the tattered remains of the Czarina's feather pillow, trying to fend them off with it. Finally, one of the guards snatched it out of her hand. His comrade tried to stab her with his bayonet but the blade was dull and she grabbed it with both hands, holding it away from her. Incredible. Eventually, one of the others stabbed her in the chest. He swore in frustration, unable to remove the blade. He fixed his boot on her stomach as she slid down the wall and heaved until it came free with a sucking noise. Then the others started on her. Now the game was over they took out their frustrations, stabbing again and again. The damned woman was still screaming.

Men were milling around, clubbing at the bodies with their rifle butts. Yurovsky walked out. He felt as if all the blood in his body had drained into his boots. He had never suspected it would be so damned difficult to kill a few people. For the first time in his life he experienced the gnawing of superstitious doubt; perhaps they were enchanted, after all.

Impossible. Nonsense from fairy tales. It was that sort of thinking that had got Russia into this mess.

When he went back into the room, the Letts were still at work, sweat shining on their faces. One man was stabbing at something, but became distracted by the dog, which was whimpering in the corner. He went over and smashed in its head with his rifle butt.

Yurovsky looked at his watch. He couldn't believe it. Where had the time gone? Why couldn't these people just die?

48

The shooting had stopped. Anastasia tried to call out, but no sound came, so she supposed she must be dead. Then why could she not move around, as ghosts did? She felt something heavy lying across her chest and she remembered Olga falling on her.

She was lying on her stomach. Her eyes blinked open but she could see only shadows in a fog of cordite. She heard buzzing in her ears and then everything went black.

Yurovsky stepped out into the garden. His shirt was damp with sweat which cooled quickly and the fabric stuck to his back. He ran a hand across his face. Wouldn't do to let the men see him so unnerved. The truck driver was still racing the engine. He ran over and shouted for him to turn the damned thing off.

Idiot.

There was ringing in his ears and his cheek was stinging like fire. He touched it gingerly, realised he had a powder burn from one of the Latvian's Nagan revolvers.

Pull yourself together.

He walked back down the passageway. The Letts were finished. He checked his wristwatch. Thirty minutes since he had fired the first shot. The whole operation was supposed to have taken two minutes.

The local guards were crowded in the corridor whispering, eyes big as soup plates. He knew what they were thinking: just fifteen months ago the Czar was still divine. They were deeply frightened. Perhaps some of them really believed they had murdered a god tonight.

Yurovsky entered the room and began checking for pulses. He counted twelve bodies, realised he must have counted one of the bodies twice. He went around again, this time counted ten.

There was blood splashed up the walls. The men had savaged Demidova and her guts were spilling onto the floor, she looked like something you'd find in the back of a butcher's shop. So much for making as little mess as possible. He picked up the feather pillow she had clung to so desperately. It was incredibly heavy.

There was a metal box inside it, punched with bullet holes. He took it out and prised it open with a knife. Inside were bracelets, brooches, icons, gold, diamonds, silver, the treasure they had been looking for since the family first arrived at Ekaterinburg. A fortune.

No wonder they had been unable to kill the damned woman.

He checked the Czar's body. The wristwatch was missing. 'Where is it?' he snapped.

Silence. The shuffling of feet, no-one would meet his eyes. Latvians. Couldn't shoot straight, couldn't be trusted.

He could feel the situation slipping from his control.

'When I come back into the room that watch had better be back on his wrist,' he said and walked out with Demidova's bullet-riddled metal box under his arm. Get this put away, under lock and key. Then come back and deal with these bastard Latvians.

Voronin couldn't control the trembling in his limbs, tried to pretend that he was just cold. He hefted one of the bodies under the arms – the face had been so badly mutilated by rifle butts he couldn't be sure if it was Krupp or the doctor – and he and another guard, Beborodev, carried the corpse out to the truck. Limbs hung over the tray from under a tarpaulin, which was sticky with black blood, some of it leaking through the wooden boards and onto the ground. As they threw back the tarpaulin to heft the body onto the truck he saw one of the young girl's faces staring up at him, her expression frozen in a grimace of terror.

For the love of God.

He wondered if he would be called to account for this day, if not in this life then certainly the next. Lenin's workers' paradise sounded all very fine but when you had the Czar's blood on your hands his Bolshevik principles weren't as convincing. They could outlaw the holy blood, but they couldn't wash it off your hands; they could deny the existence of God, but that didn't mean He wasn't there waiting for you at the end.

The bodies were piled on top of one another, like carcasses at an abattoir. He wondered which one was little Anastasia.

God forgive me.

Once I was just a factory worker. I may have been poor but I had my honour. And then, as in a fable, I meet a princess and she smiles at me. I suppose I should despise myself, for feeling so ennobled by her. But I was better man when I gave her the eggs than I am now. Before tonight, I was no traitor, and I was no butcher either.

They threw the tarpaulin back over the bodies, as another commissar called Ermakov and that arrogant little bastard Yurovsky climbed in the front next to the driver, Lyukhanov. Voronin and Beborodev got into a second truck and they followed Yurovsky and Ermakov out through the gate.

There were lights on all around the square. Everyone was awake, the whole town had heard the shooting. Yurovsky had told the men this was going to be done in secret! It would be all over the Urals by morning.

The beams of their headlights picked out the frozen tableaux of the night: a stray dog picking at the stringy guts of some morsel it had found by the road; the orange eyes of a cat or fox on the edge of the woods; a crazy old man standing in the middle of Ascension Square, shouting at them as they went past.

Neither Voronin nor Beborodev spoke. It was cold inside the cabin and the heater wasn't working; Beborodev drove; Voronin just sat there, shivering and staring at the road.

'It would be a travesty if she was the one to survive. Olga was her mother's daughter; Tatiana was regal and serene; and Marie was an angel. Anastasia? She was the devil in the guise of a fat little girl.'

The road got steadily worse, jarring their spines as they bounced over the frozen ruts.

'Does Yurovsky know the way to the Four Brothers in the dark?' Beborodev said, breaking the silence.

'He couldn't find his own prick without the light on,' Voronin said.

It was like driving through a tunnel, the woods around them drew them in, black and cold and silent. Yurovsky's truck was caught for a moment in the wash of their headlights, Voronin saw an arm hanging loose from under the tarpaulin, could not take his eyes from it.

I am crazy to get mixed up in this. The Whites are just a few miles away, if they find out I had a hand in this, God knows what they will do to me. He had heard of Red cadres being crucified in some places. What would they do to a man who laid a hand on the divine Nicholas?

They were going over softer ground now and he saw the wheels of Lyukhanov's truck sink in the wet mud. Lyukhanov gunned the motor and the wheels dug themselves in deeper.

'He's bogged,' Beborodev said. 'Fucking idiot.' The oath hung like a curse over their heads.

We're all idiots, Voronin thought. Just for being here.

'He's going to overheat the motor,' Beborodev said.

They stopped the truck and got out. Lyukhanov had ploughed his truck deeper into the swamp, sending a spray of mud high into the air. Voronin still could not take his eyes from the pale arm hanging from under the tarpaulin, and he fought the insane urge to tuck it neatly away.

'That fucking idiot Lyukhanov,' Beborodev repeated.

Yurovsky got out of the truck. His face was pale with frustration. He shouted something to Lyukhanov, who turned off the engine and got out of the cab. They stared at the back wheels, now up to the axles in the mud.

'You need planks,' Beborodev said. 'You'll never get it out of there without planks.'

'And water,' Voronin said. 'You need water for the engine.'

They could hear it, now it was quiet, the radiator hissing

and popping. Beborodev was right. Lyukhanov had cooked the engine.

Yurovsky swore violently under his breath. Voronin avoided his eyes. The man had a temper and he didn't want to get in the way of him. Not his fault things had gone wrong, of course, but you never knew where you were with these Cheka bastards.

Yurovsky felt himself starting to sweat again. There would have to be reports written to Moscow later and it was important for his future that nothing stood in the way of a glowing commendation from Lenin.

Beborodev pointed through the trees. 'What's that?' he said.

Now Yurovsky could see it, too, a yellow light, about two hundred yards away through the forest.

'The railway line is just over that way,' Lyukhanov said. 'The light must be from a serial booth.'

Yurovsky put his hands on his hips, trying to think. He must not let these clods know how close he was to panic. 'You're sure?' he said.

'I've lived in this town all my life,' Lyukhanov said, as if it was something to be proud of.

Yurovsky went to fetch a torch from the truck cabin. He could hear Ermakov snoring in the front. He had passed out, drunk. Useless peasant. He leaned into the cab and shoved him roughly. 'Wake up.'

He shone the torch in his face and Ermakov groaned and tried to shield his eyes.

'Get out here,' Yurovksy said.

They were supposed to meet Ermakov's rabble in the woods somewhere near here, they were bringing carts with them to take the bodies the rest of the way. Yurovsky still had to find the rendezvous point.

Ermakov slid out of the cabin, fell into the mud.

Disgusted, Yurovsky went back to the others. 'Go over to the signal station,' he said to Lyukhanov. 'See if they have water and planks.'

'I don't have a torch,' Lyukhanov protested.

'Walk towards the light.' He heard Ermakov stumbling to his feet. 'We'll look for the rest of the party. Voronin, you and Beborodev guard the bodies.'

He let Ermakov lead the way into the darkness. It would be light soon. They had to get the bodies out of sight before dawn. He remembered when he had come this way a few days ago, he could see the rail tracks from the Four Brothers mine site. They couldn't be seen burying the bodies or, when the Whites came, someone would show them where they were. Moscow had insisted that the execution was to remain secret.

He could feel the threads unravelling, his plans coming apart.

'Let's get back in the truck,' Beborodev said, but neither of them moved. They stood there, staring at the pale arm protruding from under the tarpaulin.

Above them the cold and indifferent stars; the forest closing in around them.

Beborodev lit a cigarette. 'Did you hear that?' he said.

Voronin stilled his breathing to listen. Nothing.

'I thought I heard something.'

Then he heard it, too. Someone moaning.

'Holy Mother of God,' Voronin said.

Neither of them moved.

It sounded like a child sobbing.

'What do we do?' Beborodev said.

If we have any sense, we will pretend we heard nothing, Voronin thought. We get back inside the truck cabin and smoke cigarettes until Yurovsky and Ermakov get back and then we do whatever they tell us to.

'One of them's still alive,' Beborodev said.

Voronin thought about the Czar, who had offered him one of his cigarettes and shared a few remarks on the weather; the little Czarevitch, lying crippled in his bed, playing with his tin of bits and pieces; he thought about the funny little princess with her plump cheeks and gold curls, how grateful she had been when he gave her those eggs.

Ermakov and Yurovsky must be at least two hundred yards away by now, Voronin thought. Far enough.

Beborodev drew so hard on his cigarette, Voronin could hear the tobacco crackling like firewood. He was waiting for Voronin to make the first move.

Voronin threw back the tarpaulin, recoiled at the smell of blood and ordure. Close to his face, the owner of the pale arm had her face turned up towards him in a silent scream, the features battered beyond recognition by rifle butts. Execution was one thing, he thought, but Yurovsky and his Cheka were just animals.

He saw movement among the twisted pile of limbs, a fluttering of fingers, like a small bird trying to move its wing. 'Here,' he said. He pulled at one of the corpses.

Voronin stopped to listen for footsteps. If Yurovsky came back now, it was all over for him. He went back to the tray and lit a match, peered among the tangle of corpses.

An arm twitched and he heard a moan. It was one of the princesses. Her dress and corset had been ripped apart by a bayonet. Beborodev put his finger in the rent, pulled out a fat necklace of fire-white diamonds.

'Holy Mother of God,' he swore in wonderment. That was why they had died so hard. Their corsets had been sewn with diamonds, had acted as armour against the bullets and knives. Dear God.

Voronin held the match close to the girl's face. Her hair was matted and black with blood, one side of her face swollen to the size of a melon. But he recognised her.

'Anastasia,' he said.

PART TWO

Shanghai, 1921

MICHAEL

Some men don't fall in love; they get lost. I was lost from the moment I saw Anastasia Romanov in the taxi club that first night.

It started like any other evening in Shanghai; drinks at the American Club until dark, then everyone went home to dress. The uniform was white mess jacket, soft white shirt and black trousers. Most nights I headed for the Carlton, for dinner and the cabaret, before I left my respectable married colleagues and their wives and hit the town on my own, perhaps an absinthe at the French club on the Rue Cardinal Mercier and then over to the Ambassador or the Casanova or the Venus and their sprung dance floors. The White Russians worked them all, charging from ten cents to a dollar for a dance ticket, you could tango all night with princesses and countesses and still come out with change from a twenty.

I don't pretend I had any illusions about what kind of girls worked in those places and I wasn't looking to redeem anyone, least of all a Russian whore. After three years in Shanghai, I considered myself immune to the tricks and devices of the taxi club girls, no matter what colour they were. But the problem with me, the problem with most men, is we don't go out at night looking for happiness. We go searching for something we can't have.

Anastasia Romanov was not exactly unattainable, not in that way. She didn't stand out from the other elegantly dressed professional dancers in their bright red lipstick and clicking heels. She came over to me as soon as I walked in and asked me to buy her a glass of champagne. It's not champagne, of course, it's cold tea, and none of the girls will touch it. You're buying their time, and their time belongs to the house.

Sometimes you meet a woman with a certain quality you can't define, something that attracts you despite yourself. You perhaps try to attribute it to some physical feature; the way they walk, the timbre of their voice, or, most often, something in their eyes. Anastasia's eyes were the saddest eyes I had ever seen. Even when she was looking right at you, you knew she was thinking about something else, as if she was bleeding to death right under that dress and trying to cover it over. Her eyes had the faraway look you see on people in hospital beds when they know they're dying.

And yes, she was beautiful, but no more so than a hundred other women I'd seduced or paid for in my young life. She had fair hair, a good figure – perhaps a little too skinny for my taste – and yes, the saddest, bluest eyes I'd ever seen in my life.

She had no technique; I was not seduced. She hit me for a glass of cold tea and then just sat there, staring off into space and smoking her cigarette, didn't try to persuade me to sleep with her, like the other girls did, which was the only reason single white bachelors like me came to the taxi club. But she really didn't care.

You see how it happened; I always want whatever isn't on offer, anything I'm not supposed to have.

'Will you sleep with me?' I said, and these were just about the first words I ever said to her.

'Twenty dollars,' she said, which was an outrageous price. I couldn't afford that sort of money, so I tried to haggle with her and she completely ignored me. Went on smoking her cigarette like I wasn't there.

Normally I would walk away from this. You never get what you pay for anyway in the taxi clubs. The girls just lie there, looking at the ceiling, thinking about the rent or their kid at home in Whangpoo, and wait for you to finish so they can move on to their next customer. I don't know what made me do it. I agreed to pay her twenty dollars for what I could have got for five anywhere in town.

She pulled her dress over her head and let it slip to the floor. And then she stood there, naked, with this look on her face, almost contemptuous, as if she couldn't believe I'd paid so much for so little.

But I suppose any woman finds it hard to imagine what a man gets from an encounter like this. You're not buying love, or even a counterfeit of it. You bring your own fantasy to the moment and whatever pleasure you get you make yourself. She let me push her onto the bed and then she lay there while I took what I'd paid for.

You are warned about this kind of girl, you hear the stories when you're at school; go with girls who do it for money and you'll get a disease. Well, I'd always been careful, until then.

My one night with Anastasia Romanov left me with something in my blood but it wasn't any kind of sickness like the sailors picked up in the brothels down by the docks. It was much worse than that; it would have been better if I'd walked under the wheels of a trolley car on the Bund.

ANASTASIA

I am a taxi girl, that's all I am, that's all I have ever been.

You tell yourself: it is just business. You look at a man, you think: how much will he pay? It doesn't matter that he is fat like a pig, that he stinks of garlic, money is what matters, Stushi, the sale not the buyer.

But it does matter, deep down; sometimes at night I lie in my bed and think of some old man, sweating and grunting on top of me, and I want to scream, I want to throw myself in the river.

I wonder if in that other time, my not-remembered time, if I ever looked at some man and thought: I would like to kiss him, I would like to dance with him. Not for money, not for anything else but because I think he is nice.

My best customer is Chinese. Chinese will pay a lot to sleep with a white girl, even if she is just a Russian white girl. I wonder if one day I can buy myself out of this place just by sleeping with Chinese. They don't want all this other business, like some of the fine Mr Englishmen, don't want the nice talk. Mister Chinese doesn't like me either; he wrinkles his nose and closes his eyes when he does it, just like I do. But afterwards he can go tell his friends: I fucked a white missy. And next time, when Mr Englishman won't let him in his park or his club, he can stroke his secret like a little revenge, for face and for good luck and for consolation.

When he walked in, he didn't look like he had much money, so none of the other girls went over. I wonder now what made me get up and walk over; perhaps I was tired of the fat old Chinamen and the pale Englishmen with their cold eyes. This one had this cowlick over his right eye, very black hair and eyes so dark and blue they made you think of water. But he looked like he had been drinking, maybe even looked a little crazy. I didn't mind if he was dangerous, not any more.

I gave him some sweet talk, and he smiled at me. His eyes seemed unfocused and when I stood close I could smell the whisky on his breath. He spoke English with a Yankee accent, and I thought this one is bad news for me, because Americans were cheap back then.

But he agreed to pay me my price; he didn't argue or tell me I was a penny whore looking for a dollar, like some do. I had to hold him up when we got outside and he stumbled into the rickshaw, and when I climbed in next to him he gave the coolie his address. It was a hot night, no stars, sampan horns booming on the river. I didn't feel anything. I had done this so many times.

I thought we would go to some cramped little room in Whangpoa, but no, he lived in the French quarter, a nice house, not bad. His servant looked at me like I was dog meat, I wanted to slap him; just some Chinese coolie and he treated me like I was a yellow whore.

We went upstairs to his bedroom. He made me take off my clothes while he sat there in the dark, smoking a cigarette.

'What's your name?' he asked me.

'What do you want my name to be?'

'I don't want it to be anything.'

'Anastasia.'

'Russian, right?'

I didn't want to talk: I do the business, the guy gives me the money, that was the way I preferred.

'What do you like?' I knelt in front of him and ran my fingernails up his leg. He was hard, I could see how stiff he was through his trousers. I started to undo the buttons.

He gripped my hand and pulled it away. Maybe he is going to act crazy and beat me up now, I thought. It had happened before.

'You're beautiful,' he whispered.

Of course I am. Every girl is beautiful in the dark.

'I've got to have you now,' I told him. It is not easy to make it sound real when you are so tired you just want to lie down and die.

I put his hand on my breast. He lifted me up and carried me to the bed. He had a nice body, lean and hard-muscled, and I let him do the business, made sure he did not tear my new silk knickers, or get any stains on my dress. I had to wear that dress when I went back to the taxi club.

It didn't take long, and then I rolled him off me. Soon he was asleep. I put my dress back on and just as I was about to go I saw his jacket hanging on the back of the chair. Inside his wallet was one hundred American dollars and that was what I charged him. It was more than he wanted to pay, but I always thought whatever my customers bought was never as much as I was selling. They just got sex; I gave away a little piece of me.

I put the money in my purse and hurried downstairs and through the courtyard. I found a rickshaw in the street and got back to the club to dance a tango with a fat Chinaman. He bought me three cold teas. The boss was very happy with me that night. He said he would make a taxi girl of me yet.

MICHAEL

The Chinese call it *jenao*; there is no one word in English that means quite the same thing. It is like an overwhelming clamour on the senses. *Jenao* summed up Shanghai perfectly. Back then it was a free city, which meant you didn't need a passport to live there, and it attracted every kind of freebooter, adventurer and refugee.

The first day I stepped onto the Bund it terrified me. Everything came at you at once, assaulting you in some way; the beggars, the rickshaw drivers, the clatter of the trams, the hawkers pulling at your clothes, and that particular stink of urine, garlic and something else, something I've never quite tracked down after all these years, perhaps it's just sweat. In the first five minutes on the wharf I saw three things I'd never seen before: a beggar with leprosy, a ten-year-old Chinese girl offering me sex, and a dead body lying uncovered on the street.

I paid too much for the rickshaw, and somehow got myself and my luggage onto the little carriage. I just wanted to get away from the dock, find my hotel and hide. As my sparrow-legged coolie carried me through the streets, Shanghai happened around me and I felt like a kid on his first visit to the zoo, gawping at everything, understanding nothing.

I saw Englishmen in bowler hats stepping over bundles of rags with outstretched hands holding naked babies; Sikh policemen in scarlet turbans frantically blowing whistles and waving at the oncoming traffic; Chinese girls in sheath-tight cheongsams weaving through the bedlam of rickshaws and trolley buses, utterly exotic, achingly beautiful.

I had come to Shanghai to make a living as a journalist. Well, I guess that's not quite true; I had come to Shanghai to get as far away as I possibly could from my parents. Journalism in those days did not pay a wage that a man with a taste for life's pleasures could live on. Fortunately I had an independent income; my family had financed my absence from New York. The sole condition of their benevolence was that I shouldn't come back until I had grown up. My father's words.

We parted in an atmosphere of mutual contempt.

They helped me find employment in my new home. The *China Press* was considered the best American newspaper in Shanghai and the editor, John B Powell, was a friend of my parents. On joining his staff I received two instructions from the editor: one, the prestige of the United States was to be upheld in my reporting at whatever cost to the truth; two, don't try to learn Chinese, it turned you queer.

I rented an apartment in the French Concession and set about doing whatever was necessary to avoid 'growing up'. Shanghai was certainly the place to do it; it lived and breathed opium, extortion, prostitution and gambling. You could get anything you wanted in Shanghai. In the sailors' bars in Blood Alley you could have sex with a twelve-year-old behind a curtain for the price of a glass of watered-down beer; heroin was delivered by room service in one of the hotels behind the Bund.

All I wanted was to drink, sleep with easy women and not worry about tomorrow. I was doing okay at it until I met Anastasia Romanov.

I don't believe in coincidence. We are where we are at certain times in our lives because things were meant to happen that way, no other reason. A man misses a ship or ferry, matter of minutes, the boat sinks, everyone on it drowns. To me, it means that wasn't the day he was meant to die, simple as that. Not luck, not fate; nothing happens by chance.

I don't think it was pure chance that I was crossing the bridge that night just as she was climbing on the parapet.

I'd drunk more than was good for me, as usual, but then, when you're twenty-four years old you don't think much about what's good for you. It was two o'clock in the morning, I was sprawled in the back of a rickshaw heading over the Whangpoa Bridge on the way home from some taxi club. I looked across the bridge and there she was, fair hair hanging around her shoulders, her heels kicked off and lying on the sidewalk, her dress hooked up to her knees as she climbed onto the balustrade.

I saw her tossing bank notes into the river. They drifted away in the ghost-light of a three-quarter moon. Then she lifted her arms like some exotically beautiful and scarlet-shimmering bird stretching its wings to the sun. I don't know how long she stood there like that. A few seconds is all. My coolie had strained and puffed to the crest of the bridge and now he was scampering down the other side, paying no attention to the crazy white-devil ghost in the red dress.

I shouted, 'Hey!' But it was too late, she didn't hear me, or she didn't care. A flash of red silk and she was gone.

'Stop here!' I shouted and jumped out of the rickshaw. I ran back to the middle of the bridge.

Had I recognised her? Of course not. Recognition came later. All I saw was a beautiful white woman jumping off a bridge, and it was my unthinking, intoxicated reaction to dive right in after her and save her.

ANASTASIA

I am still not sure when it was that life didn't seem worth living. Just staying alive was exhausting; you do this, you do that, so you can eat and drink and have somewhere to sleep, but then you have to do it all again tomorrow. One day I just decided it would be easier not to do it any more.

Some people have told me I felt this way because there were no memories to sustain me, that with a past, I would have had something to hold onto. Perhaps they were right. All I had was bad memories, all the fat Chinamen and Englishmen who treated a girl like toilet paper, use you and then throw you away after.

That night I felt so tired, so empty, so dirty. I had all this money in my hand, and nowhere to go but back to the taxi club. So I climbed on the bridge and let the money go, watched it drift like snow into the dark river. It floated there on the surface, curling and darting with the current, until it disappeared out of sight into the darkness.

And I thought: there goes all the bad business. There goes my sin.

I rose up on my toes, spread out my arms and looked at the black sky. I said to God: catch me. Then a slow arc that carried me down in perfect grace, and for just this weightless, wonderful moment I thought I could fly.

MICHAEL

The state I was in, I was lucky I didn't drown in that river myself, or catch some deadly disease; God alone knew what filth Shanghai dumped in that damned sewer. The shock of the cold water when I hit sobered me up fast and made me realise what a fool I was. The water was oily dark and there was a strong current running. Summers in the Hamptons had made me a strong swimmer; as it was I barely reached her.

She was a dead weight, I thought perhaps she'd hit her head on the way in. I struck out for the shore, towards a light on the other side of the bridge. I heard a whistle blowing, voices calling out in Mandarin. I recognised just two words: *Qiu ming*! Save life! It was only fifty yards to the shore but swimming across the current in my condition with the girl it might as well have been five hundred. I was just about done when I got there.

My coolie had scrambled down the bank, he was the one doing all the shouting; perhaps he thought I'd jumped in the river so I wouldn't have to pay him his fare. There was someone with him, holding a torch. When I reached the bank I saw it was a Sikh policeman. He must have been close by on patrol. He threw out a hand to me when I reached the shallows, tried not to get his uniform too wet, and dragged me onto the bank. I picked up the girl and carried her onto the Bund, my coolie still yabbering at me.

And you know, I still didn't recognise her. It was dark and her hair was plastered across her face and she was throwing up on my shoes. Water, mostly. At least she was alive. I sat down on the road and put my head between my knees and tried to catch my breath. I started to shiver, partly from the cold of the water and partly the adrenalin pumping through me. It occurred to me I hadn't been that far from drowning.

'What happened, sir?' the Sikh policeman was asking me, in English now.

'I saw the lady fall in.' He shone his torch on her. She was choking and limp and covered in mud and filth from the river. She didn't look like a lady; bright red lipstick smudged across her face, one shoulder strap ripped.

I wondered what the hell I should do now. I could take her to the hospital, but she wasn't sick. I couldn't walk away and leave her, though, not after almost killing myself for her.

'Are you all right?' I said, a monumentally stupid thing to say.

Her eyes opened but she didn't answer me.

'What the hell were you doing?'

Still no answer.

'You want me to take you some place?'

She shook her head: no.

The policeman tut-tutted, gave a despairing shake of the head the way the Sikhs do, like the whole world was mad except for him. I don't think he knew what to do with this crazy American and the half-drowned white woman. Hoped I would make the decision for him, I guess.

Which I did. I picked her up, like a bundle of wet rags, and deposited this madwoman in the rickshaw and told my coolie to take us back to my place on the Nanking Road. He was still shouting and waving his arms and didn't really shut up until we reached my apartment and I deposited two soggy American dollars in his hand for his trouble.

Gordon looked at me like I had dragged a corpse off the street and wanted to bring it inside. Gordon was my houseboy, and in those days no white household could survive in Shanghai without one. He was in his nightshirt, and he had this expression of reproach on his face, like my father's when I got home late from a cocktail party. I was paying his wages, for Christ's sake, but you wouldn't have known it.

The girl was leaning against me, he must have thought we were both drunk. I had my arm around her, holding her up, as I steered her towards my bedroom.

'Wanchee two towel, two dressing gown,' I told him.

He frowned at the puddles we left on his clean floors, but went off to get what I wanted.

'You'd better get out of those wet things,' I said.

I lit the lamp. I got a good look at her for the first time. I still didn't recognise her. She had been crying the whole time in the rickshaw, her eyes were swollen and red like she'd been in a fight, her hair was matted over her face. It didn't occur to me that I knew her.

'Why are you doing this?' she said.

It was the voice I recognised first, torchy, and accented with Russian or German. I remembered bringing home a lovely fair-haired Russian from a taxi club, a vague memory of drunken fumbling and waking in the morning with my wallet lying empty on the floor, a monumental hangover and a vague smell of perfume in the bathroom.

Surely this isn't the same girl?

She ran a hand through her wet hair, a puddle forming on the silk carpet. 'The Chinese say if you save a life you are responsible for that person until the day they die. Is that what you want?'

'Is that what you want?' I asked her. She lowered her eyes.

'What were you doing on the bridge?'

'I was looking for the way out of Shanghai,' she said, and slumped down on the edge of my bed, sat there pigeon-toed, looking for all the world like a lost schoolgirl. I realised the foolish assumptions I had made. One thing to save a life; it doesn't always mean someone wants to be saved. And she was right, about the Chinese, they think of life as a burden, that you have enough loads to carry without taking on another's.

'You'd better get out of those wet clothes,' I repeated.

I meant for her to go into the bathroom, or behind the screen. Instead she stood up, stripped her dress and slip over her head, and then kicked off her underwear, but without the artistry she had displayed at our first encounter. What a sight we must have been; me standing there with a puddle growing around my shoes, and this beautiful fair-haired girl, naked, shivering, skinny and unabashed.

Gordon came in, stood there in the doorway, staring at her. 'Thanks,' I said and snatched the towels and dressing gowns out of his hands and shut the door.

Her helplessness stirred some ember of humanity in me. That was my real weakness, I suppose. I still wanted to save her.

'Here,' I said and held out the towel and the gown. She stared at them as if she had no idea what they were for.

'I wanted to die tonight,' she said. There was accusation in her voice.

'I guess I screwed it up for you.'

She took the towel and started to dry herself. She caught me watching her. 'I suppose now you want to sleep with me.'

'There're easier ways of getting girls than jumping in the river.'

She put one long leg on a chair and dried it, then the other. 'You can sleep with me if you want,' she said as if she didn't care, and that decided me. Already, I wanted her to care, and I didn't even know her then.

'It cost me a hundred bucks to sleep with you last time. I've used up my girl allowance for the year.'

It was the first time I saw any reaction from her. What was it? Amusement? Surprise? Shame? I wasn't able to read her at all.

'You don't remember?'

She shook her head, no, and crushed me. 'Well, a man likes to know he's made a good impression.'

'I'm sorry,' she said, as if it was of no account.

She started to dry her hair. Christ, she was lovely, standing there in the burnished glow of the lamp. Like any man, I suppose, I never tire of looking at the lines of a woman, wondering at them. I couldn't look away even if I'd wanted to. I disgust myself sometimes.

She threw the towel on the floor and put on the dressing gown. She gave a small sigh, not of sadness or resignation but of accommodation, the sigh of a survivor adjusting to new and unexpected circumstance. She looked around the room as if seeing it for the first time. And perhaps she was. The last time she was there it was dark and anyway she was utterly focused on my wallet.

'You've made a puddle,' she said finally, looking at the floor.

I took off my wet clothes, too. Perhaps I hoped to establish some intimacy between us, but she turned away and did not look at me, not once; I had been unable to take my eyes off her. And so she won her first victory, her first revenge on me for robbing her of her escape from Shanghai and her miserable life.

'I don't remember your name,' I said.

'Anastasia Romanov,' she said. Anastasia; the city was full of them. Being an open city, Shanghai had filled with White Russians after the revolution, and Anastasia was a common Russian name.

'You'd better sleep here,' I said.

She nodded, as if it had already been decided. I suppose it had. She didn't ask me where I would sleep, showed no curiosity about me at all, beyond that first question: why are you doing this?

Why did I do it? I don't know.

I watched her climb into my bed and I hesitated; should I climb in beside her or sleep on the living room couch, like a gentleman?

I went into the living room and slept on the couch. If I had got into the bed I knew I couldn't trust myself not to touch her. If I made love to her, she would see it as repayment for saving her life, and that would have cheapened me. Besides, I wanted her to be grateful to me, to find me as intriguing as I found her.

And that was my first mistake.

ANASTASIA

I will never understand this man, what made him jump in the river in the middle of the night to save some girl, some stranger. And then there's this: he knows I stole all his money that one night, then he let me sleep in his bed and leaves his wallet there again, right there on the dresser. Like he is saying to me: please, hurt me again. Prove to me I cannot trust you.

But, of course, he can trust me now. He saved my life; I am his burden. A burden will always be there, even when you are tired of it.

Next morning I sat at the window with the tea his amah had brought me. I threw open the green-painted shutters, watched the sparrows playing in the cherry tree. Down in the little dirty courtyard the wash boy was banging the wet laundry against the sides of the trough.

A wedding procession wound its way between the houses in the laneway, the bride in her red lacquer sedan chair, her servants shouting as they cleared a path for her. More servants followed, carrying her dowry: chairs, big lacquered vases, geese. The sound of the wedding gongs was deafening.

'The Chinese can never do anything without making a big noise about it,' he said.

I had not heard him come into the room. He was wearing a white dressing gown, open at the neck, the black curls of hair on his chest tight and wet from his bath. He was holding a cup of American coffee, the smell of it was very strong.

'I see my amah brought you tea. Would you rather have coffee?' I nodded and he gave me his cup. 'I wondered if you'd still be here this morning.'

'Where else could I go?'

He shrugged. I saw him glance at his wallet there on the dresser. Like I was a thief. Last time I was over-charging, not stealing. I would never steal.

'It is all there. Do you want to count it?'

There was suddenly a high colour in his cheeks, like polished bronze.

I drank his coffee and handed him back the cup. 'More sugar next time.'

'I see you're feeling better.'

What a thing to say. He didn't understand; it was not a matter of feeling better. I didn't feel anything at all.

He was standing very close, there were nice smells: soap, cologne, coffee.

'Why did you do it?' he said.

He had saved my life and now he had the right to ask me all these questions. 'I felt bad about taking your money,' I said. 'I could not live with the guilt.'

At first he didn't understand that I was making fun of him. It was a cruel thing to do but that was the problem with being Anastasia Romanov. She did things I didn't really understand and I could only stand by and watch.

He went to the ancient armoire in the corner and took out a shirt and suit and started to get dressed, right there in front of me, like we were husband and wife. Perhaps he thought he owned a little part of me now.

I looked out of the window and wondered what to do with this new day I never thought I would have. I could go back to the taxi club as if nothing had happened. Or I could just sit here and do nothing and

73

see if he threw me out. If he did, it was not so far to walk back to the bridge. Or perhaps he would let me stay and I would let him look after me, like his burden, just like the Chinese said.

MICHAEL

The English and their clubs.

The Shanghai Club, at number 3, the Bund, boasted the longest bar in the world, one hundred feet from one end to the other, you could stand there with a gin and tonic in your hand and look out over the docks and slums of Shanghai and feel superior to just about everyone, which is what the English do best. Or there was the Shanghai Race Club: no women, no Chinese thank you, you had to be introduced to the committee by a sitting member and grovel at their feet and beg them to accept your subscription fee. They had a clock tower out at the racecourse known as Big Bertie. The English are like that: they give affectionate names to things as if they were people; they treat people like things and keep them at a formal distance, even if they've known them for years. The other great institution of Shanghai was the British Club: sixty five acres of landscaped gardens on Bubbling Well Road, its own ballroom, tennis courts and swimming pool.

That's where I'd arranged to meet Mackie.

I'd always liked Mackie. He was a Scot, so he probably hated the English more than I did, though he did a better job of disguising it. Except when he'd had too much gin. He was a doctor, worked at the American Hospital, but kept a Chinese mistress. This arrangement consigned him to a sort of netherworld, as no-one in the *Concession* was ever quite sure how to treat him; whether to defer to him because he was a doctor, or cut him because he'd gone native.

We always got on just fine, united in our contempt for the common foe.

I'd asked Mackie to examine Anastasia for any ill effects after her swim in the river; that's what I'd told her, anyway. The truth was I was looking for more. I was hoping he could give me some clue as to who she was, and why she'd tried to kill herself.

He bought me a gin and then he folded his reading glasses into his pocket. 'Fascinating woman,' he said.

I didn't respond, didn't need to. I knew jealousy was part of it, pity was another. Anyone could have told me no good could come of a relationship with a White Russian taxi girl.

'You've examined her?'

'Physically she seems fine. There're a few medical peculiarities. For instance, the big toe on her right foot is bent right over, the medical name for it is hallux valgus. In her case, it's so pronounced it must have been present from birth. She has a small white scar on her right shoulder blade.'

'But how does she seem to you?' When he hesitated, I added: 'Mentally.'

'I'm not trained in psychiatry,' he said. He lit his pipe. It stank, God alone knew what kind of tobacco he put in it, the little tin he kept it in said Player's but he had refilled it so many times it could have been anything.

'You think she's crazy?'

'No, I think you are.' He held my stare.

He was right, of course. What itch for self-destruction would draw a man towards such a woman? She was a prostitute, and perhaps even slightly unhinged. But I was unable to resist such a terrible, fragile beauty. Hell, I knew I was stupid. But if I'd wanted an easy and uncomplicated life I would have stayed home in New York.

'She says she can't remember anything before Harbin,' I said.

He fussed with the pipe. It was only ever good for two or three puffs and then it would go out. I think he enjoyed fussing with it more than smoking it. 'That is what she contends. It's possible.'

'Something terrible must have happened to her in Russia.'

'Terrible things happened to everyone in Russia. I suspect there may be a physical as well as an emotional cause for her present state.'

'But you said she was fine physically?'

His hand went to his temple. 'She has a scar, right here, and an indentation of her skull which could be the result of trauma from a blunt object. There is also a scar behind her right ear that could have been made by the passage of a bullet.'

'You think that's it?'

'I have no idea. It's just a hypothesis, Michael. Impossible to say. As I said, I have no training in psychiatry or neurology.'

I wondered what a life without a past would be like. It's history that anchors us in the present, and tells us who we are. I'd spent every day for the last ten years trying to disgust and disappoint my father, was still doing it, though he was ten thousand miles away in New York. It wasn't rational, and it wasn't very bright, but that was who I was; such conflicts defined me.

He finished his whisky and went back to fiddling with his pipe. 'You're a mad bastard,' he said.

'Why?'

'No shortage of women in Shanghai. Why go to so much trouble over this one?'

'I don't know.' I called over the Chinese waiter and ordered two more G&T's. 'Send me your bill, Mack.'

'It's on the house.'

I shrugged. I knew he'd say that.

'She's just another dance hall princess,' he said, his head wreathed in a cloud of pungent smoke.

'Yes, I know,' I answered, but I didn't believe it. Anastasia Romanov was unlike any other woman I'd ever met, I'd convinced myself of that. And having convinced myself she was different, I was going to make her different whether she was or not.

You have to understand what it was to be a White Russian in Shanghai in the twenties.

After the Revolution refugees flooded into the international settlement through Harbin. They were people without a country, without passports, and at first people felt sorry for them. They were white like us, and a few Europeans even wanted to help them. Many of the refugees were middle class, businessmen, ex-army officers, and university teachers, in background and education they were not that different to us. Some found employment as chauffeurs, watchmen or bodyguards, others taught languages or horse riding. But in the end there simply wasn't sympathy enough to go round, and when the people saw them pulling rickshaws or having the indelicacy to starve to death in the street, opinion turned against them.

It was when the Russian girls in the taxi clubs started sleeping with ordinary Chinese that the British banker sipping his G&T in the Shanghai Club and the American matron eating canapés on the roof garden of the Carlton really took exception. One thing for a man to sleep with a Russian girl, and a lot of us did; when a Chinese did it, it blurred the lines of privilege. The colony stopped thinking of them as White Russians; they thought of them as White Chinese.

So taking in a White Russian whore was not just a social gaffe; I was thumbing my nose at the whole foreign settlement.

Imagine. It is a sticky monsoon evening. You come home to the familiar and comforting bedlam of your Chinese household, the amah screeching at your number one boy, chickens squabbling in the yard, songbirds trilling in their bamboo cages. You go up the stairs, let yourself in to your apartment, and hear an adagio from Bach. You listen for the scratching of the gramophone, but instead you see a woman, her back towards you, sitting at the ancient piano you inherited with the other oddments of furniture that came with the lease.

What do you do?

I stood there, entranced, and listened. Anastasia sat ramrod straight, long white fingers moving precisely over the yellowed ivory keys. The piano needed tuning, it sounded tinny and flat, but it wasn't the music that moved me so much as the look of profound concentration on her face. She wasn't looking at the keys, she was staring at the wall, and the lines of her face were immobile.

I felt a chill along my spine.

The first flurry of rain hit the roof like a barrage of copper nails and Anastasia stopped playing. She turned around and saw me staring at her. Her face was pale in the eerie ghost-light of the storm.

'You're home,' she said.

'You can play.'

'Yes.' She stood up quickly and retreated from the piano as if she had been sleep walking and was surprised to find herself out of bed. She wiped her hands on her dress as if they were soiled.

'You play beautifully. Where did you learn?'

A painful smile. 'I don't remember.'

I ran my fingers along the edge of the piano. 'I don't think anyone's ever played this old thing for years.'

It was as if she felt guilty at being caught out. My hard case, my taxi girl who had seen too much of life at . . . what could she be? Twenty, twenty-one years old? She was just a romantic, after all, a romantic who liked Bach.

I noticed there was no sheet music on the piano.

'You played from memory,' I said.

She shook her head, as bewildered as I. The storm was rushing in, it grew ominously dark, rain leaked from the gutters and poured in sheets into the cobbled courtyard.

Why should her talent for music surprise me? Whoever she was, it had been apparent from the beginning that she had been well educated. She spoke English fluently, despite certain idiosyncrasies. I assumed that at the least she was from the middle class of some large Russian city. Yet there was something else, something in the way she held herself, that particular arrogance that comes with money and having a flunkey to pick up your dirty clothes and bring your break-fast and lay out your bed at night. I wondered if there was a title left behind in Russia, along with kin.

'I wish you'd keep playing,' I said.

'I don't feel like it any more.'

She sat down on the windowsill, stared at the chaos of traffic on the Nanking Road, trolley cars ploughing through streets already ankle deep in water, rickshaw men sopping and miserable while their fares shouted at them to hurry and get them out of the rain.

A single yellow lamp threw her chiselled features into sharp relief. Her sadness was indescribably beautiful. It only made me want her more. 'I wasn't sure you'd still be here,' I said.

'Where else could I go?' she said.

'I don't know.'

'I told you. You are responsible for me now.'

'You're mine,' I said.

'Yes. I'm yours.'

But, of course, that was a lie.

The Bund was a seven mile curve of waterfront running south from Soochow Creek, a testament to Western magnificence and the leverage of opium. There were banks, hotels and clubs, all boasting façades of bronze and granite; Jardine's, the great Asian taipan; the *North China Daily News*; and the massive edifice of the Hong Kong and Shanghai Bank, which was still under construction then; they rose into a hot, grey sky, the domes and columns reminiscent of London and Paris. A number of upright Englishmen had their statues down there, looking severe and virtuous; you could be forgiven for thinking the British Empire had been built on the profits of religion, not a debilitating drug. In the yellowed photographs I still keep from that time, it looked impossibly romantic and appealing. But when you stepped outside, it still smelled like China.

The Bund looked as if it had been there for centuries, but it was the work of a few short years. Such permanence was an illusion; the émigré Russians could have told us that.

The Shanghai Club sat at the top of the Bund, its great cupolas forbidding and eternal. As you entered from the street you passed beneath towering columns of Ningpo granite into a vast and echoing hall of black and white marble, ascending a staircase of white Sicilian marble to the library, reading room, billiards hall and dining room.

Here, if you were a member, you could eat a breakfast of kedgeree, bacon and eggs, as you looked across the Whangpoa River to the slums on the other side, which were always more appealing from a distance. In winter Chinese waiters in white jackets would serve steaming porridge with toast and Oxford marmalade. Your morning newspaper arrived at table freshly ironed.

On this evening during the monsoon of 1921 I was signed in by my friend Mackie. We made our way upstairs to the oak-panelled Jacobean bar, halloo Henries standing eight deep along the length of it. At the far end it curved to the left and ran a short distance parallel to the Bund, and from here you could look over the balcony and watch the junks on the river. The heads of the banks reserved this favoured section of the bar for themselves.

Mackie ordered two pink gins and we tried to find some elbow room further along the bar. Some banker friends of Mackie's waved to us and we went over. I knew one of them, Crichton; he had a braying laugh and pink cheeks that lent a strangely youthful air to a man fast losing much of his wispy blond hair.

Like much of his breed, Crichton felt superior to everyone else because he had been born in England, and the last time I'd met him he'd made some snide remarks about America and Americans that I ignored for Mackie's sake. Mackie didn't like him either; but he was his brother-in-law and so he tolerated him.

There was some desultory conversation about cricket, which went on interminably. And then, without warning, Crichton turned to me and said: 'I hear you've found yourself a Russian princess.'

I didn't answer him. It wasn't a question, and as a conversational gambit it seemed rude to me. Unfortunately he mistook my silence for encouragement.

'Lot of them about. Slept with the Czarina last night. Talbot here says he slept with the Czar. But you know Talbot.'

The others laughed.

'It's all right as long as you don't let them move in with you,' he said to the others. 'Most of them are inbred, like the Welsh. They only want your money and they stink like badgers.'

Oh, he was really playing to the gallery now. Mackie was the only one not laughing. And me, of course.

'Does it bother you?' I asked him.

'Does what bother me, old boy?'

'Being this stupid.'

He gave me a smile, which made him look particularly vicious. One of life's legion of bitter souls; God knows how they get to be that way.

'Good fuck, is she?'

I went for him, he knew I would. But his friends were there, stepping in, cooling things off, while he shook his head and gave me a forbearing smile, making me look like the hothead. I excused myself and left, preserving some dignity before they threw me out.

And I had made myself look a fool, no question. Sleeping with Russian princesses was one thing, keeping one in your apartment, defending her honour in public, well, that branded you as socially inferior. Two strikes against me; I was an American and I kept a White Chinese in my apartment. I might as well have walked into the Carlton with a pig under my arm.

Christ, they're a miserable lot, the English. They think they're God Almighty and that Jesus Christ was an old boy of their school.

Nothing is worse than the illusion of love. I wanted this girl more than I ever wanted anything; I wanted her because I couldn't have her and because she showed no interest in me at all. I wanted her because she was beautiful, and because she was aloof, and because she was mysterious. She embodied all the mysteries of the other sex.

One night I heard her talking to someone. I couldn't hear what she was saying above the rain beating on the roof. I got out of bed. She was sitting by the window, with the shutters thrown open, so that rain had flooded the floor. She was staring down into the courtyard and did not look up as I walked in.

She was talking on the telephone.

I experienced a stab of jealousy; Anastasia had a lover. My first instinct was to snatch the receiver from her hands, to shout and rage. Wasn't this my apartment, my telephone, didn't she owe me something for all I had done? But something in me urged caution. So I stood there in the shadows, watching, felt the prickling of tiny hairs on the back of my neck.

She was silhouetted against the storm night sky, and illuminated briefly by sheet lightning far away over the China Sea.

I strained to hear what she was saying. Then I realised she was speaking in Russian.

She suddenly put down the telephone without hanging up the receiver and got back into bed. I picked it up and listened. There was, of course, no-one there. I replaced the receiver on the wall and went out. I never asked her about the incident and it never happened again. I never made sense of it, never found out who was on the other end of the line at three o'clock in the morning.

I doubt there was ever anyone there at all.

The *North China Daily News* had been founded in 1854, it was the largest British newspaper in Shanghai, and the most prestigious. Some people considered it the only newspaper worth reading.

Over at the *China Press*, we were always short staffed, and usually in financial trouble, and most of the other dailies were in the same straits. So those of us from the smaller papers stuck together, created our own roster, working as one team instead of several. Every morning we gathered at the Broadway Club, a bar near the Astor Hotel, to divide the day's work between us. One of us covered the law courts, someone else the Central Police Station, others the incoming shipping, the rest wrote up the main sporting events. At the end of each day we wrote our copy and dropped off a carbon at the club for each of the others.

This worked well most of the time. But one day one of

the boys decided to spend the afternoon with his mistress instead of covering the football match between the Lancashire Fusiliers and a team from the Municipal Police, as agreed. He subsequently wrote a piece about the Police winning the game by four goals to two and devoted two hundred words to the story. The actual score was seven–one to the army, but every daily in Shanghai except the *North China Daily News* reported that the police had won, and it was the *News* who earned a bad reputation from the incident, as the only paper in the whole colony running a different score.

Being an American, I didn't give a damn either way, and as the result did not reflect badly on the United States of America and as none of it was written in Chinese, my editor wasn't concerned either. It just shows you, if you need telling, that if enough people believe it, legend becomes truth.

Ask Anastasia.

I'd arranged to meet Mackie at the Race Club for a drink. We were sitting in the coffee room; I remember the club was enormous, the coffee room had a vast brick fireplace and the walls were panelled in dark teak. There was even supposed to be a bowling alley and a Turkish bath somewhere. It had a huge marble staircase in the entrance hall but that was for the exclusive use of male members, there was a separate one for the women, to stop these so-proper English gentlemen from looking up their skirts as they ascended.

It was the kind of Shanghai scene that made my teeth ache; gentlemen in wicker chairs smoking cigars and talking about money, not a woman in sight. It always appeared pleasant enough but there was an underlying tension. These men reminded me of gangsters I had seen in New York. Transport these taipans from the Race Club coffee room into a Lower East Side bar and they would not have been out of place. The looks on their faces were just the same; blank and hard as shovels.

'Have you seen this?' Mackie said to me.

It was one of those souvenir postcards the tourists buy to send home to their families in Oxford or Chicago. When I turned it over to look at the photograph, I realised it was different; the picture was a portrait of a family group. I recognised it immediately, for it seemed the whole world had been fascinated with these people and their fate for the last three years. It was the last Czar of Russia, Nicholas, with the Czarina and their five children, a famous photograph, one of the last taken before the Revolution.

'They sell hundreds of them every day in Little Russia,' Mackie said.

I wondered what this was about.

'Look at the girl on the far right,' he said. 'That's Anastasia, she was the youngest daughter.'

I saw a dumpy adolescent with long fair hair and a solemn expression. It hit me with a jolt that there was something familiar about her, but the notion was so absurd I started to laugh.

'They said she had brilliant blue eyes,' Mackie said.

'A lot of people have brilliant blue eyes.'

'Statistically,' he murmured, 'not that many.'

'You're out of your mind.'

'I just think there's an uncanny resemblance. Don't you?'

'Not really.'

He raised an eyebrow. 'No?'

I tossed the postcard back at him. 'It's impossible.'

'I agree. Impossible. But it's a remarkable resemblance.'

'The Bolsheviks killed them all.'

'Still, one does hear rumours.'

The rumours: that one of the Romanov daughters had escaped from the Urals in 1918; that just before the Whites arrived in Ekaterinburg the Bolsheviks had conducted desperate searches in the area, searching every train in and out of the town, looking for a young woman. But then there had been other crazy rumours as well: the Czar had been shot but his family had escaped and were living in exile in Peking; the Czar had been seen walking down Regent Street in London; the whole family had been seen holidaying on the French Riviera.

All through history despots have hung their enemy's heads on spikes on the city walls; let the people see their former heroes rot there and be eaten by the crows, and then they can never come back to haunt you. But shoot princes in a cellar, and you invite impostors and rumour mongering.

'It looks nothing like her,' I said, though it plainly did. Why did I baulk? The idea that I might be harbouring a Russian princess in my two-bedroom apartment in the French Concession seemed just too bizarre. And yet there was a part of me that was uneasy, that didn't want to invite the world's curiosity about my Anastasia Romanov. If a man uncovers a mysterious object in his garden, he wants to understand it before he gives it away, and loses possession of it for ever.

I suppose that was it. I wanted to possess her; I was not ready, did not know if I would ever be ready, to give her back to the world.

Late one afternoon we were sitting in the living room of my apartment, listening to the muffled calls of the street hawkers on the Nanking Road. Anastasia sat on the chaise longue under the window, her legs drawn up beneath her, wearing a green silk kimono I had bought her in the market.

I got up and went out onto the balcony. Throw open the windows and the city would hit you in a wave of noise, day or night; the tinkling of bicycle bells, the clamour of car horns, the shrill piping of tenders out on the river. Endless. It never stopped.

In the winter Shanghai was grey; grey stone of the buildings on the Bund, grey overcast, the slick grey ribbon of the Whangpoa winding through the city like a greasy snake.

The table lamp threw a pale light into the room. I could make out the beat of pulse at her throat, and the fine hairs on the backs of her arms where the sleeve fell away from her wrist.

'Tell me what you remember,' I said.

She sighed. 'Why is the past important? The past is over.'

'The past is what makes the present. It's what brought you here.'

A long, trembling breath.

'Do you remember how you came to Shanghai?' I persisted.

'I remember living on the street in Harbin. I had no money. Some men, Chinese, they took care of me, bought me a meal, found me in a room in a hotel. Then they told me I had to pay them back.'

'Triads.'

She shrugged, it didn't matter to her what label I put on them. 'They put me on a boat to Shanghai with four other girls. They made us sign contracts, they were written in Chinese, but it doesn't matter, does it, it's not like they will take you to court if you run away, they will just slash your face with razors, right?'

Trafficking in White Russian women was big business in Shanghai. Because it was an open city, you didn't need papers to get in; you only needed them to get out, and once these Russian girls were in the international settlement they were trapped there, with no hope of repaying the money the traffickers said they owed them for getting them out of Harbin. A lot of the taxi club girls were recruited that way.

'What about before Harbin?'

She shook her head. 'Did you ever wake up in the morning and try to remember your dreams? They are right there, you can almost feel them, but no matter how hard you try you can't get them back.' She drifted away, and when she spoke again her voice was soft, dream-like. 'I only remember being on a train, it must have been before Harbin, but then, when I try to think harder about it, it's like I have just imagined it . . .'

'Perhaps your family was rich.'

'What good will that do me now, remembering when I was rich and perhaps when I was happy? I am here now and there is not a thing I can do to change anything. You see? The past is no consolation. Why do I want to bring it back, just to torment myself? Why do you care so much?'

'Perhaps it's important.'

She turned away. 'No, it's not.'

She's wrong, I thought, the past is important. There was some part of her that remembered, I was sure. Why else did she never smile?

ANASTASIA

The city was hushed in a shroud of fog. Foghorns from the cruise liners and warships echoed along the river. The stink drifting from the docks seemed worse on these grey still mornings, a fug of seaweed, raw sewage and coal smoke.

I sat on the windowsill, staring at the margin of river afforded from the balcony. It was dusk and lights were twinkling along the Bund.

'What is America like?' I said.

Michael smiled, as if I had said something amusing. 'You wouldn't like it. It's full of Americans.'

'How do you know I don't like Americans? Are they all like you?'

'Not all of them.'

'So there you are.'

He grinned, drew up a knee on the sill, lit another cigarette, cupping his hands to the flame.

'Where were you born?'

'New York.'

'Your family is not very rich, I think.'

'Why do you think that?'

'You have to work. Write stories.'

Again I seemed to have amused him. Finally, he said: 'My old man is a stockbroker. He has an apartment overlooking Central Park and a beach house on Long Island. My mother's related to the Vanderbilts somewhere along the line. But I don't suppose you've heard of the Vanderbilts.'

'So your family is rich?'

He nodded.

'So why do you live here in this little house?'

'Long story.'

'I shall sit quietly and listen.'

'I don't get on with my father. I think he's an over-bearing bastard and he thinks I'm a waster and a drunk. I left New York so I didn't have to see his shadow every time I looked over my shoulder. I still remember this look of disapproval people got on their faces when I introduced myself. "Oh, you're JB Sheridan's son." Everyone over there either loves him or hates him. If they loved him, they didn't like me because I was the wayward son who'd caused him so much pain. If they hated him, well, I was just another Sheridan, spawn of the Devil. So I got out of New York to make my own way, be my own man. Prove to him I wasn't a waster and a drunk. Haven't made a very good fist of it so far, have I?'

Hearing him talk this way made me wonder, yet again, what my own mother and father were like. Did I love them, or despise them, as Michael did his? 'At least you have a place to go back to.'

'I suppose so, if I ever want to throw away every ounce of dignity and self-respect that I have.'

Easy to talk about dignity and self-respect when you have food in your belly and a roof over your head. I traded dignity and self-respect to stay alive and at the time I thought I had a bargain.

He flicked his cigarette away and I watched the glowing butt arc away into the dark.

'You have brothers and sisters?'

'One brother, a stockbroker like the old man. All he can talk about is yachts and the share market.'

'You don't miss your family?'

A sigh. 'There's nothing wrong with starting over with a clean slate. You get to find out who you really are.'

'I have the clean slate, Michael. You have the other side of the old one.'

'Very cute,' he stood up. 'You want to go out? We can have drinks at the American Club, make a night of it.'

'You want to show off your new girlfriend?'

'Hardly a girlfriend.' He reached out his hand and stroked my cheek. I wasn't expecting it and I jerked my head away, as if it was a slap.

'Am I that repulsive?'

How could I explain to him? How my skin crawled every time a man touched me, how I closed my eyes and willed myself not to run away when I danced with those men in the taxi club, how it made me gag when they pawed me? I did it for money, it didn't mean I ever liked it. It was thanks to him that I didn't have to go back there and I did not mean to hurt him.

'I'm going out,' he said and the door slammed behind him.

MICHAEL

The Line had a discreet brass plate on the front door. The madam, a charming American woman by the name of Grace Gale, had furnished the house with mock Chippendale furniture, Oriental rugs and the most extensive foreign library in the whole city. Gentlemen were encouraged to treat it as a club, a place to drop in after work to read the newspapers or read a good book with a brandy in hand, or to trade gossip with friends. The Line happened to be a legitimate place of business for me, it was where a good journalist could pick up information on everything from the stock market to the latest warlord manoeuvres. It wasn't like a real brothel at all.

Grace served only French champagne and employed a top rank Chinese chef called Fat Lu, who had once cooked for the Imperial Russian delegation in Peking. The girls were all Americans, and my personal favourite – for her conversation – was a girl known as Big Annie who sat in a chair and knitted scarves and woollens when business was slack. Grace used the chit system; you signed off for your entertainment and at the end of the month she sent her

Chinese shroffs to collect payment from your office. It was the only place I have known in the whole world where a man could get a woman on credit.

Four in the morning found me in Grace's parlour, drinking brandy and politely refusing Big Annie's half-hearted requests to give her an alternative to her knitting. There was nowhere else to go at that time of the morning, except home to the crazy Russian girl who wouldn't let me touch her. So I'd decided to stay out, brood and drink.

Over the past few months I had struck up a friendship with the local Reuters man, a tall Cambridge graduate called Sebastian Beaumont. Seb, as he liked to be called, was a chameleon who seemed to fit into whatever social group he found himself, an admirable quality in a journalist.

Sebastian was a bachelor like me and we often found ourselves in the Line in the early hours of the morning, sharing a bottle of brandy. His background was not unlike mine; he had been born to money and privilege, nursed a disdain for both, but discovered he couldn't survive without them either. We traded stories about our appalling fathers, the American and British girls in the colony we would have liked to have slept with, and stock market tips.

Suddenly he said: 'I hear you're in love.'

I was immediately wary. 'Who told you that?'

'Mackie. He said you've got some Russian girl living with you. From what I hear, she's a corker.'

Corker. The English had a lot of schoolboy expressions like that. I shrugged my shoulders and wondered how to field this question; trying to explain my relationship with Anastasia was much too complicated.

'Her name's Anastasia Romanov,' was all I said.

He drew on his cigarette, raised an eyebrow, let me know Mackie had told him the rest of it.

'Like the Grand Duchess,' I added.

'Romanov is a pretty common name in Russia,' he said. 'So is Anastasia. I have had about a dozen Anastasia Romanovs since I've been in Shanghai.' A redhead called Lotus climbed on a table holding a champagne bottle and started an impromptu can-can. Sebastian sipped his brandy, and I thought he was going to let the subject drop, but then he said: 'Still, there are these rumours.'

'Yes, I know.'

'Still. You're probably not sleeping with the Grand Duchess of all the Russias.'

'No, I don't think so either.'

'I slept with two Duchesses and a Grand Duke last week,' he said. 'If I'd paid five dollars more I could have had Rasputin as well.'

'Sometimes she just acts like a princess,' I said.

'All women do until you marry them.'

I must have fallen asleep in the chair. When I woke up, Seb was gone and Lotus was asleep on her back, half naked, the champagne bottle clutched to her bare breasts like a lover. I crept out, hailed a rickshaw, went back to my apartment and got dressed to go to work.

ANASTASIA

One day I gave in, I let him take me out, just like a girlfriend.

It was a garden party at the home of a man called Tony Keswick, a big taipan at Jardine Matheson. There was a military band playing in the garden, under a pavilion, and everyone pretended it wasn't raining in torrents all afternoon, as only the English can. The women all wore long frocks, chattering away under their umbrellas with the hems of their dresses trailing in the puddles, high heels sinking into the lawns.

A man came up to me, very English, very affected, like they say. He was smoking a cigarette in an ivory holder, and he had a certain look on his face, and I started to panic. I often had this feeling when I met someone new, this suspicion that perhaps they knew more about me than I knew about myself.

'So you're Michael's Anastasia,' he said.

'Do I know you?'

'Sebastian Beaumont,' he said, and held out his hand.

I was not sure what to do. Michael had left me standing there alone, he was on the other side of the room, talking to some financier, working, getting gossip and news. It was his job, he said.

'He talks about you all the time.'

'Does he?' I did not know what to say to that. Everything Michael did made me feel indebted to him. He talked to everyone about me as if I was special, when I knew I was just a taxi girl, an opportunist trying to survive in a hall of mirrors. I could see it in this Sebastian's eyes: he knows what I am and that I have no right to someone like Michael.

'You're Russian? Your English is very good.'

'Thank you.'

'Michael's a prince,' he said and smiled, like it was a joke.

'He is a journalist.'

'Just an expression. It means he's generous, good-looking, charming, he'd do anything for anyone. A prince. I'd hate to see someone take advantage of him.'

'You think that someone is me?'

'He won't marry you, you know,' he said, as if that was what I wanted from him. 'If you want a passport, just ask him. He'll fix it up for you, it's the way he is. You don't have to tell him these stories.'

'What stories?'

'Making out you're a Russian princess. You must be spectacular in bed. He's not usually so gullible.'

I wanted to slap his face, but a taxi girl gives up the right to slap a man's face when she starts sleeping for money. Besides, I didn't blame him, Michael was his friend and he wanted to protect him. 'That's not what I want from him. I don't know what he wants from me.'

'Isn't it obvious?' he said.

'No. Ask him. If you find the answer, you can tell me.'

I left the party and walked home in the rain, in the new white gown Michael had bought for me. By the time I got home it was a sopping rag. Gordon looked at me like I was a wet dog, didn't even offer to bring me hot water for a bath. I towelled myself off the best I could and then curled up naked in the bed and, for the first time I could remember, I started to cry. I hadn't even done that when the men from the taxi club beat me up, or when I was so hungry in Harbin I ate weeds growing in the street.

I don't know what made me cry then. I think it was because I had started to like Michael a little bit, and because I knew his friend Sebastian was right. He was a prince and I was just a taxi girl, and I had no place in his life.

I woke up one night, heard arguing from down in the courtyard. I went to the window to see what was happening. There was a splash of light in the yard from an open door, and I saw two Chinese men, I recognised them straightaway, gangsters from the taxi club. They were yelling at Michael, I heard them say my Chinese name, Little Pigeon. Michael was shouting right back, said he didn't know what they were talking about.

I thought: I cannot cause any more trouble for this man. It is time to go back to the taxi club, live like before.

I packed up all the clothes and pretty things he had bought for me; the little brush with the tortoise-shell handle, the silk dressing gown with the embroidered dragon, the silver bracelet I knew he could not afford. His friend was right about him; he was a prince. Why did I not realise it before? I don't know. Perhaps because I was so miserable I did not think anything about anyone except myself.

The shouting in the courtyard stopped and I heard Michael's footfall on the wooden stair.

The door swung open and he stood there, leaning against the jamb. 'They were looking for you.'

'You are not going to send me back?'

'No, I'm not.'

Why not? He doesn't want me for sex, so what does he want me for? I knew those triad gangsters would not give up like that. Maybe they would watch the house, try to grab me off the street or perhaps give Michael a beating for keeping me. I was worth a lot of money to those men.

'What do you want from me?' I asked him.

He shrugged his shoulders like that was answer enough, like I was supposed to know what was going on in his head.

'You want me to sleep with you?' I asked him.

'Do you want to sleep with me?'

Why would I want to sleep with him, sleep with any man? But he had been kind to me, and if that was what he wanted in return for everything he had done for me, I would happily give it to him.

When I didn't answer, he sighed: 'We have to get you out of here.'

'It would be easier if I went back to the taxi club.'

'And one night you'll just throw yourself off the bridge. Only next time there'll be no-one to fish you out again.'

'What does it matter to you?'

'Damned if I know.' He was waiting for me to say something, do something. I was grateful to him, of course, but I felt frozen.

'I must be out of my mind,' he said and shut the door gently behind him. I wondered later if there was something I could have said, some kindness that I could have shown him, that would have changed what he did next.

MICHAEL

Sometimes you can be lying in the dark, about to fall asleep, and you hear a mosquito buzzing in the room. You are too tired to turn on the light and search for it, but the buzzing keeps you awake and tossing restlessly in your bed. In my case the mosquito was that postcard Mackie had showed me; it wasn't sleep it kept me from, it was my peace of mind.

There were Russian bookstores springing up all over the city and I went into one and bought myself a copy of that postcard portrait that Mackie had showed me. I brought it home and stared at it for hours, surreptitiously compared the little girl on the right of the picture with my own Anastasia Romanov, hiding the postcard in the pages of a book so she did not know what I was doing.

The similarities were there; but the little girl in the picture was plump, well fed, had spent her whole life a pampered princess; my Anastasia had starved on the street and worked as a prostitute for Chinese gangsters. I imagine that changes you, not just emotionally, but physically as well. Comparisons become unreliable.

My Anastasia made no claim to be other than what she was; a refugee with no memory of the past. If anyone was to unravel the mystery, it would have to be me.

You have to understand, the White Russians were not an anomaly in Shanghai. They were as much a part of the fabric of life there as the Chinese. They lived in the poorest and the richest areas. They were everywhere and they were nowhere.

After the Revolution the lucky ones with a bank account fled to Europe. The rest drifted across Siberia to Vladivostock. After it fell to the Bolsheviks in 1920 they settled in Harbin or found their way to the Treaty Ports of Tianjin and Shanghai.

You found them all over the city, but particularly down the Avenue Joffre in the French Concession, most of them unemployed, hanging around the cafés, waiting for something to come along – and there wasn't a street in the Concession that didn't have at least one Russian restaurant. Even the shop signs were written in Cyrillic script. You walked down the street, you smelled warm bread and cakes from places like De De's, heard Russian shouted from the cafés as they argued and debated politics, the sound of a violin drifting from an open window. They loved music, those Russians. Music meant everything to them. They could be piss poor and living in some damp cellar but the last thing they'd pawn would be their cello or their piano.

Anastasia had never shown any desire to go to any of these places. I wonder what would have happened to her, to us, if I'd kept her away from Banischevski. Perhaps nothing. She would have gone slowly insane living there in that little room, staring at the Bund day after day.

For things to happen in your life you have to risk. Life, real life, is all about risk, isn't it?

I knew Banischevski would be holding court at the Golden Bear café that day. Unlike the other pretenders strutting around the streets of the Concession he really had been a part of the Czar's inner circle. He had a fancy address overlooking the Bund, was treated like royalty by the refugees.

I took Anastasia there that day because I wanted to see what Banischevski would do when he saw her. I wanted him to turn away without a second glance; I wanted his reaction to confirm for me that she was just another poor Russian émigré. I wanted him to look at her with disdain, like he did everyone else.

And what if he had? What would I have done? Would the obsession have been over? Would I have told her to pack up and get out? But if I examine my motives honestly, I know I can't be sure what I would have done if the mystery of Anastasia had been solved so easily.

Banischevski's full name was Count Andrei Sergeiovitch Banischevski, and he had been a member of the Czar's inner circle until Nicholas's abdication in 1917. Of course, in those days every other Russian claimed to have been either the Czar's closest military adviser or a member of the Empress's sewing circle; but with Banischevski it was demonstrably true. I'd seen the famous photograph taken at Coburg in 1894 when the Czar got engaged to Alexandra, and there was Banischevski standing at the back of the group behind Victoria and the Prince of Wales. He appeared in another well-known photograph also, at Mogilev in 1916, him and the Czar and Duchess Tatiana.

He had been a general in the Czar's army, though he had never done much soldiering himself: he liked the uniforms, just like the Czar.

Provocatively, I bought Anastasia a white and unfashionably long ankle-length dress, of a kind similar to those the Grand Duchesses had worn in the postcard. I made her wear it, even borrowed a string of pearls from an ex-girlfriend.

When we arrived Banischevski and his entourage were at a corner table, arguing politics. It was the only topic of conversation among the exiles, every day they worked over the past, like a dog with an old bone, bored and caged and nothing else to do with their time; if the Czar had done only this; if only the Empress had behaved this way; how things would be different next time.

Next time. They lived for next time.

It was mid-morning, the café was thick with the cloying fug of strong Russian cigarettes. The White Russians in their suits and tie pins and faded elegance were stark counterpoint to the shabby surrounds, the rickety chairs and faded sepia photographs of Czarist royalty on the walls.

Anastasia and I sat down. There was a Chinese shoeshine boy wandering around the tables, he had a palsy and one side of his face looked like it was made of melted wax. I gave him a few coins and let him shine my Oxfords, more for his sake than mine.

'Why did you bring me here?' she asked me.

'You've never been?'

She shook her head. I waited to see if she would pick up the Russian newspaper on the table but she ignored it. In fact, the only time I'd heard her speak Russian was that night when she was sleep walking – if that was what it was.

She was staring at the old photographs on the walls, shivering like a rabbit caught in the glare of a torch.

'Are you okay?' I asked her.

'I don't like this place,' she said.

I glanced over at Banischevski's table. He was staring at us, he had this look on his face, a frown like he was trying to remember something, and there was something else – what was it? Fear. As if he'd seen a ghost. Finally he got to his feet and came over.

I stood up. He held out his hand and gave a little bow. 'Count Andrei Sergeiovitch Banischevski,' he said.

'Michael Sheridan. We met once before at an American Embassy dinner.' I could see he didn't remember. He shook my hand but he wasn't looking at me, he was staring at Anastasia. 'This is Miss Anastasia Romanov,' I said.

He gave me a look, like he thought perhaps I was playing games with him. He took her outstretched hand and gave a little bow over it and clicked his heels together. 'And have we met before?' he said to her.

'I don't think so,' she said.

He stared at her a little longer than was polite and she flushed and turned her head away. 'I am sorry. I must be mistaken.'

He returned his attention to me, albeit reluctantly, and looked at me down that long aristocratic beak of his as if I was one of his soldiers on a parade ground. I was, after all, only an American; in his eyes, I had no culture, no breeding, and my ancestors were revolutionaries.

I knew him only by reputation; a liking for cocaine and the sexual appetites of a tomcat. He was tall and spare, with lips like a woman's and the hands of a concert pianist. A receding hairline had left him with a forehead that seemed to take up most of his head, and he wore an expression of disdain, as if he had just bitten down on something foul. He was well into his forties, and wore more jewellery than was good for any man. He went nowhere without his ebony cane with ivory handle, which he would lean on even when sitting down.

'You must excuse me,' he said to me. 'The young lady's face is very familiar. I thought I knew her.'

'Who does she remind you of?'

He was not accustomed to my colonial bluntness. Instead of answering, he contrived to look confused. 'So many names, so many faces. Most of them are dead or buried in the past. I did not mean to be rude.' I thought he might leave it there, but instead he indicated the chair between us. 'May I sit?' he said.

Now, too late, I wished I hadn't done it, wished I hadn't brought her here. I was a kid with some secret treasure, finally showing it to the world to risk having it reclaimed, or its magic tarnished by another's contempt.

Banischevski clicked his fingers in the air and the Russian waiter immediately appeared at his shoulder. He spoke in quick fire Russian, and the waiter scurried obediently away. Just like the old days, I thought.

He sat down beside me but all his attention was focused on

Anastasia. 'May I ask how long you have been in Shanghai?' he said to her.

'I think . . . a little over a year.'

'I thought I knew every exile of good family from the Mother Country. I am amazed I have not met you before.'

'What makes you think she is from a good family?' I asked him.

He seemed irritated by my interruption. 'She is, isn't she?'

She was sitting ramrod straight, and she had not learned that working in taxi clubs.

'May I ask where you are from?' he said to her.

She looked at me, then back at Banischevski.

'She doesn't remember,' I said, answering for her.

'Doesn't remember?' He arched an eyebrow. 'What do you mean by that?'

He was getting on my nerves. 'What do you think I mean?'

The waiter reappeared with coffee, the thick black mud the Russians favoured. Little tendrils of steam hovered over the rims of the tiny white cups.

'Her doctor thinks she may have a traumatic amnesia.' Mackie had said no such thing; it was something I had discovered myself, reading a medical book he gave me.

'The poor girl,' he said. He propped the ivory-handled cane between his legs so he could rest both hands upon it and affected an expression of superhuman thought.

Anastasia seemed embarrassed by the attention he was giving her. She looked desperately to me for support.

'You remember nothing before you came to Shanghai?' he asked her, in Russian. I had tried to learn a little of the language since Anastasia had come to live with me. It was rudimentary, I could understand more than I could speak.

'I was in Harbin for a time.'

'So how did you get to Shanghai?'

He ignored me completely now, like I was a servant who had fetched some errand and was waiting to be dismissed. I was getting angrier by the second.

Anastasia again looked at me, wondering if I would tell him she came to Shanghai as a bonded prostitute.

'There are gaps in what she remembers,' I said in my halting Russian.

Banischevski looked up sharply, probably astonished that I understood what he was saying. His friends and sycophants were watching us, wondering what was so interesting to him about the American and his young companion.

He shook his head. 'I can't help thinking I have seen you before. I am sure, if I had enough time to think about this, perhaps ask some more questions, I might be able to fill in some gaps for you.'

But instead of asking more questions, he made some desultory small talk.

Anastasia answered in monosyllables, looking for all the world like an animal caught in a trap. We listened to him prattle on about his work in the Russian exile community, about long forgotten conversations with the Czar, what would happen when the Bolsheviks were finally overthrown. I guessed he was fishing for some reaction from her, and if that was the case he must have been greatly disappointed.

We finished our coffees and I got up to leave. He seemed disappointed and said – to her – that he hoped it would not be too long before they met again. And then he whispered something to her, in colloquial Russian, at that time beyond my vocabulary. Anastasia looked startled, but did not reply.

'What did he say to you?' I asked her when we got outside.

'It was just Russian for goodbye,' she said.

But I knew she was lying. As we rode back to the apartment I wondered what I'd done. I thought I would discount my suspicions that morning in the Golden Bear. Instead I had compounded my doubts.

ANASTASIA

It was the noise from downstairs that woke me, Gordon and the amah shouting to each other in high-pitched Mandarin. There was thumping on the stairs. I put on a robe and went out to see what was wrong.

Gordon was helping Michael up the stairs, the amah fussing behind, shouting instructions. Michael's shirt was soaked with blood. His eye was cut, there was dried blood in his hair, his lip and his nose were bleeding. One eye was swollen shut.

'You should see the other guy,' he croaked when he saw me.

Gordon pushed past me and dragged Michael inside the apartment, laid him on the ancient chaise longue by the window. Gordon and the amah shouted at each other some more and then the amah rushed out of the room, returned with a cloth and a bowl of water.

She tried to help but Gordon pushed her away. Then Michael said to him: 'No wanchee you my side, wanchee missy do it!' and Gordon threw the cloth into the bowl in disgust and took a step back. He gave me a look of absolute ferocity, before stamping out of the room. He thought of Michael as a personal possession; he did not want to give him up to me.

After Gordon and the amah had left, I dipped the cloth into the bowl and tried to clean the blood off his face. 'What happened?'

'Fight.'

'Where?'

He shrugged off the question.

'You need a doctor.'

'I'll go and see Mackie in the morning. It's not as bad as it looks.'

'You can't see how it looks.' There was a big cut just over the eyebrow, almost an inch wide, the flesh was swollen, and split open like rotten fruit. There was another cut just back from the hairline, a bigger one. One of his teeth was loose. 'This was a very bad fight.'

'Been in worse.'

There was alcohol on his breath. He had been drinking again. Perhaps what his father said about him was right: a drunk and a waster. Maybe so, but he was my drunk and my waster, for now.

I cleaned him up as best I could. He wouldn't tell me the truth, kept saying it was just a bar fight. After a while he complained that I was hurting him and snatched the cloth out of my hand and told me he'd do it himself. He sent me off to bed.

Next morning when I woke up he was gone. All that was left behind were some dried bloodstains on the chaise longue and the bloody water left in the bowl.

He came to see me one day when Michael was not there. Gordon told me that I had a visitor and when I went into the parlour there he was, diamond tie pin glittering at his throat, a thick ruby on his little finger, another diamond on the index finger of his other hand. He bowed as if it was some great lady walking in, not the do-nothing Russian mistress of an American journalist.

I remembered what he whispered to me that day when we were leaving the café: 'I never thought to see you again, Highness.'

Ever since I had wondered what to make of this. Which Highness did he take me for? Was this why Michael was always asking me questions about things I could not remember?

'Your Highness,' Count Andrei Sergeiovitch Banischevski said to me.

I did not know what to do, had no idea what to say to him. He seemed to be waiting for some reaction from me, as if I had some secret that I was keeping from the world and he had given me its password.

Gordon was standing there watching. Andrei snapped at him to go and fetch chai. It was clear that he was a man accustomed to giving orders. He sat down in Michael's favourite armchair, making a little steeple with his fingers. I sat down, too, wondering what he wanted, in what way my life might be about to change.

'I hope you don't mind,' he said.

'Mind?'

'That I call on you like this. Unannounced.'

'Perhaps Michael will mind.'

He made a face. 'Mr Sheridan. Yes.' He picked up a packet of Michael's cigarettes from the table, a cheap American brand. He replaced them with a look of contempt. 'I am still curious. Where did you meet him?'

'Here in Shanghai.'

He smiled; we were playing games with each other now. 'Is it really true, that you remember nothing?'

'I remember coming here to Shanghai. I remember some things in Harbin.'

'But you are a Russian, and you so obviously have noble blood in your veins. You must be tormented not knowing where you are from, who your family is.'

Just then Gordon returned with the chai. Andrei looked at him as if a pig had just walked in off the street. He tapped impatiently with his fingernail on the handle of his ebony cane while Gordon poured the steaming tea into little cups.

Finally Gordon went out again but Andrei made no effort to pick up his teacup. Neither of us wanted the chai; Andrei, because he only enjoyed strong Russian coffee, and me, because I knew he had made Gordon lose face and so to pay him back Gordon had almost certainly spat in the teapot.

'What do you want from me?' I asked him.

A manicured fingernail caressed the ivory tip of the cane, tapped twice more. His lips were pursed in thought. 'I thought perhaps I recognised you from the old days.'

There was a small bird trapped in my breast, a tiny fluttering, a beating of wings that was just the quickening of heartbeat. Hope and fear are twins; if he really did know, would it be better or worse for me?

What things might he be able to tell me? Was my mother kind? If she is dead, then how did she die? Was my father a monster who beat me or a gentle man who suffered for my sake? Did I have brothers and sisters? Was I proud, was I good, was I gifted, was I poor? And why did I not remember any of these things?

Could this man tell me who I am and what I am like?

Oh, I had told myself over and over that it did not matter to me any more, that even if I knew where I was from and what life I had had before, I would still only be like all these other wretched refugees here in Shanghai; whether I was a duchess or a schoolteacher I would wake up tomorrow with no future and no way home. But there is something in every one of us that needs to understand our own history, without an identity we are dust.

I waited for him to tell me more, but he just smiled and waited for me to make the next move, knowing I was trapped in his web. If he knew me in Russia, then I must have noble blood in me, for he was once a confidant of the Czar himself.

'Who is it that I remind you of?'

'If I told you, and I am wrong, I make myself look a fool and torment you unnecessarily. It seems to me you have suffered enough.'

From what little I knew of him, he did not seem the kind of man who disturbed himself unduly over the suffering of others.

'Is that why you came here today, Andrei Sergeiovitch? To play riddles with me?'

'No, I wanted to be sure I was not mistaken.'

'And are you sure?'

'Unfortunately, no. The young woman I remember, if you are her, was not as . . . beautiful, if you will forgive me for saying so. She was plumper and much different to you in temperament. Yet you do have a certain troubling resemblance. What are we to make of it?' He sighed, theatrically. 'How did you meet Mr Sheridan? Are you his mistress?'

'That is an impertinent question.'

'And will you answer it?'

'No. I think I'd prefer it if you left immediately.'

What made me say that? I was aching to know how much he knew, or had guessed, about my identity. I wanted to leap across the table and scratch his eyes out, I was so furious with him for playing these games. But another part of me was too proud to let him see how angry I was. Perhaps it was just lies anyway.

'Well, you're haughty enough to be her,' he said, with

a smile and then, tapping his cane twice on the carpet, he stood up. 'Goodbye, *malenkaya*.'

What did he call me? Little one. I stared at him in blank confusion.

He seemed disappointed that I did not respond.

'Before I go, may I see your right foot?' he asked.

I was frightened now. Was he deranged, perhaps even dangerous? Some of my former customers at the taxi club had obsessions with feet.

He smiled at my confusion. 'The girl I remember. The bone structure of her right foot was . . . distinctive.'

I took off my shoe. The smile fell away, was replaced by something else. What was it? Confusion, uncertainty. He stared hard into my face. 'Is there nothing you remember about Russia? Not one thing?' His voice was suddenly different; it was almost as if he was pleading with me.

I shook my head.

And with that he bowed and left. I watched from the window as he climbed into the rickshaw that was waiting for him in the street. I wanted desperately to run after him, beg him to tell me everything he knew, or even just those things he suspected, but even then I was too proud. He had given me hope and there is nothing like hope to torture the soul.

I lay awake that night, staring at the stars through my window, trying to navigate my thin scrapbook of memories, fix the precise moment when I crossed the border between memory and void. But it was impossible, there were only fragments before Harbin, it was like crossing the Whangpoa on a foggy evening, a glimpse of lights here, a sound there, but nothing so well defined that you could fix your bearings.

I could not get Andrei's expression out of my head, how his eyes bored into mine, how he made me feel that I was somehow important. I had stopped believing that a taxi girl like me could be important to anyone.

MICHAEL

We all lived high off the hog in Shanghai and it was Chinese labour that made it possible. Chinese servants were cheap, they were reliable, and for the most part, they were honest. Or rather, they were honest after the Chinese fashion. They would not blatantly cheat you, but they always took a commission on any service rendered. I kept a watch on this practice, to make sure it did not get out of hand.

One night soon after our meeting with Banischevski I sat down at my desk to go through the household accounts. Gordon stood by my shoulder, obviously agitated about something. I went through the chits and receipts more meticulously than usual, thinking he had something to hide.

I knew from experience that Gordon was ingenious at supplementing his income with little extras he thought I'd miss. I once caught him out billing me for cat food, even though I didn't have a cat.

'What thing every month belong five dollar cat chow?' I had shouted. 'You savvy plenty well master no belong cat. I no wanchee see any more cat chow five dollar.'

So next month there was a new item on the accounts. 'One cat, ten dollar.'

'What thing you lookee sad?' I asked him.

Gordon kept his eyes on the floor.

I banged my fist on the desk. 'What thing?' I shouted, fed up with this game.

'That missus,' he mumbled. 'That man one time come this side, talkee missus, drinkee chai, no good, boss.'

'This day?'

'This day, boss.'

Well, what did I expect from a taxi girl? The mystery was an illusion of my own design. She was just another Russian whore, wasn't she?

She hadn't asked me to help her, she hadn't asked me for anything. I must have been crazy keeping some girl I didn't know, that I wasn't even sleeping with.

'Go catchee missus,' I said to him. 'Bring my side, chop-chop.'

Gordon went off to find her. I stared at the wall, sweating in the summer heat, scratched irritably at the prickly heat under my arms. She'd made a fool of me, I decided; no, I'd made a fool of myself.

Astor House on the Whangpoa Road was the premier hotel in Shanghai. When I telephoned Banischevski, we arranged to meet there for lunch, on the understanding that he would pick up the bill.

I made my way through the palm garden to the restaurant. It now boasted a famous French chef, he'd worked at Maxim's in Paris, and was supposed to be one of the best in Europe. It was crowded with bankers, diplomats, arms dealers, socialites. The talk was about stocks and shares, whether to take a forward position in silver, sell short on the US dollar, buy wheat futures at Chicago, sell a thousand bales of Liverpool cotton. Everyone was making money these days. It was fashionable, it was easy, and it was fun.

I donned Yankee attitude at the door, all arrogance and bad manners, knowing my old man could have bought and sold just about everyone in the place. I wasn't out of my league, just angry that I looked it.

Banischevski blended easily into the surroundings; the silver service, the Irish linen, the fine colognes, the French wines, the diamond tie pins. He looked as relaxed as if he was sinking into a warm bath. When the waiter came over the Count ordered turtle soup and lobster and then sat back and surveyed the room, granting a smile here, bestowing a nod of the head there.

I wondered how he did it. There were no more royal stipends, no estates to finance this lavish lifestyle. They said he'd escaped Russia with a fortune in roubles, and I wondered how large that fortune was. 'You came to see Anastasia the other day,' I said to him. Anastasia had told me finally, when I confronted her about her mysterious visitor. I thought she was whoring on my time; I was furious Banischevski had gone behind my back.

'No small talk then?' he said. 'No refinement?'

'I'm not one for refinements.'

'Yes, I saw that about you from the moment we met.'

I let that one go, but another remark like that and I promised myself I would pick him up by the throat and toss him into a potted palm. Anyway, I wanted to have my lobster first. It was a long time since I'd eaten lobster, the old man's remittance wasn't that generous. 'What's your interest in Anastasia?'

'I was wondering the same thing about you, Mr Sheridan. Are you sleeping with her?'

'Is that any business of yours?'

'That's what she said.'

'Good.'

'Did she tell you what we discussed?'

I shook my head. 'Clammed up about it.'

'Clammed up, like a clam, an oyster, yes? A delightful expression. I haven't heard it before.'

'I'm surprised. Your English is pretty damned good.'

'Better than yours, I think. But then, you're an American.'

I smiled back. 'And you're an arrogant son of a bitch living on past glories. At least I've got a passport.'

He smiled at that. 'You misjudge me, Mr Sheridan. You see, I have a passport also. My mother was German. But that's another story.' The soup arrived, Banischevski smoothed out his napkin and breathed deeply in, enjoying the aroma as if it were a vintage wine. He sipped the soup, his concentration focused on it, and then he said unexpectedly: 'Who do you think she is, Mr Sheridan?'

'I have no idea.'

'I doubt that.'

That should have given me some satisfaction, I suppose. Instead I felt a surge of protectiveness for her. God alone knows why, for until then she hadn't shown me even a scrap of tenderness.

'Who do you think she is?' I asked him.

'I think we both harbour similar suspicions, only it seems

too fantastic to be true, does it not? But the difference between you and I is that I am in a position to do something about this extraordinary find. You are not.'

'I'm a journalist.'

'You wish to profit from her then?'

'That's not what I said.'

He returned his attention to the soup. 'Is everything to your satisfaction?'

'The soup's fine.'

'Exquisite would have been the word I would have chosen, but that's another difference between us. I am a connoisseur. I put great store by fragile and beautiful things. And you, you are a journalist.'

'You have a point?'

He wiped his mouth with his napkin, but did not answer. He was right, of course, about the difference between us: subtlety.

'Is this true, do you think, that she remembers nothing?' he asked me.

'Why would she lie?'

'Indeed. It is a tragedy if it is true. Along with you, along with anyone who hears her story, I would like to know how she escaped from Russia.' The waiters removed the soup plates. 'Do you love her?'

'No,' I said.

'Well, that surprises me. After all, she lives in your house, is dependent on your charity. Why else would a man support a woman this way?'

'I'm a philanthropist.'

He laughed, made a theatrical display of wiping tears from his eyes and then said: 'So. We have a man digging in his garden. He finds perhaps the greatest treasure he has ever seen in his life, a treasure that may change the shape of history. What does he do with it? A poignant dilemma.'

'What about your dilemma?'

'What can I do? I neither possess this treasure, nor can I prove that it is authentic until I can take it somewhere to be examined by experts. So, tell me, Mr Sheridan, what is it you want?'

'One thousand dollars.'

He blinked. I guess he did not expect that sort of directness, even from me.

'You are willing to sell her?'

So I told him the story. As I painted the sordid little picture for him he fell quiet, said nothing when the lobster arrived, his face creased into a frown.

'You're right,' I said when I had finished, 'there's nothing I can do for her, no matter who she is. She doesn't give a damn about me and she's a strain on my finances. If you don't take her off my hands, I'll kick her out anyway.'

I meant it at the time, or I thought I did. I told myself she was more trouble than she was worth and I thought this way there would be no losers, and I could still feel good about myself.

'One thousand dollars,' he said, and tasted the lobster.

There and then, we made the arrangements. I would send her over to him, like I was forwarding luggage. After-wards, as I walked out of the Astor into the steaming afternoon sun, replete with fine seafood and French wines, I felt relieved, as if a burden had been lifted from my shoulders. I could go home tonight without looking over my shoulder, get my bank balance back on track and bring women to the apartment any time I wanted. I wouldn't look in the mirror and see some fool who'd been taken for a ride by a taxi girl. I told myself that once she was gone I'd never think about her again.

What a fool. But then, I was only twenty-four.

ANASTASIA

I woke suddenly. Michael was in the room, throwing open the blinds. He pushed open the window and let in the sound of the street, the shouts of the rickshaw drivers, the rattle of the tramcars on Nanking Road. He started throwing clothes into a battered brown suitcase.

'What are you doing?'

'You have to leave here,' he said.

'Why?'

'Why do you think?'

I didn't know but I had no right to argue. He had been kind to me, he had fed me and given me somewhere to sleep and bought me clothes and asked for nothing in return. Now he was tired of me and wanted me out.

I was like a leaf, blown from one place to another, just something that fell to the ground and when the wind changed I was taken in another direction. I didn't care.

I got out of bed, took off my nightdress and looked for clothes to wear. Michael was staring at my naked body, I knew he wanted me; this was my last revenge on him for throwing me out. Now I was leaving I wanted to stay, I wanted to live in this room for ever and not have to go back into the world.

He threw some clothes at me. 'Get dressed.'

'I have nowhere to go, Michael.'

'Your friend Banischevski is going to look after you.'

'Andrei?'

'Does that surprise you?'

'You want me to go to Andrei?'

'Sure I do,' he said, and clicked the locks on the suitcase. The snap they made was like the shutting of a door. I suddenly realised I would miss him.

'Be ready in ten minutes,' he said. 'Banischevski will be here to pick you up. I have to go to work.' And that was our goodbye.

Going to live with Andrei was not as strange as I imagined. It felt like coming home.

He had a house on the Rue Cardinal Mercier, in the style, he said, of an English Tudor cottage. There were lattice windows and fake timbering, the beds had monogrammed sheets of Irish linen and there were black and white tiles in the bathroom. Every morning a servant brought the local Russian newspaper, freshly ironed.

I needed no instruction from him on what silverware to use at the table – I didn't know where I learned these things, just as I didn't remember where I had learned English and French – and Andrei was delighted when he discovered I could play Mozart and Chopin on the white grand piano in the parlour room.

That first afternoon he took me to Madame Garnet's, the most expensive dress shop in Shanghai, to buy me a new wardrobe of clothes; pencil thin dresses in French silk, hand-stitched jerseys. I liked the way the staff fawned over me because I was with Andrei. I found, like the silverware and the piano, that imperiousness came easily to me.

I knew he was watching me, every little gesture, every word I spoke, like a detective with a suspect, waiting for me to incriminate myself in some way. I was nervous, of course, but because I did not know what he wanted, I had no idea how to behave.

I assumed he would want to sleep with me but when we got home that evening his number one boy showed me to a bedroom at the other end of the house. All this time I had been sleeping with men for a few dollars; now I had a whole new life, and it was free.

It was because Andrei thought I was someone important. I only wished he would tell me who.

The photograph albums were bound with soft green leather, and smelled of dust. Black and white photographs had been lovingly pasted into position, rows of them, the parade of a life now gone. He placed them in front of me and waited – for what? A sigh of recognition, a finger placed absently on some image, perhaps, as a reluctant memory was coaxed to the surface.

I did recognise some of the people in the photographs, but picture postcards of the Czar and his family were commonly for sale in every Russian café and restaurant in the French Quarter, a whole industry had grown up around them. They had become the equivalent of religious icons for the émigrés of Shanghai.

He did not say anything to me, kept turning the pages, waiting for me to say or do something. I could feel my anxiety growing. I wanted to please him. If he threw me out now, where would I go?

I tried to concentrate.

Andrei himself featured in many of the photographs. He murmured a commentary: here I am following the Czar down the staircase of the Kremlin; here I am walking behind the Czar and his family in Peterhof, see the Czar's daughters in their white dresses and black stockings; here I am with the Grand Duchesses for a dance on the deck of the royal yacht *Standart* on the Dowager Empress's name day in 1912; here I am at lunch with the Czar and other officers and aides at Stavka, the Russian army headquarters during the war.

He placed a reverent finger on each photograph as he spoke, as if tracing the contours of a familiar face, feeling the rough wool of a uniform, the warmth of a hand. His face lost its habitual coldness, and when he looked up at me I knew he was searching for this same nostalgia in me. But I felt nothing at all and I knew I had disappointed him.

He continued to turn the pages, endlessly reciting the names of grand dukes and duchesses, counts and countesses. He knew each of them without hesitation, their familial relationship to the Czar, and to each other. As the singsong of the coolies chanting in the street and the boom of the Blue Funnel liners navigating the river drifted through the open windows, he conjured a forgotten world from shadows and light, and I felt the stirrings of pity for him.

When he finished one album he took up another, lifting each in turn from its box and its wrapping of soft paper. By the time he had finished, the afternoon was almost gone. Wall sconces threw a pale yellow light across the table.

'Which one of these women do you think I am?' I asked him.

'Don't you remember any of this?'

I shook my head. 'Perhaps you are mistaken about me.'

'Perhaps.' He leaned in so close that I could smell the taint of strong Russian cigarettes on his breath. 'It has to be you.'

The hairs rose at the nape of my neck. I wanted to scream at him to tell me: Who am I?

'It seems you have forgotten everything but your name,' he said.

I stared at the last page of the album, not a photograph but a postcard, bought in a bookstore right here in Shanghai, a portrait taken in 1916, the Grand Duchesses of the last Romanov Czar: Olga, Tatiana, Marie and Anastasia.

I was not shocked, or surprised, or overwhelmed. The notion was just too bizarre for me to take him seriously. 'Impossible,' I said.

'I am going to make you her whether you are or not.'

He slammed the photograph album shut, got up and went to bed, left me sitting there in the dark, wondering what he meant.

When I came downstairs the next morning he was standing at the French doors, watching the monsoon turn the carefully trimmed lawn into a lake. He had his hands behind his back, as if reviewing a battalion of soldiers.

'Do you want me to get you out of Shanghai?' he said.

'I don't know what I want, except to find out who I am.' I heard myself say the words and they sounded strange, like a phrase in a foreign language I was trying out for the first time. Before this I had not cared about myself or my past.

He sat down, in the manner of a man about to broach a matter of discipline with one of his children. 'I have to go to Berlin.'

114

'Berlin?'

'A provisional government in exile is to be established there. Naturally, I wish to be a part of it. I cannot live here for ever.'

Berlin. Once more, a leaf in the wind.

'I want you to come with me.'

'I'm not Anastasia,' I said.

'You don't know who you are. How can you know who you're not?' The photograph albums were still lying open on the table. He picked one up, found the postcard of the four Duchesses. 'I cannot be sure either . . . there is an uncanny similarity but . . . I last saw the Duchesses a year before the Revolution. It's five years ago now and the mind plays tricks . . .'

'You think I am that fat little girl in the . . .'

'The fat little girl would be much thinner after starving on the street in Siberia and Harbin.'

'I see no resemblance.'

'You did not know her.'

I tried to gauge my own feelings, but I felt numb inside, frozen. I wanted now so desperately to discover my own identity; I had never imagined that with it would come this terrible burden of responsibility. I didn't believe him; a man will always see what he wants to see. I remembered what he had said to me the night before: I am going to make you her whether you are or not.

'If that was me, I would know. I would remember something.'

'Would you?'

I could not answer him. He was right: would I?

'I have to take you with me to Berlin. If I am right this will cause a sensation.'

'And if you are wrong?'

He shrugged. 'You can go back and live with your American journalist. Is that what you want?'

What I want: not to go back to the taxi club. Not to dance with men for cold tea, not to sleep with men for money. All I have to do is pretend and I am good at pretending. I can pretend to like making love to a man, if he pays me enough. If I can do that, I can pretend to be a Grand Duchess, if that is what Andrei wants.

115

'I can get you a passport, I have friends at the German Embassy. But first it will be necessary to conduct a marriage.'

Conduct a marriage. The words were spoken with distaste.

'Marriage?'

'But of course. What did you think?'

We were married at the German Embassy. A man in a dark morning suit read the ceremony from a printed card, it took three minutes.

Andrei invited no-one. He said he did not want any of his friends to see us together here in Shanghai. He said it was important for our plans in Berlin, as if I had had some hand in formulating them.

We ate dinner at the Astor and then returned to the house on the Rue Cardinal Mercier for our wedding night. It was a bloodless coupling, as quick and as joyless as any time I had done it for money, and afterwards Andrei put on a dressing gown and returned to his own bedroom without a word.

I sent one of Andrei's houseboys to Michael's apartment to tell him I was leaving. There was no reply. Two days later we sailed out of Shanghai on the Orient liner, *Kashmir*. I stood on the docks before we boarded, staring at the grey battleships moored in the river, at the coasters heading out to sea trailing choking plumes of black smoke, and I waited for him to come. Even until the moment we stepped onto the sampan that would take us out to the *Kashmir* I expected to see him on the dock, waving.

Two hours later, as the sun faded to a dirty orange ball over the slums of Pudong, the *Kashmir* sailed down the river towards the sea, and Michael did not come.

PART THREE

Berlin, 1923

ANASTASIA

I am a virgin sheet of paper that no pen has touched, a ball of potter's clay ready to be shaped, a history waiting to be written. I am his creation, the canvas on which he has painted his memories and his hopes; yet he feels nothing for me, nothing at all. I am a story with no beginning. I long for an archive of my own, and I long for love.

I am prized like a jewel yet spark no desire. In Shanghai it was enough that I took off my clothes. In Berlin I have nothing to sell but a past stolen from others' memories.

I wonder why he makes love to me at all. There are times when he speaks idly of children, but children are a product of love and passion and there is none in our life together. There are times he takes me to bed and kisses me with such desperate ardour, like an actor portraying the part of a lover on the stage. But he is a very bad actor.

Afterwards he rolls away from me, puts on his silk dressing gown and, lighting a cigarette, walks out of the room. I lie in the bed, disappointed not in him, but in my life.

Because I know it can be different for me; I'd see them sometimes, the lovers of Berlin, as they walk hand in hand along the Unter den Linden, or huddle in doorways late at night, or whisper to each other in the cafés on the Kurfürstendamm. And though their faces and their clothes are different, I recognise this man and this woman by the way they have shut out the world. They are alone with each other even in the crowds on the Friedrichstraße. And I envy them.

They have something you cannot find in the taxi clubs of Shanghai or along the Chaussiestraße, no matter how much money you have in your pocket. They are foreigners to loneliness. They do not lie in their bed late at night, as I do, watching the snow drift onto the windowsill, feeling as remote from the earth and all the people on it as the moon in the night sky.

One day I would like to be the woman waiting impatiently for her lover in the café. I will count my history from then.

From the moment I arrived in Berlin I began my education about myself. I was required to learn my own past, if that's what it was.

I left Shanghai a taxi girl; I arrived in Berlin a grand duchess. This was how he introduced me everywhere and I was met with either awe or disbelief; there was not, could not be, any middle ground. I would have been universally derided for such a claim, if not for Andrei's sanction. Everyone knew of Andrei Banischevski; if he thought I was *the* Anastasia Romanov, most were prepared to suspend their ridicule, at least to my face.

There was not one Russian émigré population; there were hundreds, thousands. They had formed their own cliques, depending on their political affiliation, and there were more of those than it was possible to count. Andrei soon attracted his own circle of followers, those who believed in the restoration of the Romanov dynasty, and believed, too, that I was the sole survivor of Nicholas's family. I think he hoped my presence would rally support for his own cause; if that was what he wanted, then he must have been disappointed by the paucity of that support in Berlin. I still do not know whether he truly believed I was Anastasia, or was using me for his own purposes. But I will say this for him: he never gave up.

The Russian community in Berlin was a society turned on its head; there were Russian archdukes driving taxis, while their fares, who ten years before had been stoking boilers on trains, argued in the back seat over anarchist principles and communist manifestos; counts worked as doormen in hotels saluting former factory workers attached to the new Bolshevik Embassy in Berlin.

The desk clerk at our hotel had been a field marshal in the Czar's army.

Berlin was a mad hatter's tea party, and no-one expected the city to recover its sanity any time soon. In this looking glass world did Anastasia Romanov, Grand Duchess of all the Russias, really matter so much any more?

Andrei sometimes took me to a restaurant called the Allaverdi, on the Kurfürstendamm. Although the Allaverdi's patrons were almost all monarchists, there was one table in the corner of the restaurant that was reserved solely for the use of the Soviets. Karl Radek, Lenin's personal envoy, often went there. Some said he came because the shashlik was the best in Berlin; I suspected he came to be waited on by former archdukes.

One day I was there with Andrei and the rest of the crowd. There were the usual arguments going on; whether the Czar should have taken a firmer stand with the Empress over Rasputin, whether he should have left the running of the war to the generals, the usual rehashing of history.

Bored, I looked over to the Red table, saw a man sitting there with Radek in the peasant-style military uniform the Soviets favoured. He was thin, with a dark beard and the blackest, most penetrating eyes I had ever seen. I found I could not look away. Perhaps he felt my stare, for he turned around and trained those terrible eyes on me. It was like a shock of cold water.

Here, at last, I told myself, was a memory, and for a moment it stirred something in me. I thought to capture this remembrance but it was like grasping at a tendril of smoke. Almost at once, it had gone.

Andrei turned to me. 'Are you all right? You are quite pale.'

'Who is that man over there?'

'That's Radek.'

'Not him. The other one.'

He shrugged. 'I don't know, I've never seen him before.' He turned back to the others and started arguing loudly that if it had been up to him, he would have shot Rasputin himself.

Next day, Andrei came home from a meeting of the Supreme Monarchist Council, sat down in his armchair, opened his newspaper and said to me, almost casually, 'That man you saw. The Bolshevik in the restaurant. His name was Yurovsky.'

The name meant nothing to me at all.

We had been in Berlin perhaps six months when I discovered why Andrei found loving me such an arduous task. He rarely let me leave the house on my own, but I had been having persistent headaches and I went to see a doctor about it. Perhaps he did not hear me arrive home; when I walked into the bedroom I found him sitting in front of the dresser, applying my lipstick. I screamed, thinking him an intruder; he had on a tight red dress, the one he had bought for me at Madame Garnet's, and high-heeled red shoes. He wore a fashionable hat, tilted at a rakish angle, and beneath it was a blonde, bobbed wig. The rouge on his cheeks accentuated his age.

We stared at each other in shock.

'Andrei,' I murmured.

He set down the lipstick and cast an affectionate gaze at his reflection in the dresser mirror.

'What are you doing, Andrei?'

'What does it look like I'm doing?'

'Why are you wearing my clothes?'

'I paid for them,' he said, as if that was explanation enough, and stood up. I don't know, perhaps he'd just decided to bluff it out. He towered over me in the high-heeled shoes.

'You look like one of the whores on the Kurfürstendamm.'

'You should know.'

'Why are you wearing my clothes?' I repeated.

'Because I want to,' he said and slapped me hard across the face with the flat of his hand.

It must have given him a taste for it because he slapped me again, harder. He did it twice more. To my shame and horror I fell to my knees under the blows. Then he started kicking me, with my own red shoes. I curled into a ball, my knees up to my chest, I heard myself screaming, but he still kept on kicking and after a while I blacked out.

When I came round, Andrei had changed back into his own clothes and was wiping the lipstick off his mouth with a monogrammed handkerchief. He seemed pleased with himself. 'I hope we understand each other,' he said.

What could I say? The flood of fear that had taken possession of my body when he struck me was bewildering. He slapped like a woman. Why had I shrunk away like that? I sat up, not trusting myself to stand, my knees were still shaking.

'Who are you really?' he said.

'I am who you tell me to be.'

'You think this is a game?'

'I don't know. If it is, I didn't win it.'

'You thought it was you I wanted?' he said, which struck me as a strange thing for a man to say as he wipes your lipstick off his mouth.

'I am not so vain as to think that.'

'I think you just wanted my money and a passport,' he said and walked out. The evening shadows crept across the carpet, I curled up on the floor, like a dog hiding away to lick its wounds. Two more years I lived with this cold, strange and difficult man, two years of pretending to be this Anastasia, whoever she was. I stayed because I had nowhere else to go, and no-one else to be.

MICHAEL

I arrived in Berlin in the summer of 1923 and immediately became a rich man. In New York I would have been just another hack trying to file stories for the *Tribune* or the *New York Times*, but in Berlin you could live like a king on what would have been a pauper's wage back in the States. In Shanghai I had servants; in Germany I could have rented rooms in the Reichstag. The capital of one of the great European countries had turned into a lunatic asylum.

Berliners lived as though they were at a railway station, as if tomorrow they were off to somewhere better, but for today they must live out of a suitcase and make the best of it they could.

Life had become an affliction, to be borne stoically, like a toothache. Men who had been crippled in the Great War sold bootlaces outside the gates of the Tiergarten, sang folk songs for copper coins in the echoing caverns of the underground railway. But foreigners like me lived like royalty. For one hundred US dollars a month you could live in a fancy apartment with not one, but two, maids, and eat at the most expensive restaurants every night, while the locals drank turnip coffee, put ersatz honey on mildewed bread and decided which of their possessions they would sell to pay for tomorrow night's dinner.

But the Germans were not quite at the bottom of the social scale. There were nearly half a million Russian refugees in Germany, one hundred thousand of them living in Berlin. In fact it was as much a Russian city as a German one in those days; there were Russian churches, Russian clubs, Russian movie houses. There were even three daily newspapers published in Russian. You heard Russian spoken everywhere; and as you walked along the Kurfürstendamm at lunchtime the sound of balalaika music and gypsy violins from the restaurants all but drowned out the rattle of the trolley cars.

Much of eastern Europe's former royalty could now be found sleeping on benches in the Tiergarten or in the men's room at the Zoo Bahnhof. Former dukes and countesses wrapped themselves in discarded Russian newspapers to try to keep out the cold, but when winter came most of them would freeze to death anyway, dreaming of costume balls in the Winter Palace and French champagne and cocaine. Some people said it was a kind of poetic justice, for none of them had given a damn about the millions of peasants who froze and starved in the Czar's Russia, but I still felt sorry for them.

The Russians had not fled from their country's conflicts; they had brought them with them. There were monarchists, anarchists, fascists and, of course, the communists. If the French invented sex, the Russians invented politics. Everywhere you looked there was a poster or a banner for some political association or other, shouting its message in strident Cyrillic lettering. The White Russians used the term of their exile as the Bolsheviks had: to plot, to plan, to draw up charters, to argue. Everyone knew the Reds could not last and so the monarchists prepared for their imminent return to Holy Mother Russia. They were, after all, the keepers of the flame.

It was politics, too, that brought me to Germany. Soon after Anastasia left Shanghai, my friend Sebastian Beaumont got a job at *The Times* in London. A few months later he wrote to me saying that there was an opening at the newspaper, if I was interested. I took it. In the year or so I was there I worked hard, and had some political pieces published under my own by-line. I must have impressed a few people because Reuters offered me a posting to their agency in Berlin. The first thing they did, as soon as I was settled into an apartment, was send me down to Munich for three weeks; but when I got back I went looking for Banischevski. It didn't take me more than a day to track him down. I'm a journalist, after all. Like a cop, I know how to find people.

It was a Sunday and he was in the courtyard of the Russian Memorial church on the Unter den Linden. He was selling all the usual monarchist junk; hastily written and badly printed histories of the civil war, from the point of view of the radical right; photographs and postcards of the Czar and his family; leaflets calling for all Russians to return and fight for their homeland. I picked up one of the leaflets and read through it. In essence it claimed the Revolution had been a Zionist conspiracy and espoused the same sort of anti-Semitic views I'd just heard from an angry little man in Munich.

The courtyard suddenly crowded with people flooding out of the church, exiles most of them, former dukes returning to their one-bedroom apartments behind the Nollendorf Platz, admirals to wait tables in the Russian tearooms. As the summer sunshine warmed the cobblestones, they stopped to fuss over the books and postcards, assuring each other that the great days would soon return.

After half an hour most of them had drifted away and the usher started to close the gates. Banischevski had been busy with his friends and until then had paid no attention to the young man in the homburg reading the assortment of pamphlets piled on his stall.

'Can I help you?' he said, when the last former army officer had paid his respects and left.

I took off the homburg and smiled. 'Count Andrei Sergeiovitch. Do you remember me?'

It took a moment. When it came, the only measure of his recognition was the briefest flicker of irritation. 'The American,' he said. 'From Shanghai.'

'Michael Sheridan.'

'What are you doing in Berlin?'

'Working.'

'Not that American rag you wrote for in Shanghai?'

'I'm with Reuters now.'

He raised an eyebrow, to indicate surprise that such an august institution would employ someone like me. 'What do you want?' he said and busied himself packing away the books and photographs.

'How is Anastasia?'

'If you are referring to the Grand Duchess, I do not think that is any of your business any more.'

The Grand Duchess Anastasia. Well. 'There're an awful lot of grand duchesses in Berlin. I was referring to the woman of our mutual acquaintance from Shanghai.'

'How much do you want?'

'What?'

'That's why you're here, I suppose.'

'I don't want your money.'

He didn't seem convinced. 'You're here to make trouble, aren't you?'

'I just want to see her. See that she's okay.'

'She's in the best of health. And she doesn't want to see you.' He continued packing the books and postcards into two battered brown suitcases.

'Is she . . . have you established her identity?'

'I paid you off once.'

'Like I said, I don't want your money. She is all right, isn't she?'

He sighed heavily and turned to face me. 'As you have pointed out, there are many fraudulent claims being made regarding the Romanov dynasty at the moment. It has taken a little longer than I had hoped to establish my wife's true identity.'

'Can I see her?'

'Absolutely not.'

'Will you tell her you saw me and that I asked about her?'

'Of course,' he lied.

But was it chance, any of it? From the moment she left Shanghai a part of me was plotting some way of finding her again. I hadn't wanted to admit it but here I was, again, making a fool of myself over a woman. I had tried to get her out of my mind. I couldn't. Some Europeans brought back an addiction from their time in the East; usually it was for opium rather than a woman.

In London I had a flat, a girlfriend, a life on track. But my addiction gnawed away at my soul, and my resolve to forget her had unravelled when the chance had come for me to go to Berlin.

Still, a man has to make himself a fool over something, unless he wants to die of old age with a mountain of regrets. The alternative to being a young fool is to be young and sensible, and no-one ever had a story to tell by being sensible. There are worse things to make a fool of yourself over; horses and whisky, for instance. I only ever really had one vice, and that was women, and Anastasia, I guess, most of all.

'*Zu später*,' I mumbled, in my appalling German, and wandered off. I could feel Banischevski's eyes burning into the back of my neck. I suppose he knew I was going to find a way to ruin all his plans for him.

If that was what he was thinking, well, he was right.

ANASTASIA

There was a restaurant on the Kurfürstendamm called The Eagle, it was Andrei's favourite, we went there all the time. It was as if God had reached down and snatched a café from old Saint Petersburg and put it here in a Berlin street, he said. He could become quite sentimental about Russia; it was the only thing he was sentimental about.

The noise. You walked into a wall of noise; the clatter of plates, the twang of balalaikas, waiters shouting in Russian. Photographs of the royal family crowded the bare, brick walls. Andrei and I always made a grand entrance, and as we walked between the tables it seemed everyone wanted to bow and take my hand and extend their compliments. We were the royalty these lost souls had thought never to see again in their blighted lives; even those who did not believe I was Anastasia called me Duchess. They wanted to believe and that was enough for them.

What dinner companions we had most days; there was always a duke, or a countess, at the very least, and a certain young man who seemed extraordinarily fond of Andrei and whose eyes were remarkably bright. Cocaine, one of my dinner companions whispered to me once.

On this particular day our guest of honour was a handsome middle-aged countess just arrived in Berlin. Andrei assured me she had known the Czar and his daughters, and had been well connected at court. Her name was Natasha Ludmilova. 'You are to impress her,' Andrei had commanded me before we left the house. 'It is vital that we have her support.'

As always, I was on display, playing the role of Anastasia for him. There was not a moment in Berlin that I did not feel eyes on me, holding me to the closest scrutiny. Small wonder that I longed more and more for my own company and the solitude of our house in the Grünewald.

The waiter, a silver-haired man with a huge moustache, brought our food to the table with a manner of unfathomable hostility and rudeness. He had once been a duke, was a contemporary of Andrei's, though in his present circumstances he and my husband hardly spoke a word to each other. The Countess Ludmilova told the others, in an affected whisper, that she had known him in Russia, had attended a ball at his estate outside Saint Petersburg. A vulgar man, she suggested. His great grandfather had disgraced himself at Austerlitz, allowing himself to be captured by Napoleon.

Plates appeared on the table; zakuski, blini, shashlik, borscht.

I felt the woman Ludmilova's eyes on me, watching everything I did. Suddenly she leaned towards me and everyone around us stopped their conversations to listen. 'Don't you recognise me?'

'I am sorry. I am sure everyone has told you. I have no memory of Russia.'

She was staring at me so frankly I had to turn away. 'It's uncanny, the likeness,' she murmured to Andrei. She seemed in the grip of some powerful emotion. 'Oh, Your Highness, you can't have forgotten me.'

I wanted to find something that might placate her. It was always this way, this feeling of guilt, as if I should repay some long-forgotten debt. Andrei's continual coaching had only made things more difficult; I was never sure if the images that came to me were actual recall or a fantasy inspired by his harping on legend and hearsay and his own vague recollections.

Everyone was staring, waiting for me to be acclaimed or denounced. But Natasha Ludmilova merely shook her head. 'It's so long ago,' she said.

From the corner of my eye I saw Andrei's face, saw his disappointment, his disgust. His creation had not enjoyed the success he had hoped for. 'You said you met her many times,' he hissed at Ludmilova.

'She was just a girl then. She's a woman now. The memory plays tricks.'

Just then the waiter stopped at the table with another plate of shashlik. 'If this woman's the Grand Duchess,' he announced to the table, 'I'm Vladimir Lenin.' And he walked away.

Andrei threw his napkin on the table and stood up. 'That bastard was a bloody lousy general,' he said, 'and now he's a prick of a waiter. I'll have him thrown in the street!'

He stormed out of the room, shouting for the manager.

There was an appalled silence.

When the old waiter came back into the room, he was grinning into his moustache, apparently delighted with the furore he had caused. As he went past, I put out my foot. He went down, the plates of borscht circumscribing a perfect arc and then hitting the floor with a crash. Soup sprayed up the walls, some of it landing on a photograph of the royal family, like spatters of blood.

I stared at the poor old man, horrified at what I had done. He looked up at me from the litter of plates and beetroot soup, with a look of such hatred that I had to turn away. What on earth had possessed me to do such a thing?

Andrei walked back into the room just as Natasha Ludmilova shouted: 'That's just what Anastasia would have done!'

And then this complete stranger, smelling of cheap

perfume, actually came around the table and threw her arms about my neck. Everyone cheered and clapped and wept and Andrei called for champagne. Once again I was the centre of everything, the vortex for all their hopes. I felt no sense of accomplishment, only a deep and abiding horror for my predicament.

Amidst this scene of acclamation I saw the old duke slip away, his white jacket stained beyond repair, his duty to the royal crown finally done.

Behind the bar at The Eagle was a circular stairway that led down to the after hours club in the cellar, where, if you had the money, you could sprawl on sofas in a badly lit room and drink French champagne and eat pickled mushrooms until the sun rose. There was usually some poor émigré playing the violin for tips on a tiny stage.

Countess Natasha Ludmilova was exquisite from a distance. It was only when you came close you saw that the beauty was artifice, and you knew from the lines on her eyes and neck she was very probably ten years older than you had thought. Her skin had the waxy appearance of butcher's paper and her flesh was wasted, probably by tuberculosis. She smoked too much and her paroxysms of coughing would often leave her struggling for breath for minutes at a time.

Like all émigrés, her conversation was of the past; of this party and that costume ball, of friends dead or impoverished or missing, social seasons long forgotten, of grand houses and fine families now disappeared for ever. She coped with her new life in Berlin by pretending that it did not exist.

'Do you remember the Czar's brother, Highness?' she asked me, and then immediately apologised. 'I am sorry. Of course you don't remember. I keep forgetting.' And then she laughed at her little joke.

I found it disconcerting the way some people called me Highness, and others didn't, depending on the depth of their belief.

'I've seen pictures of the Grand Duke,' I said to her. All my so-called memories came from photograph albums. My past – if that was what it was – was etched in sepia tones. My history was manufactured from Andrei's anecdotes and remembrances.

'He was a wonderful man. Such fun. I had an affair with him.'

I wondered what I was supposed to say to this. She had had an affair with my uncle. Did that make us intimates?

'He was a ladies' man. Not at all like Andrei.'

A spiteful smile. She put a cigarette in an ivory holder and lit it.

There was a woman on the stage, one of the most beautiful women I had ever seen. She was slender as reed, with a mane of blonde hair, and a haunting, exaggerated quality to the way she moved. Her high heels accentuated the muscles in her calves, and she possessed a face of such ethereal beauty it could have been carved from marble. As a woman, I felt a stab of jealousy. Andrei was devouring her with his eyes. He had never looked at me like that, I was sure.

She started to sing, an old Russian love song from before the Revolution, accompanied by a violin and balalaika. The room was still.

'Of course Andrei just wants your millions.'

'What?'

Natasha, reclining on the sofa like an empress, watched my reaction from beneath half-lidded eyes. 'They say there's an absolute fortune in bullion and jewels in the Bank of England. If that old bird in Copenhagen ever decides you're the real thing, you get all the money.'

Old bird. The Dowager Empress.

'I suppose he deserves something for everything he has done for me.'

'More than something, dear. If you get the nod, it's the regency for our Andrei.'

It was the first time I truly appreciated the stakes for which these people were playing. Once the Bolsheviks were thrown out – and Andrei said it was a matter of months, the way things were going – there would be a

132

squabble over the vacant throne. I still could not quite accept the notion that Andrei was prepared to lay my claim to it. The idea was too ludicrous.

No matter how often Andrei introduced me as the Grand Duchess, all I could think was how this particular duchess had once slept with fat Chinese and tight-jawed Englishmen.

'I wonder if he's got it in him to produce an heir?' Natasha said.

I saw Andrei staring at us, angry that we were talking through the woman's song. To hell with him.

'Do you really think I could be her?' I asked her.

I held my breath as I waited for her answer. Could I be this elusive ghost called Anastasia?

But Natasha couldn't, or wouldn't, answer. Instead she leaned in to me and whispered: 'Look at these people. They are all living in a dream world. Idiots!' And then she collapsed into convulsions of coughing. Andrei glared at her, and then returned his attentions to the beautiful singer on the stage.

MICHAEL

My boss at Reuters was Jeremy Sanderson; Oxford educated, five languages, hair parted with a slide rule, spoke like he had a marble in his mouth. He was the kind of Englishman I was ready to detest on sight, another braying halloo Henry with an insufferable superiority complex. But Sanderson was not an easy man to dislike, even when you were predisposed to it; he had charm, a dry sense of humour, the Military Cross for valour in the Great War, and an inexhaustible supply of cigarettes. It's hard to know which of these many fine qualities won me over.

As soon as I arrived in Berlin, Sanderson took me under his wing, explaining everything from the complexities of German politics to the best way to tell a girl from a man dressed as a girl – the Adam's apple – in the bars off the Friedrichstraße. So it was to Sanderson, of course, that I went for advice on the mystery of Anastasia Romanov.

'Look,' he said, 'the Romanovs are big business right now. There's this Anna Andersen woman, for instance, right here in Berlin. Just last year there was a woman in Paris who claimed to be the Grand Duchess.' We were in one of the sidewalk cafés on the Kurfürstendamm, watching the passing parade, the sway-hipped transvestites, the middle-class émigrés promenading in their pearls, shuffling beggars selling shoelaces for a few groschen on the pavement. 'This isn't about a lost princess. This is about politics.

'It is about the fight over the succession. If Anastasia was still alive, it would complicate everything. You see, sport, there're three main pretenders for the Russian throne. There's Grand Duke Nicholas, in Paris, popular, quite an intelligent man, by all accounts, but his actual lineage is questionable. Then there's Kyril, the Czar's brother. He should be next in line but no-one's in a hurry to forgive him for what he did.'

'For what he did?'

'In 1917, he marched down the Nevsky Prospekt with his soldiers and offered his services to the Duma in the fight against the Czar. At the time the Duma president was actually trying to keep Nicholas on the throne, so he told Kyril to go home. Kyril went back to his palace and hoisted the red flag on the roof. Most Russian monarchists would rather see Lenin on the throne than Kyril.'

'Who's the third pretender?'

'The Duke of Hesse, Nicholas's other brother. The Dowager Empress – she's living in a castle in Denmark – remains the titular head of the Romanov family and would probably support his claim over Kyril's, but what she won't do is admit that her darling Nicky's feeding the worms. That's the main sticking point. Whoever is chosen needs the old bird's imprimatur.'

'And Anastasia?'

'She's dead, along with the rest of the family, old sport.'

'But if she wasn't. Just say.'

He shook his head, but went along with the game. 'First you'd have to find someone who could reliably identify her. Trouble is, the family retreated to Tsarskoe Selo for the last few years, lived like hermits. There're only a handful of people still alive who might remember her from that last couple of years. Don't forget, she was the youngest of the four daughters, so she wasn't considered very important.' He drained his coffee cup. 'How long ago did you leave New York?'

'Four years.'

'Ever been back?'

I shook my head, no.

'Okay. Suppose everyone who knew you then, your family, almost all your friends, disappear in a massive tidal wave. Who's left? An aunt, your nanny from when you were a kid, a schoolteacher. You show up back in New York and claim you're the heir to the family fortune. Only some cousin you've never even met doesn't want you to have it, so he says you're a fraud. How easy do you think it would be to prove who you were without papers?'

'Well, if my aunt remembered me . . .'

'What if you've changed, what if you weren't the physically stunning specimen I see before me now? Suppose you'd got fat or lost some hair and aunty's gone a little soft in the head herself. Your teacher isn't sure, it's been a long time. The nanny only remembers you from ten years ago. It goes to court, there're people who saw you a couple of times and they're pretty sure it's you until some clever lawyer gets them on the stand and trips them up, puts doubts in the jury's minds. In the end everything comes down to your old granny. Only granny is a cantankerous old bitch, half mad with grief, who always preferred your cousin to you and has a vested interest in pretending you're not who you say you are.'

'Why would she do that?'

'Because then she'd have to accept that her favourite son is dead. And she's so mad with grief she's fooled herself into thinking he's still alive somewhere. That's what's happened to the Dowager Empress. Olga, Tatiana, Marie and Anastasia might have been her granddaughters, but it was Nicky that she loved. Nicky was everything to her.'

I saw his point. After all, the Romanovs were famously eccentric before the Bolshevik uprisings. I had read the biographies: when the Czar was at the frontline during the Great War and tens of thousands of Russian soldiers were being slaughtered all around him every day, Nicholas's diary concerned itself almost entirely with the weather. His wife, meanwhile, was taking counsel on medical and political matters from a depraved and itinerant monk.

'So even if this girl I've told you about is Anastasia, you're saying she could never prove it.'

'Right. Although as a woman she could not inherit the throne through Pauline law, if she were accepted as genuine her rulings on matters of imperial succession would be unquestioned. Hesse isn't going to let that happen, he intends the throne for himself. None of her family, for different reasons, actually want Anastasia to have survived. And because they don't want to believe, they won't believe it.' He leaned in. 'Then, of course, there's the money.'

'The money?'

'Rumour is that old biddy in Denmark got out of Russia with millions of dollars in diamonds and jewellery. They say she keeps them under her bed in a large leather trunk. Anastasia would be entitled to a share of the dough. Sorry to say it, but some of this comes down to who gets the money.' He raised an eyebrow. 'You don't really think this woman you know is the real thing, do you?'

I shrugged, as if it was unimportant to me, that it was just a story that had fired my journalist's instincts. 'Not really,' I said.

He smiled. 'You know, it's a clever trick, the amnesia.'

'A trick?'

'Old sport, if I was going to impersonate someone, it's what I'd do. Doesn't matter how good an actress you are, you'll get caught out sooner or later; the name of a pet dog, or a servant, your favourite food. You can never know everything about another person's life, it's impossible. But if you say you've lost your memory then everything comes down to the physical resemblance and then no-one can really prove anything either way. In other circumstances Banischevski might have pulled it off.'

'I don't think she's faking it,' I said.

'Think about it: your memory is who you are, old sport, it's the sum total of your personality. If you have no memory, you don't know where you're from, you don't know what events shaped your life, you don't know anything at all about yourself. It's your soul. If this girl really doesn't remember anything, she's lost her identity. It means she can invent a new one.'

He was a journalist; cynicism came with the territory.

'I suppose you're right,' I murmured.

I thought about Anastasia as I first saw her that night in the taxi club: a girl without a soul. It fitted her perfectly. Only now she did have a history and I was a part of it. I knew what events had shaped her, I had been there and I had helped make them happen.

In other words, she was part of my history now, part of who I was. I knew I had to see her again, to exorcise the ghosts, get her out of my mind, and out of my life.

The atmosphere inside the Douglavary Egel was thick with the cloying smoke of strong Russian cigarettes. The dreary scratching of a violin drifted from a dark corner, a waiter shouldered past carrying plates of blini and shashlik. Every photograph on the sombre, oak-panelled walls was of the dead Czar or his family; here was Nicholas arriving at the Winter Palace for the 1913 tricentennial of the Romanov dynasty; here he was again, in his grey uniform and peaked cap, reviewing the troops in some muddy field; over there, in a white naval uniform posing for a formal portrait with his family.

The restaurant was crowded, and it took me a few moments to find who I was looking for. Banischevski was holding court at a corner table at the rear of the restaurant, a slight, fair-haired young man on his right, a matronly Russian woman, handsome rather than beautiful, on the other. Gathered around him was the usual ragbag of exiled nobility in all their faded glory. I heard him from the other side of the room, scoring some political point. Then everyone at the table started talking at once in Russian and none of them paid me the slightest attention. I stood at the end of the table staring at Anastasia.

She had changed, of course. I remembered a waif, haunted and pale, with shadows under her eyes, and bony hands that moved restlessly, like some pale butterfly fluttering from place to place. She had recovered her health, it was clear; there was colour in her cheeks now, and flesh on those delicate bones.

But the greatest change in her was not physical; it was a metamorphosis of spirit, apparent in the way she sat, her chin resting on her hand, her eyes bright. She was attentive and assured. Somehow my Anastasia had reconnected with the world.

When she saw me her eyes went wide. She touched Banischevski's sleeve and he broke off what he was saying and looked up. His face clouded with anger and, I think, fear.

Suddenly everyone stopped talking and looked along the table at this stranger who had arrived unannounced at their little gathering.

'Hello, Anastasia,' I said.

'Michael.' Perhaps she was pleased to see me, I couldn't tell. I always found her face impossible to read.

'Andrei Sergeiovitch,' I said, nodding my head at Banischevski.

He must have known that I would look for her, I had given him warning of my intentions in the courtyard of the Russian Memorial Church. With some grace he held out his hand and I shook it. 'This gentleman is an acquaintance of mine from the Far East,' he announced to the rest of the table. 'A journalist.'

I looked back to Anastasia. I had forgotten how beautiful she was, how deeply she affected me. There was no way to explain it, to myself or to anyone else. There was no sense to it. I looked at her and I felt myself start to burn.

'Andrei, you are forgetting your manners,' the handsome woman said, 'shouldn't you be offering our guest a seat?'

He looked as if he would rather cut my throat with a razor. But he fell in with the charade and asked if I would like to join them. He was transparently relieved when I declined. Instead I reached into my waistcoat pocket and produced a business card. I gave it to Anastasia. 'I'm working in the Reuters office here.'

You could see that Banischevski wanted to snatch it out of her hands and tear it to little pieces but that would have been a little obvious, in front of everyone.

'Reuters?'

'Can't be a bum for ever.'

The look on Banischevski's face. Utter contempt.

'You look wonderful,' I said to her.

'Thank you.'

'It's good to see you again. Give me a call sometime.'

I left, wondering as I walked out into the sun what that had achieved. I only knew I had to see her again, alone, but I didn't really believe she would ever call me, and she didn't disappoint.

ANASTASIA

My feelings on seeing him again were as powerful as they were unexpected. I had thought of him often since leaving Shanghai, sometimes damning him for the life he had consigned me to, at other times saying prayers for his soul, for he had saved my life.

One morning soon after we arrived in Berlin Andrei and I were having breakfast in our villa on the Kurfürstendamm, and my husband had pointed out to me an item in the newspaper about communist riots in Shanghai. Michael's name was mentioned and I had made some fond recollection of him. Andrei had that look on his face I had come to recognise; it meant he was about to say something particularly vicious.

'Well, he certainly thought well of you.'

'What do you mean?' I had asked, knowing he was longing to tell me.

'I didn't tell you at the time because I did not wish to upset you. But he actually demanded money from me when I told him I wanted to take you with me to Berlin.'

'You paid him?'

He dropped the newspaper on the table and looked at me with such condescension I wanted to slap him. 'You poor thing. You didn't suspect? One thousand dollars was the asking price. I paid it, happily, of course. But he really is such a mercenary bastard.'

One thousand dollars.

So, my white knight had traded me like a piece of meat. But that wasn't the only reason I came to hate him. As I realised the hell into which I had descended with Andrei, I looked back on Michael's flat off the Nanking Road with fonder recollection, for it had been my sanctuary and my haven, and I hated Michael for making me leave it. You might wonder at my gratitude, or lack of it; after all, if it was not for his courage in fishing me out of the river I would not have found my way there. What can I tell you? There is no logic to the heart.

But fondness survived, sometimes even flowered, beneath the wintry fields of my contempt. In my foreshortened history, there was only the taxi club and then Michael. There were moments with him in Shanghai that were the only kind memories I had of my brutal past.

And what was his legacy? Kindness and courage tempered by greed and self-interest. He saved me then sold me. What was I to make of him?

MICHAEL

In the summer of 1923 the flower shops along the Unter den Linden were a riot of colour. The cafés were filled with elderly matrons in Paris fashions, while on the other side of the Weidendammbrücke little girls sold themselves to middle-aged men and children died from tuberculosis in the parks.

Andrei Banischevski arched one black-painted eyebrow and draped an arm languorously across the back of his chair. 'I want you to stay away from her,' he said to me.

I had arranged this meeting here, told him it would be to his benefit. He had finally agreed to talk to me, albeit reluctantly.

I watched the drab parade of clerks and minor government officials pouring along the Friedrichstraße on their way to lunch. The Brandenburg Tor was silhouetted against a pale blue sky.

'Did you hear what I said?'

'I want to interview her.'

'What?'

'I think she's a good story. And you need the publicity.'

His face underwent a transformation. 'Is this still about money?' he said, and there was a note of wonder in his voice.

'Coming from you, that's rich.'

'Without me, she would still be working in a taxi club in Shanghai.'

'Sure, pal,' I said. Let him think that, if that's what he wanted.

Two transvestites flounced past, arm in arm, girls out for a stroll. I saw a naked hunger in his eyes. In the bright sunlight the ravages wrought by his addictions were more noticeable; I had heard he was addicted to cocaine, among his other vices. Drugs, champagne, his pretty boys, it was a profligate lifestyle and it must be straining even his extensive resources. He needed his little investment to pay off soon.

'So what do you say? It will only take an hour, maybe two. You can be in the room the whole time, if that's what you want.'

He shrugged his thin shoulders. 'I might be able to arrange it, for a fee.'

I laughed.

The coffees arrived but I didn't want to prolong the conversation. I threw my card on the table. 'Give me a call then,' I said and left. I knew my mark, and I knew he wouldn't let this opportunity pass. He was a desperate man.

If he only knew it, so was I.

He lived at the end of the Kurfürstendamm, in the Grünewald. The houses were crowded together in a dark and drab pine wood, quiet except for the barking of pinscher dogs bought by their owners to keep out intruders.

I was greeted at the front door by a housekeeper in a white apron. She told me I was expected in the tone of someone expecting the undertaker to call. She led the way inside.

It was an echoing rococo villa, that smelled badly of ancient mould. The house was cluttered with the treasures the Count had collected during his sojourn in Shanghai; Ming vases, jewelled opium pipes, a sandstone head from Khmer or Siam. This eclectic collection jarred with the dusty gilt-framed paintings that crowded the walls; wounded Cossacks reclining in heroic poses on smoky battlefields, looking tired and careworn, as if they had just come from a riotous cocktail party. There were no dismembered limbs or shattered skulls, the horses appeared furious but did not spill their entrails on the ground and no women were raped or children butchered. Past Russian glories as men like Banischevski wished to remember them.

They were waiting for me in the drawing room, posed together like a portrait. He was wearing a smoking jacket and smoking a cigarette in an ivory holder, a parody of himself. Next to him, in a wing-backed chair, was Anastasia. She wore a long-sleeved white dress with lace border, evocative of other photographs I had seen of the Grand Duchesses, taken just before their father's abdication. She looked pale, serene and ethereal.

Which, I supposed, was what Banischevski intended.

I sat down and the housekeeper hurried off, at Banischevski's command, to fetch coffee. I took out my notebook and pen, feeling Anastasia's eyes on me the whole time.

'Thanks for agreeing to talk with me,' I said, which was how I began every interview.

'Andrei said he gave you one thousand dollars for me. It's a lot of money, especially when you got me wholesale. You turned a nice profit.'

I looked at Banischevski. His face was as flat and expressionless as a new shovel.

My Anastasia had changed, I thought. Where had she found this sharp tongue? Her husband's influence, no doubt.

'Not a bad night's fishing,' she said, pressing the point.

Should I tell her? No, to hell with her. 'No, not too bad,' I agreed.

'You should have held out for more. Some people seem to think I'm a Grand Duchess. A thousand dollars? Andrei was cheating you.'

'Well, you know, I was desperate to get you off my hands. He didn't know what you were like to have in the house.'

Her cheeks flushed. Grand Duchess or not, she had certainly acquired the temper of an aristocrat in Berlin. She looked as if she would have liked to have her footman whip me for my impudence. 'Still scribbling away?' she said.

'That's right.'

'How did you manage that? Haven't Reuters read your work?'

'I guess not,' I said, not rising to the bait. In many ways, I preferred her like this, with some fire in her belly, than that sad, fragile creature I knew in Shanghai.

'Can we get on with this?' Banischevski snapped.

The housekeeper delivered the coffees – real coffee, not ersatz – and I started the interview, asking questions for which I already knew the answers: if she remembered anything at all of how she escaped Russia; how she had been received by the émigrés of Berlin. If she faltered, Banischevski quickly stepped in and guided her back to the answers he had undoubtedly rehearsed with her. I had the impression of a great actress, overwhelmed with the size of her part, and a backstage prompt.

I asked myself again why I was doing this; did I want to see her succeed or fail? Certainly an article coming through Reuters would attract attention, would do something towards hastening the result.

'What would you say to those people who claim you're a fraud and that your memory loss is no more than a ploy?'

'Is that what you believe?' she asked me, as if by asking such a question I had somehow betrayed her.

'It doesn't matter what I believe.'

'You were the one who started this.'

Banischevski couldn't contain himself. 'Many people who knew the Czar and his family before the Revolution have recognised her immediately, as I myself did. We have sought all possible medical assistance for her to try to recover her memory, which I believe will prove, without doubt, her true identity.'

I looked at Anastasia, who gave a slight shrug of the shoulders. She had heard this little speech a thousand times.

'There is another woman here in Berlin, also claiming to be the Grand Duchess Anastasia. Her name is Anna Andersen. You have heard of her?'

'Of course.'

'Do you not think that having two Anastasias in the one city damages your claim?'

'I am sure it does.'

'This doesn't trouble you?'

The clear blue eyes looked at me, and through me. 'It troubles me, but there is nothing I can do about it.'

'What are your thoughts on the Romanov succession?'

She opened her mouth to answer but Banischevski interrupted once more. 'The matter of the Romanov succession will be decided once the Grand Duchess has been lawfully recognised.'

'By the Dowager Empress?'

'Yes.'

'And when do you think that will be?'

To his surprise, and mine, Anastasia answered without hesitation. 'I long to see my family again. I long to know who I am, and how I came to be here. I only pray that the Dowager Empress will agree to see me and tell me if I am her grand-daughter, or if I am not. I just wish to know who I am.'

'You will not print that,' Banischevski said to me.

I ignored him. 'Do you ever think about Shanghai?' I asked her.

Banischevski was on his feet. 'This interview is terminated,' he said.

Anastasia's ice blue eyes were on mine, and the effect was unsettling. I felt sick with desire. I had wanted her for so long, and in that moment I resolved to do anything to take her back from him.

'I trust you to keep your word and do nothing that will discredit my wife to the world.'

'I have one more question.'

'The interview is over.'

I put away my pen and my notebook and stood up. He was standing between Anastasia and me so I was unable to wish her good afternoon. Banischevski put a hand on my arm and

I shrugged him off. He never knew how close I came to breaking his nose.

I left, heard the door slam behind me, starting the dogs barking again all through the Grünewald. A bright summer's afternoon. The warm sun stirred the blood. I had to have her back.

ANASTASIA

Andrei forbade me to leave the apartment, had to watch over me all the time, censor what I said, what I did. But he couldn't be there to watch me all the time. He tried to set the servants against me, but they despised him, and if I ever went against his instructions they lied to him for me. It's the price you pay for arrogance.

Natasha Ludmilova, alone in the coffee house, the elegance of her fox fur and ersatz pearls displayed for strangers who would pass her at her table and never speak a word. Appearance was everything in Berlin, it was all many had left. She would sit there and drink her ersatz coffee, looking proud and formidable, her salt and pepper hair drawn into a tight bun at the back of her head. I counted her as my only friend and confidante among the satellites drawn into orbit around my dazzling husband.

I was never clear about her position in Saint Petersburg society before the Revolution; she said she remembered me, that she had recognised me from the first moment she saw me. It was comforting in many ways, to be confronted with such certainty. She, more than anyone else, convinced me that I was who they said I was, that the trick was simply to learn to play myself again.

Or perhaps it was just that, a trick. Now when I looked at the photographs on the walls, the ache I felt in my chest was a real physical pain. I mourned the loss of a family I did not remember, I could even make myself weep for them. Once I caught others at the table in the restaurant watching me, and I realised I was crying. They nodded to each other, exchanged knowing looks, my tears confirmed for them that I must, indeed, be Anastasia. And so the illusion compounded itself.

It was one of the first days of autumn, Andrei had taken himself off to the country for another meeting of the Supreme Monarchist Council. If the Bolsheviks could be defeated with talk, he and his friends would have massacred them long ago. When he was gone I went alone, against his strict instructions, to meet Natasha, to while away a few hours and watch the queers in their beautiful dresses prance down the Kurfürsten-damm.

After the scene in the restaurant, Natasha had wanted to know all about the handsome American who had come to our table in the Douglavary Egel. Was he my lover in China? Had he followed me here? It seemed the whole world was besotted with crazy notions.

'He's just looking for a good story,' I said.

'He could write about me any time he wished,' Natasha said, and laughed deep in her throat, almost a growl. 'I should like to drape myself across his typewriter and he could scoop me.'

Today we talked about the other Anastasias; there were several in Paris and here in Berlin, Anna Andersen was the newspapers' latest darling. I tried not to think of them as rivals, tried to remind myself that my own claim might be some dreadful mistake. But slowly, day by day, I was absorbing the certainty of Natasha and Andrei and the rest of our clique, and I found myself becoming as outraged by the other pretenders as they.

Once, I had been my foremost cynic. Now I was

almost persuaded that they were right. They all seemed so certain.

After we had drunk our coffee, Natasha asked me to visit with her at her apartment. She had some photographs from the old days, she said, that she would like me to see. I dreaded such invitations. I searched photograph albums as parents searched the woods for lost children, first with hope, then overwhelming desperation. Each fruitless search convinced me I would never see my own Anastasia Romanov again.

But I agreed. I knew Andrei would not be back tonight. And in Natasha's invitation I recognised a lonely and ageing woman looking for my kindness.

Those grey medieval streets intimated a lost grandeur, those rundown alleys a perfect refuge for exiles mourning the Old Russia. Heraldic devices and stone eagles presided over every arch and doorway, layered with a century of grime and soot. Our footsteps were muffled by a blanket of chill autumn fog.

A train clattered on the railway bridge as we passed underneath. Two men were sitting side by side on the kerbing, one of them had found a stub of a cigarette in the gutter and lit it, sharing it with his companion. I fumbled in my purse for something to give them. Once a few groschen would have been sufficient. Now a million Deutschmarks might buy a sausage between them.

'You shouldn't do that,' Natasha scolded me, as we passed on, 'it encourages them.'

'They looked as if they needed encouragement.'

An old man was playing a concertina in the doorway of some fine house that had become a crumbling tenement slum. We passed into a murky courtyard and Natasha fumbled for her key.

'You live here?' I whispered.

'You get used to it,' she said.

Until then I thought that all émigrés lived as I did, in musty sad-looking villas hidden in the woods. Natasha's tiny flat smelled of damp and decay, its windows looked out over a grimy courtyard, rusted drainpipes and dark soot-stained brick walls. There was an armoire, a bed, a tiny kitchen, a table and a few hard-backed chairs. As I stood there and looked around in dismay, I had the feeling that Natasha was showing off her poverty. Look how much you have, the dismal room seemed to say. Now look at what I have. Now you have seen·this, you owe me something for my loyalty.

We drank coffee made from turnips and then Natasha produced her photograph album, handled it reverently, as if it were a locket of hair from a dead child. In that moment it was not her frailty I recognised, but my husband's. He had inflated her importance to disguise the paucity of his support in Berlin, to elevate himself in my eyes. As we talked I realised with a sinking despair that Natasha was no countess; the pretence dropped away and without confession, without apology, she announced herself not as the Countess but as her children's tutor. It was as if she had thought I had known all along.

Perhaps she was right; there was a part of me that had always known, I supposed.

'Do you remember the costume balls?' Natasha said, as rain leaked down the grimy windows, 'What fun they were! I remember the Countess used to wear the most outrageous costumes. Once she dressed as an Indian slave girl.'

The Countess. As if the Countess were her oldest and dearest friend and not her former employer. What illusions my fellow émigrés had created of their lives.

'Where did we meet?'

Natasha's eyes shone. 'It was at the Winter Palace, the tricentennial celebration. I was there to watch over the children during the service.'

'We spoke?'

She laughed. 'Of course not. You were with your dear mother and father, in the procession. You were no more than arm's length from me, though. I remember your face as if it were yesterday.'

Ten years ago! You convinced me that you knew me intimately; but your certainty is based on a glimpse of my face ten years ago?

'I cannot believe the Dowager Empress will not see you,' she said. 'That she could abandon you, her own grand-daughter! These other upstarts are to blame, of course, but I still cannot understand how she could delay the reunion for so long. When she discovers what she has done she will never forgive herself.'

She closed the album and caressed the plain binding with a loving hand, as if it were velvet.

It was cold in the room: there was no heating. We sat in the autumn gloom and I realised what hopes I carried with me, on my pretender's shoulders. It is not truth or order these people want, I thought: they want a vanished princess. They want beauty and romance and dazzle. They believe in me because they need to.

'Remember we are all devoted to you, Your Highness,' Natasha said, and she placed a hand tentatively on mine. A contract had been signed. I had found a devoted subject and in return I was to rescue her from the damp and the cold.

So there we were, duchesses and tutors alike, looking for rescue, and for hope.

MICHAEL

Berlin was not so much different from Shanghai. Any city I've been to in the world, the currency is vice, tempered to local taste. In Shanghai it was opium, in New York it was prohibition liquor, in Berlin it was cocaine. And sex, of course. It was the sex that gave Berlin its salty taste. Berlin specialised in dark sex, in the depravities that find their way into any city when money becomes worthless and tomorrow no longer matters.

On the Chaussiestraße child prostitutes patrolled the pavement, none of them over twelve years old. They wore pigtails and skimpy dresses and swung their handbags like hardened streetwalkers, skipping off with their clients to any one of the cheap hotels that crowded the area.

Their older sisters catered to different tastes. One day, walking along the Tauentzienstraße a woman leaned out of the shadows and whispered as I passed: 'Want to lick my boots? Just three billion marks and a cigarette. It's a bargain, *liebschen!*'

I turned around. She was wearing high black leather boots and sporting a riding crop. Her boots had been polished like a sergeant major's. She winked at me. I made a polite refusal and moved on. Three billion to lick those boots. A bargain to be had nowhere but Berlin.

The prettiest girls on the Kurfürstendamm were men. In the dimly lit honky tonks between the Kaiser Wilhelm Church and the Zoo, powdered and rouged government clerks supplemented their meagre incomes by courting drunken sailors and foreign diplomats, offering them androgyny and blowjobs.

Easy to see now why national socialism took hold.

Not that I lived like a monk. A man is still just a man, even when he's in love. There was a string of German girlfriends, attracted by cigarettes and silk stockings and the dinners I could buy them in restaurants. We helped each other out and they didn't love me either.

But I could not get Anastasia out of my head. I wrote the article, as I promised I would, and coloured it in such a way that I knew would attract the attention of a certain Dowager Empress in Copenhagen. I all but gave her Reuters' imprimatur to her claims.

Then I waited for Anastasia to ring me. I waited so long I almost gave up hope.

The Friedrichstraße and the Kurfürstendamm were the arteries of the city, but it was in the cafés where its soul was to be found; places like the Café, des Westens, the Josty, the Schiller, and the Monopol. It was here that Berliners went to read the newspapers – even though all the news was bad –

where they went to meet friends, to exchange gossip, and to argue politics.

We had arranged to meet in the Romanische café, just across the road from the Russian Memorial Church. It was as big as a *bierkeller*, could seat one thousand customers at a pinch. That's why I chose it.

When Anastasia arrived, she looked around, fascinated. The customers were a ragged and bohemian bunch; some with hair straggling over their collars, others with their heads shaved; some in rags, some in furs; there was even one young man dressed as an American cowboy in boots and spurs.

'What is this place?' she asked me.

'You've never been here before?'

'We go only to Russian cafés.'

'Everyone comes in here, the communists, the anarchists, the Dadaists, the Marxists. I like to sit here and eavesdrop, pick up snippets for my pieces. See those two guys playing chess over there? The one on the right is Emmanuel Lasker. He was the world chess champion for nearly thirty years. Some Cuban beat him for the title two years ago.'

'So if he invites me for a game, I shouldn't bet any money?'

I smiled. 'That's about it.'

The waiter brought us coffees and I watched her, sitting there so properly, like her spine was one steel rod. She had that same poise in Shanghai, I remembered, someone had trained her to sit like that. On its own it proved nothing, except that she was probably not middle class.

Although much about her had changed, there was still much that was the same; those haunted eyes, the long silences, the feeling you had that a part of her was missing. She was a lost passenger at a foreign train station waiting for her missing luggage, a lost child in a midtown police station, wide-eyed and afraid. But at least she had rediscovered the will to hang on, the instinct that had slipped away from her that night in Shanghai.

'You look . . . beautiful,' I said.

She inclined her head, accepting the compliment as if it were a cheap bouquet thrust into her hands by some stranger. I felt suddenly gauche and clumsy.

'How are things with Banischevski?' I said, quickly, to cover my embarrassment.

'He treats me well enough.'

'It's good to . . . know that you're okay. I've thought about you a lot.'

Again a slight nod of the head, but no clue to how she felt about seeing me again. That was how it was with her; you never knew what she was thinking, or planning. Perhaps the chess champion at the other table might not find her such easy prey, after all.

'Why did you call me?' I asked, vainly hoping she would give herself away.

She took a breath. 'There are only two people here in Berlin who know what I was . . . before. One of them is my husband.'

'Your secret's safe with me.'

She frowned, as if she wasn't quite sure about that. I felt insulted. But there was a chasm between us now; my mysterious taxi girl was just a memory now, a painful one.

'So. Grand Duchess Anastasia,' I said, making a joke.

'That's right,' she said, and it shocked me, the way she said it, for she was deadly serious.

The irony of it; I was the one who had started the whole crusade, now I was devil's advocate. I wanted my taxi girl back, perhaps. 'Are you scared?' I asked her.

'I don't know. What is my choice? Anonymity.'

'Some of us get by with it.'

'I don't think I could, not now.'

That rocked me, too. I suppose fame, destiny, whatever it's called, once you've been touched by it, you can't live without it, as she just said. Like cocaine, like opium, its dreams are sweeter than the drabness of life. Banischevski had given her the taste. Now she wanted more.

'If only I could remember just one thing. It would put an end to all this.'

'Would it? This Anna Andersen remembers many things and most people still aren't convinced.'

'But I look like Anastasia. She doesn't.'

'You look like Anastasia to Banischevski.'

We drank our coffee and talked, but the conversation led us nowhere. I wondered if she had agreed to meet me as an act of rebellion against her husband; as for me, well, I had made myself fool enough. Perhaps I would never really understand this strange and disturbed young woman, and it

152

struck me for the first time that whatever had happened to her had robbed her of the capacity to love a man.

She wanted the dreams Banischevski had whispered to her. She seemed more remote to me than ever.

I had my pride. I told myself it was time to cut my losses.

We shook hands and parted company in the street. As I walked away I told myself that was the last time I would see her. She would become a story told late at night to other men over port and cigars. Her mystery would remain; she would be my unfulfilled passion, and perhaps the better for it.

I would walk away and never look back.

ANASTASIA

The house was empty, it was the servants' day off. Something different about the hallway; a Ming vase and a jewelled dagger both missing from the ornamental table beside the mirror. I took off my hat and coat and dared a nervous glance at my reflection. My face was flushed, I had that look that women have when they are having affairs. Any other woman would notice it straightaway, of course, but I was confident I could fool Andrei.

I stopped at the foot of the stairs, held my breath, listening. There was someone else in the house. A foreign scent; two glasses on the drawing room table, one smeared with bright red lipstick. I felt strangely wounded. It was only my pride, of course. Was I so repulsive that he could make love to another woman but could not bring himself to make love to me?

There was a black leather shoe, with a high and narrow heel, on the carpet. I picked it up, planned to hurl it at his head. There was two years of rage stored up in me, stockpiled against his slights and demands and neglect.

I stopped and listened at the door. Like two animals rutting in there.

I walked in. Two heads twisted towards me from the tangle of bed sheets. One of them belonged to the singer from the Douglavary Egel, only now she was without her blonde wig. Her real hair was short and fair, and without it her face acquired a certain familiarity. Behind the rouged cheeks, the smeared lipstick and pencilled eyebrows, was the young man from the Douglavary Egel who often sat beside Andrei, drinking anise.

At that moment my husband was astride him, clutching his hips. He had entered the singer's changing room, as it were, by the stage door. His own face was heavily made up, but in the spirit of the performance he, too, had lost his dark wig. I decided then and there, that if I should go bald on the crown, like my husband, I would stop wearing cosmetics. The effect was ludicrous.

What a fool I had been. My husband's dissolution must have been obvious to everyone except me.

We all stared at each other. I took a few moments to adjust to this new perspective; another defining moment in my small history.

I watched a droplet of sweat course down my husband's temple. 'Shut the door as you go out,' he said.

And I did.

November; all colour had been leeched out of the world.

Berlin existed only in shades of grey, everything dripping with rain; the smell of the city was the smell of damp clothes, steam rising from wet coats, umbrellas leaving puddles of rainwater beside café radiators. The trams clattered into the fog, the girls on the Kurfürstendamm huddled in doorways, sharing damp cigarettes. Berlin's miserable and tubercular homeless shuffled

154

under bridges or died quietly in the Tiergarten by night, nameless and unmourned.

On the eighth an Austrian rabble rouser called Adolf Hitler and the former chancellor, Ludendorff, interrupted a speech given by the governor of Bavaria in a Munich *bierkeller* and, surrounded by a mob of Brownshirts, had assumed the government. There was a pitched battle in the streets a week later and Hitler was arrested. It was all anyone wanted to talk about in the cafés.

That, and how to find enough to eat. The value of the Deutschmark had sunk from one million to the US dollar on August the first, to a rate of one to one and a half thousand billion German Deutschmarks.

In effect Germany no longer had a currency.

Every day something else went missing from the apartment. It was as if we were the victims of a progressive thief, but we were too polite to discuss the matter between ourselves and too delicate to inform the police. It began with the vases and other light, moveable objects. Then the paintings disappeared from the walls, the Chinese carpets from the drawing room and the bedroom. I knew what was happening, but as there was nothing I could do about it, I simply kept my silence and fretted.

Andrei became increasingly morose, sometimes violent. I learned to stay out of his way. But then one day, finally, it happened.

He was drunk when he got home. I had just retired to bed, and heard him stamping about the house, calling for the servants to bring a bottle of champagne from the cellar. Then he threw open the bedroom door.

'Wonderful news,' he said.

He stood there, swaying, a sheen of sweat like dewdrops on his forehead. I could make out the high-lights of rouge against his high, pale cheekbones.

'The Grand Duchess Olga is coming to Berlin,' he shouted. 'She has permission to come from the Dowager Empress herself! She wants to meet you!'

Olga was the Dowager Empress's niece; the great dame herself never left her castle in Denmark, sent Olga to run her errands for her throughout the world. She must finally be convinced of my claim to legitimacy. Andrei had been sending letters to Denmark for months, had been lobbying everyone on the Supreme Monarchist Council, and now, of course, Michael's article had stirred interest in my cause again. I could not believe it had finally happened.

'As soon as she meets you, she will know who you are. The waiting is nearly over, for all of us. As soon as she meets you, she will know who you are.'

He had gambled on me, confident of winning. These were high stakes, too, long odds; belief placed like casino chips on this outside chance Duchess, winner take all, control over the Romanov succession, and so over Russia itself.

Andrei had drunk too much champagne, relief and desperation had added to his euphoria. My own reaction surprised me: it was dread. The moment had finally arrived, Olga would examine me as an antique dealer might inspect some rare piece of china, declare me either genuine or fraud. What if she was disappointed, what if I failed the test?

At some point I, too, had become a true believer. Like Natasha, like Andrei, I believed because I had to, because there was no other palatable choice. I did not wish to go on living if I was, after all, just another desperate refugee. Without Anastasia, there was no hope.

Our housekeeper brought champagne and Andrei tore the foil from the neck. The sound of the cork flying out of the bottle was like a gunshot. Froth bubbled onto the carpet. He filled two glasses, spilling most of it onto the floor, and thrust a glass into my hand.

'To the Grand Duchess Anastasia,' he shouted. He drained his glass. 'We have much to do to prepare you. She will be here the day after tomorrow. Out of bed.' He pulled back the bedclothes. 'We have to be ready!'

And so it began. I was like a student cramming before an important examination. Andrei would not let me rest. Books lay open everywhere, on the coffee table, on the sofa, on the floor. The Russian libraries and bookshops of Berlin were full of leather bound volumes and magazines about the Romanov family, and Andrei had bought them all. There was no shortage of information to be learned and absorbed.

He paced the floor in front of me, like a schoolteacher. 'Your father had a scar just here,' he said, touching his forehead. 'When he was a young man, still the Czarevitch, he went to Japan on an official state visit. As he was walking on the street in a place called Otsu he was attacked by a policeman wielding a sword. The man swung at him and the sword caught him a glancing blow across the temple. It left a small, white scar. Everyone in the family called it the Otsu mark.'

'I don't remember any of this,' I said.

'You don't have to remember it from before, I just want you to remember it now. The Otsu mark,' he repeated and returned his attention to the book he held open in his left hand. 'You loved animals. You loved every kind of animal.' He stopped, thinking. 'Perhaps I should buy you a pet. A spaniel, perhaps. A King Charles spaniel.'

'What are you talking about now?' I said. My head was aching. I had had hardly any sleep at all these last two days.

He thumbed through the pages of the book. 'Here we are. Your sister Tatiana had a dog, it was called Jemmy. Can you remember that? Jemmy. Jemmy. You loved that dog. You carried it with you everywhere as if it was yours.'

I shook my head.

'What was the name of the dog?'

'Jemmy.'

'Again.'

'Jemmy!'

'Good. Now see here, your little brother was crippled. He couldn't move his left knee, his illness had left it permanently crooked. There were two sailors who went with him everywhere, bodyguards, and they carried him around in their arms. Their names were Andrei Derevenko and Klementy Nagorny. Say it.'

'I don't remember.'

'It doesn't matter. Say it!'

I jumped to my feet. 'No! I don't remember any of this! Why should I say I remember things when I don't?'

The slap stung my cheek. 'Because I tell you to! Because I pay for the food that goes into your mouth, and for the roof over your head! Because I am your husband and I command it!'

I felt my knees give way underneath me. How shameful to be this terrified of him, but I couldn't help it. He was standing over me now, his hands balled into fists. I was terrified that he would hit me again. I heard myself sobbing, begging him not to hurt me.

But he was in a rage, and contrition had no effect. He pulled off the ruby ring on his finger, held it under my nose. 'See! Look at this! Tomorrow I have to sell it! Don't you understand, you stupid little bitch? Two years we have been living here in Berlin, where do you think the money comes from for this house, these fine clothes that you wear? If we don't convince the Duchess that you are Anastasia we're both out on the street.'

When he finished his rant his voice was hoarse and droplets of spittle glittered like dew on my dress. His breathing sawed in his chest, it sounded as if he had just run all the way up the stairs.

'Now do you understand why we must learn these names?'

'Andrei Derevenko and Klementy Nagorny,' I said.

'I don't care that you lost your memory. Perhaps it helps us. But a few memories will not hurt. I can tell you things you cannot find in any of these books, things that will convince even that old bitch in Denmark that you are her grand-daughter. How could she not be moved by her own poor grand-daughter?'

'Andrei Derevenko and Klementy Nagorny.'

'Good.' He was calm again, the storm had passed. 'Now let me tell you something about Nagorny,' he went on, his voice completely normal now. 'He had this habit of putting his little finger in his ear and scratching, like this. This is something I saw him do myself many times . . .'

And so we began again, the second-hand memories, the borrowed history, the only schooling I ever remembered, Andrei was my only teacher, poring through books in our dank little villa in the Grünewald long into the night until my head ached and I was so tired I dreamed each time I closed my eyes. And each time he would shout at me and shake me roughly awake.

Anastasia stalked the room like a scourge.

The whole morning waiting, waiting. I rose at dawn to brush my hair a thousand different ways, try on every dress I had, rehearse the family history a thousand times more. Finally it was twelve o'clock, the appointed hour, and there was nothing to do but stare out of the window while Andrei paced the floor, chain-smoking cigarettes with trembling fingers, snapping at the servants, snapping at me.

Both our lives would turn on what happened in the next few hours.

A black Sunbeam drew up in the street. I strained for a glimpse of the occupants through the curtains, but Andrei called me away from the window to wait, like a nervous schoolgirl, by the door.

The Grand Duchess Olga.

I had expected something grander. I had imagined tiaras, regal condescension and jewellery. Instead, my first impression was of a large woman in an old-fashioned dress, smelling faintly of rosewater. Her escort was a man who called himself General Radzinski, a pompous middle-aged man in a military uniform, who looked as if he might, at any moment, fall flat on his face with the weight of the medals on his chest and the decorations on his uniform. If one single Russian had been that brave the Bolsheviks could never have won. He and Andrei seemed to know each other, and I had the impression from their stiffly formal greeting that there was bad blood between them. But I never found out if there was any truth to that.

The Duchess was staring at me, and I submitted to this unabashed inspection. I was by now accustomed to such scrutiny, to strangers studying my face in every detail, as if trying to identify a criminal from a photograph. Olga seemed as nervous as I felt. She looked at me, then at Andrei, and her bottom lip began to tremble.

'Your Highness,' Andrei said, bowing, 'may I present the Grand Duchess Anastasia.'

She seemed unsure of what to do. I gathered up my skirts and curtseyed, as Andrei had coached me. 'Aunt Olga,' I said.

Aunt Olga. His idea.

For a moment I thought she was about to embrace me. 'Are you really her?' she whispered.

Now was my cue to say something. Andrei had coached me in this, also, something like: 'Please, Aunt Olga, I long to see my grandmother again,' or some such drivel. I didn't even know what this grandmother of mine looked like, even the photographs I had seen of her had been taken ten years before. The lie caught in my throat.

'Are you really her, child?' Olga repeated.

I could feel Andrei's eyes on me, urging me to play the part he had written for me. But then I heard myself say: 'I don't know.' If it wasn't a very clever answer, at least it was the truth and it was all I could manage. And so we both stood there, with the servants and General

Radzinski and Andrei looking on, both of us tongue tied
and lost in our own dilemmas.

Andrei had spared no expense over lunch. He sat there
in his Riviera flannels, seemingly poised and without a
trace of nerves, while the servants fussed around the
table, serving borscht, shashlik, blini pancakes. He had
spent a small fortune on the best French wines.

I had no appetite. The food sat in my stomach like
cold fat.

It was clear that Olga had come prepared to be disappointed but now was not sure what to think. She could
not keep her eyes off me. As we ate, Andrei gave her a
sanitised version of how he had found me in Shanghai,
but she hardly seemed to be listening.

When he had finished she said to me: 'So you
remember nothing, my sweet?'

She was not at all like the formidable princess I had
expected. I was disarmed by this kindly if sentimental
spinster, and struck dumb, overcome, I think, by the
gravity of our meeting. Andrei had rehearsed with me
over and over what I should say and do, but I could not
deliver the performance.

'No, I'm sorry,' I said.

'Perhaps the odd thing, here and there?'

I shrugged and shook my head again. Andrei glared at
me, his face pale with rage, but I could not do it, not for
him, not for her, not for me. I wanted so badly to be
Anastasia, you see, that I would not buy her with lies.

'You used to have a little dog, I remember,' Olga said.

'It was Tatiana's,' I said and for a moment I saw a
smile of triumph and relief on her face. 'But I think
Andrei told me that.'

He would have jumped across the table and throttled
me there and then, I think. His eyes were like pinpoints.
Olga, of course, did not notice.

'You loved that dog, don't you remember?'

I shook my head. 'I'm sorry.'

161

She lapsed into a disappointed silence.

If I was Anastasia, I decided, then sooner or later someone would discover it. If I was not, I would not pretend.

And to hell with him.

Finally, Olga murmured: 'You are so like her,' and then added: 'You are so like her, *malenkaya*.'

Malenkaya. Wasn't that what Andrei had called me once? The name meant nothing to me, but apparently, it should have done. She was looking at me for some start of recognition, I knew. It was an old trick, had been tried on me many times, by different people, using different words or photographs. As if they could creep up and take my memory by surprise.

'It was the name your father had for you,' Olga said.

'I must be honest with you. People tell me that I look like Anastasia. Many people. But I remember nothing, nothing at all. I'm sorry. I know you are all looking for a sign from me. I wish . . .'

There was a stone in my throat. I got up and fled the room. I had had enough. I was no-one without Anastasia; they would all of them love me if I was her, dismiss me without thought if I was not. I needed Anastasia to live. But Anastasia was a monster, had tortured me now for two years and I could not bear her any longer.

Perhaps it was my transparency that swayed her. It was precisely because I didn't try to persuade her that I was her niece, as Andrei had suggested, that Olga convinced herself that I was. I do not know how else she could have arrived at the conclusion she did that afternoon.

From the bedroom I heard her talking on the balcony to Andrei.

'Is it really her?' Olga said.

'For myself, I have never had the slightest doubt,' Andrei said, sounding like someone who believed just the opposite.

'Is that why you married her?' Olga asked him. Really,

I had thought this mild old lady did not have it in her to say such things. I almost cheered.

'I know what you think of me, Your Highness. But I love her. I would love her even if she were not Anastasia, even if she were just a peasant in the fields.' A huge lie, enormous, breath-taking. Yet such things slipped off his tongue with such ease, it was hard not to believe him.

'Still. It must have made it easier for you.'

'It was not the reason I married her.'

'I wish I could believe you, Andrei Sergeiovitch.'

'Your Highness, with respect, it is not my sincerity that is at issue here.'

Well, for all the world I hope not, I thought. If it is, we are lost.

'Am I mistaken?' Olga wondered aloud. 'How could she have survived for a year in Siberia on her own?'

'Only she knows that, and the answer is locked somewhere in her mind. What is done cannot be undone. It is left to those of us who knew her and loved her to put her suffering at an end.'

Such a speech. How smoothly he drew her in to his conspiracy. Did he mean what he said, despite everything? With a man like Andrei, it was impossible to know.

'It is so hard to believe again after so long.'

'It need not have been so long, Your Highness. I have written many times about this matter to your revered mother. She might have ended this whenever she chose.' It was a gentle admonishment.

'My mother is a stubborn old woman,' Olga said. 'She does not want to believe that Nicky and the children are gone. Perhaps it has blinded her to what is in front of her face.'

'It is up to you now, Your Highness. What do you think should be done?'

A long and aching silence. 'For myself,' I heard Olga say, finally, 'I think she is so like her. I want to be convinced. If only she could remember something. Something that would put the issue beyond doubt.'

'What will you say to the Dowager Empress? Will you leave my poor Anastasia to suffer without the love of her own dear family?'

I heard the words I had not dreamed I would hear: 'You may rest assured that upon my return you will hear directly from the Dowager Empress. There will be a reunion very soon. It seems to me it has been delayed far too long already.'

I put my knuckles in my mouth and bit down. I could not believe my ears. The ordeal was finally over.

There were tears in her eyes when she left. I suppose there may have been tears in mine, also.

Yet in truth, I felt utterly detached, as if I was watching myself from the other side of the room. If I felt anything at all, it was an overwhelming pity for the downtrodden spinster who had come here at the behest of her tyrant mother to search for the damaged remnants of a family irretrievably lost to them both.

I even wondered about her judgment of me, rebellious now to my own cause. Had I really known this sad and kindly woman in that other lifetime? Perhaps one day the dark and silent gates of my memory would open again and allow me entry to my lost self. If they did not, then Aunt Olga was gatekeeper to my soul.

We stood on the threshold, she looked at me with terrible longing and then, suddenly and without warning, she wrapped her arms around me. The embrace lasted for just a moment, long enough that I felt her hot tears on my cheek. She gasped with grief as she threw herself out of the door, General Radzinksi making a brief farewell before hurrying after her.

For a long time we both stood there. I knew Andrei was furious at me for disobeying his instructions; yet he must also have been elated, for he had won the victory he craved.

In the end he neither congratulated nor admonished me. Perhaps he could not believe what had happened either. I suspect he thought I was a fraud all along and could not really believe his little scheme had worked. But I think he was scared, too, knowing how he had treated me until then. So it was easier to say nothing. He simply turned and went into his study, shutting the door gently behind him.

I had played my part, improvised from a script of my own creation. Now I had to wait in the wings until it was my cue to perform again.

MICHAEL

The Deutschmark continued its free fall; shopkeepers changed price tickets every day, then every hour. A wheelbarrow piled with Weimar Deutschmarks couldn't buy a loaf of bread. The favourite song in the nightclubs was: 'Tomorrow's the End of the World'.

There was one poor bastard in our office, old Jürgen, lived with his wife in a little apartment by the Tiergarten, acted as our driver and interpreter, answered the telephone, ran messages. Two of his sons had been killed in the war, the other had lost a leg and couldn't work, and he was glad of the job. Inflation was so crazy we had to pay him every day, we put bundles of Deutschmarks in a sack, he'd grab it and run straight out of the office looking for something to buy; shoes that didn't fit, stockings, cuckoo clocks, once even a second-hand bicycle, anything that might hold its value and could later be traded for something else.

He was over sixty by then, had worked as an English professor at the university, had retired with one hundred thousand marks put away for his old age. Three months later it wasn't enough to buy a tram ticket.

Under the damp, black trees of the Tiergarten, peasant boys, driven out of their villages to look for work, froze solid overnight on the benches, while tubercular whores shivered in the alleys behind the Kaiser Wilhelm.

That was Berlin in the winter of 1923: tomorrow's the end of the world.

We sat in the Café Josty, huddled in our overcoats, icy rain dripping steadily from the awnings and onto the pavement, a few miserable souls with their heads down, hurrying past, crouched under their umbrellas.

I warmed my hands around my cup of ersatz coffee.

A few customers still made a show of preserving the life they remembered from before the war, stoically chewing cakes made from frost-bitten potatoes, smoking Havana cigars rolled from cabbage leaves steeped in nicotine. Poor bastards. The winter stretched ahead interminably, December the first stop on this endless journey called winter, long days to fill and endure, nowhere to get a decent meal, no station on the line to step off.

I had promised myself I would not see her again. But one day, unexpectedly, she called me, asked if we could meet. I should have said no, I wanted to. I couldn't.

'You look tired,' I said.

She sipped her coffee, winced, added two more teaspoons of sugar. 'Andrei is having an affair.'

What was I meant to say? Was she angry, was she hurt, was she relieved? I knew about Banischevski's lifestyle, of course, even when I was in Shanghai. He liked cocaine, dressing in women's clothes and sodomy, and not necessarily in that order. It's what happens when you allow people to inbreed and give them a lot of money and free time.

'Is it a man or a woman?' I said.

'A little of each.'

'I'm sorry.'

'Why? Why are you sorry? You brokered the deal.'

'I thought I was giving you the chance of a better life.'

We stared at each other. She looked away first. 'I suppose you did think what you were doing was for the best. For both of us,' she added.

'What about the Dowager Empress?' I asked her. The visit was supposed to have been a secret, but it was all over Berlin inside twenty-four hours.

'Not a word. It's been two weeks.'

'It will work out.'

'I don't know what's going to happen. His money's running out. There's hardly anything left in the house, he's selling it all from under our feet.'

Now I knew why she'd called me. She was looking for her white knight. 'You don't have to stay with him,' I said, on cue.

'Where would I go?'

'I could help you.'

'Why would you want to do that?'

'For old time's sake.'

All the time she lived in my apartment in Shanghai, I don't think she once looked at me in the face. Her eyes always roamed the room, as if she was looking for a way out. For the first time I felt the full force of those ice blue eyes. 'How would you do it?' she said, and I realised I had just allowed Anastasia back into my uncomplicated life.

'I can get you papers. It's easy enough. Bribe an official in the right department. You can buy anything in Germany if you know who to talk to.'

'And then?'

I stirred my coffee. And then, indeed.

'I have to go back to England at the end of the month. This was only a temporary posting. You could come with me.' It was a lie, all of it, but it sounded right.

She shook her head.

'Why the hell not? I'll take care of you.' I sat there, waiting for her answer, wanting her more than I'd ever wanted anything. So much for getting on with the rest of my life, so much for letting it be.

'You want to rescue me again?'

'Something like that.'

She tried to make a joke of it. 'The last time you rescued me I ended up in Berlin with a man who sleeps with boys in dresses.'

Of course. She would wait on the Dowager Empress in

Denmark, would not compromise any announcement that might yet come from Copenhagen. No matter about Banischevski now, what he did, how he treated her. She didn't want to be pulled from a muddy river again. She wanted to be Anastasia, the Grand Duchess of all the Russias.

I finished my coffee. The rain on the Kurfürstendamm had turned to sleet.

'What if that mad old woman in Denmark says you're not Anastasia?'

'Is that what she'll say?'

'I don't know.'

'Neither do I. I have to find out.'

I smiled at the irony of it. I looked at my watch. 'Why did you call me?'

'I needed to talk. You're the only real friend I have.'

I don't know, perhaps she meant it. 'I have to go.'

She reached out and put her hand on mine. 'Thank you, Michael.'

'For what?'

'For everything.'

That the touch of a hand could cause such profound regret. I wanted this story to end differently. But now, this time, it really must be over.

'One thing you should know,' I said. 'The money your devoted husband gave me. That wasn't for me.'

'Don't tell me. Your sick mother needed an operation.'

'Those friends of yours from the taxi club were looking for compensation.'

'A thousand dollars?'

'A thousand dollars I didn't have.'

She turned pale, and I took some satisfaction from that. I could walk out now, leaving her feeling bad about the sick mother joke, but this time I did not want to leave her thinking I was without honour, for all that mattered to a man like me. It was more important to me that she would never know how much I still wanted her.

'I'm sorry,' she said. 'I didn't know.'

'You didn't ask,' I said, and feeling I had finally evened the score, I got up and left.

ANASTASIA

Life is fair; no matter what people say, it always gives you choices.

You can starve to death or you can become a prostitute; it's a choice. You can go back to that life, or you can marry a complete stranger and depend on his charity and patience. Another choice. You can leave him to follow another man, and gamble on the chance of love, or you can stay behind and risk discovering not only an identity for yourself, but a destiny.

I made my choice; but I was not prepared for the regret that squeezed my insides like a fist as I watched my tall and handsome American turn his collar up against the December rain and walk out of my life for ever.

The house was almost bare. Hardly any furniture left, bright rectangles on the wallpaper where the pictures had been. Bare floorboards in all the rooms. And cold inside, the smell of rot and damp rising from the cellar. Even the Khmer head had gone, the last of the antiques from Shanghai to be sold off. It must have been very valuable.

As I entered, our housekeeper came rushing down the stairs in her hat and coat, tears streaked on her face. 'Ilsa?' I said.

She pushed past. 'I'm not coming back, Highness,' she said and was gone.

Ilsa was the last of the servants. I took her departure to mean she had been told there was no money to pay even her. A house without help; no-one to take my coat or fetch me a glass of hot chocolate. I looked around. The fire was cold in the grate because there was no money for coal or for wood and no-one to light it if there was.

I felt suddenly helpless. How quickly we become accustomed to privilege. In Shanghai I ate in the street and counted myself lucky to have a bed for the night. Now I fretted because there was no-one to fetch me a warm drink.

I found Andrei upstairs in the bedroom, staring out of the window at the dirty mist blanketing the pine wood. There was a bottle of vodka in his fist.

He was dirty-drunk and vicious. 'Where have you been?' he growled.

'I thought you were in Bad Reichenhall.'

'I said where have you been?'

He frightened me when he was like this. I kept my coat on, and glanced towards the door. 'I had coffee with Natasha.'

'You're a liar,' he said.

I could not find my voice.

'Cat got your tongue?' he demanded.

'I went . . . to the Tiergarten.'

'Alone?'

'I don't have to tell you who I was with. You don't own me.'

'Of course I do. Without me, you freeze to death in the street.'

He meant it literally, of course. The marriage papers were in his possession, I had never seen them. Without him I would be back where I started, with no papers, no money, and no shelter.

He was right, he did own me.

'You were with that American,' he said.

He slapped me hard across the face. The slap was terrible, an open hand, but delivered with the brute force of a man. It made my head ring and took my breath away.

I knew what was going to happen next so I turned on my heel and rushed for the stairs. He came after me, but he was drunk and slow. I heard him shouting at me, but already I was out of the door and running.

Evening turned rain to ice, sleet to snow. I saw a bundle of rags underneath the rail bridge, most likely a corpse. Perhaps one of the men I gave money to. Ice hung from the girders, a hard sheen of ice glistened on the tramlines.

My breath formed white clouds on the frigid air as I made my way up the stairwell to Natasha's flat. I leaned against the door and rapped with my knuckles.

She was bundled in her overcoats, one worn over the other, a scarf wrapped around her face. She could not afford to heat her apartment even in the dead of winter, I realised. There were purple rims around her eyes. She was sick.

'You,' she said.

'Can I come in?'

She stood aside. No smile, no 'Your Highness' today. She watched me from the door. She was wearing mittens and sweating even in this icebox of a room.

'You're not well,' I said. 'You need a doctor.'

'Who can afford a doctor?' She looked me up and down. 'What are you doing here?'

'I had nowhere else to go,' I said, and was about to tell her about Andrei. I had to tell someone.

'He threw you out. I knew he would.'

Once again, I was a spectator to my own life. Natasha knew something I did not and I steeled myself for bad news.

'She won't see you. Did he tell you?'

Natasha relayed her bad news with relish. Olga had run her errand but the Dowager Empress had refused to validate her niece's judgment. Or perhaps Olga had changed her mind on the journey from Berlin to Copenhagen. Whatever the truth of it, Andrei's gamble had failed.

I felt myself sway on my feet. Yet in a way, I was relieved. It was over, at least.

'You're in the same boat as me now,' Natasha said, and there was real spite in her voice. 'Not so high and mighty any more.'

'Natasha, I . . .'

'What are you going to do? You won't be able to live in that fancy villa any more. You'll be just like the rest of us. Worse.' She leaned closer and I could smell her hot, foul breath. 'There's no work, you know. We've all tried.'

'I thought you were my friend.'

'I thought you were the Grand Duchess.'

She pushed me back out into the corridor and slammed the door.

The door to the house was swinging open. There were shards of glass in the hallway, the remnants of a vodka bottle that had been thrown against the wall. In the drawing room one of the curtains hung askew from the rail.

I did not feel afraid. I had decided this grotesque man would not terrorise me any more.

I went upstairs. It was dark, and the bedroom was frigid. I went to the table by the window and turned on the lamp.

'So you've come back,' Andrei said. I turned around. He was sitting in a wing-backed chair, a bottle of warm French champagne in his right fist. As if he was celebrating. His lips were wet and he slurred his words; he was drunker than I had ever seen him.

A contemptible man. I had more dignity as a taxi girl than as this man's wife. All for a few mumbled promises.

'Have you heard the news?' he said. 'That old cow in Denmark has denounced you as a fraud. So much for your loving *babushka*.'

'I never claimed to be Anastasia. That was your story. You told me I was her.'

'If you had done what I had told you, we might have convinced that fat bitch. Now you've thrown it all away.'

'It wouldn't have mattered what I did. They all want Anastasia dead. We will not convince them otherwise, no matter what we do.'

He tried to get out of the chair. 'You ungrateful little minx.'

'You disgust me.'

That stopped him. I had never spoken to him that way before and for a moment he veered on the brink of self-pity. 'It's all gone, you know. The money. I've sold everything to support you, and what thanks do I get for it?'

'You did it for yourself, not for me.'

'I suppose they'd let me be a waiter at the Douglavary Egel.' He lurched out of the chair at the third attempt. 'Your Highness,' he said to me, and bowed in mockery, his voice slurred.

He staggered, bounced off the wall and went into his study. I wondered what to do now, where to go. It was obvious I could not stay here. I thought about Michael; Michael, who had saved me once before; Michael, who had, in fact, saved me twice if you counted paying off the gangsters who had come looking for me in Shanghai; Michael, who had mysteriously reappeared in Berlin at this next crisis in my life. Michael, the only friend I had in the whole world.

Andrei stood in the study doorway. He was holding a gun in one hand and in the other he had a fistful of bullets. He dropped several on the carpet as he tried to load the ancient revolver.

'What are you doing?'

'There's only one honourable way out,' he said, and I believe he meant for both of us.

He managed to fumble a couple of rounds into the chamber and snapped it shut. He was already raising the revolver when I came at him with the champagne bottle.

But I was too late. I was staring down the black eye of the muzzle and I heard a voice scream 'Papa!' from a very long way away. He squeezed the trigger and there was a click as the hammer came down on an empty chamber. I swung the bottle as hard as I could and it struck him on the side of the head. He went straight down and the back of his head hit the corner of the hearth.

The bottle had not broken, which surprised me. I must have hit him with the base. I raised it over my head a second time, ready for him when he got up and came at me again. But he didn't move.

The revolver lay on the floor at his feet. I kicked it across the room.

He lay there, his eyes half open. Dark blood formed a widening pool on the parquet floor. His body gave a series of violent twitches.

I realised what I had done.

I dropped the bottle and ran to the door, then stopped and turned back into the room. I didn't know what to do.

I felt numb. It was an accident, I didn't mean to hurt him, not like this. Would anyone believe me?

What was I going to do?

I opened my purse, found Michael's business card with the number of the Reuters news agency in Berlin. I dialled the number, taking long, slow breaths, trying to control my breathing.

When someone answered the telephone, I was surprised at how calm I sounded. 'Hello,' I said, 'this is Countess Anastasia Nicolaevna Banischevski. I would like to speak to Michael Sheridan please. Please tell him it's urgent.'

MICHAEL

I had been working late in the office, typing up another story on the Munich *Bierkeller Putsch*, when I got the call from Anastasia. She sounded quite calm but insisted that I come to her villa in the Grünewald straightaway. She didn't tell me what was wrong, just said that it was urgent.

I had told myself it was over, thought I would never hear from her again. But all I wanted was an excuse and I knew, sooner or later, I would have one.

When I got there, the house was in darkness, and the front door was wide open. It was as cold inside the house as it was outside, I could see my breath on the air even in the hallway. 'Anastasia?'

There was no answer. I looked around, felt the hairs rise on the back of my neck. I remembered the last time I was here, the huge gilt pictures on the walls, the vases, the antique statuary. Now the house was almost bare, the carpets were gone, most of the furniture as well. 'Anna?'

I went up the stairs. There was a single lamp burning in the bedroom. I made out a woman's silhouette in a wing-backed chair by the window.

'Michael,' she said. 'I knew you'd come.'

There was a man's body lying on the floor beneath the mantelpiece. I switched on the light. 'Jesus Christ.'

There was no doubt that he was dead. His face was mottled blue, his eyes had that filmy sheen I'd seen on the herring at the fish market. Blood had congealed around his head in thick purplish globs, and glistened darkly in his hair.

I needed to sit down. I slumped on the edge of the bed, and we just sat there for several minutes, neither of us saying anything. I tried to think.

'What the hell happened?' I said, finally. My voice sounded hoarse.

'He came at me with a revolver.'

The sound of her voice unsettled me, it reminded me of the night in Shanghai when I heard her talking on the phone in her sleep. She seemed unnaturally calm; I suppose we both did, sitting there, ignoring her dead husband lying there on the floor as if he were a throw rug that had slipped off the back of a chair.

I felt the heel of my shoe connect with something hard. I looked down and saw the revolver lying on the carpet between my feet. On some irrational impulse I nudged it further under the bed with my shoe.

'What do you want me to do?' I said.

'I don't know.'

'What did you hit him with?'

'A champagne bottle.'

So, it was the drink that finished him off, I thought and gave a short barking laugh. Just nerves.

I went over to the body, bent down to take a closer look, was careful not to touch anything. There was a deep laceration to his right temple, going right back into the hairline, but I decided that wasn't what killed him. The back of his head lay against the edge of the tiled hearth, and this was where most of the blood had come from. There was a thick purple swelling on his skull, like a bruised plum, and some blood and fluid had leaked out of his left ear.

I stood up. 'Well, there goes the meal ticket.'

'What am I going to do, Michael?'

Or, more to the point, what are you going to do, Michael? Walk right out of here, if you have any sense. Berlin police were notoriously unreliable. What would they make of this? Banischevski was only Russian, after all, and what was one more or less in a city like Berlin, which was overflowing with refugees? Would they accept Anastasia's version of events; or would they take the Prussian point of view, that a dead husband, even one holding a loaded revolver, is worth more than one frightened wife? She would certainly go to prison for this. The question was, would they hang her?

This would be a heaven-sent opportunity for her enemies, in and out of Germany, to get rid of this troublesome pretender. Men like the Duke of Hesse had the power to interfere with police procedures and the courts.

And where did that leave me if I helped her and made myself an accomplice? But I had been a fool for her ever since I jumped into the Whangpoa River and fished her out, and apparently I saw no reason to stop now.

'Where are the servants?' I asked her.

'Gone. There's no money to pay them.'

'How soon will he be missed?'

'He has friends everywhere . . . I don't know . . . he has lunch at the Douglavary Egel every Friday.'

'Two days then, at most.' Not nearly enough time to get

176

her out of Berlin. 'Does anyone know about you and me?'

She shook her head.

When she went missing they would think she had fled Berlin. That would be the logical thing. Who would think that some American journalist would put his career and his liberty at risk for a Russian refugee?

'You don't have to help me,' she said.

'Then why did you call me?'

'There was no-one else.'

'That makes me feel a lot better.' I looked back at Banischevski. I'd seen a lot of dead people in my job, taken photographs of quite a few, especially after street riots in Shanghai; Christ, I'd even stepped over a few frozen corpses on the way to work in the last few weeks. But Banischevski was the first dead person I had seen that I had actually known in life, and it unnerved me. And, of course, I was worried about my own neck.

Then I looked at Anastasia. 'Get your coat, and pack some things,' I said. I looked around the room, wondered whether I should rearrange things for the police, put the gun in Banischevski's hand, perhaps, lay the bottle beside his head, arrange a tableau that even the most stupid Prussian investigator could understand.

I decided to leave things just as they were.

'Should be a while before he starts to smell in this weather,' I said, thinking aloud.

Anastasia shivered. I put my arms around her and held her but she just stood there, rigid. I might as well have tried to comfort the poker in the hearth.

'It will be all right,' I told her.

'Nothing will ever be all right,' she said, which seemed to me an altogether too gloomy appraisal of things. It was not as if Count Andrei Sergeiovitch Banischevski would be a great loss to the world. The problem now, it seemed to me, was merely one of logistics and expediency.

A woman can dress in a man's clothes but it's a rare female that can walk and talk like one. I admit, there were a few creatures

I'd seen walking down the Kurfürstendamm that summer who had given me pause for thought, but on the whole, given good lighting and a reasonable state of sobriety, a woman in a man's clothes will always look just that.

And Anastasia wasn't about to fool anyone.

She sat cross-legged on the other side of the train carriage, in a suit and stiff collar, wearing tartan socks and carefully polished black Oxfords. Her hair had been cropped short, and she had a neat parting on one side, but the effect was to make her look not so much like a man but like one of the underage boys you could pick up for a packet of cigarettes in any of the clubs behind the Kaiser Wilhelm, if you had a mind to. She was reading *Der Zeitung* and trying to affect a masculine arrogance, but there was absolutely nothing manly about her. Her bones were too slender, there was no hair on her knuckles, for God's sake, and even without make-up she was too beautiful to be mistaken for a man. Still, that might work in our favour, I thought. Others would be suspicious of our relationship, but for the wrong reasons; they might think us degenerates but not fugitives.

Another man, a business traveller by the look of him, joined us in the first-class carriage at Zoo station. He kept staring at us, and I knew what he was thinking. I tried to ignore him, but when I finally looked up he gave me an unctuous smile to let me know he was a man of similar, dissolute tastes. He thought Anastasia was my bum boy.

The ticket collector must have thought so, too, but unlike my travelling companion, he was a Prussian of the old school, and wanted to spit on the floor at my feet.

Anastasia lowered her newspaper, so that I could see her face.

Everyone's staring at us, she mouthed at me. They think I'm queer. They think you are, too.

Well, if only my father could have seen me. I remembered when I was ten years old and he thought I was spending too much time reading books. I overheard him talking to my mother one night, when I was in bed: 'You don't think the boy's queer, do you?'

Next day I found the biggest kid in the street and punched him on the nose. The kid's name was John Sanderberg. Johnny just stared at me, a look of disbelief on his face: 'What was that for?' he said, so I hit him again, and watched two trails of blood leak out of his nose. He put his hand up to his face and when he saw the blood his expression changed to something much less benign.

He practically killed me: a couple of roundhouse rights and I was lying on my back on the sidewalk. Then he jumped on top of me and kept hitting me until I blacked out. When I got home my face looked like raw hamburger. My old man looked up from the *Wall Street Journal* and asked me what had happened. I told him I just picked a fight with some kid and that I'd won. He said good boy and went back to his newspaper.

He stopped worrying about me being queer and I went back to my books.

It was the last time I'd tried to get his approval. I got beat up for him and he didn't even put down his newspaper. After that our history was one of rebellion, daily skirmishes, and finally major revolt. He wanted me to be like my big brother and be an A student, so I flunked college. He wanted me to go into the family firm; I told him to shove it and got a job with a newspaper in New Jersey.

I suppose it was my old man then that led me to Anastasia; she mourned a past she didn't have, I mourned a past I couldn't run from. A past forgotten, a past remembered, brought us both to Shanghai. The road to Anastasia had brought us here to this train compartment, with Prussian conductors thinking we were queer. If you look hard enough, there seems to be a symmetry to everything.

The train pulled out of the station and started its slow procession across the countryside. I tried to read my newspaper, took deep breaths to try to calm my nerves. Several hours to the border, we would wake up next morning in France or a Berlin jail.

'Do you have a light?' Our travelling companion leaned towards me, with a cigarette in his mouth. I was sure there was a perfectly good box of matches in his pocket and this was just a conversational gambit. But I lit his cigarette for him anyway.

'You are Russian?' he asked me, in German.

'American.'

'Ah, American,' he said, as if that explained everything. 'You work in Berlin?'

I nodded and pretended to read my newspaper. I hoped my demeanour would deter him, but there're people who miss or choose to ignore the little signals the rest of society lives by. My friend was so desperate for conversation, he didn't mind that I wasn't.

And I think he was curious about Anastasia. He kept looking at her, a hungry look in his eyes. I wondered if he would have felt the same way if he'd known she was a woman.

'My name is Petrovski, Serge Petrovski,' he said, though I didn't ask. 'I am an émigré, yes? I have to run away from Russia after the Revolution. Now I have my own restaurant, in Tauentzienstraße.'

I did my best to look bored. I was too nervous for small talk. I looked at my watch again, though we were still in the Berlin suburbs.

'Your friend doesn't say much,' Petrovski said, throwing another lean look at Anastasia.

'Who is this boring old fart?' Anastasia said, without even looking up from her newspaper, playing her part to perfection. The spoiled brat with the sugar daddy; the sugar daddy was me.

A sharp intake of breath as Petrovski realised he had been mortally insulted. He looked at me for a sign of apology or retraction and, finding none, gave Anastasia a bitter look before returning to his newspaper. It was the look of a man rejected by a hoped-for lover.

I glanced up at her; a look of conspiracy. Then I reached forward and laid a hand on her knee, knowing she could not brush it away, establishing a feigned intimacy for the benefit of our travelling companion. I had not touched her since Banischevski's death. She had remained hidden in my apartment for two weeks after that and we had not slept together. Our love affair had never gone further than that first night, a drunken twenty-dollar fumbling, with an eighty-dollar tip.

A hundred dollars and I didn't remember a thing about it. I could have had her whenever I wanted, how could she have refused me after all I'd done? But here in Berlin, as in Shanghai, I made a pact with myself: if Anastasia ever took me back into her bed it would be because she wanted me there, not because she had no choice. Our next time would not be like the first.

Petrovski was staring at my hand on Anastasia's knee. He was plainly envious.

'Your young friend is very beautiful,' he said, trying again.

Anastasia shook her newspaper in irritation.

'She isn't German, is she?'

I shook my head.

'I'm Russian,' Anastasia said, from behind *Der Zeitung*, 'from the aristocracy. And I don't care what Lenin says, I still don't mix with the middle class.'

His face went the colour of boiled beetroot. He finally gave up, returned to his own newspaper, and I tried not to laugh.

He got off at Middelburg, and the police got on.

We saw the blur of uniforms as the train pulled into the station. I glanced at Anastasia, saw my own fear mirrored in her eyes. Neither of us spoke. We had to stay calm. I've always thought guilt is what catches most criminals.

I pulled down the window and leaned out. The air was frigid. Through the steam from the boiler I saw two policemen climb aboard the very last carriage, next to the guard's van. I shut the window and sat down again.

'Do you think they're looking for us?' Anastasia whispered.

I shook my head. 'Just routine,' I said, but I wasn't as certain as I sounded.

The train rumbled on. I went back to my newspaper, let Anastasia see that I wasn't concerned, but I couldn't concentrate. I kept reading the same sentence over and over.

Were they looking for us?

I heard the connecting door to our carriage click open. I lowered the newspaper and looked down the corridor.

'Is it them?' Anastasia whispered.

I nodded.

'What are we going to do?'

'Unless you want to let fly with a champagne bottle again, we just sit here and read our newspapers.'

They were making their way along the corridor, going into each compartment, checking papers. Were they really looking for us? For a few days her picture had been in all the newspapers, but the sensational murder of some minor

Russian count did not hold the public interest for long when Hitler and Ludendorff were standing trial in Munich, and the French were marching through the Ruhr.

Anastasia's new passport was in my jacket pocket. It had cost me all my savings. I would find out if I had got my money's worth sooner than I thought.

The police were in the next compartment, the train was travelling at top speed through the Prussian countryside, there was no escape. I felt a droplet of sweat make slow passage down the back of my shirt.

Anastasia stood up, went to the door, perhaps thinking to slip past them in the corridor. I put my hand out to stop her. 'No,' I said.

'They're looking for me.'

'Sit down.'

'We can't just wait for them to come and arrest us.'

'We don't know it's you they're looking for.'

At that moment there was a commotion outside. A man ran out of the next compartment, the two policemen shouted at him to stop and chased him down the corridor.

Anastasia looked up at me and smiled. 'You were right,' she murmured. 'You saved me again.'

We were ten minutes from the border. We abandoned the charade with the newspapers. Anastasia tapped her foot restlessly. There was sweat on her upper lip.

'What happens when we get to London?' she asked.

'That's up to you.'

'I don't understand. Why do you risk all this for me and never ask for anything back?'

'I don't want to ask. I want you to give it.'

She just stared at me, her face impossible to read. We heard the grinding of metal as the driver applied the brakes, and the train began to slow.

I reached inside my jacket and took out the passports, mine authentic, hers an elaborate forgery. A clerk inside the German Foreign Office had ensured his family's survival for at least a year by smuggling it out for me. He said the passport was good enough to get her out of Germany, perhaps even into England. I hadn't thought past that.

The train slowed to a stop. We were at the border. We held our breath.

PART FOUR

London and Sverdlovsk, 1924

ANASTASIA

I remember – a strange thing to hear myself say even now – I remember the customs official at Dover, his features still as vivid in my mind as the face of a lover; the nest of hairs under his chin that he had missed when he was shaving; the slick strands of black hair under his uniform cap; the small mole above his right eye. He took my passport with brusque formality and then looked up into my eyes. I felt myself wilt, like some night creature before an unexpected flame. I knew he could see through my pitiful disguise, that he would recognise my papers as forgeries. I would be hauled out of the line and sent back to the Berlin police and a murder trial. I imagined a grey prison yard, a black robed priest, a thick manila rope. But instead he tossed the passport back to me and waved me through the barrier, turning his attention to the next person in the line. It felt as if a spotlight had been turned off. I saw Michael waiting for me, a bland smile on his face, as if he had never expected the result to be otherwise . . .

I had to carry my own suitcase.

We arrived at Waterloo station on a cold winter evening. I stepped onto the platform, watched the steam from the engine curl under the girders overhead, and prepared to do battle with another faceless city.

Porters brushed past with trolleys piled high with cabin trunks and hatboxes. Michael shepherded me through the din and the crowds, to a line of hansom cabs waiting outside the great porticos. I was immediately assaulted by the smell of a strange city; chimney smoke, fumes from the trolley buses, the manure of the waiting horses, ripe and rich. Around me I heard harsh Cockney accents I did not immediately recognise as English.

I stared out of the cab window as we crossed the Thames. London was shrouded in fog, the mist creating haloes around the gas lamps on Westminster Bridge. I was safe, I realised; I had done the worst thing in the world and I was safe. This stranger, my best friend in the world, had saved me again.

We stopped outside a row of Regency houses in a place called Kensington. This time Michael picked up both suitcases and I followed up some stone steps to a green door. His flat was on the second floor, up a narrow flight of stairs. The flat smelled of damp, the furniture was hidden underneath white cover sheets. It was bitterly cold.

Michael turned on the lamps, and bent over the grate, fumbling with a box of matches and some rolled-up newspaper.

'I'll get a fire started,' he said.

I looked around. It seemed so drab, so small. Now that I was safe, I wondered what I had come to.

'Do you want anything?' he said, and I shook my head. I just wanted to sleep, hide from the world.

He took me through to a bedroom and lit the little gas lamp beside the bed. 'You can sleep here tonight,' he said.

I was suddenly overwhelmed with gratitude, choked with it. He had risked so much for my sake. Exhausted as I was, I reached up, put my arms around his neck and pulled his face towards me. And I kissed him, I kissed him on the lips, kissed him so hard I felt as if my lips would bruise. I had never kissed Andrei on the lips, the whole time we were together, even on the few occasions that he made love to me I never did that. And I never kissed any of my customers in Shanghai.

A kiss was the most precious thing I had to give.

I was still wearing my men's clothes and I imagined how we might look to some casual intruder, two people in dark suits, locked together. I fell back onto the bed, Michael on top of me. I could smell the damp wool of his suit. I felt safe in his arms, safer than I had ever felt in my whole life, and I never wanted him to let me go.

'Thank you,' I whispered, 'thank you.'

I felt his body go rigid and he pulled away from me. I tried to pull him back onto the bed but he was too strong. He disentangled himself and stood up.

'What's wrong?' I said.

'I don't want a professional at amateur's rates,' he said.

Such a cruel thing to say, it took my breath away.

'Go to sleep. We're both tired.' The door closed gently behind him.

I had hurt him somehow. A disjointed life, fractured and without recall, met by loneliness or contempt. I ached in my bones. But I had seen melting footprints in the snow; there was a belief in me now that there was a path to follow, a place to go.

Just not tonight.

MICHAEL

I woke up to a bright Kensington morning, the mist melting away under a distant sun. I heard the clatter of horse's hooves from a milk cart, the clink of bottles left at the door, the tuneless whistle of a milkman. There were noises in the kitchen and for one insane moment I thought Anastasia was making us breakfast. I don't know why I thought that; my princess didn't know how to tie an apron.

I put on a dressing gown – after so many months, it reeked of mothballs – and went into the kitchen, lured by the smell of frying bacon. Someone was making one of those English breakfasts where everything is thrown into a frying pan and cooked in lard and butter.

It was Angela.

Angela – Angie to those of us who knew her – was Sebastian Beaumont's sister. A flapper, they called them in

England. The last place I would have expected to find Angela Beaumont was in the kitchen; this was the Beaumont family equivalent of the red carpet. There was scrambled eggs in the pan – my guess they had started sunny side up – and bacon and fried bread. She looked at my silk robe and tousled hair as if I was a child that needed improvement and instruction.

'So you're up.'

'How did you get in?' I said, more surprised than anything.

'You gave me the key,' she said, and then I remembered that just before I left for Berlin I had asked her to keep an eye on the flat for me. Angela had been the natural choice because she had spent many nights here and knew her way around. I remembered making vague promises that we might take our relationship further when I got back from Germany. Like most men I stumbled towards marriage like a blind man bumping into the furniture in a strange room.

'Seb told me you were coming,' she said. Seb had probably asked her to discover what exactly was going on.

Bacon fat spat out of the pan and she squealed and jumped back. I took the spatula from her and took over. The fried bread was already starting to burn.

'How was Berlin?' she said, taking off the apron and waiting for me to kiss her. Something that, for obvious reasons, I was avoiding.

'Fine.'

She put her arms around me and nibbled my ear, which I used to like. I tried to concentrate on the eggs. 'No kiss for me?' she said.

'There's something I have to tell you.'

Too late. She was standing in the doorway, wearing one of my long dress shirts she found in the wardrobe and with her hair so short she looked like a teenage boy. It must have gone through Angela's mind that I'd gone queer. Turned public school, as she called it. Then Anastasia shifted her weight against the door frame, the swell of her breasts and the shape of her hips altered the contours of the shirt entirely and the expression on Angela's face changed with it.

'Who's this?'

'This is a friend of mine, from Berlin,' I said. 'Anastasia Romanov. Anna, this is Angela Beaumont.'

Angela did not wait for further explanation. She threw the

apron on the floor and pushed past my new houseguest, picked up her coat and hat from the sofa and went out, slamming the door behind her.

It opened again, she threw the spare set of flat keys across the room and then the door slammed a second time.

'What was that about?' Anastasia said.

'She thinks we slept together.'

'We did.'

'A long time ago.'

'That's playing with words.' She seemed to think it was funny.

I took the pan off the range and left the contents on the sink to congeal.

'Who is she?'

'A girlfriend.'

'I'm sorry.'

I sat down, fumbled for my cigarettes. The packet was empty. Angela had taken my last one.

Anastasia looked around the flat; two bedrooms, a kitchen and a living room, nothing like the grand villa Banischevski had provided for her in Berlin. She looked like a lost little boy sitting there in the oversized shirt. And so pale.

'I have caused you a lot of trouble,' she said.

A breath-taking understatement. I had got beaten up for her in Shanghai, now I'd made myself an accomplice to a murder in Berlin. Was it murder? She hadn't meant to kill her husband, not as she told it. She had struck out at him in self-defence, she said, but I only had her word for it. A cold shadow lay between us. When I kissed her last night, I found myself wondering just how hard she hit him.

But we were safe, for now, the German police could not reach her here, and there was nothing to link her to me. I could go back to Berlin and to Reuters, if that was what I wanted.

'What are we going to do?' Anastasia said, reading my mind, perhaps.

'You can stay here for the time being.'

'What about your girlfriend?'

'I don't think there's enough room for the three of us.' The joke fell into the silence like breaking glass.

After a while, I said, 'Angela's my problem, not yours.' I looked around for something to eat. There was coffee, hardly fresh, no milk and no sugar either. Well, there was a little in the bottom of the bowl, but it was set hard like volcanic rock.

'You should have let me jump off the bridge,' she said. 'Now I'm not just stateless, I'm a stateless murderer.'

'No-one's going to miss him.'

'His friends will miss him.'

'He didn't have friends. Just hangers-on.'

'He didn't deserve to die.'

'Not many people do. It happens anyway.'

She started to cry. Good tactics. I went around the table and held her; held her like you'd hold a wounded bird, afraid that if I squeezed too hard she'd break. She was skin and bones under the shirt. I rocked her in my arms and told her everything was going to be all right and wondered how I'd got myself in so far, because there was no mistake about it, I was in love with her, no other woman came close. She had everything I had ever wanted; beauty, mystery, intelligence and best of all, she was utterly remote, beyond my reach.

Sebastian didn't want to meet in the office. He chose the saloon bar of a public house near his Fleet Street office. I dodged buses and taxi cabs crossing the street, a motorcar klaxon horn blared as its driver swerved around me, two bright young things squealing in the back seat, scarves flying. There was another enraged shout from a cyclist on his way back from Covent Garden, boxes of carrots and tomatoes balanced precariously over the front wheel.

I didn't get across without getting horse dung on my shoes.

The bar was gloomy and overheated. The wall sconces were on, dull yellow light was reflected on the mahogany panelling. The stained-glass windows that faced the street were the colour of dried egg yolk. A fug of tobacco smoke and hops cosseted the patrons from the bitter English winter.

I found Sebastian in a corner booth. 'Roads are a disgrace,' he said, looking at my shoes. 'City's no place for horses now. Be a damned sight cleaner the day we have just motorcars on the street.'

I set down two pints of Whitbread's and he pretended to study the front page of the *Times*, which lay open on the table next to his bowler hat. Lenin was dead. The world mourns.

We talked about the news for a while, and the weather, and the traffic, then came the pregnant silence we had sought to avoid with our small talk. No question about it, I had let him down, and badly. First, professionally, in Berlin; then personally, with Angela.

Sebastian plunged in first. 'So, what have you been doing to my little sister?'

'It's a long story.'

'I warned her about you. It's her own silly fault. I told her you weren't to be trusted.'

'Thanks.'

'She had this daft notion that she was going to marry you. I told her not to be so damned stupid but young girls don't listen to their big brothers any more.'

'I appreciate the recommendation.'

'Well, I was right, wasn't I?'

Beside the point, in my view. If it wasn't for Anastasia I could have been persuaded to do the right thing. But perhaps that was why I'd gone looking for my princess in the first place. Anastasia was always going to be there, in the back of my mind, waiting for me to go out and find her again.

'Who is this girl?'

'It's not what you think.'

'Look, I'm not Angela, I don't care if you've slept with her or not. I'm just curious.'

He was getting testy. He did care, for Christ's sake, of course he did: Angela was family. In his own reserved and bitter way an Englishman cares about honour as much as a Sicilian or a Turk. It would be a civilised vengeance when it came. It was my job, not my balls, on the line.

Whatever, I owed him an explanation. 'You remember the Russian girl in Shanghai? Anastasia Romanov?'

He looked incredulous. 'It's the same girl?'

I nodded.

A smile: or was it a look of pity? 'You went looking for her.'

'It was a coincidence.'

'Of course.' He finished his pint and went to the bar for another round. It gave him some time to think this through.

When he came back, he said, 'So, what happened to the Russian? Banischevski, wasn't it?'

Well, he had to know the answer to that. Sanderson had filed the story on the wire service. Sebastian stared at me, daring me to lie for her.

'He died,' I said, simply.

'Died.'

'Tragically.'

He didn't press it. Instead, he asked: 'So why is she here with you?'

'She has no money.'

A raised eyebrow was verdict enough on my hopeless behaviour. 'I hope she's worth it,' he said, which in those days was how a well-bred Englishman asked you if the sex was sensational. He sipped his beer, watching me over the rim of the glass, and then asked me the other obvious question: 'How did you get her into England?'

'I managed to organise some papers for her.'

'Is that a fact? Must have been expensive.'

He studied me over the rim of his glass. 'Pity you left Berlin in such a hurry. The stories you filed were pretty damned good. Even the one on that Austrian, what was his name, Hitler? I dug it out again after the trouble in Munich.'

'I'm not going back.'

'Because of a girl?' He sounded incredulous.

I didn't answer him.

'I don't know if I have any work for you here.'

'Seb, I'm a good journalist, anything you can do –'

'You humiliate my sister and then you come crawling to me for another job. If you don't go back to Berlin, who's going to hire you again?'

'I'm good at what I do.'

'Are we talking about women or writing for newspapers?'

I suppose I deserved that.

'If you're short of money, have you considered returning to the fold and living in the manner to which we would all like to become accustomed?'

'You mean my father?'

'It seems the obvious thing.'

'I'd rather go begging in the street.'

'That could happen.' He finished his beer and put his coat

on. I thought that might be the final verdict but then he relented. Perhaps I appeared sufficiently penitent. 'I'll see what I can do,' he said.

'Thanks, Seb.'

'This girl, this is the one you thought was . . .?'

I nodded.

'You don't still think so?'

I shrugged my shoulders.

'You've got to be off your rocker, old chap. They're all dead. The Bolsheviks shot them all. Is that what you're angling for here? Is that what she is to you? Another story? Or is this for the money and the glory?'

'None of those things.'

'What are you going to do with her? No-one here cares about the Romanovs.'

'It's not about the Romanovs.'

He sighed. 'What am I going to tell Angela?'

'Nothing. I'll tell her myself.'

'Be gentle, old chum. Poor girl was in love with you.'

And that was the problem. I didn't want to love anyone who wanted to love me back. It was as simple as that.

I took the underground railway to Highgate station and hired a taxi cab to take me out to the house. Doctor Bernard St John Beaumont lived in Highgate, in a gloomy Gothic mansion with a crenellated tower and green stained-glass windows. It was surrounded by a high wall that deterred both burglars and the sun.

And so quiet, that was the thing you noticed first. In Kensington there was always noise from the traffic and the barrow boys, but out here you could hear the wind rustling the bare branches of the oaks and the elm trees.

Angela still lived with her father. It was an idyllic existence for the idle, and Angela was happy in it. She was shockingly spoiled, content to live off her allowance, go to the clubs in Mayfair and Soho at night, sleep by day. She left chocolate wrappers around the house for the servants to pick up. She would have made a perfect princess.

I rang the bell, heard the scratchy sound of a gramophone from inside the house. The Black Bottom. Angela was risen and it was not yet eleven o'clock.

A servant led me to the sitting room. It was dark and forbidding and pretentious like the rest of the house, gilt-framed oil paintings on the walls, red-coated British soldiers with abundant facial hair massacring Zulus and Sikhs, Prussians and French. The room was dominated by a round mahogany table piled with leather bound books. Angela reclined languidly on a chaise longue, F. Scott Fitzgerald's *This Side of Paradise* lying open beside her, a copy of *Ulysses* discarded carelessly on the floor, as if she had been reading it. There was lively cross-Channel smuggling of James Joyce and DH Lawrence in those days. Pornography for the well-heeled and well-read.

Angela uncrossed her legs and called for the maid to bring a pot of tea. There was a coal fire burning in the grate. I warmed my hands on it.

'I owe you an explanation,' I said.

But I'd left it too late. This was a different Angela from the one I had surprised in my kitchen; this one was scornful, poised and bitter. 'You don't owe me anything,' she said.

'Angie, you were the last person I expected . . .'

'That was obvious.'

'I didn't sleep with her. I let her stay with me, that's all. She had nowhere else to go.'

'You want me to believe she only gets half-board and lodging?' She put a cigarette in an ivory holder and lit it. 'Not like you. I've always found you very hospitable. Very hospitable indeed. Who is this Anastasia Romanov, darling?'

'She's a Russian refugee.'

'Bringing home waifs now. I suppose it requires less technique if your victim is grateful.'

'That's not it at all.'

'Well, tell me how it really is. I can't wait to hear it.' And she crossed her arms and glared at me.

'I didn't mean to hurt you,' I said. How lame that sounded.

'No, I'm sure it wasn't what you intended. You wanted to make love to another woman and get away with it. I can understand that.'

'That's not how it was.'

'When did you meet her?'

'A few years ago, when I was in Shanghai.'

'How exotic. You two go back a long way then. Must have stained a lot of sheets in that time.'

Angela had the propensity to be stunningly crude. Vulgarity and a plummy Home Counties accent are a formidable combination.

'She looks like a public schoolboy. Changing your tastes?'

I didn't say anything to that. I couldn't explain to her how I'd smuggled her out of Berlin. But Angela had an uncanny knack for locating the rawest nerve.

'All the mystery. Did she murder someone?'

Something on my face must have given me away. Whatever expression she saw, it impressed her. For a moment she seemed deflated.

'Well, I can't compete with that,' she said.

'No-one's asking you to.'

The maid returned with a pot of tea. Silver service. The girl started to pour but Angela shooed her out of the room and did it herself. Manual labour, now; Angela's brave attempt to break down the class barriers.

'So, how long is she staying?' she asked, passing me a cup of dark brown Ceylon tea.

'I don't know.'

She picked up her teacup but her hand was shaking and she put it down again so it couldn't betray her. 'Sebastian is so angry with you.'

Was that the real reason I had come here? Did I want to square things with Angela because I was genuinely sorry I had hurt her feelings, or was I just worried about getting another job?

'You love her, don't you, Michael?'

'I don't know what I feel.'

'It's all over your face. It's so obvious.'

'I didn't sleep with her,' I said and I felt genuinely outraged because it was the truth. It was the only thing that really irked Angela at that moment, not that I had betrayed her in other, more elemental ways.

'So where does that leave me?' she said. 'You've ruined me for marriage.'

'Oh, come on.'

'What I mean is, I loved you,' she said with unexpected and exquisite gentleness. 'Where am I going to find another man who'll match up?'

It was humbling, hearing her say something like that. If only it were true. 'I didn't know you felt this way,' I mumbled.

'Would it have made any difference?'

'I do care for you, Angie.'

She closed her eyes. 'But that's not the same thing, is it?'

'I guess not.'

'Oh Michael, you are such a darling man. She's going to break your heart, you know. And I shall be there on the sidelines cheering.'

I nodded. I knew she was right about that.

'Seb told me all about her. Why on earth did you fall in love with someone like that? What does an aristocrat want with someone like you?'

'Thanks.'

'You're really set on her, aren't you, you poor thing.'

'Don't feel sorry for me.'

'Oh, don't worry, I won't.'

It was true, of course, that I was about to have my heart broken. She was a woman and women are always right about these things.

After Berlin, where the price of one loaf of bread had risen to two billion marks, London seemed like a paradise. Yet England was also a country in deep crisis. Its younger generation was on a collision course with the Victorian past, and the nation's economy had been shattered by the cost of the Great War. More than five years on, men in khaki uniforms still begged in the street, their war medals pinned to their chests, their caps on the pavement and one sleeve or trouser leg pinned up, holding a chalked sign: 'Wounded in the Great War, wife and five children to support.'

Among the young a new phenomenon had taken hold; a generation of women had appeared who had thrown their parents' values aside and were intent on just having a good time. You found them among the daughters of the upper classes, and there was a name for them, 'flappers'; they smoked hard, drank hard – 'got blotto' – and danced till the small hours with effete young men in clubs like the Silver Slipper and Rector's. You saw them squealing, paisley cashmere scarves flying in the breeze, in the dicky seats of Renault sports cars, or in the sidecars – 'flapper brackets' – of Triumph and Harley-Davidson motorcycles.

The changing fashions reflected their attitudes. Modern girls cut their hair short, in bobs, shingles or Marcel waves. I had seen a cartoon in *Punch* magazine: 'Grow your hair, man, you look like a girl!' Cloche hats were almost a uniform item, and girls raided their brother's wardrobes for ties, scarves, even pyjamas. The invention of rayon had put flesh-coloured stockings within the reach of every working girl.

Their boyfriends wore Oxford bags, sack-like trousers that trailed around in the mud, and long, loose woollen jumpers. They modelled themselves on matinee idols, slicked their hair back, parted it in the middle, and tried to grow pencil-thin moustaches like Ronald Coleman. Everyone smoked, it was considered a social grace, an accessory to good conversation. But it was bad form to offer cigarettes from the packet; you decanted them, like sherry, into a silver cigarette case, Turkish on one side and Virginia on the other.

All the talk was about the Stock Exchange, money, and the latest cocktails. The long established music halls were swept aside by clubs that played the new Dixieland jazz and picture houses showing Charlie Chaplin and Buster Keaton and Rudolf Valentino moving pictures. The latest crazes were chewing gum, saxophones and gramophone records.

I was twenty-six and I was starting to feel old around these people.

But among Londoners in those days an American was considered highly fashionable and I never lacked for social invitations. Everyone who met me wanted to know what the latest craze in New York was, and they seemed disappointed when I said I hadn't been back there for almost four years.

But not everyone was finding life such a thrash. Unemployment had risen to two and a half million, and shoeless children roamed the East End streets where bronchitis, rickets and polio exacted a heavy toll among the young. For at least half of the country, the roaring twenties never roared.

Britain, with its ingrained class system and desperate poverty, mirrored the Russia of 1917. It was a nation ripe for revolution, and the ruling classes knew it. The well-off murmured fearfully about the Bolsheviks, and in the clubs and the salons and the tearooms everyone agreed it was the communists who were behind the latest wave of strikes. Social justice became somehow inextricably linked with anarchy, and the Reds were blamed for all the country's evils.

Yet Russia remained strangely fashionable. Its faded glories and radical politics exuded a certain charm, for the middle class, at least. I sometimes wondered what Anastasia would have made of that. But she could not remember, so what was the point of asking?

In Hyde Park, horses cantered along the riding paths, the women riding side-saddle and wearing bowler hats with veils, the men in tweed hacking jackets and cavalry jodhpurs. The oak trees were grey, skeletal, and there were patches of snow and ice on the grass. But it was a clear day, even though there was no warmth in the yellow sun. From our seats on the top deck of the bus we could see across the park to Kensington Palace.

I pointed out the sights to Anastasia, enjoyed playing the role of guide. We pulled the weather canvas over our knees against the cold, and I slipped her hand into mine. Considering our history, it was a hopelessly romantic gesture. I had known her body as intimately as any man could, and yet when I felt the answering pressure of her fingers, it affected me as deeply as if she had taken my face in her hands and kissed me passionately on the lips. I construed it as her first gesture of the heart towards me.

So there I was, feeling like a boy again. I had long ago shed the suffocating skins of my innocence but at that moment, after all the dives and bars and dance halls of Berlin and Shanghai, it seemed like the most erotic thing I had ever experienced.

Later that day we fed the ducks in St James's Park, for Christ's sake. I smiled at other couples, baker boys out on this cold, bright morning courting chambermaids. We were of the same brotherhood. Afterwards I took her to Lyon's Corner House. Just me and the Grand Duchess of Russia, I remember thinking. Taking tea together.

The gas lamps were on in the street by the time we returned to my Kensington flat. It was bitterly cold. You didn't openly display affection in public in those days but there was no-one to see us so I put my arm around her.

As we went up the stairs, the door to the downstairs flat flew open. My neighbour's name was Mrs Stanton, and we'd only spoken a few words to each other in the eighteen months I'd lived there, good morning and good evening, the way the English do.

But on this afternoon she looked up at us on the landing, gave Anastasia a poisonous look, hissed 'trollop!' and shut the door again.

As quickly as that, the spell was broken.

What would a good Englishman have done? Made a cup of tea, I suppose. Instead, when we were back inside my flat I went to the window and lit a cigarette. A gloomy habit with me, I smoked whenever I was nervous or frustrated. Anastasia busied herself with lighting the fire in the grate.

'I don't know why it should bother me,' she said. 'But she's right, isn't she? That's all I am. Ever since Shanghai, a man's kept me.'

'It still doesn't seem quite fair.'

'I must be the most expensive tart you never had.'

'Don't call yourself that.'

She stood up and walked over to me. She still had her coat on, her fists plunged deep into the pockets. 'You can take me to bed, if you want. I don't mind.'

'Rent?' I said. That was deliberately cruel. I said it because I wanted her to mind when I took her to bed. I wanted her to mind very much.

'If you want to look at it that way.'

'Will I still have to check my wallet in the morning?'

For a moment there were bright tears in her eyes, but then she recovered. 'Well, knowing the sort of girls you bring home with you from your trips, I suppose you should never be careless.'

She shivered. The fire would take many hours to warm the flat. I thought how it would have been, warming each other with our bodies. But that wasn't going to happen, Mrs Stanton had made sure of that. She would have been hugely satisfied if she'd known. Two more souls saved from the sin of loving.

'I don't know what you want,' she said.

She didn't know, and I wasn't going to tell her. That would ruin everything. If she knew, she might fake it.

'You paid to sleep with me once. Now you can have me for nothing, any time you want, and you act like a monk.'

I put my hand up to her cheek but she flinched away.

'You don't like to be touched but you'll let me sleep with you.'

'It's what you want, isn't it?'

'No, princess, it's not what I want.'

And we stared at each other in utter incomprehension. Finally she went into the bedroom. She left the door ajar, but that night I slept on the couch again.

ANASTASIA

Why did I draw away when he tried to touch me? What is so terrifying about a small token of human affection? How can I explain it? Like a beaten dog, I could not trust any hand that reached out to me.

Michael wanted to use me in some way, of course. That was what I hoped, it was something I could understand. But he was a complicated man. All the strangers in Shanghai, rutting and grunting on top of me, had never demanded as much from me as he did.

I felt as if my personality had fractured; wherever I was, I was not. I am Anastasia, I thought, and a princess;

202

I am also Anastasia, taxi club dancer and whore. One moment I would feel so far above Michael, above everyone; I tossed them the crumbs of my personality, a smile here, a word there. But then I would remember that other Anastasia and I was so ashamed, like dirt at his feet.

If I am Anastasia, he does not deserve me. But if I am just some Shanghai White Russian tart, I do not deserve him.

Michael took me to a party in Mayfair, thrown by a friend of Sebastian's who lived in a studio off Grosvenor Square. It was crowded, everyone there were strangers except for Angela and Sebastian. In other words, I knew no-one except the two people in London who had most cause to despise me.

I clung to Michael's hand. Of course he knew everyone and was inexorably carried away by the crowd. I stood in a corner and stared at the young men in their huge trousers, so wide you couldn't even see their shoes, their girlfriends in tight calf-length skirts dancing to the Charleston, all flapping beads and frenetically waving arms.

I had not drunk real champagne since Berlin, and I grabbed a glass from the table and drank it down. I wished I had never agreed to come. I had thought this would be a small party, just a few of Michael's friends, imagined that I would get to know some people, that he would show me off as a princess.

I saw Angela moving through the crowd towards me.

'So, Michael brought his refugee with him,' she said.

She had cause to hate me. I didn't bite back. 'Stateless again, I'm afraid. Have you seen him?'

She pointed. Michael was dancing with some skinny girl, all bare legs and arms.

Someone put another champagne glass in my hand and I drank that straight down as well.

'I should hate you,' Angela said, 'but I suppose it's not your fault.'

So there we were, both of us staring at him. It was not that he was classically good-looking with that boxer's face and cowlick falling over his right eye. Perhaps it was that crooked grin that made him so irresistible. At least, every other woman in the room seemed to think so, for we were not the only ones looking in his direction.

I wondered why I hadn't fallen for him as hard as Angela had. There must be something wrong with me.

'He's hopelessly in love with you, you know,' Angela said.

It was obvious he loved me, it had been obvious for a very long time. So why did hearing her say the words affect me so deeply? Why couldn't I just love him back?

'You're a lucky beast,' Angela said, and then some young man grabbed her by the arm and begged her to dance with him.

Hopelessly in love or not, I had lost Michael for the night. He was settling scores with me, and I didn't blame him. He had finished dancing with one girl and now another was hanging on his arm, begging him to Charleston with her. These girls were so obvious. I had disguised my intentions rather better in the taxi club.

Lucky Michael, so many eager young women to choose from.

Poor Michael. He had chosen me.

'Hello,' someone said. I looked around. A tall, fair-haired young man was leaning over me, holding two glasses of champagne. 'Brought you shampoo,' he said, leering. He was drunk. So was I.

I took the glass.

'Roger Worthington.' He held out his hand. 'Friends call me . . . well, they call me Roger, actually. You're a pretty little thing. Are you here on your own?'

'I'm with Michael Sheridan.'

He squinted across the room; Michael was surrounded by three young women, all laughing a little too hard at his jokes. 'He seems to be rather busy. I say, what's your name?'

'Anna. Anna Romanov.'

'Russian, are you?'

'Yes. How did you guess?'

'Well, obvious isn't it? Romanov's a Russian name. Rather gives it away.'

No facility for irony, this one.

'Michael does rather look like he's abandoned you.' He put the palm of his right hand flat against the wall by my head and leaned in close.

I finished the champagne. Here was a chance to play Michael at his own game. But wasn't kissing a man like Roger Worthington rather a heavy price to pay to even the score? And what had Michael done to deserve my enmity anyway? Such petty vindictiveness was graceless after Berlin.

'Have to find the powder room,' I said and moved away.

The bathroom door was open. There was a young woman crouched by the hand basin sniffing cocaine off the marble vanity. She looked up and grinned. 'What a thrash,' she said and went out.

I stared at my reflection in the mirror, didn't like what I saw. Every day I reinvented myself, every day there was someone different, someone a little more contemptible. I felt cheated. I should be a celebrity, feted wherever I go; I was meant for better than this. When I walk in a room every head should turn to stare.

Or was I deluding myself? Had I invented these feelings of destiny, conjured them from the hopes and promises of others? Was any feeling I had really my own?

I splashed cold water on my face. The room was starting to spin. Too much shampoo. I tried to focus on the skinny woman in the mirror, the stranger with the cropped fair hair and startling blue eyes. Pretty, but no more so than any of those other girls out there.

What makes you special?

I felt sick, needed to get some air. But when I came out of the bathroom, Roger Worthington was waiting for me.

'Feeling all right, are we, old thing?'

'Just need . . . some air.'

'I'll walk you.' He took my arm and led me down the stairs.

A young man was crouched over by the railings, heaving. A girl was standing a little way off, watching him, her face twisted into a grimace. You could hear the sound of the party down here in the street, see the silhouettes of the dancers against the curtained windows of the flat.

Roger manoeuvred me into a doorway. It was a cold night and I sobered up quickly. I started to shiver. His fingers were hurting my arm.

'You really are a pretty little thing,' he said and tried to kiss me.

I pushed him away and staggered. It was suddenly hard to stand up, I felt like I was going to pass out.

'Oh, come on, just a little kiss,' he said.

I started to get frightened.

But then there was Michael, my guardian angel, standing there with that crooked grin, his hand on Roger Worthington's shoulder. 'Mine, I'm afraid, Rog,' he said.

When Roger saw Michael, he grinned sheepishly, shrugging his shoulders like a naughty boy caught out in some little mischief. 'Sorry, old boy.' He ambled off. Roger was harmless, I realised. I had overreacted, again.

'My escort abandoned me,' I said to Michael, realising I had slurred the words.

'How much have you had to drink?'

'Just a couple of glasses.'

'We'd better get you home,' he said. He took off his jacket and wrapped it around my shoulders against the chill. Then he hailed a hansom cab and poured me in.

I don't remember the journey home. I propped myself against his shoulder, the world spinning, and tried not to be sick. I do remember one thing; at some point in the journey I nuzzled his cheek and whispered, 'I love you.' I heard myself say it, and I meant it at the time, but I was drunk, and by tomorrow I would probably forget.

I woke up, fully dressed, on his bed. I looked at the clock; it was five in the morning. I didn't remember getting up the stairs. I lay on the bed sheet, in the dress I'd worn the night before, covered with a blanket. I sat up, looking for him.

The light was on in the living room.

Michael was asleep on the couch, a book open on his chest, the table lamp still on. I knelt on the carpet and watched him. His breathing was shallow and even, and a lock of hair fell across his face, he looked for all the world like a small boy asleep with his homework.

I took the book off his lap and laid it on the floor. On some impulse I leaned forward and kissed him gently on the lips.

His eyes blinked open.

'I've been waiting three years for you to do that,' he said.

He took my face in his hands, touched my forehead with his lips. I could see our reflection in the wall mirror. How many men had there been before Michael? Too many to count. This was the first time I ever wanted a man as he wanted me.

'You didn't try to sleep with me.'

'You were drunk.'

'For an American, you are such a gentleman.'

I slipped off my dress, felt the warmth of the gas fire on my bare back. I didn't remember our first time together and I wondered if Michael did, if he was thinking of it now.

I knelt down to undress him, eased his shirt off his shoulders. I could not remember what his body was like. There had been so many men from the taxi club, and our own brief encounter was so long ago.

Here was a new and delicious experience; a man kissing me on the mouth. I felt an equally unfamiliar spreading of warmth to my belly and my groin. Tonight I will try to be good for him; I know how to please a man, of course. I just never really wanted to before.

And he was so gentle, as if I was a virgin. It moved me that he was so concerned with my own pleasures. He cupped my breasts in his hands, such large hands, and then knelt down in front of me, his tongue tracing the contours of my belly. I knew what he was about to do and no man had ever done that.

I tried to pull away, some unknown puritan instinct rebelling at the thought of it. But he held me tightly and I submitted; I was too tense to enjoy what he did, but it broke a barrier between us. Afterwards I did to him what he had done for me, first taking his nipples sweetly in my mouth, teasing him as he had teased me. When I finally sat astride him, I lowered my face to his and kissed him again. If only I could have held onto that feeling, Michael inside me, his face in my hands, his tongue in my mouth, joined for that instant, in body and heart.

I pretended a little, of course. It didn't seem to matter so much, in a lifetime of pretending everything.

'I love you, princess,' he whispered.

'I love you,' I lied. I wanted to mean it. And if he had believed me, I wonder what he would have done.

A cold February morning, frost on the roofs of Kensington. I was alone in the flat. Michael had lost his job with Reuters, was now a court reporter with the *Daily Telegraph*. It paid poorly, and he hated it, but he said there was no choice.

There was a knock on the door. I opened it, Angela was standing there, looking cool and stylish in her tight cloche hat and sheath skirt. I was in one of Michael's dress shirts, a pair of old slippers on my feet. I felt like Cinderella.

'Oh,' I said and stared at her.

She looked me over, rather coolly. 'Is Michael here?'

'He's at work.'

She raised an eyebrow, as if to say: 'Who would employ him?' Then said: 'May I come in?'

I stood aside.

She wandered through the flat, looking things over, as if she was thinking of buying it. She took a cigarette out of a silver case, put it in a long ivory holder and lit it. She cocked her head to one side and studied me. 'You really landed on your feet, didn't you?'

'I beg your pardon?'

'He says you're Russian.'

'Is that a crime?'

'Where did he really find you?'

I just stared at her.

'Some men like to pick up strays. It makes them feel useful.'

I wasn't going to just stand there and take it this time. Some people use glamour and money like a weapon, they bludgeon you with it, think they have the right. 'You can say what you like about me,' I snapped back, 'but I won't let you say anything bad about Michael. Twice now he has saved my life. He's one of the kindest, most courageous men I've ever known.'

A good speech, no anger, no histrionics. I was proud of myself, for once.

I don't think Angela was expecting me to defend him. She seemed lost for words. Finally she said: 'What do you mean, he saved your life?'

I wasn't about to tell her about Andrei so I said: 'In Shanghai, I had nowhere to go, I was starving. I threw myself off a bridge. He jumped in and saved me, afterwards he let me stay with him and he looked after me.'

'Why?'

'I don't know.'

'What did he get in return for his kindness?'

'Not much,' I said and looked at her, hard. 'You're right about me. You're wrong about him.'

She thought about this. I don't know what it was, perhaps my candour disarmed her. She looked me up and down. 'Haven't you got anything else to wear?'

I shook my head. I had left all my clothes in Berlin. Michael said that if our luggage was searched, dresses and women's underwear might look suspicious if I was travelling on a man's passport. 'I only have what I wore to the party.'

'We'd better see what we can do,' she said.

I had heard so much of England, seen so much of the British in Shanghai, expected that they all lived in marble palaces with their own bevy of servants. It shocked me to see ordinary Englishmen in working clothes, instead of Panama hats and white linen suits. The granite and marble domes and Regency arcades were stirring, but what impressed itself on me most was that there was so much misery, even here.

We took the underground railway to Charing Cross. I stopped outside the station to stare at an organ grinder with a monkey that rushed to take coins from passers-by. I gave the monkey a penny from my purse, to Angela's irritation. 'You shouldn't encourage these people,' she said.

We went up St Martin's Lane, past the buskers and the sandwich-board men. A policeman with an enormous handlebar moustache rode past us on a bicycle. 'Stop gawping, they'll think you're up from the country,' Angela snapped as I stopped to stare at two toffs – which is what Angela called them – hurrying past in top hats and tails in the direction of Shaftesbury Lane.

Angela had dressed me in one of her own outfits, a tight-fitting suit with a hem up to the knee, a cloche hat to hide my boy's haircut, severe even for a modern twenties woman. She even lent me her make-up. A few young men turned their heads to stare. I thought we must look like two proper flappers, as Angela called them, and stopped to admire my reflection in Lyon's coffee house window.

Angela said she would treat me to an afternoon tea.

We were shown to a seat by the window. It was crowded inside, and there I was, the Grand Duchess, staring like some potato picker at the waitresses in their black dresses and white aprons rushing to serve cream cakes and pots of tea to the customers. Berlin already seemed like another lifetime.

I let Angela talk, prattle on about fashion, dance clubs, parties. My new and unexpected friend had decided to take me under her wing and now she gave me a potted introduction to London society. It was a benediction of sorts. I had been forgiven; next I was to be redeemed.

Or was it just a way to distract me, ingratiate herself, so I would confide in her, reveal weaknesses she could exploit to get Michael back? Trust, you see, did not come easily to me. I noticed how tenaciously she always steered the conversation back to Michael, Michael, Michael.

'You simply have to go to the Brissenden party next week,' she said.

'The Brissendens?' I said, playing my role of wide-eyed novice.

'Hasn't Michael mentioned it to you?'

'Perhaps he hasn't been invited.'

She stared at me in confusion, as if I had suddenly reverted to speaking in Russian. 'When you're Michael Sheridan you don't have to be invited. He's a friend of Sebastian's and devastatingly handsome. It's just expected that he'll show up.'

'Well, I guess we will be going then.'

'Of course, Michael hates these kind of parties. He's probably told you that.'

Well, he hadn't.

Angela cocked her head to one side, her cigarette poised in the air like a flaming torch. 'You must love him very much,' she said, and by her expression you would have thought I'd just been told I would have to have my limbs amputated. As if I was a creature to be pitied.

'I don't know if I love him at all,' I said, to shock her. And perhaps it was true. I relied on him, which was not the same thing. He was all I had, after all. I had let him make love to me, once for money, and twice more, almost, out of gratitude. But did I love him? I was incapable of it.

'I adore him,' Angela said, and I heard reproach in her voice.

'I'm not your rival,' I said to her and she gave me this look, as if she knew better. 'I'm not,' I repeated.

'But he loves you.'

How could anyone love me? There must be something wrong with a man who would allow himself to fall in love with a prostitute, I had decided, and who would then risk his life and his career for a murderess. I closed my eyes and saw Andrei lying on the floor of the flat in Grünewald, his brains leaking onto the parquet. The image was indelibly etched in my memory. It seemed unfair that I should remember that, when I had forgotten so much else.

And what did I really feel for Michael? If someone throws you a lifebelt in the freezing ocean, you reach out and grab it, hold on for dear life. You don't first wonder what the lifebelt thinks of you.

'If I had the courage I would clear out, let him be,' I said.

'If you disappeared, he wouldn't come back to me, he'd go looking for you.'

Angela's eyes were full. She reached into her bag for a handkerchief and angrily brushed the tears away. 'I wish I knew your secret. Michael's had so many girls.' She stirred her tea, staring into the milky brown swirls. 'You're not really a Russian princess, are you?' It was not so much a question, as an accusation of fraud.

'No,' I answered, 'of course not. I never said I was.' Another lie, spoken for her benefit.

If I wasn't Anastasia Romanov, who else was there to be?

MICHAEL

I had arrived in London with no plan other than to get Anastasia out of Berlin. She stayed with me one night, then two, then a week, then a month.

Sebastian didn't come through for me, and I can't say I blame him. I'd lost the Reuters job and it looked like I'd lost a friend as well. I got a job at the *Telegraph*, working the crime beat, spending long, dull hours every day in the Old Bailey, reporting the sordid parade through the criminal courts.

At night I accepted love from Anastasia like a beggar accepting coins.

I knew that what fascinated me about her was what was unknown. And I wondered: when I know all there is to know, will I still be in love with her?

There was nothing, as far as I could see, that I could give her that she could not get somewhere else. What did I have to offer? Looks and charm were for hire anywhere. I had turned my back on things that can be fully measured; influence and money and power, possessions that make even the most unprepossessing of men attractive to women. I had spun the reverse of the vanity coin; I could have had all these things, they were my birthright, and I had spurned them for an ordinary life. It was a test on the world and a test on all women; I wanted to see if they would love me anyway.

The game had rebounded badly; in my ordinariness, I didn't see how the woman I loved could possibly love me.

But she owed me, that much was certain. I had gone out of my way to put her in my debt. But I didn't want to be repaid, I wanted to be wanted. The game was spiteful and the rules I had made ensured I could not win.

I had abandoned my quest to discover Anastasia's true identity, the murky world of émigré politics in Berlin had cured me of that. Banischevski had found out, the hard way, that no-one was interested in whether Anastasia was a Grand Duchess or not. People are curious about the truth, but it's politics that makes the world.

For me, Berlin was the end for Grand Duchess Anastasia Romanov. Her past, real and imagined, would remain our secret, or so I told myself. Perhaps my beautiful enigma would settle for happiness, not as the wife of a count or a duke, but lifetime partner to Michael Sheridan, talented but hardly wealthy journalist.

This was surely what I had risked so much for in Berlin. I was like a rogue gambler, dumping money on a horse that never won, thinking one day my luck would change. I'd tried to walk away from the gamble so many times, but I always came back for one more risk, thinking this time I would recoup all I had lost.

One day, I got home and I knew, from the look on her face, that she'd been brooding. She'd had all day to do it. I sat down and crossed my arms and prepared for the onslaught, the ingratitude, the unconcern for the debt she owed me.

She was queenly in her resentment, and it reminded me of all those things I hated about her; the way she never came to greet me when I walked into a room, I must always go to her; the assumption that food would arrive before her, at regular hours of the day, without taking a hand herself in its preparation; the way she left her clothes strewn about the bathroom for me to pick up.

'When are you going to throw me out?' she said.

'Why do you think I'm going to throw you out?'

'Then what do you want from me? Why do you keep me here?'

'I don't keep you here. You're free to go whenever you want.'

'You want me in your debt.'

'God forbid you should show me any gratitude.'

'You see?'

We stared at each other, combatants in a shadow play.

'Do you love me?' she said.

'I suppose I do.'

'You suppose?'

I had never seen her like this. What was this about? 'You haven't given me a moment's encouragement.'

'Is that what you want? Encouragement?'

'I want you.'

'Why?'

I couldn't answer that question; at least, not answer it honestly, without leaving myself utterly vulnerable. I remained silent.

'I don't want you,' she said. 'I don't deserve you. I deserve someone like Andrei, someone who can help me get what I want and treat me the way I deserve to be treated.' She was crying. I stood up intending to comfort her, but she pushed me away. She kept talking, as tears ran down her face. 'I hate you. I don't want anyone decent and kind. I don't deserve it. At least Andrei understood me. You're like a dog, a faithful dog, all I want to do is kick you. You're always chasing after me, showing up like some good angel, I don't want a good angel, I don't want to be saved!'

She stopped for breath, her lower lip trembling, her face twisted with emotion.

I didn't know what to say to her. I had been attacked by women for being many things, never for being dependable.

'I'm sorry,' she murmured, 'you didn't deserve that.'

Still, no words suggested themselves to me.

'You made me cry,' she said, and wiped her face with the back of her hand, smearing mascara across her cheek.

'It's all right,' I said, filling the silence with a meaningless platitude.

'You're better off without me.'

'I always knew that.'

'I warned you. I can't trust myself. You shouldn't either.'

'I'll take my chances,' I said.

She tried to kiss me. Her first reaction was always to offer her body in exchange for affection or security. To a man like me, I'm afraid, bodies were common currency, accepted everywhere. But not with Anastasia. What I wanted was to hear her say she loved me back. I wanted this mysterious and silky creature with the piercing blue eyes all for myself. I wanted her desire, not her gratitude.

She started to unbutton her dress, but I stopped her. I turned her face up to mine, made her look at me.

'Do you feel anything at all for me?' I asked her.

'Of course.'

'What? What are you thinking? Right now?'

She shrugged, helplessly. 'I don't know. What do you want me to say?'

But I couldn't, wouldn't, prompt her. It had to come from her. 'I'm tired of chasing shadows,' she whispered, and then she kissed me again, to stop me asking any more questions. I kissed her back, my lover, my mistress, my beautiful enigmatic liar.

One night I heard her talking in her sleep. I reached out for her, but her side of the bed was empty. I put on a dressing gown and went out into the living room. It was late, not even the rattle of the trolley cars on the Bayswater Road. The only sound was the cackling of a prostitute in a doorway on the street below, propositioning a passer-by.

Anastasia sat on the windowsill, the curtains were thrown open, and her face was lit by the yellow splash of gaslight from the street lamps. She wore only a long white nightdress, looked like a ghost.

'He deserved it,' I heard her say in Russian. 'He did.'

Her voice sounded odd, high-pitched, and there was something jarring in its tones and inflexions, it was like hearing a piece of familiar music played at a different beat, then realising with surprise that you know it. There were long silences each time she spoke, as if she was waiting for some unheard voice to answer.

'I can try,' she said.

I felt I was listening to one part of a telephone conversation, and the sensation was so immediate and so alarming that I felt the hairs rise on the back of my neck. I wondered, not for the first time, if my Anastasia was insane. Had I allowed a madwoman into my life, into my home? I only had her word for what happened to Andrei. I even checked to see if she was holding a weapon. But her hands were empty and very still, folded on her lap like a pair of white gloves.

'What will I learn, Papa?' she said.

Should I interrupt this reverie? Was she really asleep? Her eyes were open, but she seemed unaware of my presence in the room. And so I hesitated. I had heard that waking a sleep-walker could be dangerous, and so I stood and watched, feeling like a voyeur.

'Is that what you are, Papa?' she said. 'Gracious?'

I felt somehow tainted, standing there, listening to such intimate conversation. I should go back to bed and leave her. Or should I wake her, break this spell? Might it shake some slumbering memory from her consciousness, send it tumbling from its hiding place like a secret lover? Or would I only send her further into retreat and sadness?

I went back to bed. The murmuring continued in the other room for a long time. Finally I felt her cold body slip into bed beside me and I rolled over and held her in my arms. I thought she might respond; I wanted her then, as badly as I ever wanted her, needed to own a part of her mystery. But she was asleep, and would not be woken.

It only deepened the mystery of her for me. I was like a fly

216

caught in a sticky web; the more I struggled, the more I became entangled in Anastasia's trap.

One day I gave her a one pound note to go to the shops and fetch groceries. She came home empty-handed, the money gone; or not exactly empty-handed, because she brought with her a stray dog. What had she done with the one pound?

'There was a man sitting by the road. He was holding a sign, he had lost his arm in the war and he had a family to feed and no money. So I gave him our one pound. We can afford it, can't we?'

And yes, I suppose she was right, we could afford it. If we didn't have any supper that night or the next.

The dog was a mongrel, it had fleas and it wasn't house-trained. I told her that she would have to find another home for it the next day. But two days later it was still there and I could no more turn the dog back out onto the street than I could her.

Anastasia was changing. While I struggled with the same dilemmas, she became something else. Like the starving cur she had brought home, she began to thrive. With regular meals, and without the fear of being beaten, they both started to make their own rules, and took over my life.

One day I came home from work and she was not there. At eight o'clock that night, when she finally appeared, she confessed she had been working in a soup kitchen near Hyde Park, ladling out soup and rolls to London's poor. Her sleeves were rolled up like a washerwoman's, and her hair – the curls were slowly growing back – was hidden beneath a knotted scarf.

Two months after our escape from Berlin, she said to me: 'I need a job.'

'A job?'

'I cannot live on your charity for ever.'

I wanted to stall her, keep her in my thrall, as Banischevski had done. 'Impossible. What skills do you have?'

She tossed her head. 'You know what skills I have. You've seen them for yourself.'

'Apart from those.'

'I can dance. I can speak three languages. I can impersonate royalty. And I can play the piano.'

I went to the window, gave myself time to think. A chill fog had settled over the city. The trees in Hyde Park seemed to scuttle in and out of the mist like spies. 'Any ideas?'

'Perhaps a job in a honky-tonk specialising in European clientele,' she added, and I heard the self-reproach in her voice.

She could not possibly get a job. She could not type or file, had no secretarial skills whatsoever, and there were two million people unemployed out there.

Out of the fog emerged a crowd of perhaps three hundred men and women, marching slowly towards Speaker's Corner, surrounded by mounted policemen. 'We-want-work, we-want-work!'

There was a scuffle in the crowd between one of the protesters and a policeman. It looked as if there would be trouble. Her hand reached for mine, gripped it tight. 'What's happening?'

'You're not the only one looking for a job,' I said.

I was shocked by the look on her face. It was only a small demonstration, those poor bastards were just trying to make a point. But Anastasia looked as if she was watching a wall of molten lava heading in her direction. She started shaking.

'What's the matter?' I said.

She didn't stop trembling until the demonstration disappeared into the park. Our discussion about work was dropped and by the next day I had forgotten all about it.

But while I was at work Anastasia went out looking for a job, giving her name as Anna Sheridan. She must have confounded her would-be employers, for though she spoke impeccable English, her accent was still a hybrid of German and Russian.

As I warned her, she found there were no jobs for a girl without typing or secretarial skills. She couldn't even get work as a seamstress; and as she had no facility with money, shopwork was ruled out. I could have tried to keep her at heel but I knew it was futile. So finally I decided to help her and called in a marker; a friend of my father's ran a law office in Temple Bar and he needed a receptionist, was even willing to train her.

Anastasia had her first job.

And so, chameleon that she was, she blossomed into her next incarnation as a young middle-class Englishwoman with a secretarial job in the city; I was the only one who knew she was Anastasia Romanov, stateless person and royal pretender, wanted for questioning in Germany for the murder of a displaced Russian count, her only identification a forged passport in the name of Gerd Netzer. She was my secret, my house guest and my obsession.

I knew Sebastian had something for me. He asked to see me in his office, which was always a good sign. This time he didn't mention Angela, or Anastasia. Another good omen. His secretary brought me a cup of coffee and then it was straight down to business.

'How are things at the *Telegraph*?' he said.

'I'm going out of my mind. They could train a chimpanzee to do my job.'

'I suppose they felt that an American was a good compromise then,' he said, with a bland smile. I let that one go. 'You were meant for better things, Michael. You'd get them, too, if you could keep your mind on the job.'

'I'd do it all again, Seb. I don't regret it.'

'Perhaps you haven't spent long enough in the Old Bailey. I should leave you in purgatory a while longer.'

Again, I didn't rise to the bait. I told myself he hadn't invited me to his office just to torment me.

'How's your Russian?' he said, and I felt my pulse quicken.

'Rusty, but it's still there. I got by in Shanghai and I picked it up again in Berlin.'

'I've got a proposition for you. If you can tear yourself away from London.'

'An assignment or an actual job?'

'An assignment, freelance commission if you like. It could lead to a salaried job, if it comes off. There's a new editor-in-chief here now, needs to be convinced about you. This is your chance to redeem yourself.'

'Have I ever let you down?' I said, and we both smiled at that.

'I want you to go to Russia.'

I didn't say anything.

'It's a long journey, and it won't be very comfortable. Means being away from London for a month, perhaps longer. How are things at home, by the way?'

He meant Anastasia. 'I'm happier than I've been in my whole life,' I lied.

'Congratulations.' His tone implied no felicity. He still hadn't forgiven me; which was reason to be suspicious. As it turned out it was the mark of the man that he didn't let Anastasia stand in the way of our friendship. I misjudged him.

'So is there going to be a Mrs Sheridan?'

'I can't afford to get married.'

'Then you can't afford to say no to an opportunity like this. After all, it's to do with your young lady,' he said.

I knew what was coming.

'We have a correspondent in Moscow these days, man by the name of Roper. He filed a report last week, rumour he's heard floating around Bolshevik circles. Unsubstantiated, of course. There's a chap in Sverdlovsk been saying he was the one who shot the Czar. I don't think anyone's quite sure what to do about him. The Komintern haven't decided on their position on this yet.'

I knew the story better than anyone. In the months following the Czar's death the Bolsheviks met all demands for information about the royal family with obdurate silence. When the Whites retook Ekaterinburg – albeit briefly – in 1918, they sent a team to investigate the murder of the Romanovs, headed by a former policeman called Sokolov. The investigation was thorough, but they were unable to find anyone who would admit to being inside the house the night the executions took place. One man, called Voronin, had talked about it to his family but he couldn't tell Sokolov's men much because royalist sympathisers had already crucified him. They found his body in the woods about a mile out of town.

In his report, Sokolov concluded that the Czar and his family had been shot in the Ipatiev house and their bodies burned and buried in the woods. He even unearthed a finger that he claimed belonged to the Czarina, and a belt buckle that belonged to the Czar, but his conclusions were based on hearsay and primitive forensic evidence. He had not found any of the bodies and therefore no-one could know exactly how the Czar and his family had died.

When the Bolsheviks reopened the borders to the West, a few Westerners, journalists and diplomats had travelled to Sverdlovsk, as the Bolsheviks now called Ekaterinburg, but like Sokolov they had not found anyone willing to talk about what happened that night.

Until now, apparently.

'Why doesn't Roper go down there himself?' I asked.

'We don't pay him to run around the largest country in the world chasing rumours. Takes three days on the train from Petrograd just to get to this place. There may not even be a story in it.'

'But you want me to go?'

'You're perfect for the job. You're available, you speak the language, you're experienced, and above all, you have a personal interest in getting this story told. More than anyone I know.'

'Sverdlovsk,' I said.

'It was called Ekaterinburg before the Soviets took over, but I suppose you already know that. How're your finances, by the way?'

I didn't like where this was leading. 'I have a little put aside.'

'What about Daddy?'

He was needling me now. The 'daddy' jibe got under my skin, as he intended. 'I don't take his money.'

'Any more.'

'Right. Any more.'

A slight twist on the truth. When I didn't come home after a year in Shanghai, the cheques stopped arriving. I suppose he thought it would change my mind about rebellion, but it only made me more determined to survive without Sheridan money.

'Reuters isn't prepared to send you to the other side of the world on a wild goose chase. But, if, for the sake of argument, a freelance reporter came back with a verifiable story, perhaps even photographs, we'd reimburse all his expenses and pay handsomely for the story. We would probably think about employing him again, too.'

'That's the deal, is it?'

'That's the deal, as you so elegantly put it.'

It was a perfect arrangement for him; it would cost nothing out of his budget, and he knew I couldn't refuse the bait. 'What makes you think the Bolsheviks will let this fellow talk to me?'

He sipped his tea. He even had a biscuit to nibble on. These Englishman are so damned genteel. 'He's already talking, if what Roper tells us is right. We just need someone to go there and verify his story.'

I still hesitated. Perhaps I didn't want to know the truth after so long. The worst thing about a verifiable truth is its finality, its lack of imagination. The truth can be so inflexible.

Sebastian leaned forward. 'It's a golden opportunity from where I sit. There's not a newspaperman in the world who's going to chase this story harder than Michael Sheridan. Do this well and you'll have a by-line in newspapers all over the world.'

I shook my head. 'You know I can't afford this.'

He looked unimpressed and unconvinced. He sipped his tea, like the blue-blood Albion bastard that he was. 'Lay the ghosts to rest once and for all, Michael.'

It would take all the savings that I had. I would risk losing my flat and my job. It was a huge gamble, but it might relaunch my career. And that wasn't all; the dancing lure on this particular stretch of bright water was Anastasia. I might finally uncover the truth about a mystery that had obsessed me for the last three years.

I thought it over and shook my head. 'Not a hope in hell,' I said.

He shrugged. 'Well, if you change your mind, you know where to come.' And he smiled.

The next day I did change my mind, of course. He knew I would. That was why he asked me.

Anastasia was sitting at the old piano I had installed in my flat for her particular use. She had got home from work at six o'clock, an hour before me, and had sat straight down to play.

It was not her way to think of preparing dinner for us. Always the Grand Duchess.

Her hair had grown back, and she had had it styled into a modern shingle. Although we had little money she still found enough to put aside for the latest fashions.

She had her back to the door and did not hear me come in. She was playing a Bach étude. I should have been irritated. Instead I stood in the doorway, listening, drinking in this private vision of my dream girl, my mystery. How would she survive while I was gone? She had not a practical bone in her body and I had no money for servants.

She stopped playing suddenly and turned around. She gave a little gasp. 'I didn't hear you,' she said.

'I wanted to watch you play.' I sat down in the chair by the window and wondered how to tell her. 'I went to see Seb Beaumont today,' I said.

'Did he offer you a job?' she asked me, and her face brightened.

'In a way. Not in London. It would mean going away for a while.'

There was a long silence while she considered the ramifications of this. 'Where?'

'Russia. Sverdlovsk.'

Down in the street the lamp lighter pedalled slowly between the lamp standards, a long pole over his right shoulder. He stopped, lifted the pole to turn the key in the base of the lantern outside the flat, and ignited the gas. The lamp glowed to life, a tiny halo forming in the mist. He put the pole back over his shoulder and pedalled on to the next one.

'You're going looking for me,' Anastasia said, putting it more succinctly than I could ever have done.

'I suppose so.'

'How long will you be gone?'

'I don't know. A month, perhaps.'

She knelt down at the floor by my feet, put her head on my lap. I tried to talk more to her about it, but she wouldn't be drawn about her feelings. That night, though, she made love to me with an urgency I had not known in her before.

Afterwards, as I lay in bed, Anastasia's head on my chest, I stared at the shadows on the ceiling and wondered if either of us really wanted an answer from Sverdlovsk. There is always disappointment inherent in the solving of any mystery, for the unknown has greater cachet than the truth. When I returned from Sverdlovsk would I still be as fascinated by a refugee and taxi girl, a daughter of minor nobility fallen on hard times? Perhaps my Anastasia was wondering that very same thing.

ANASTASIA

Coming out of a cold, lost season that had started long ago in Berlin. I had grown tired of the weary winter landscape. I longed now for spring and sun and hope.

Michael came home at night weary of his job and weary, I suspected, of me. Where was Anastasia now, when he needed her? He had traded her for a law secretary, passed in the romance of the Shanghai and Berlin bars for this dreary street in Kensington, with its gas lamps and smell of damp, suspended in fog and freezing drizzle.

One night I caught him staring at me from his chair by the fire and I knew what he was thinking: what have I done to us?

And now, here was a chance to lay the ghosts to rest for ever. I suspected that he was afraid of what he would find in Sverdlovsk. He had no choice but to go, I understood that. But if he came back without his Russian princess, what would happen to us?

I watched Michael as he slept, his arms stretched above his head, his chest rising and falling in deep, even breaths. Tomorrow morning he would leave for Russia, the mythical place of my imaginings, the grey dreamworld that had born me, but of which I remembered nothing. He was going where I could not go, like a surgeon investigating my own heart, or womb. It frightened me to think of what he might find.

As did his leaving me. There was no reason for fear. There was money for when he was gone, though not much of it, and there was a roof over my head. But I would be alone, and the prospect of aloneness frightened me. Since that night on the bridge three years ago, there had always been a man to watch over me.

I wondered what I might do with that freedom.

Michael would leave on the morning train for Dover, no promises made or expected. We were still creatures of the moment. I could not talk of yesterday, and Michael never talked of tomorrow. But the future was something I could no longer push from my thoughts. I could not ignore it, as I could not ignore the soreness of my breasts that had nothing to do with our lovemaking. I wondered if I should tell him my suspicions.

But no.

Michael, I had decided, was a man who was meant for taxi club girls. He rescued princesses from the swirling waters of a Chinese river and would move on, eventually. If I gave him this gift of permanency, he would hate me for it, I was sure.

Let him sleep.

Perhaps tomorrow, before he goes, I'll tell him. If he wants this sullied princess, then I will know from the look in his eyes. If he doesn't, I will know that, too, and I will be gone before he returns.

Wait till the morning. Tell him then.

MICHAEL

I stood on the steps of the rail carriage, buffeted by crowds of people, the din of other farewells drowning out my own last words to Anastasia.

The moment was defined by what did not happen. She did not cry; she did not wave; she did not run alongside the departing train as other lovers did. She stood there and did not move.

I cannot tell you what I felt. I knew in that moment that I had lied to myself; I had made myself believe that my devotion to her had touched her somehow.

On that day, at my leaving of her, she remained Anastasia, beyond reach and beyond definition. I knew then, as I knew from that first moment, that I still wanted something I could not have. There was nothing to do but stand on the running board and watch her disappear through the steam, lost among the crowds of a grimy Waterloo.

ANASTASIA

The house was cold when I woke. The postman made his first delivery of the day. I heard the letterbox bang. I got out of bed, the bare boards cold on my feet, and went into the living room to light the fire, put some coins in the meter for the electric light.

I went into the bathroom, filled the basin with warm water, and took off my nightdress to wash with a flannel and a bar of soap. My breasts still felt swollen and sore; I had missed my bleed last month. How strange. All those months in Shanghai, all those men. I hadn't cared what happened to me, or my body, back then. Life could sometimes be kind; it had waited for me to find a man who would help me before allowing consequences.

But I was terrified; not of the birth, but what it would mean. I tried to imagine the years ahead, as the wife of a struggling journalist, and a mother to his children. I was convinced Michael would hate me for doing this to him. He did not need a nest; he needed to fly.

And what did it mean for me? For a time Andrei convinced me that I had a destiny of my own. I wondered, now, how I would live without that bright and shining dream. A dream is real, after all: it has boundaries, can be as tangible as any possession. Already, I was grieving, mourning its loss.

I towelled myself dry and dressed quickly. Michael's photograph was on the mantel above the fire. I traced the contours of his face with a finger.

Come back soon, I whispered. I was frightened. Not for him, but of me.

MICHAEL

I met up with Roper in Moscow. An old Etonian; as soon as he heard my accent he treated me as if I was something his heel had skidded on in the street. I had the impression he was sorry he'd filed the rumour about Sverdlovsk. He was like a man watching his former wife dance with strangers; although he didn't want her for himself, he got nervous and hostile if anyone else showed interest.

I got a briefing from him, if you could call it that, in his grim and cluttered office. I waited for an invitation to dinner, but it didn't come. The next night I was on a train to Petrograd and I never saw Roper again.

My hotel window looked out over the city; the domes and golden spires appeared raw and grey on this April morning. Petrograd, they called it now. A socialist workers' paradise.

It used to be Saint Petersburg, the city built by Peter the Great on the marshes of the Gulf of Finland. During the eighteenth and nineteenth centuries it had the richest upper class in the world, all of them striving to outdo each other in the splendour and ostentation of their palaces. It boasted one of the most lavish public squares in all Europe, the greatest art collection outside the Louvre in its Hermitage Gallery, and summer palaces that rivalled those at Versailles.

If you could forget that all of it was built on the misery of the poor, you might grow nostalgic for what had gone.

I put on my overcoat and went out into the drab morning.

The old Nevsky Prospekt had been one of the most famous shopping thoroughfares in the world. Under the Bolsheviks it was the Prospekt October 25, its half-empty shops selling dingy goods manufactured exclusively by the state. The furs and Fabergé eggs were long gone and the workers on the street would not miss them. There had never been ermines and baubles enough for them.

But the Revolution, it seemed to me, had changed little. The old world had possessed both glamour and misery. All Lenin had done was take away the glamour.

Unshaven workers wearing overalls were hurrying to work, while women in sack-like dresses already queued outside the butcher's shops and the bakeries, clutching their ration cards like hungry children. Not many Soviet heroes about this morning.

I turned up my collar against a mist of rain, kept my frozen hands in my pockets and headed towards Saint Isaac's Cathedral.

As I went up the steps, the granite columns reared above me to a sky the colour of lead. The cathedral had been turned into an anti-religious museum, the gilt icons on the walls replaced by garish cartoons depicting monks in drunken orgies and crazed priests firing machines guns from the belfries of their churches, mowing down women and children in workers' demonstrations. Even the intricate and beautiful mosaics were all but hidden behind crude posters proclaiming the wonders of the new Five Year Plan and others that proclaimed: 'RELIGIOUS ART IS A TOOL OF THE CAPITALISTS'.

I did not stay long.

Everywhere it was the same. The glories of the old regime had not been torn down, merely adapted to other purposes.

The Czar's Winter Palace, where Nicholas had celebrated the tricentennial of Romanov rule just thirteen years before, now housed armies of apparatchiks. Refuse littered the dried-up marble fountains and in the bookstores the only literature available were biographies of Lenin and histories of the Revolution.

I crossed a bridge, stared at the Fortress of Peter and Paul on an island in the Neva. The Czar had imprisoned Bolsheviks inside it. Another museum now, I guessed. I didn't go there.

I passed the palace where Yusupov had murdered Rasputin, now the House of Culture and Rest. Beyond, in the suburbs, the new Petrograd, the people's city, rose in grim concrete around the contemptible glories of the past. Everywhere construction crews were at work; the sound of the Revolution was the rumble and shriek of steamrollers and bulldozers and riveters. Utopia rising.

The next day I went out to Tsarskoe Selo to see for myself where the Czar and his family had spent their days. If I ever came close to Anastasia, it was here. To truly understand someone's life you must see the place where they grew up, and what else was there to Anastasia Romanov but the story of a childhood?

To my relief there were no posters proclaiming the wonders of the new Workers' Party, its tractors and sausages and nails. The palace was as the Romanovs had left it, kept as monument to the decadent lifestyle of the former Czar.

I was guided around the main palace by a suitably disapproving young woman, who pointed to the murals with such revulsion one might have thought the walls were built from human skulls. And perhaps in a way they were, I thought. Magnificent as they now seemed, I wondered how many people had starved to death for want of a few kopecks while the Czars lavished their millions here.

But then Nicholas despised this place as well; it was in a smaller palace that Nicholas and his family had lived, and that was where I went next.

At my request, my guide showed me the billiard room where Nicholas and his generals had consulted their war maps, and the hidden balcony above where the Czarina had eavesdropped on these discussions. She had then shared everything she heard with Grigory Rasputin, and after obtaining his counsel, used her influence with her husband to assist or block the war plans as she – or Rasputin – thought fit.

I soon formed the impression that this was not the home of an Emperor and Empress, but the refuge of two strange and eccentric people, a committed family man with child-like obsessions and an English housewife with unrestrained religious mania. There was the little vegetable garden where the richest man in the world grew his own potatoes; the study where he kept obsessive weather reports in his diary even at the height of a war in which tens of thousands of his soldiers died every day; the room the Czarina had decorated entirely in purple floral chintz ordered from a London mail-order catalogue; her bedroom, perfectly preserved, with hundreds upon hundreds of religious icons filling every space on the walls and the bedside tables.

The Czar's bedroom also gave an insight into the man; his bedroom was cluttered, not with religious icons, but with framed family photographs, hundreds of them; on the tables, walls, and cabinets, sometimes four deep, lined up with military precision, like soldiers on a parade ground.

This was the man the Bolsheviks had labelled a monster. Instead of a beast, I had the impression of a man guilty of neglect, a Czar more interested in his vegetable garden than his country, a father who considered the politics of state a bothersome intrusion on the time he would rather spend with his family.

And I was still looking for Anastasia.

I found her in one of the formal reception rooms, where the children's toys were set out. Arrayed below the crystal chandeliers was a wooden slide Alexei and Anastasia would have played on during rainy afternoons, together with a miniature automobile with rubber tyres and cut-glass lamps in which the Czarevitch would have ridden around the corridors of the palace.

I tried by force of will to imagine myself standing there ten years ago, to picture Anastasia, see the world as she saw it, find the key that might unlock her memory. But such an exercise is a bitter and fruitless effort. You cannot share another's memories. The secrets and sounds and smells and experiences are uniquely locked away, and imagination becomes a poor and hopeless thing.

For three consecutive days I stood in a line at Petrograd station, trying to buy a first- or second-class train ticket to Sverdlovsk. Eventually it was explained to me that all such tickets were taken by Party functionaries. Privilege had not been eliminated from the new Russia. It had just changed carriages.

So I travelled third class for the three-day trip. The journey was a nightmare; my fellow passengers and I packed into hard wooden benches, together with luggage and live-stock. We were crowded in to the point of suffocation, and after three days the smell would have offended a slaughter-man. There was no water, no food and no electric light, no chance to sleep, even to read. I endured it, somehow, but I was unable to emulate the same stoic fatalism of the Russian peasant, to whom hardship is a fact of life, like breathing.

Through the long and sleepless nights, when my muscles ached from cramps and my bones screamed for rest I stared at the frozen darkness beyond the windows and thought of Anastasia, her warm body and scented hair, pretended I was with her, telling her everything would be all right.

But I knew it would not be all right. After Sverdlovsk, everything would change.

ANASTASIA

Felix Rifkin was a big man, fleshy, and well over six feet tall. He was dressed with immaculate precision, in a charcoal Savile Row double-breasted woollen suit, with diamond tie pin, gold fob watch and homburg. There was a diamond signet ring on the little finger of his left hand that caught the light as he moved. The clothes he wore were worth more than the wages I would make in an entire year.

My job was to answer a telephone, make cups of tea, file documents and smile prettily at clients as they walked through the doors of Renfrew Bannister. There were women who had been with the firm for twenty years, doing these same things day after day. I imagined sometimes that I saw dust in the lines on their faces. I wondered if that was to be my destiny, too.

Until Felix Rifkin.

He emerged from the lift holding a leather briefcase in his right hand. He took off his homburg and approached the reception desk where I sat. I waited for him to introduce himself and state his business. Instead, he just stared.

'Good morning and welcome to Renfrew Bannister,' I said, with a well-rehearsed smile, 'how may I help you?'

Felix Rifkin continued to stare.

I had never had anyone look at me that way. 'How may I help you, sir?' I repeated, feeling the beginnings of panic.

'Anastasia,' he said.

He recovered from whatever shock I had given him. He leaned across the desk. He wore an expensive cologne. 'What are you doing here?' he said.

What could I say to him? I think I knew then that he was about to change my life for ever and for a brief moment I tried to hold on to Michael, to the whisper of that other life I could have had. But then it slipped away.

Felix looked confused. 'I'm sorry, I must be mistaken,' he said. And then he added, in Russian: 'Stushi, don't you remember me?'

'No, I'm sorry, I don't,' I answered, in English.

He smiled. 'But you do speak Russian?'

I saw Bannister's secretary staring, watching this exchange over the rim of her spectacles. She stood up and tapped on the door of my employer's office, then stepped inside, perhaps to warn him of the unusual conversation taking place at the front desk.

'You are her,' he breathed and then he was beaming at me and for one moment I thought he might rush around the desk and embrace me. 'Stushi, it's me, Felix!'

I felt dizzy. I had been holding my breath. Not just another Andrei, someone who had seen me from a distance. Here was someone who really remembered me.

Bannister emerged from his office. He looked troubled. 'Felix. Is everything all right?' Everyone was staring at us. Bannister crossed the foyer, a severe look on his face, perhaps concerned that I was making trouble with the clients. 'Is everything all right, Mr Rifkin?'

'I think I know this girl,' Felix said to him.

I just stared at him in bewilderment.

'I knew this girl in Russia,' he repeated and Bannister threw a stern look in my direction, as if he was seeing me for the first time. Perhaps he was. Until then, I was just the girl he had hired as a favour to an old friend.

'We must have lunch, Stushi,' Felix said to me. 'Today.'

'I only have half an hour for lunch,' I answered.

'I'll talk to your boss,' he said looking at Bannister. 'I'm sure he'll make an exception for me.' He gave me a huge smile. And I thought: another knight, to carry me away, free me from the past, and the enchanted imprisonment of the present.

Felix went into Bannister's office. Everyone was still staring at me.

I went to the ladies' room perhaps a dozen times in the next hour. I couldn't concentrate on anything, all I could do was pee. Whenever I answered the telephone I forgot the little speech I had been taught and had parroted a thousand times before. My hands were shaking so much once I dropped the receiver.

I could not take my eyes from Bannister's door.

233

It seemed for ever until Felix Rifkin finally emerged and told me to fetch my hat and coat.

And that was how it was done. I came to work as Anna Sheridan, a ladder in my stocking, six weeks pregnant, living in sin in a flat in Kensington. I left for lunch as Grand Duchess Anastasia Romanov, with a past and a future.

Like it was yesterday.

I sat in the Café Royal in Piccadilly with the high society matrons and the Bright Young Things with their banker and stockbroker husbands and boyfriends, and I was blinking in bewilderment with just a bright smile and a string of fake pearls, drab and underdressed. I might as well be naked, I thought.

Yet an arrogance accompanied my shame, because I was also thinking: If only these people knew who I am.

Felix Rifkin was utterly at home here, telling the maitre d' that it was a celebration and ordering French champagne and lobster. I was a cork carried along on this wave, unable to resist. That was my defence in the confession I was already preparing for Michael.

'I can't believe my eyes,' Felix said. 'I thought you were dead. This is like seeing a ghost.'

'Perhaps you are.'

He leaned in, touched my hand, as if to satisfy himself that I was real. 'There's no mistake. Do you not remember? We played together all the time. You can't have forgotten me!'

I told him the story as I wished it might have been, and in this version there was no taxi club, no Michael, and no Russian aristocrat husband killed with a champagne bottle in our Berlin apartment. I still had no memory, of course, but in this better, happier story I was saved from the streets by a Russian count who loved me and was kind to me and died tragically of pneumonia in the bitter Prussian winter. What an accomplished liar I had become.

'You don't remember anything?' Felix asked me. The

look on his face: pity, awe and the urgent desire to help me. I had seen that expression before.

'Not before Harbin. I was living on the street there. I have vague memories of being on a train, but nothing . . .' I dropped my hands, a well-tried gesture of helplessness and frustration. 'Eventually I escaped to Shanghai.'

'This man in Shanghai, the one you married. What was his name?'

'Ludmilova,' I said, the lie coming easily, too easily. 'Count Andrei Sergeiovitch Ludmilova.'

Felix frowned. 'I don't remember him.' He reached across the table and his hand touched mine. 'But I knew you. I know who you are. You are my Stushi.' And then, a self-effacing smile. 'If I may call you that, Your Highness.'

With those two words he breathed new life into me, made me long for that lost Anastasia again. Was it really true, what he said? I wanted it to be, so much. When the Dowager Empress had told the world I was a fraud, everyone had given up on me. Now, looking into this man's eyes, I saw the truth.

I am her. I am Anastasia.

'How did we meet?'

'My father was physician to the Czarina. Sometimes he brought me with him to the palace at Tsarskoe Selo. We were the same age, and we became best friends. We used to play on the slide in the great hall; on rainy days, some-times Alexei would join in but mostly we played alone because Derevenko was afraid the Czarevitch would injure himself. We played hide and seek in the halls.'

He waited for me to say something, it must have been hard for him to accept that all these beautiful and treas-ured memories were vanished for me.

The champagne arrived. He toasted his good fortune at discovering me again. I sipped from my own glass. Shampoo. It made me think of Michael, the first night I had got drunk at that party in Mayfair.

Felix Rifkin, my old and unknown friend, stared at me, his gaze hypnotic, and we both fell silent. I heard Anastasia laugh as she played in vast and empty corri-dors. In my mind I chased her down the echoing marble halls, but she was gone. Impossible to accept, even now, that the ghost was me.

The entrées arrived, turtle soup, but I had no appetite. Felix was not hungry either, nibbled at a bread roll, let his consommé grow cold. He wanted to know every detail of my life to that moment. I took care not to drink too much champagne, for I had to carefully edit everything I told him. I repeated my story, elaborated just a little, until it sounded plausible even to me. Once again, Michael was omitted from my reconstruction, the most influential figure in my history neatly excised, as if I had told the story of the Revolution and made no mention of Lenin.

'But what about your family?' he protested. 'What about the Empress? What about your uncle, the Duke of Hesse, and your aunts in Denmark. Surely they have not abandoned you?'

'The Empress said I was a fraud. What could I do? I had no choice but to believe her.'

'But you are her!' he said so loudly that several of the other diners turned their heads to stare.

'Olga came herself to Berlin and she –'

'Olga did not recognise you, her own niece?'

'She had not seen me for many years, and could not be sure, or so she said. Is such a thing possible?'

'I suppose so,' he said, but did not sound convinced. 'The Czarina was almost a hermit. There were so few of us allowed at Tsarskoe Selo in those last few years, and she and the Dowager Empress hated each other.' He nodded to the waiter, had him take the plates away, the soup untouched. 'This is an outrage. My poor Stushi. What have they put you through?'

His anger was genuine, and it moved me.

'Have you heard of this girl, Anna Andersen?' he asked me. 'She says she is you.'

'Many women have claimed to be Anastasia.'

'I have seen photographs of this Andersen woman. She is nothing like you. How can anyone believe her?'

He shook his head in wonderment, as well he might. 'What do you do in New York?' I asked him.

'I have a stockbroking firm on Wall Street,' he said and shrugged his shoulders, as if having your own stock-broking firm at twenty-four years old was nothing. 'My family was among the fortunate ones. My father got our money out of Russia before the Bolsheviks took over. We all went to New York, he started a messenger service on Wall Street. Did rather well at it. Last year, when he died, I expanded our interests, started trading in stocks and securities. It's where all the money is, these days.'

'Are you very rich then?'

He gave me a smile that appeared shy and boastful at once. 'I do rather well.'

'You live in New York?'

'Of course.'

'What brings you here to London?'

'My mother's sister left Russia at the same time as we did, only she came to England. She died a month ago, and my mother and I came across to settle her affairs. We're only here for a short time.' He squeezed my hand. 'It's a miracle that I found you. It was meant to be.'

'Felix,' I said, calling him by name for the first time, 'could there be some mistake? Perhaps I just look like the person you remember.'

He shook his head. 'There's no mistake,' he said and that was an end to it.

I allowed myself to be persuaded and yes, to be seduced. Over high tea in London. So genteel. So befitting a lady of high birth. The world had wronged me. Felix Rifkin had come into my life to unlock the past for me. He would set all the wrongs to rights, no matter what Michael found at Ekaterinburg.

MICHAEL

There was nothing about Sverdlovsk to intimate that anything unusual had ever happened there. It was squalid and dismal like countless other towns from Tomsk to Vladivostock.

Horses grazed by the river, in a grey haze that drifted from the smelters and factories and smokestacks. Beyond the town dark pine forests melted into an endless and drab horizon.

I trudged through the mud with my suitcases. I thought about how the Czar and his family had arrived here six years before and wondered if they were as relieved to see the end of their journey as I was. There were no taxis outside the station so I walked to my government hotel. I wanted to get to work straightaway. Before I met the Czar's executioner, I wanted first to see the place where he had died.

The house was a public museum now, open to curious Russians from nine o'clock in the morning till four o'clock in the afternoon.

I looked around the square. Had my Anastasia been imprisoned here once? All I had to broach the missing years was my imagination, and a journalist can have too much of that. The Ipatiev house looked to me like just another old and shabby mansion in an old, shabby town. Hard to credit that such a celebrated and monstrous act had happened here.

I stood in the square for a long time silently conducting a conversation with Anna: Were you really here? Was this where it happened? Is everything as it was then? I wanted to commit everything I saw to memory, for there might be some detail, however insignificant it might seem, that might illuminate the past for her.

Or perhaps it was, as Sebastian had put it, a wild goose chase.

A sign in Cyrillic identified the house as the Ipatiev Prison Museum. Inside, it smelled of damp and mould, and was cold as a tomb. I was given a Bolshevik guide, a young and intense woman who referred to herself as Comrade Ivanov – she wouldn't tell me her first name – and who had the earnest, humourless demeanour of the true believer. The house had been filled with relics from the Revolution, posed photographs and portraits of local Bolshevik leaders, factory workers risen far above their imaginings and ill-suited to their long moustaches and fur hats and medals. They looked every bit as self-important as the generals and dukes they had come to dispossess. The irony was lost on my guide.

There were yet more of the posters I had seen in the churches and converted palaces of Petrograd; heroic workers waving red flags; women with corn-coloured hair and vibrant bodies working in the wheat fields with scythes; well-fed and well-shaved young men with bulging muscles, waving from their tractors and fields. It was a fantasy at odds with the reality I had seen from the train, that other world of grey-faced babushkas and undernourished men with dead eyes and dull clothes.

'Under the new Bolshevik government,' my guide told me, 'aeroplane production has increased by seventy eight per cent, tractor production . . .'

She expected me to write down all this propaganda, so that I could reproduce it faithfully for my newspaper in the capitalist West. She despised me and wanted my approbation in equal measure.

'Which rooms belonged to the Czar and Czarina?' I said.

She was unhappy that I had interrupted her monologue. 'Those ones,' she snapped, pointing to the two nearest rooms. I realised she knew nothing and cared less about the only thing that interested me at all about this house or this squalid little town.

I went along with it. 'Was that where they slept or was that where they lived?'

She gave me a look of pure loathing. 'The Czar is dead. The Czar was a murderer. He kept millions in poverty and repression. Why does the world care about the Czar?'

And she returned to her litany of heroic Soviet achievement.

I ignored her and carried on looking around. I tried to imagine Nicholas walking down these stairs under the brute gaze of his militia guard; the Czarina's wheelchair squeaking as Botkin pushed her along the corridor; even tried to picture Anastasia with her sisters in the garden below, but it was now overgrown with weeds and littered with all manner of junk, rusting truck parts and empty wooden packing crates, even an ancient bed frame.

I endured my guide's monologue, an hour's dissertation on the glories of communism. It was not that I was sympathetic towards the Romanovs, I was an American, for Christ's sake,

I didn't believe in autocracies. But I knew bullshit when I heard it.

By the end of the tour I had found only two sections of the entire building that were devoted to the Romanovs. On one of the upstairs walls a Bolshevik artist had painted a life-size mural depicting the arrival of the Czar and the Czarina at Sverdlovsk, the royal couple suitably cowed in the presence of the three disapproving Bolshevik commissars waiting to take them into custody on behalf of the people.

On the opposite wall I found several glass cases containing photographs, letters and documents relating to the Romanovs' imprisonment. There were also pages from the diaries kept by the Czar.

Ivanov frowned when I showed interest in these exhibits and did not try to hide her impatience. To spite her, I lingered longer than I would have done. Finally I followed her down a flight of narrow steps, out into the garden, then back into the house through a narrow corridor. I stopped to examine a series of framed newspapers on the walls. They were already yellowed with age.

One was the front page of the Ekaterinburg newspaper from 19 July 1918; my knowledge of the Cyrillic alphabet was rusty, but I worked it out with my dear Ivanov's help:

EXECUTION OF NICHOLAS, THE BLOODY CROWNED MURDERER – SHOT WITHOUT BOURGEOIS FORMALITIES BUT IN ACCORDANCE WITH OUR NEW DEMOCRATIC PRINCIPLES

The basement was exactly as it had been in 1918, my guide told me. It was a tiny, windowless room, it hardly seemed large enough to fit in all eleven of the Czar's party. Large sections of the wall had been removed by Sokolov's investigators. Sections of the floorboards were gone, too, the bloodstains preserved either as evidence or as icons. The room was now used to store old packing boxes, which were piled almost to the ceiling, in defiance of the imagination and its sad attempt to reconstruct the events of that night.

I wondered what my enigmatic mistress would think if she were here with me now. Would it disturb any sleeping memories? Or was my Anastasia just the traumatised daughter of the lesser nobility, of no importance to anyone but me?

Was I as deluded in my pilgrimage as my guide?

The tour was over. Ivanov and I were both exhausted by it. I left feeling cheated. I found not a trace of Anastasia in the Ipatiev house. I wondered if, when I found the man who claimed to have murdered the Czar, I would only meet with more disappointment.

ANASTASIA

In Grosvenor Square, nursemaids with high collars and white bows around their hats were pushing perambulators or sitting together on benches to gossip. The rarefied air of Belgravia and the reverential silence of the austere façades were a shock after the trolley cars and barrow boys of the Bayswater Road. I followed Felix out of the hansom cab and up the steps of the white Regency portico.

A butler took our coats as we entered a gloomy hall dimly lit by a chandelier high in the stair well. A suit of armour stood sentry at the foot of the stairs, the walnut panelling on the walls burnished by the yellow glow of the gas mantles. The house was silent save for the ticking of a grandfather clock further down the hall.

Felix led me into the drawing room. Madam Rifkin sat in a wing-backed chair of claret leather, in a long straight dress of jade duchesse satin. There was a string of pearls around her throat. She looked a little like the photographs I had seen of Queen Victoria, with her bun of grey hair and small, piggish eyes. She could have been no more than sixty years old, but her demeanour was that of a much older woman.

'Mother. This is the girl. This is Anastasia Romanov.'

I felt like an exhibit rather than a guest. Madam Rifkin weighed me in her gaze for a long time and then said: 'You'll have to forgive me, I can't see very well. But my son tells me I am talking to a Grand Duchess.'

'My name is Anastasia Romanov, Madam Rifkin. More than that, I can't say.'

That answer seemed to satisfy her, for now. 'Is it true you have no memory?'

'It's true.'

'The Dowager Empress's daughter met you in Berlin. She said you were a fraud.'

'Then I shall have to take her at her word. For myself, I've never claimed any title. How can I? I can't remember anything of my past at all.'

At this point Felix remembered his manners, guiding me to a brocade chair, smiling apologetically at me through his mother's interrogation. Madam Rifkin just sat there, firing off questions like a judge interviewing a criminal, assessing my suitability to stand trial.

'You can speak Russian?' Madam Rifkin said, slipping easily into her native tongue.

'I must have learned it somewhere,' I answered, in the same language.

'Look at the way she sits, the way she speaks,' Felix said, and I realised how badly he wanted his mother's imprimatur on his discovery. 'You don't learn that picking potatoes.'

Madam Rifkin smiled at me. 'My son is already convinced of your identity.'

'As I said, Madam Rifkin, I make no claims for myself.'

'Very wise.' She looked me up and down once more. 'What happened to this husband of yours in Berlin?' I realised the trap I had set for myself. They must have discovered for themselves what had really happened to Andrei, it had been widely reported in all the German newspapers. I could not keep to the fiction that he had died of pneumonia.

I looked Madam Rifkin in the eye. 'I lied to Felix. But you know that.'

From the corner of my eye I saw Felix sigh with

relief. Madam Rifkin just sat there, her expression unreadable.

'I lied because it is not a pleasant thing to admit to anyone.'

I looked back at Felix, then at his mother. I gave a convincing performance of a woman struggling with her own anguish.

'My husband was homosexual. Perhaps you had heard the rumours about him. I do not know why he married me, unless it was for personal gain.' I swallowed hard, as if holding back tears. 'I came home one day and found him dead on the floor of our apartment. I passed one of his lovers on the stairs. I panicked and ran away.'

It was a lie, of course, but it fitted the facts as far as anyone but Michael and I knew them.

'You know the police in Berlin are looking for you,' she said.

'Of course.'

'They think you murdered him.'

'I made a lot of enemies in Berlin. It would suit them to have me in prison, I think.'

She nodded, prepared to give me the benefit of the doubt. I had passed the first test. My palms were damp.

Madam Rifkin sighed, then looked at her son, perched on the edge of his seat beside me, awaiting his mother's verdict. 'My eyes are not what they were,' she said to him. 'I cannot say if this is her or not.'

'It's her, Mother,' Felix said. 'I am sure of it.'

Madam Rifkin gave an almost imperceptible nod of her head and turned back to me. 'I only saw you once or twice, I was never important enough to be invited to Tsarskoe Selo. On the only occasion I met the Czarina, she asked me who I was. When I told her, she congratulated me on having such a fine husband and moved on. So you see, I, too, have been touched by royalty.' After all these years she was still bitter at being so summarily dismissed by the Empress.

The Empress. My mother.

'My son is convinced you're her,' she went on when I made no reply.

'Does it matter any more?'

'Oh, it matters, young lady. And next year, or the year after, when the Bolsheviks are thrown out, it will matter a great deal more.'

When I went to work next day there were a dozen roses waiting for me. They were from Felix. After I read the note I rushed in to the bathroom and wept. Perhaps I was overwhelmed at receiving flowers. More likely, I think, it was because I was going to have Michael's baby and most mornings I was ready to either cry or vomit over the slightest thing.

We went to Gunter's tearooms, one of the most fashionable and expensive tearooms in London. I still had not told him about Michael and I did not know how this unsuitable flirtation would end.

I watched Felix as he ordered a pot of Earl Grey tea and a bowl of raspberries and cream from the uniformed waitress. He was wearing a Fair Isle pullover; I could smell the scent of the Macassar oil in his hair. Although he was about the same age as me, he somehow contrived to look much older. It was impossible not to compare him to Michael; Felix, always so fashionable, so wealthy and so, well, soft; Michael, always in debt, a man who dressed appallingly as if to draw attention to his looks, which were those of a matinee idol who had taken up boxing.

I smiled, at fond memory.

'What are you laughing about?' Felix asked.

'Nothing.'

'I wish I knew what you were thinking, sometimes. There's so much about you I don't know, isn't there?'

I looked out of the window, across the street. Two prostitutes stood on the corner of Curzon Street propositioning customers with a cheerful: 'Lookin' for a girl, dearie?' I thought about Shanghai and the taxi club; there wasn't a day I didn't think about it, didn't wonder what it would take to put me back on the street again.

Felix saw the two girls I was staring at. 'It's a disgrace, isn't it?' he said.

'They're just trying to get by.'

He gave me this look; he was shocked by such sentiments, I suppose. When you have raspberries and cream in front of you and a napkin on your lap, selling sex for money can look pretty tawdry, I suppose.

Afterwards he insisted on taking me back to the flat in Kensington in a hansom cab. I saw his look of surprise and disapproval when he saw where I lived. As we climbed down from the cab he leaned towards me. I knew what he wanted and I drew back. It's not that I found him repulsive in any way, he always smelled very nice, and was pleasant to look at. Besides, a taxi girl learns not to have misgivings about any man, if she wants to pay her rent.

The guilt sat there in my chest, the size of a fist. As he went to kiss me I turned my head away, and his cheeks flushed the colour of copper as he withdrew, flustered. 'I'm sorry,' he said. 'I shouldn't have . . .'

'No, it's not that.'

'No, I'm sorry,' he repeated, and we stood there staring at each other, both lost to embarrassment.

'Forgive me,' he said, and got back inside the hansom cab. The horse stamped its foot in impatience, almost as if the dumb beast was as astonished by my behaviour as I was.

Felix showed me a London I had never seen. I suppose it was money that made the difference. Perhaps Felix thought he seduced me; but it was his wealth that did that. I wanted to live like a princess, and he showed me how to do it.

One night he took me to the Savoy, and we danced under the new electric chandeliers to Nick la Rocca's jazz band. Afterwards we went to a jazz club on Half Moon Street, and the early hours of the morning found us eating scrambled eggs at David Tennant's Gargoyle Club. On a weeknight, too.

Another night he took me to the Forty Three, one of Ma Meyrick's illegal nightclubs in Mayfair. He pointed out the actress Tallulah Bankhead, and introduced me to the King of Romania. Knowing that the police might burst in at any moment added even more glamour to that golden evening, and some of that excitement and daring rubbed off onto Felix. Like glitter, it came off in the dry cleaning, but I didn't know that then.

I felt guilty all the time I was with Felix. It was not as if Michael and I were married, but I knew I owed him my fidelity after all he had done, and now I realised I could not even offer him that. I was living under his roof, and here I was, like a common tart, going behind his back with another man.

But I could not help myself. This was the life I had missed, and I snatched at it with my princess's greedy hands. I longed to be away from the drab Kensington flat, for I missed the high times that Andrei had shown me. There had not been the money to enjoy myself like this with Michael. London was not as cheap as Shanghai or Berlin, where even a journalist could live like a duke, and Michael's new job did not pay very well; and although I thought myself very grand and clever when I first took the job at Renfrew Bannister, at the end of a week my wage was no more than a pittance.

I wanted to drive through the streets with my Lanvin scarf blowing in the wind; I wanted to wear silk and diamonds; I wanted the latest fashions; I wanted the world to know I was Anastasia.

But my elusive and ghostly Anastasia demanded a high price from me, and the price was Michael. I tried to tell myself that I did not really love him, began the long summation of my case to a sceptical conscience. I argued and reasoned and cajoled, but my conscience remained intractable, a solemn and stern-faced judge.

I wondered if in the end I would have the courage to act, with or without the approval of my soul.

MICHAEL

Ermakov, Zachary Ermakov.

After all these years one of the executioners had broken his silence. He had been boasting about it for months now: I was the one who shot the Czar. He was not hard to track down; he was foreman at the local copper plant, everyone knew him. I wondered if his bravado might endure an interview with a Western journalist. One thing to tell the local youth brigade of the Workers Committee that you were a hero, but telling such stories to foreigners had wider implications.

I tried ringing the copper plant but the telephone system was so bad that I gave up and paid a man with a horse and buggy to take me out to the plant, three miles out of town. The air out there was sulphurous. It was like I was choking.

I rushed across the street to a nondescript brick office. I went in and told a fearsome-looking woman in a peasant's smock that I was looking for Comrade Ermakov. She told me he no longer worked there. He had lung cancer. He was dying. No, she didn't know where he lived.

I walked back outside, put my scarf around my face to filter out the smog. So, the grave had caught up with one of the Czar's assassins already. Now I knew why Comrade Ermakov had decided to break his silence. The government couldn't hurt him now.

The telephone rang beside the bed. I woke, startled. I didn't think the damned thing worked. I looked at my watch, six thirty in the morning local time. It was freezing inside the hotel room, still dark outside.

'Yes?'

'Is it you looking for my husband?' a woman's voice said.

'Who is this?'

'This is Comrade Tatiana Ermakov. You went to the factory yesterday. You told Comrade Bulgarin you wanted to speak to my husband.'

I was instantly awake. 'Yes, my name's Sheridan, I'm a writer for . . .'

'Come to the house, this afternoon, two o'clock.'

I scrabbled on the table beside the bed for pencil and paper. 'What's the address?'

She gave me instructions on how to find the house – it was on the other side of the river, a mile out of town – and then hung up. I sat there, staring at the telephone. I checked my watch again. Seven and a half hours to wait.

It was going to be the longest wait of my life.

ANASTASIA

It was cold in the flat when I woke. I lit a candle and ran barefoot to the bathroom. I had no coins for the meter.

I washed, and dressed quickly, shivering on the cold tiles. I put on the same dress I had worn the day before. I rolled up my woollen stockings, securing them to elastic garters, and studied myself in the cheval mirror. Not much like a princess this morning. I put on the new cloche hat that Felix had bought me. I should not have accepted it. It was wrong.

There was a knock on the door. I knew who it was. I ran to the window, looked down into the street, saw the hansom cab waiting. Felix.

I looked around the room; candles gone to grease on china plates, wet stockings hanging on the mantelpiece in front of an unlit fire, a cold, grey room that screamed of desperation and misery. And it so obviously belonged to a man; a woman living alone would not keep bottles of whisky and brandy on the bookshelves. Michael's homburg was on the hatstand, by the door.

Felix knocked again.

I took a deep breath, assumed a dignity I did not feel, and opened the door.

'Anastasia,' he said. He stood there, in a camel hair coat from Savile Row, fingers toying nervously with the grey kidskin gloves he held in his hands. A shy smile. 'I know this is unexpected. I had to see you. I couldn't sleep last night. Forgive me.'

I stood aside to let him in. I saw Mrs Stanton peering up at us from her downstairs flat. Any moment she would be shouting 'Trollop!' at the top of her voice.

Felix stood in the middle of the room, looking around as if he was witness to a devastating earthquake, an expression of both pity and shock. 'It's cold in here,' was all he said.

'I was getting ready to go to work.'

'I know. I'm sorry.'

'You said you couldn't sleep?'

I saw him glance at Michael's homburg. But he said nothing. 'I've been thinking about us.'

'Us?'

'Mother and I have to go back to New York soon. Perhaps as early as next week.'

Should I feel relieved or desperate? The truth of it was, I wasn't sure.

'The thing is,' he said, 'I want you to come to New York with me.'

And there, exactly at that moment, I could see my life separate, like the fork in a road. I hesitated, looking as far as I might down both ways, saw the pitfalls and the vistas, and I froze, not knowing what to say or what to do. A part of me argued for Michael; little Anastasia, my Anastasia, pleaded with me to go with Felix.

'But you hardly know me,' I said.

'On the contrary, I've known you all my life. Since I was a child. I've not thought about anything else for the last ten years.'

'But there are so many women in the world, Felix, who could be better for you.'

He shook his head. 'There's no-one.' He took my hand. It looked like a small, pale lifeless bird in his.

'I can't,' I heard myself say.

'Because of Michael?'

That shook me. And then I thought: of course, someone at the office has gossiped about me. Or perhaps Felix made it his business to find out all about me. A man does not become wealthy without knowing where to find the information he needs.

'You know about Michael?'

'Do you love this man?'

I was about to murmur, 'Yes, I think I do,' but I stopped myself. At that moment I had the chance to throw the old Anastasia away, to be rid of her for ever. Easy to say; here was a man with ease enough and money enough to buy back my birthright. The words stuck in my throat. If I stayed with Michael, the world might never call me Anastasia, and I would never discover my birthright or my destiny.

I remember thinking: why throw away everything you've dreamed of for a man who may never come back for you, a man who cannot give you a proper home for your child. What are you doing?

'Michael's been kind to me,' I answered, and betrayed him utterly with just those five words.

'How?'

'In Berlin. After my husband died, I had nowhere else to go, no-one else to turn to.'

I saw the disapproval on his face. This was not how a princess down on her luck was supposed to behave.

'Where is he now?'

'He's a journalist. He travels abroad a lot.'

He gave me a wistful smile. 'If only you could remember the promises we made to each other once.'

I looked into his face, wondered if I had made such promises. Was he just saying this to twist me to his way of thinking?

'I won't give you up,' he said.

'You have to let me think about this.'

'I want you to marry me,' he said, 'marry me and

come back to New York with me. I won't take no for an answer. Not after so long.'

Marry him, a voice inside me said. Marry him, and when the child comes, well, he'll know it's not his, but by then it will be too late. That's what a survivor would do.

And you are a survivor, Anastasia. If nothing else, whoever and whatever you are, you are a survivor.

'I have to think,' I repeated and turned away from him.

'I have always loved you,' he said. 'Always.'

I did not hear him leave, there was just the soft click of the door as it closed behind him. I watched from the window as he climbed into the hansom cab down in the street. I was at war with myself, for now, but when the truce was called, I knew what my answer would be.

That night Felix took me to dinner at the Savoy; beignets of sole, *loup de mere en croute*, crêpes soaked in grand marnier. Felix ordered a bottle of Corton Charlemagne. Afterwards we walked along the Victoria Embankment, the gaslights along the river looked like strings of pearls.

Felix told me about his own exile, after the Revolution.

'I remember the day my father told us we must get out of Russia. There had been riots every day in the street, and one day a man died on our front step. He had been shot by the soldiers. I suppose we were the lucky ones, at least we got out alive. We had relatives in New York and we arrived there the day the Bolsheviks took over in Russia. My father and my uncle formed a company, hiring out messengers on Wall Street, right in the heart of the financial district. They started off with two employees, now we have over two thousand.

'When my father died he left me two hundred thousand dollars. I poured it all back into the company, trading in stocks and securities. Now I'm worth ten times that.'

I stared at the river. What a strange thing life could be.

The rich get richer, as the song went. The world had turned full circle in five years, for those that survived.

'What are you going to do?' he asked me.

I did not answer. I stared at the mists floating on the river, heard Big Ben strike the hour.

'This is an outrageous thing that has happened to you. We have to fight to have your claim recognised.'

'We, Felix?'

'You need money, and you need powerful friends. That's why you need me.'

I watched Michael's face dissolving into the fog.

'I have some influence in the Russian community in New York, I have the money to pay lawyers. We can have your claim lodged in the German courts. It can be done, I know how to do it.'

'You forget. I'm wanted there by the police.'

'Money takes care of everything,' he said, and I wanted to believe him.

He moved closer, took my hands in his. 'I have a confession to make. Even when I was thirteen and we played on the slide, I was in love with you. I couldn't say anything then because I was just a doctor's son and you were a Grand Duchess.'

'And now I'm a secretary in a law firm and you're a millionaire. How the world turns.'

I knew that if I turned my face up to his, he would kiss me and the pact would be sealed. But I hesitated, concentrated instead on his tie pin. A diamond, emblem of that other world of wealth and privilege that was my birthright. But still, for the good of my soul, I swear I hesitated.

'Will you come to New York with me?' he whispered.

The horn of a barge echoed across the Thames. I listened to the water lapping against the embankment, tried to assemble my thoughts. I wished Michael was there, to stop it happening.

Should I tell Felix about the baby? I stood there, my head pressed against his chest, let the current carry me along, the spoiled little duchess from Tsarskoe Selo again, taking the easy way out.

'Marry me,' he whispered.

'We've only known each other a few weeks.'

'I know more about you than you know about yourself. I know about your temper tantrums, I know how you pulled your cousin's hair when she annoyed you and how you tripped up the servants when you were bored. I know you were inattentive at your lessons and I know you have a mole on your right shoulder blade.'

'Not any more, they cut it out,' I said, remembering the little white scar on my shoulder.

'I know the world has wronged you and that you have suffered needlessly. I know you have a birthright and that only money and influence is going to give you your rightful place in the world. I know I have the power to give you these things and I would want you to have them even if you didn't want me. I know you will always be the only woman I will ever want.'

And there it was; a choice between destiny and Michael, my beautiful Michael, between regaining my royal birthright and a life of comfortable anonymity. I could be happy with Michael, I thought, but happiness would not be enough. I knew, deep in my soul I knew, that I was meant for better things than happiness.

There was no such thing as coincidence, Michael had told me that. It was destiny, not chance, that had brought Felix here and tonight I could recover the course of my life as it should have been.

I had done so many hateful things in my life, had stood apart from myself and watched as I did them; or else I had turned a blind eye to myself, as you would to an old and beloved but dishonest friend. And so I tried not to think the word 'betrayal' as I raised my face to let him kiss me and when he asked me again to marry him I believe I must have said yes.

I woke next morning in Felix's Mayfair bedroom. His heavy body lay in the bed beside me, big as a mountain. Last night we had made love, in the way of casual strangers. It had reminded me of one of those nights in

Shanghai, with some anonymous customer. A transaction had taken place, something material had been promised, something material received.

I slipped into the heavy brocade gown he had left for me by the bed and went to stand at the window, looking out over the slowly waking city. Down in the street I heard the muffin man's bell.

Morning: a perfect time for recrimination. How could I do this to Michael? When I thought back on my remembered life, he had been there for me always; the night in Shanghai when I had given way to the black dog of despair; in Berlin, when I had called him from Andrei's apartment, frantic that I would go to prison. Both times he had come to my rescue. How could I betray him now?

And yet, I argued, what was I to him but a burden in his life? Like everyone else, he only wanted me because I might be Anastasia. The moment I stopped being a mystery for him, he would lose interest, I would become an impediment. He could not stay here in London for ever. He had ambitions for his own life that did not include a wife and a child, of that I was sure. There would be other women after me, as there were many women before. He would be happier without me. He might even be relieved when he found that I was gone.

I tried to imagine his face, how it might have looked if I had told him I was carrying his child. Try as I might, I could not conjure happiness from it, only a look of entrapment. At some future time he might even hold me responsible for his predicament.

He had to be free to follow his own dreams, as I had to be free to follow mine.

There. I had done it. I had convinced myself.

MICHAEL

A hovel built of ancient timber, weathered to grey, one half tilted at an angle to the ground as if the whole structure might split in two at any moment. I wondered how many years it had stood like that. I imagined endless seasons of freeze and thaw, the land constantly shifting beneath the foundations.

The house crouched among the black shadows of spruce and pine, looking over the sprawl of factories and smelters that was Sverdlovsk. A smudge of black smoke leaked from the chimney into a sky of chill blue.

There was no fence, and the yard was littered with old machinery and rusting tin. A goat was tied to a post, ice glistened in its rank coat. It stared at me with belligerent curiosity. I shivered, the tension sitting in my gut like a cold, greasy meal.

The goat gave a sudden bleating cry and I felt adrenalin shoot through my veins. I hissed a curse at the beast and climbed onto the veranda. The boards creaked alarmingly underfoot.

The front door was open but the house was dark and there was no light inside. It took a moment for my eyes to grow accustomed to the gloom. When they did I saw a pair of eyes staring at me from the doorway and I took a step back in shock.

It was an old woman, dressed in a shawl, long black dress and a man's boots. There were holes in the dress and in the woollen shawl and there was a cake of mud on her boots. She had only three teeth left in her head. Her skin hung on her skull like an old saddlebag, worn out with use and age. She smelled of wood smoke and boiled cabbage.

Although I knew she had been expecting me, she stared at me as if I had just dropped out of the sky, managing to look both curious and terrified at once. I started to introduce myself but she just turned around and shuffled back into the house without a word of invitation. There was nothing to do but follow.

Not much furniture, as you might expect; one over-stuffed armchair, a wood stove with a pair of enormous boots sitting under the grate. Her husband's, I decided. On the wall was a framed photograph of Lenin, and another of a man, dressed in black, with a bristling moustache, and a pistol held heroically in his right hand. That must be him, I thought.

The man who shot the Czar.

Zachary Petrovich Ermakov was no longer a giant of the Revolution. The only resemblance between the man I saw and the man in the photograph was the beetling black moustache. He lay on a crude wooden bed at the other end of the room, cotton quilts piled up around him. He could not have weighed any more than six stone. The flesh had wasted off him, and I could make out the shape of his skull through the parchment-like skin. There was a crust of dried blood at the corner of his mouth and dark and unidentifiable stains on his pillow. His breath was rank and it was as much as I could do not to turn away.

'You're the newspaperman,' he croaked.

I nodded. In my experience, death cowed people. You could see the fear in their eyes. Not Ermakov. His body may have shrunk but his eyes burned like coals, and there was nothing in his face but hatred.

His wife indicated the wooden chair beside the bed and I sat down. There was a bowl at my feet stained with bile. I felt my stomach rise in revolt.

'I'm dying. They told you?'

I nodded.

'It's the cancer. My lungs . . . are rotting away.'

Up close he looked like an old man but by my calculations I reckoned him to be in his forties. He regarded me with those terrible eyes.

'They said you want to know about the . . . Czar.'

'You were there?'

He smiled. His teeth were brown and rotted from ciga-rettes. His fingers, too, were stained the colour of shit. There were jagged purple scars on his wrists, the purple cicatrices livid against his white skin.

'The Czar did that,' he said.

'The Czar?'

'Nine years in the camps. Those fucking bastards.'

'You were lucky to survive,' I said, trying to establish some rapport with this creature. I had to get this story, drag everything I could out of him. I was worried he might change his mind about talking to me.

'It wasn't luck. I was tough then, and I promised myself I would survive just so I could make those . . . fucking bastards pay.' He held out on emaciated wrist. 'I was kept handcuffed for a whole year. The sores on my wrists festered for months, even after . . . after they took them off. They said I would . . . lose my hands. But I didn't. This hand . . . this hand shot that fucker in the head.'

'You shot the Czar?' I said.

'Yes. It was me. Me.'

I didn't believe him then and I still don't. Even though most of what he said was subsequently proved to be true, I still think Yurovsky killed him. In the years after Ermakov gave his version of events, half a dozen men came forward and said that they fired the fatal shot. They all wanted to be the one.

Ermakov was grinning at me, watching my reaction, pleased to have declared himself a murderer, even on his deathbed. There was no God waiting for him on the other side. Never mind communism, his eternal glory was right here, right now.

'You were one of the guards at the Ipatiev house?'

'Not just one of the guards. Me and Yurovsky were in command. That bastard took all the credit. But it was me, I was the one who did the hard work. That was why . . . that was why Sverdlov made me foreman of the factory. That was all the reward I got for . . . doing their dirty work for them . . . that was all . . .'

His voice trailed off into a fit of coughing. His face turned the colour of beetroot and his wife rushed over, grabbed the bowl and held it under his chin while he choked and spluttered for breath. I thought he might die then and there. I got to my feet, appalled and fascinated by this grotesque little scene. Finally Ermakov gasped in a breath, blood and bile leaking from his mouth.

His breathing crackled in his chest. They could have heard

him in Revolution Square. The episode exhausted him and he lay gasping for a long time, unable to speak.

Eventually he nodded to his wife to let her know he was recovered and she hurried away to empty the bowl outside in the yard. Those lucky chickens. I sat down again, shaken. He extended a bony hand and tapped a finger on the page of my notebook, to let me know he wanted me to take notes.

'I was there . . . the day the Czar and Czarina arrived here in Sverdlovsk. I was thinking he would be some great Ivan . . . with red eyes and a thick beard, the size of a shithouse, but he was just this pathetic creature, you could blow him over.' He started to cough again, but managed to get it under control. 'And her. Fat German cow. She wanted us to push her around in her wheelchair. We made the old bitch walk.'

He smiled fondly at these recollections of viciousness, as at the memory of a favourite grandchild.

'The first day that German bitch wrote out menus on these little gold menu cards, she wanted us to get her . . . all this fancy food. Like we were her servants. We soon fixed her. She got the same as us. Soup and . . . vegetables.'

I wondered how long the interview would last. He seemed too weak to talk for long before another coughing fit stopped him. The first episode had weakened him to the point where I thought if he had another he would pass out or have a seizure. I was impatient. I didn't want to know about the Czar; I only wanted to hear about Anastasia.

'Do you remember when the others came?'

'The sailor, what was his name, carrying the Czarevitch . . . ?'

'Do you remember the princess, the youngest one, Anastasia?'

He had to think about that.

'Pretty little things. I wanted us to have our pick but Yurovsky . . . now I'll never know what it's like to fuck a Grand Duchess.'

I never thought I would ever wish suffering on another human being. But as I sat there, pretending to be of a mind with this monster, a part of me cursed him to linger a few weeks more in choking agony. I had never met anyone who fed on their own hatred like this. I imagined a little sac of bitterness, a canker made of his own venom, eating away inside him like a nest of maggots.

'You don't remember Anastasia?'

He was growing irritated with these questions. 'They were all the same. Who cares anyway?'

'You were telling me . . . about the night they died.'

He smiled again, the memory of the Czar's death cheering him. 'We found these pits, about ten miles out of town . . . abandoned mines . . . Yurovsky chose it as the place. We . . . collected some big tins of petrol, firewood and acid and sent it all out there. The night of the execution . . . we got a truck and about a dozen blankets and drove it into Cathedral Square. We told the driver . . . to back up to the basement entrance, to leave the engine running, make . . . make as much noise as possible.'

'Where were you?'

'In the house. Where do you think? I wasn't going to miss the executions for anything.' My cadaver was growing fatigued. His wife brought him a glass of cold black tea. He lapped at it, then pushed the glass away without a word. She went back to sit in the shadows. I wondered what it was that made her so dedicated to him. Perhaps he had been a kinder husband than he was jailer.

Or perhaps she was afraid of him even now.

'Everything went wrong that night,' Ermakov said, his voice getting hoarse now, so that I had to lean in closer, wincing at his fetid breath. 'It was Yurovsky's fault.'

I sat there, not daring to interrupt.

'It took them nearly an hour to get ready. The girls . . . carried pillows with them . . . to sit on in the car. I thought that was very fucking funny . . . We got them . . . all down to the basement, we said they had to be evacuated . . . that the Whites were coming . . . I remember the Czar said: "Well, at last we're . . . we're going to get out of this place." Then we heard the truck.'

He stopped, exhausted. His lungs made a wet, crackling sound every time he breathed.

'Yurovsky went in and read the sentence. I was standing right behind him . . . I could see the bastard's face . . . he couldn't believe it.' He started to laugh, broke into another fit of coughing.

I drew back from that appalling breath.

'The Czar couldn't hear over . . . the sound of the truck . . . and Yurovsky had to repeat . . . repeat what he said. I knew he wanted to do it . . . and I'd promised myself that . . . privilege . . . I took out my revolver and I . . . I leaned over his shoulder and I shot him in the face.' A deep sawing breath. His eyes were alight. He spoke the words again, like an absolution. 'I shot the Czar . . . me . . . you tell the newspaper that, all right?'

I nodded, feeling sick to my stomach.

'He went down, he . . . never moved. Then Yurovsky . . . fired his Mauser . . . into the German bitch's mouth. It got crazy . . . everyone firing . . . over everyone's shoulders, there wasn't enough room in the doorway . . . I was deaf for . . . a week. The room filled with smoke, we couldn't shoot them . . . a few of them got scared . . .'

And then it started again, he had been talking too fast and he broke into another paroxysm of coughing, his eyes bulging out of his head. He clung to Madam Ermakov with a skeletal grip and I thought: this is it. His head fell back onto the pillow and I thought he was dead. But then those black eyes turned towards me, and he smiled, a terrible smile that sent a cold chill along my spine.

I waited for him to recover his strength. After a while he started again, taking up from where he had finished.

'It wasn't until later we found out . . . the women had jewels stuffed into . . . into their corsets, the bullets just bounced off them . . . it was lucky nobody was . . . killed.' He laughed at his little joke. 'Nobody of us. Finally all the bullets were gone . . . the Chekas had to finish them off . . . with their bayonets.'

Jesus Christ, I heard myself murmur.

'You don't know how hard it is . . . to kill eleven people.'

'I hope I never have to find out,' I said, in English.

'Everyone in town heard the shooting . . . I ran in to see what was happening . . . you couldn't move in the corridor and all the time that lorry driver was . . . revving the engine. Finally it was over. Yurovsky told everyone . . . to take the hats and coats off the bodies . . . find the rings and necklaces and watches . . . put them all in the corner. He was your typical . . . apparatchik, that one, everything . . . by the book. Except he was . . . a fuckwit, of course, like all those bastards . . . he really screwed up that . . . night.' He started laughing and a froth of pink foam formed at the corner of his mouth.

'We wrapped the bodies up in blankets and put them . . . on the truck. Pillows and handbags and slippers . . . everything was soaked with blood . . . blood everywhere. Just what Yurovsky said he didn't . . . want. But that's what you get . . . when you have to club and stab people to . . . death.'

Another hacking breath.

'We set off out to the . . . mines. Two in the morning before . . . we got started. The roads were just mud . . . it took two hours to go ten miles, the wheels kept slipping . . . into the mud. You could see dawn coming up . . . when we got there.'

'You burned the bodies then?'

He shook his head. 'There wasn't time.'

I could see this was the part of the story he wasn't interested in. 'Why not?'

'We didn't want to do it in daylight . . . people would see . . . the smoke. We knew the Whites weren't . . . far away. We didn't want anyone . . . telling them where the bodies were . . .'

'So what happened?'

But Ermakov was exhausted. He shrugged his shoulders.

'Anastasia survived,' I said, to get him talking again.

'No-one survived.'

'Anastasia is alive,' I repeated.

He tried to sit up in the bed, agitated now. 'They are all dead!'

'You left the bodies there all day. What if she survived the bullets and the bayonets?'

'I put a guard on those bodies! The next night I came back . . . I counted! They were . . . all there! I saw Anastasia!'

I wondered if I could believe him. 'You saw her?'

'Eleven bodies! The next night . . . we came back and we burned the faces . . . with the acid . . . and then we burned them with the petrol. There's nothing left of any of the princesses, of any of . . . them. They're all dead. And I . . . Zachary Petrovich Ermakov . . . I was the one who killed the . . .'

Another fit of coughing but this one went on and on. He gripped Madam Ermakov's shoulders as if he were underwater, reaching for the surface. He was drowning in his own blood. A fitting end, it seemed to me.

But the spasm passed. Madam Ermakov looked at me and shook her head. The interview was over. Ermakov lay on the bed, his eyes rolled back in his head, his breath sawing in his chest. A terrible noise. I left.

Outside in the yard, a distant sun warmed my skin. Dark pine forests stretched away across the vast hinterland under a washed blue sky. It was the warmest part of this spring day but I shivered inside my coat. I knew now what had happened to the Czar and his family. Anastasia, as he had said, was dead. She could not have survived the bullets and the bayonets.

This was the bitter counterpoint of knowledge. A terrible certainty is sometimes worse than tiny glimmers of hope. I knew: I wished I had not known.

ANASTASIA

My suitcases were packed by the door. I placed the envelope on the mantel and went to the window to look for the cab. Felix had said he would be there at eleven to take us to Waterloo station. From there we would catch the train to Southampton and sail for New York.

I looked around the flat for the last time, felt a sharp stab of regret. I told myself again that there was no choice.

A hansom cab pulled up in the street outside, I heard the ring of the hooves on the road, and was about to fetch the cases. Then I saw a man climb out of the cab and I realised it was not Felix. My heart clenched like a fist in my chest.

I just wanted to run. I cannot face him.

But there was nowhere to run, and nothing to do but stand there with my back to the window and wait for the door to open. I heard his footfall on the stairs, heard the key turn in the lock. And then Michael was there, holding his battered suitcase, a day's growth of stubble on his chin. He smiled, a little uncertainly, and then the smile dropped away when he saw the two suitcases by the door.

He looked at me, in my hat and coat, and I shall never forget the expression of indescribable pain that I saw there. I hated myself then, more than I had ever done, and I am someone who has much to hate herself for.

'Not the welcome home I'd been expecting,' he said.

I closed my eyes, could not bear to look at him. God forgive me.

'What's happened?' he said.

'I'm leaving.'

'To go where?'

'New York. I've met someone else.'

I opened my eyes again, watched his face, could see emotions tumbling one upon the other, anger, confusion, disbelief.

'Someone else?'

'I'm sorry.'

'You're sorry. Is that it?' He waited for me to justify it somehow and when I didn't, he said, 'I've only been away a month.'

'It has nothing to do with you.'

'What are you talking about?'

How could I explain it to him? I couldn't.

'I'm sorry,' I said.

'Sorry,' he repeated, as if it was an obscenity.

'Michael. I am her. It's true. I've met someone who knew me from before.'

'Another Banischevski?' He swallowed hard. 'I hope he has life insurance.'

'He remembers me from Tsarskoe Selo.'

'Who is he?'

'His name is Felix Rifkin, his father was . . .'

'I met someone who knew you from before. When I was in Sverdlovsk. He knew you very well because he was there the night you died. He helped the Cheka club you to death with the butt end of a rifle and then he poured acid on your face and buried you in the woods ten miles out of town.'

I thought I was going to be sick. 'You're making this up.'

'He was there. I don't know what this Rifkin told you, but he's a liar. Grand Duchess Anastasia is dead. I don't know who you are, but you're not that Anastasia Romanov. Are you listening to me?'

But I wasn't listening. I had seen the truth in Felix Rifkin's eyes. My whole existence was a hall of mirrors. Felix had finally brought me certainty. I wouldn't believe Michael now, I couldn't.

'Michael, he even remembers the mole I have on my right shoulder.'

'That doesn't prove anything.'

The strangest thing: I felt as if I was arguing for my life. I felt a real sense of desperation. 'This Russian you talked to, how do you know *he* wasn't lying? Would he really want the world to know he botched the job? The Bolsheviks lie, everyone lies.'

'Even you, apparently. You said you loved me.'

Felix's cab pulled up outside. 'I'm sorry,' I said, 'I can't do this,' and I picked up my bags.

I thought he might try to stop me, but he didn't. So like him. Hadn't that been our story from the beginning?

'I can't believe you're doing this,' he said.

'Neither can I,' I answered and walked past him out of the door.

I heard the downstairs door open and Mrs Stanforth peered into the hall. 'Trollop,' she hissed as I passed her for the last time.

I looked up once as I got into the cab. I thought I might see Michael's face at the window. I didn't.

There was nothing else to be done. Anastasia Romanov got into the cab with Felix Rifkin and went in search of her destiny in New York.

PART FIVE

New York and Shanghai, 1929

ANASTASIA

I woke to the alarm clock, one of the new mass-produced clocks you could buy in any department store in any city in the United States. It was fashionable these days to be woken by such a device, instead of by a servant. The clock even had a luminous dial so that you could see the time in the middle of the night. The world had changed so much since the war.

The maid had already run my bath. Afterwards I dressed and went through to the dining room where the maid was serving breakfast. Madam Rifkin was already there, with her morning coffee. Sophie, Felix's sister, was still in bed. Unlikely we would see her much before noon.

Felix would already be in his office. Every day he left just after dawn and did not return before seven or eight o'clock in the evening.

We now lived in an apartment on Fifth Avenue, one of New York's most fashionable addresses, eleven rooms decorated in the latest Art Deco style. Besides keeping the three of us, Felix maintained three live-in servants, as well as a seamstress, laundress and a chauffeur for the Hispano-Suiza. He had kept his promise to keep me in the style to which I was accustomed. Whose life? I sometimes wondered. Whoever's life it is, it is a very easy one.

I murmured good morning to Madam Rifkin and sat down at the table. One of the maids poured coffee. Even up here in our eyrie we could hear the murmur of the traffic on Fifth Avenue through the terrace windows.

I picked up the *New York Times*, turned the pages, looking for something of interest; more food shortages in Russia. It was the fifth year of Josef Stalin's New Economic Policy, and food production was still to return to the same levels as when the Czar was on the throne. So much for feeding the masses. It had been so easy to blame Nicholas for everything that had been wrong with Russia. Now they had had their Revolution and their blood-letting and the poor still had nothing to eat.

The headlines were all about the soaring stock market prices. There was hardly anyone in New York who wasn't in the market, every day you read something in the *Times* about this latest craze; a Park Avenue matriarch complaining she had lost her cook because she wouldn't give her her own personal ticker in the kitchen; a dowager in Queens complaining that her chauffeur would not report for work until after the market had closed. Even the Rifkins' own seamstress had stunned Felix one morning by asking him whether he thought the latest break in the market was the end of the bull run or just a technical readjustment. That the servants should know about such things.

It was like a madness that had seized the entire city, the entire country. Movie houses and theatres wanted to place tickers in the foyer for their customers.

Felix was one of the big players, of course. His own trading house could not match the might of houses like JP Morgan's, but he was in the market for around five million dollars, and his own success had mirrored the burgeoning trade of stocks on Wall Street.

I turned the page. In England there was a new Labour government under Ramsay MacDonald; Leon Trotsky was asking for asylum there. In Paris, America, Britain and France had ratified the Young Plan, which would allow the Germans to pay off their war reparations by 1988. It made me think about my time in Berlin as Countess Banischevski, people freezing to death in the parks and drinking coffee made from turnips. They could look forward to another sixty years of it.

An advertisement caught my eye. A familiar face, one of Felix's friends, an Italian count, expounding the value of a new stock issue, claiming it assured the security of his estates near Milan. On the next page a French aristocrat claimed she would serve only one kind of ginger ale to her broker friends. Ginger ale! No broker I knew would be so crass as to serve soft drinks to his guests. Prohibition was for the poor.

Money, everything was money. I wondered what would happen if I ever got my day in court and proved to everyone that I was the Grand Duchess of the Russias. Would I be deluged with offers to sell soap and cigarettes?

'What are you doing today?' Madam Rifkin asked me.

'I've arranged to have coffee with the Metrevellis at eleven.'

'I think I shall come with you.'

For a moment our eyes met; another long and exhausting day stretched ahead of us with nothing whatsoever to do. Our most important decision would be which shoes to wear with which dress. After the Metrevellis we would lunch at the Waldorf-Astoria or the Ritz, take in a private art viewing at three o'clock, a committee meeting of the Saint Catherine Orphanage Fund at four, and another hectic day in the trenches would be over. Back home for cocktails and a late supper with a husband who was often exhausted and invariably distracted by work.

My life as a princess.

I envied Felix. He had places to go where he would be missed if he did not appear. Meanwhile, here was I, trapped in my Art Deco castle, dragging myself through another endless, glamorous day.

> *Picture a little love nest,*
> *Down where the roses cling,*
> *Picture the same sweet love nest*
> *Think what a year can bring . . .*

The scratchy sound of Sophie's gramophone drifted from the drawing room where our young princess lay on a chaise longue with a cold compress on her aching head, recovering from another night in the speakeasies. Poor, pale Sophie, suffering bravely on.

Rachel ran in, her nursemaid Maggie shuffling along after her. Rachel was screaming because the head had broken off her doll. It was one of the newfangled toys, it could say 'mama' when you pulled the string in its back. It had a plastic face instead of a china one and the man in Macy's had said it was unbreakable, but there was no such thing when you put a toy in the hands of a small child.

'Rachel, dear, don't scream, there's a good girl,' Sophie groaned. 'Your aunt Soph's got the most awful headache.'

> *He's washing dishes,*
> *And baby clothes*
> *He's so ambitious,*
> *He really sews . . .*

I scooped Rachel up in my arms and nodded to Maggie who was apologetic that I should be so disturbed. I carried my angel into the kitchen and sent Maggie off to find some glue, see if we could do some mending ourselves.

> *But don't forget folks*
> *That's what you get folks*
> *For makin' whoopee.*

After I had comforted Rachel, I set to work on the doll. At last, something useful to do. As I worked, I thought about what was known in the Rifkin household as The Case. A curious thing, but recently, and I didn't remember exactly when this started, I had begun to wonder if any of it really mattered any more. If a judge ruled that I was Anastasia, would it really make me content? Was becoming Anastasia going to change the way I felt?

I really wasn't sure I knew the answer to that now.

The Dowager Empress had died the previous year and now her daughters were living in Windsor under the protection of King George. The Romanovs had settled into exile like an old marriage, in Berlin and France and New York, getting greyer, talking less and less of Nicholas and Saint Petersburg. In Russia, Stalin showed no signs of losing his grip on power despite widespread starvation and his country's isolation from the rest of the world.

Anastasia really didn't seem to matter any more.

Felix was still determined to pursue her. He had retained a lawyer, Martin Lachter, to file a claim in the German courts seeking to establish my identity and clear the way for a claim to the Romanov succession. It was going to be a long and difficult road, for mine was not the only suit; the woman that Felix referred to as 'that Polish peasant', Anna Andersen, was living out on Long Island now, and she had retained a lawyer, too.

Felix sent me to a psychiatrist friend of his, and I spent many afternoons lying on a couch in the Upper East Side. He told me I had repressed my memories because they were too painful for me to recall. To please him I recounted fantasies inspired by the memories of others, scenarios woven from photographs and anecdotes gleaned from people I had met in Berlin.

The psychiatrist told Felix we were making real progress and word went around the Russian colony that the doctor was willing to testify in court that I really was Anastasia Romanov.

The only person not convinced was me.

Felix took me to another psychiatrist friend who had been experimenting with hypnotism. He put me in a trance state, in order to delve into what he called my 'subconscious mind' and retrieve the memories he said were locked away there. He, too, claimed to have made a breakthrough, but he was a fraud, and I was the only one who knew it. These doctors needed Anastasia more than I did.

At Lachter's request Felix also admitted me to Mount Sinai hospital for a full physical examination. The results were encouraging. I had always been self-conscious about my feet; the big toe on my right foot was bent at the joint, forming a rather ugly bunion. The doctors had a clinical name for it, hallux valgus, and apparently it was one of the physical peculiarities possessed by the Czar's daughters, just as Andrei had once told me.

They found a small white scar on my shoulder blade from a cauterised mole, exactly in the spot where Anastasia was known to have had such a birthmark. More significantly, according to Felix and Lachter, the doctors also found a one inch groove behind my right ear that they agreed could have been caused by the passage of a bullet. The triangular scar on my right foot was apparently consistent with the contours of a Russian bayonet.

They also took X-ray pictures of my head, which revealed that at some stage I had sustained a severe fracture to the right temporal region of my skull. The doctors told Felix that such injuries could have resulted in what they called traumatic psychogenic amnesia, which meant that there might be an actual physiological reason for my loss of memory, as well as an emotional one. Damage to the right temporal cortex, they said, could lead to extensive memory loss.

My husband and his lawyer were ecstatic with these findings. But perversely, I had ceased to care so much. All I knew was that I was tired of being Mrs Felix Rifkin. I was a princess now in everything but name, and the road ahead looked dull and pliant and filled with luxury; it was also more tedious and loveless than I had ever thought to contemplate.

MICHAEL

The liner's massive screws stirred the dark waters of the Hudson as she headed upriver past Staten Island and the Statue of Liberty towards the towers of Manhattan. Smoke belched from the three blue stacks, staining a cloudless sky. I stood at the rail watching the city rise from the water. From here it looked for all the world like a fortress, the concrete towers merged into one. I hadn't seen my home town from this perspective too often. When you live here, it mostly just closes in and folds itself around you.

The sun was refracted from cascades of windows, so bright it hurt the eyes and I had to turn away. Nine years since I had been back here, so many demons lurked in these canyons of shadows and light; my family, who no doubt would swoop down to bring me back to the nest; and Anastasia Romanov.

After I returned from Sverdlovsk I had won some degree of celebrity with my by-line on the murder of the Czar. It had won me back my job with the Reuters agency. I worked as a correspondent in Paris and Berlin and then replaced Roper as bureau chief in Moscow. But a year in Moscow, that drab and paranoid city, was enough for me and when I got an offer from the *New York Times* I took it. Looking back, I suppose it was less of a career move than a final opportunity to lay some ghosts to rest.

The liner nosed further up the Hudson River and New York's true vistas revealed themselves; the smoke stacks on the Jersey side, the mushrooming pinnacles of commerce and wealth on Manhattan Island. The greatest city in the world, they said, surely the richest. I had left Europe on the other side of the Atlantic, with its kings and castles and decaying courts. That was the past; this was the future, right here, and right now.

It wasn't until I was looking down at the quay that I realised how much New York had changed while I had been gone. The dock was crowded with horse-drawn cabs the day I sailed away; nine years later there was not a single horse down there, just rank upon rank of black shiny automobiles. New Yorkers, too, had undergone a transformation; the women wore knee-length suits and helmet-like cloche hats, all chic straight lines, boyish and brassy. Some of them even wore garters, below the knee, styles that would have had the grey-beard burghers of my youth scurrying away to get the police.

Even the men had thrown off their conservative shackles. New York's go-getters now wore lightweight cottons, in blues and greys. The pace of the city had changed, you could feel the buzz in the air.

The old man had sent the Packard to pick me up. I recognised our chauffeur, Davis, in his uniform, ten years he had been with us when I'd left, and he was still holding doors for the Sheridan family. He tipped his cap to me as if I had never ever been away. 'Good afternoon, sir. Mr Sheridan asked me to come and fetch you.'

'That was nice of him,' I said. I had no intention of getting in. The Packard was just the opening gambit of the game we would play over the next few weeks, my heart and soul as stake.

'He asked me to tell you there's a room made up at the house for you. Unless you have other arrangements.'

I thought about Anastasia. This was what she had been unable to give up, I supposed. Living like royalty has many compensations. Outside the customs sheds, people were fighting for the few chequered cabs.

I hesitated, but only for a moment. 'Give him my regards, Davis. Tell him I'll be in touch.' I picked up my cases and went on by, joined the scrimmage on the dock, just one of the people now, one of those poor suckers without the velvet cushion of wealth and privilege.

Welcome to New York.

ANASTASIA

We were out on Long Island for a polo match, Felix's Wall Street firm against the local pony club. Two chukkas in, and I had earned a wave from my dashing Jewish polo-playing husband like a true Ivy Leaguer, and then we went out for the treading-in. Our darling Sophie had come along, no doubt she had her eye on one or all of the polo team.

The sun was fat and yellow and lazy in a baking sky. Another simple day of boredom and ease in my somnolent life. I had no premonition of his return, was not expecting to be jarred so savagely from my diamond life.

'Anna,' a voice said and I started, as if someone had touched me with an electric wire. I felt the hairs rise on the back of my neck and heard the blood pulsing in my ears. I spun around.

He had not changed at all; his hair was shorter, and styled a little differently, but it was still Michael, my Michael, as I always remembered him. He stood there, hands in the pockets of his grey suit, a mocking lazy smile on his face, the sun glinting on the gold chain at his waistcoat pocket.

I just stared and stared. I felt as if I had been hollowed out with a spoon. Finally, I heard myself say: 'What are you doing here?'

He raised an eyebrow. 'This is my home town. You're the one who should be showing your invitation to the footman.' He was enjoying this; he had had time to prepare.

I wanted him to tell me how much he'd missed me, how good I looked. He didn't say any of those things.

Instead: 'Felix is riding well.'

Was he making fun of me? Probably.

'What are you doing here, Michael?'

'I have a new job with the *New York Times*.'

'You must be doing well.'

'Not really. I get by. Only bankers and brokers make money. But I expect you already know that.' Another taunting smile.

'How have you been?' I asked him, not knowing what else to say.

'Fine. How about you?'

'Fine.'

He stared, and I stared right back, and that was how we were when Sophie came over; Sophie, with her ravenous expression and slut's eyes.

'Anna, I see you've met someone interesting. Who's this?'

Damn her. Go away, Sophie. Not now. 'This is Michael Sheridan. He's an old friend of mine, from London. Michael, this is Sophie Rifkin, Felix's sister.'

'Ma'am,' he said, and gave her his special smile, probably for my benefit.

'From London? You don't look English. You don't sound it either.'

'How do the English look?'

'A little more refined,' Sophie said, 'and not as attractive.'

Typical of Sophie to flirt so outrageously with a man she had only just met.

'Are you enjoying the game, Miss Rifkin?' Michael asked her.

'I always enjoy the game,' she said, shamelessly.

I felt my face grow hot. The little trollop. Michael saw me flush and grinned.

'Would you like to join us for a glass of champagne?' Sophie asked. She indicated our little party sitting on deckchairs near the Hispano-Suiza, the wicker picnic hamper balanced on the running board.

He saw Rachel, scampering in the grass after someone's puppies. His expression changed. 'Is she your daughter?' he said to me.

I nodded, did not know what to say to him.

'She's beautiful,' he said.

'Thank you.'

He turned back to Sophie. 'I would love to have the pleasure of enjoying your hospitality,' he said, 'but I'm afraid it's impossible. Perhaps another time. It was nice to see you again, Anna. And very nice to meet you, Miss Rifkin.' He took off his homburg and gave a slight bow. Charming, when he wanted to be.

As he turned away, I felt a flaring of panic. 'Will I see you again?' I almost shouted it at him.

He just gave me a self-satisfied smile and walked away, without another word. For a moment I almost ran after him. He disappeared among the crowds.

Sophie looked bewildered and, of course, utterly fascinated. 'Who was that really?' she said.

'No-one,' I snapped and went back to join Rachel and Madam Rifkin under the trees. I searched for his face among the crowds for the rest of the afternoon but he had disappeared. I fidgeted in the car on the way home and I couldn't sleep at all that night. Felix, I'm sure, wondered what was wrong, and I thought dear little Sophie was certain to tell him. But sometimes people surprise you. She didn't say a word.

276

The Waldorf-Astoria had been built in 1893, red brick and sandstone in the German Renaissance style. Before they pulled it down it stood on the corner of Fifth Avenue and 33rd Street, facing a wide and tree-lined pavement that was always crowded with black and white chequered cabs.

The management kept a private suite where the women of New York could go to deceive their husbands. The drapes were kept permanently closed, the lighting discreet, and no men were ever allowed inside. From ten o'clock in the morning until three o'clock in the afternoon they came, wealthy wives with time on their hands; young blondes wearing too much lipstick and smoking too many cigarettes; middle-aged dowagers with guttural German accents and diamonds on their fingers the size of small rocks; spinsters with sparrow-like movements and dresses to their ankles; wives of doctors, wives of professors, wives of lawyers. They lounged on davenports with pens and notebooks watching two blue-smocked girls changing figures on a blackboard. It was a noisy room, filled with the chatter of scores of women and the clatter of a bank of ticker machines on the far wall. Here they all gathered, my fellow travellers on the American miracle, the Lady Bulls.

The gossip was not of minor infidelities and scandals and clothes and servants. We talked instead about rails and industrials, coalers and grangers, motors and sugars. We cheated on our husbands in the most shameless and fundamental way; we brought home the bacon; we paid our way. They would have preferred us to have screwed the chauffeur.

It was in this room that I lost sight of the destiny I had clung to so tenaciously, for it was here, finally, that I turned profit-taker over princess.

I did not need my father's millions. I could make my own.

MICHAEL

I rented a small apartment in Greenwich Village, close to Union Square. Having just left Moscow, I guess it made me feel at home. Back then the Village was teeming with communists, every day you saw them marching in the street, carrying picket signs in Yiddish and Russian and English, singing the Internationale. Most of them worked in the garment factories that had sprung up in the nearby tenement district. One day I saw the police charge them with horses and take some of the protesters away in paddy wagons. Never a dull moment.

The First World War had changed the whole world, not just the geography of Europe. While France and Germany had been beggared by the war, America had become a creditor nation for the first time in its history. Russia had its workers' revolution; America had a revolution of its own soon after. It was not the proletariat worker but the advertising man who took over the streets.

The clamour and sweep of this new order exploded from the street hoardings and the new and colourful magazines; gramophone players that could play twelve records at once, refrigerators that did away with the need for an icebox, even electric toasters.

The brash new America was reflected in the scandalous new fashions and music. Around America ministers of religion railed against the Charleston and the Black Bottom, which were declared an offence against womanly purity. The modern woman modelled themselves on the 'it' girl, Clara Bow; they plucked their eyebrows, lined their eyes with kohl, smoked and drank and had affairs. When I left America, women's dresses finished just above the ankles; now you could see their suspender belts and garters when they sat down, if you looked hard.

And I did.

Nothing mirrored this new liberalism better than the changes in my own business. Broadsheet newspapers like the *New York Times* were being seriously challenged by smaller, more compact dailies called tabloids, which appealed to people's more prurient appetites, rather than just providing news on politics and current affairs. Bernard McFadden's *Evening Graphic* epitomised the new press, with headlines such as 'TWO NAKED GIRLS BEATEN IN REFORM SCHOOL'.

Conservative America was fighting its rearguard actions at night. Like the rest of the United States, New York had had prohibition since 1920. By the time I arrived there were over thirty thousand speakeasies in New York. That may give you some idea what New Yorkers thought about temperance.

As far as I could see, the only ones who benefited from prohibition were the Sicilians, and they owned machine guns. They also owned a lot of the speakeasies.

The speakeasies were like brothels; everyone knew they were there, they just pretended they didn't. The difference with a speakeasy was that you could take your girlfriend along.

They were everywhere; you'd find them in the basements of Fifth Avenue mansions and in Greenwich Village cellars; in Park Avenue penthouses and behind soft drink parlours; behind restaurants and over barber shops. Over in Harlem you could go to the Cotton Club and watch beautiful half-caste dancing girls – 'high yallers' – doing the Cotton Club Stomp to Duke Ellington's jazz band, or you could slum it at the Sunset Club dancing to Louis Armstrong. The Algonquin set went to Jack and Charlie's Luncheon Club, which sold real imported wines and spirits. But the most exclusive place in town was Club El Fey on West 40th, where the hostess, Texas Guinan, greeted her customers with, 'Hello, suckers!' And she wasn't kidding. A watered-down Scotch would set you back a dollar fifty a glass and you were slugged twenty-five bucks for the aerated cider they called champagne.

Apart from the liquor, the other great thing about the speakeasies was the music. Jazz was the sound of the twenties. I saw Louis Armstrong play once, and when he hit the high notes he would run around the stage punching the air and the crowd just went crazy. None of us had ever seen anything like it. It disgusted people like my father and I guess it was why we liked it so much.

The speakeasies were full of girls in flapper hats and scanty, pencil-slim dresses, jerking bare arms and legs to Negro rhythms of trumpets and brass. While they jiggled and shook on the dance floors, the rich boys who'd brought them smoked cigarettes out of long ivory holders, and tried not to choke.

It was at a basement dive on the Lower East Side that I saw Sophie again. Two in the morning and the place was packed, cigarette smoke thick as gauze. Laughing girls in skimpy, fringed dresses, damp with sweat, crammed in shoulder to shoulder with young men flashing money and cigarettes. A Negro jazz band played frenetically on a narrow stage. It was the last place I expected to see Felix Rifkin's sister, perhaps the last place she expected to see me.

I recognised her at once. She looked like an Asiatic princess, olive skin and a hooked nose, her exotic looks accentuated by a headband with a spray of black osprey feathers. There were diamonds at her throat. Anastasia said about her that she could flirt with a man from a hundred paces when she was only half awake; and it was true, Sophie said everything she had to with her eyes.

I remembered the way she had come on to me at her brother's polo match. But I still wonder what it was that made me go over. Was I interested in Sophie or was it a way of getting back at Anastasia?

'Sophie, isn't it?'

She looked around at me and smiled, as if she hadn't seen me come over. Her smile was as delicious as it was mischievous. Okay, perhaps she found me attractive, but the thought of putting one over her sister-in-law must have made me irresistible. I think we both knew that.

'Michael, isn't it?' she said, mimicking me.

'That's it.'

'From England.'

'From New York. I've been around a bit the last few years.'

'Good for you,' Sophie said. 'So have I.'

I bought her a drink and lit her cigarette for her and we talked. Of course, the first thing she wanted to know was how I was acquainted with her brother's wife. I danced around that one a bit.

'We met in Shanghai,' I told her. 'I was working for a small newspaper over there.'

'Were you lovers?' She rolled this last word around her tongue, drawing it out.

'No,' I said, but she didn't believe me. Little minx.

Sophie was a looker, let me tell you. Hair the colour of coal, fashionably bobbed, to-hell-with-you eyes and a mouth like a bruised plum. Her dress revealed most of her arms, which were long and very brown. She could have had any man in the room. The way she talked, she gave the impression she already had.

A high yaller was dancing on one of the tables. I savoured the moment. I knew where this was headed straight off. Such a twist of fate was as rich and potent as illicit brandy.

Sophie leaned in close. 'Does my brother know about you?' she breathed.

'There's nothing to know.'

'Not the way she looked at you at the polo field. You're more than old friends.'

'We go back a long way.'

'But you're not the kind of man to kiss and tell.'

'No.'

'So if you were to kiss me, you wouldn't tell anyone?'

'Would you?'

She bit her lip. 'Why? Are you worried about your reputation?'

'I don't have one in New York.'

'Would you like to have one?'

She was more than a little drunk. I would be taking unfair advantage. Did I feel ashamed of myself? Not really. I'm a man, conscience is something we only suffer from when things go wrong. And there was a reservoir of spite built up over the last five years.

'Does Felix know you're here tonight?' I asked her.

'I'm old enough to do what I please,' she said and there

was both challenge and invitation in those fathomless black eyes. And I was not the kind of man who would refuse either.

I woke up next morning to Sophie's dark curls on my pillow. I could hear her softly breathing. I kissed the curve of her shoulder and she murmured softly in her sleep. I still wasn't sure how I felt about this. Not the first time I'd had a stranger's head on my pillow, but this was not just a single man's licence. I had made some sort of statement here.

She opened one eye. 'You're thinking,' she said.

I traced the contours of her spine with a finger. 'Thinking about you.'

'You're thinking how you can get me out of here without promising to marry me.' She turned towards me, ran her fingers through the hair on my chest, and one long pink fingernail followed the line of muscle down my stomach to my groin. The corners of her mouth curled into a most unladylike smile.

She rolled onto her back, and the sheet fell away, revealing the soft curve of her breast. She covered herself up again, quickly, as if it had been an accident.

I tried to kiss her but she pushed me away. She got up, taking the sheet with her, which she wrapped around her body. She pulled back the curtains. A hard, bright day in New York. I felt naked with the curtains open; perhaps because I was. I got up, found my dressing gown hanging on the back of the bathroom door.

'How Bohemian,' she said, looking around the room, the ancient armoire, the faded curtains, the worn carpet.

'It's not the Ritz.'

She gave a little scream. 'My God,' she said, pointing, 'what's that?'

'It's just a roach.'

'I thought it was a dog. How can you live like this?'

'Most of New York lives like this. Didn't you know that?'

'Most of New York doesn't have manners and breeding.' She found a packet of de Rezke cigarettes on the table and put one in her mouth. It was my cue to produce a light for her.

'Do you ever smoke when you're on your own?' I asked her.

'Sometimes. Why?'

'Just wondering if you knew how to light one,' I found a box of matches on the bedside table and lit it for her.

She seemed to like being insulted. Darling Sophie. She held the cigarette poised in the air, like incense. I put my arm around her and this time she didn't try to wriggle away. It was cool in the room, and there was gooseflesh on her skin. I put my arms around her, kissed the long curve of her neck, each tiny mound along her spine, breathed in the warm fragrance of her hair, the mustier scents of last night's love-making.

The horns and clatter of Greenwich Village outside the window were suddenly a long way away. I slipped my hands under the bed sheet, felt her nipples growing hard under my hands. I kissed her neck again and she sighed.

'Why did you bring me here, Michael?'

I had been around long enough to know that when a man wants to make love and a woman wants to talk, trouble isn't far away. With your hands on a woman's body, you can't think straight, and they take advantage of you. Sophie wasn't the kind of girl who wanted to hear me tell her I loved her. Still, you could never be sure about that.

'Are you sorry?'

'I don't know. It depends on your reasons. Was last night about me, or about Anastasia?'

I didn't answer straightaway, because I didn't know how to. She pushed herself away and sat down on the bed.

'How much did she tell you about me?'

'She won't talk about you at all. Which means there must be an awful lot to tell.'

'Did she tell you how she met your brother?'

She shook her head. 'He went to London to tidy up some domestic affairs and came back with a Grand Duchess.'

'You believe that?'

'Of course not. I think she's just a little gold-digger. Hit a rich vein with my brother, didn't she?' My beautiful Sophie had a pinched and vicious look about her this morning. Perhaps it was the light. 'What was she doing in Shanghai?'

'She was a refugee. She didn't have much money. I looked after her for a while.'

'She always lands on her feet, doesn't she?' Sophie said, and gave me a knowing look.

I didn't like the way she said that. But perhaps she was right, my princess was just a manipulative minx.

'You still love her, don't you?'

She crossed her legs. Hard for a man to think straight when a woman does that, too. Was I really over Anastasia? How could I be?

'You should forget about her.'

'I have. You're the one who keeps talking about her.'

'Because I know what she's really like. She has my brother on a string, she still has you moon-eyed after all this time. Men really are stupid, aren't they?'

'I can't argue with that.'

She turned around to find an ashtray and the sheet fell away from her shoulders. How can you think straight when you have just been afforded the promise of a coffee-brown nipple?

'Do you know how old Rachel is?'

This came at me from nowhere. Sophie saw the look on my face and gave me a vicious smile. She was a poisonous little witch. God doesn't give perfect breasts only to angels, apparently.

'Rachel.'

'Their daughter,' she said, prompting me, and I remembered the little girl I had seen at the polo field, and now I tried to think back, picture her more clearly.

'She'll be five years old in October,' Sophie said.

'I don't understand.'

'Think about it.'

Five years old in October. Born in October, 1924. Back nine months: January. Anna and I, in the flat in Kensington.

I felt suddenly dizzy and sick. The little girl I had seen running across the polo field was my daughter.

'Aren't you going to say anything?'

But there was nothing to say. My throat had closed up and I couldn't speak.

I threw the first thing that came to hand. The sofa cushion didn't do enough damage. I followed up with the lamp.

'I'm sorry,' Sophie said. She seemed appalled by what she had done. She ran into the bathroom. I heard her crying through the door.

I stood in the middle of the room and tried to imagine what was going through Anastasia's head when she did this to me. She must have known she was pregnant with my child. And not a word. She still walked out, never told me, never meant for me to know.

Perhaps she thought I would not want to know, I thought, already rushing to her defence, an unfortunate habit of mine. It's true some men would not have approved.

But I was not some men. I wanted to marry her. Didn't she know that?

I dressed quickly and went out. I walked for hours through the Village, but even today I cannot tell you where I went or what I did. All I could think about was Anastasia, trying to understand what she had done and why. When I came back Sophie was gone.

ANASTASIA

Sophie dragged herself out of bed just before noon, appeared in the dining room in a pale blue silk dressing gown with a Chinese dragon embroidered on the back. She drifted around like a wraith, smoking a cigarette from an ivory holder. There were dark bruises under her eyes and she carried around with her an air of dissolution. I imagined it draped around her like a tattered battle flag.

'Where was it last night? Morgan's? The Cotton Club?' I recognised spite and envy in my voice. I resented her having such a good time while I played the dutiful wife.

She blew out a long stream of smoke. 'God knows where I was. It's all a blur, darling.'

'Does Felix know?'

'Only if you tell him.'

Why did I hate Sophie so much? Because she was having fun; because she didn't have a five-year-old daughter; because she wasn't married to Felix.

'Guess who I saw?' Sophie said, pouring herself a dry martini. Barely noon, for God's sake.

'Who?' More gossip about our incestuous little circle of rich friends.

'Michael Sheridan.'

Like a blasphemy, hearing Sophie say his name. I knew Michael would never suffer for female company, but to think of him with Sophie, well, I couldn't bear it. Irrational, perhaps, but there it was.

I wanted to scratch out her eyes. Instead I pretended to read my magazine.

'I can understand why you were attracted to him,' she said.

'Really?'

'I've never had a man kiss me like that.'

I felt my fingernails bite into the flesh of my palms.

'What I don't understand,' Sophie said, 'is why you let him go.'

'What did he tell you? About me?'

'Not much. He's the strong, silent type. But the way you looked at him the other day at the treading-in, it's obvious there was something between you.'

'Stay away from him, Sophie.' I couldn't help myself, the words just came out.

'What was that again?'

'He's no good for you.'

'Oh, I think he could be.'

'Just stay away from him!'

Sophie gave me her special look. She was enjoying this so much. How delicious to have something your despised sister-in-law secretly wanted for herself. '*Au contraire*, sweet. The attraction is purely physical. He's such a man, if you know what I mean. And an absolute animal in the boudoir. A stud.'

I was shocked. Not Sophie's style to be quite so blatant at home.

'Nothing against darling Felix, of course, he's my brother and I love him madly. But he must be a bit of a

286

cold fish by comparison, surely. Or do you have little secrets you don't want me to know about?'

'You have a dirty little mouth.'

'That's what Michael says. Only in a rather more appreciative tone.'

I wanted to hit her, and perhaps she wanted me to. The imprint of my hand would not stand out quite as pinkly as it would on my own pale Slavic skin, but it would still be a formidable battle scar to parade before her mama. And it would mean she had won.

And I did miss Michael. I didn't know what I had until I threw it away, and then it took the passage of a year to fully impress itself on me. I had never considered myself a passionate creature; I was content to be calculating. I don't know when I changed. Somewhere I lost the coldness necessary for survival.

When I thought about him in bed with Sophie I hated her, and I hated him. It was an image I was unable to bear. Perhaps I had sacrificed too much for Anastasia.

Sophie bit speculatively on a fingernail. 'I love his hands. Big hands for a man.'

'For God's sake, Sophie.'

'I'm just picking up the pieces. No-one to blame but yourself.'

'You're jealous of me and Felix.'

'Not jealous, sweet. I think you're a gold-digger. You were only ever using him and the way you still feel about Michael only proves it, doesn't it?'

There is nothing anyone can say that will hurt you worse than the truth. Bluster all I might, I knew she was right about me. Slapping her face, throttling her senseless, as I would like to have done, was not going to change that.

I slapped her anyway. It was what she wanted, after all, and it made me feel better. Otherwise I would not have been able to sleep that night at all. She gave me a look – a sneer, really – and flounced out of the room. I knew I had just made a complete fool of myself. And whatever hurt I was feeling, well, I had it coming.

MICHAEL

I followed them from their apartment on the Upper East Side to Central Park. She was skipping, holding the hand of her grey-uniformed nanny, who was slim and shingled and not at all like the nanny I had when I was her age, a roly-poly Irish woman with an accent that could have cut glass and the makings of a beard.

I kept a discreet distance as they crossed Park Avenue and walked down the leafy boulevards of the park. The young woman in grey sat on a bench while Rachel chased ducks around the pond. I stood on the bridge, smoking a cigarette, and watched.

My daughter was a dumpling, with a mop of fair hair, dimpled knees, and a face like a cherub. There was nothing of me in her at all. Good for her. In fact, there was an uncanny resemblance to the photographs I had seen of the young Anastasia, though I knew it must be my imagination, for I was now convinced my Anna had never been royal.

It was never my intention to let Rachel see me, or to say a word to her. So after a while I just walked away. The sunlight was dappled through the branches, the hum of the city was muted; all any passing stranger would have seen was a man walking with his head down, distracted by his own thoughts.

Something happened to me in New York. I started playing games. Anger, I suppose. I got a delicious thrill out of it, while hating myself for my duplicity.

Like a chess master, I kept two games going at once; Anastasia on one hand, my father on the other. I imagined myself a tactical genius, a feint here, a double play there. I took perverse satisfaction from it.

Sophie stayed over for the night at my apartment in Greenwich Village. It must have been difficult for her; no gold fittings on the bath faucets, no-one to buff her toenails or bring cold compresses for her headache. I had no illusions about what she thought about me or my apartment; my new girlfriend was slumming it.

She rose after lunch, as usual. I hardly ever saw her eat. The only sustenance the poor girl got were the olives out of her martinis.

When she was finally bathed and primped and perfumed and recovered from the previous night's drinking and dancing – about three in the afternoon – we took a taxi to the Upper East Side. I didn't even tell her where we were going.

Time to say hello to the old man.

I had been in New York for almost a week and my family had not heard from me since I turned down Davis's offer of a ride into the city. I had not seen them for nearly a decade and this was our reunion, me showing up unannounced at four o'clock in the afternoon with my good-time girlfriend. Poor Sophie.

I should have gone alone but I knew it would really disgust my parents if I took my slutty rich-girl Jewess. Why do we do these things? Everything with the old man was a test, wanting him to prove to me he wasn't the pompous asshole I thought he was. He never passed a single one of the tests, of course. But I didn't come off much better this time around, provoking him, using Sophie as bait.

'What's going on?' she asked me, as our cab pulled up outside the marble mansion on Fifth.

'I said I'd stop by and see Dad,' I explained, pulling her out onto the sidewalk.

'With me?'

'Why not?'

Sophie was thrown. She looked up at the gingerbread balconies and towering windowpanes, four floors of them. She bit her lip. 'Well, all right, godammit,' she said, and for the first time I felt a surge of real affection for her. I don't know why, something in the spirit of the girl. A real trooper, my Sophie.

We were met at the door by the old man's new butler, and ushered into a marble hall. A grey-uniformed maid took my coat and Sophie's wrap. Another maid, slightly older, inspected Sophie with the disapproval of a Lexington Avenue matron.

The butler, Phillips, led us upstairs. I took Sophie's hand, it was damp.

He took us into the first-floor drawing room, burgundy velvet curtains drawn across towering windows the height of four men. The walls were crowded with Raphael paintings and Renaissance tapestries. Yellow roses were elaborately arranged in a crystal vase on an antique table. Their scent did not quite overcome the smell of furniture polish.

I had seen the room countless times as a child, but I had never realised: it looked like a Venetian bordello.

And there he was.

He hadn't changed that much; more grey in the hair, the Silver Fox they called him on the Street, probably made up the name himself and got a minion to spread it around. He wore a French-cuffed white shirt with heavy gold cufflinks and a striped silk tie. There was a gold signet ring on the little finger of his left hand. He looked rich and imposing and forbidding.

After nine years I got a cool, dry handshake and a swift appraising glance. Was I expecting more? You could say we deserved each other.

Mother was at her icy best, pearls and a Chanel gown and French perfume coming at you in waves. We all sat down and the servants brought tea and sandwiches.

It took us about five minutes to talk through the years. They didn't want to know a great deal about Shanghai or Berlin or Moscow or my career in something as vulgar as the newspaper business. I had the impression they were looking for newsprint stains on my fingers. For myself, I wasn't much interested in how much richer the old man was, or how well my brother had fitted into the firm.

It was all very polite. They asked me where I was staying and when I told them, I thought the old man would choke on his tea. A Sheridan living in Greenwich Village; I don't know if he felt insulted or just astonished.

During the hour I stayed, there was no weeping or embracing or heart-to-heart exchanges. The good name of the

Sheridans would not be sullied in front of someone as common as a Rifkin. We drank our tea and chatted politely and then I left, with a promise to return shortly. I had outmanoeuvred the Silver Fox by bringing an interloper to the reunion.

I departed with my soul in tatters and my smile in place.

'I didn't realise you were one of *the* Sheridans,' Sophie said.

'Well, it's not an uncommon name.'

'Felix talks about your father as if he's some sort of god.'

'The old man would want it that way.'

As the cab sped away, I cast a diseased eye at my father's Fifth Avenue world, the fake French chateau on the corner of 45th, the crenellated brick towers and slit windows of Carnegie's medieval fortress, the elegant mansions of the New World barons. We headed downtown towards the earthier corners of the city, where Michael Sheridan still held out for independence.

'What happened between you, Michael?' Sophie asked. 'Did they throw you out?'

'No, I left.'

'Why?'

'If it doesn't sound too pompous, I wanted to live my life on my own terms.'

She was quiet for a while. Then she said: 'You could have been rich.'

'Money isn't free.'

'But don't you miss it?'

'Miss what?'

'Life could be so much easier for you, Michael.'

'Is your life easy?'

'Of course it is,' she said. If someone thinks that having everything easy is all there is to life, you're never going to persuade them differently. They have to find out for themselves. The lucky ones never do.

'I really don't understand you,' she said.

'Why I'm a journalist and not on Wall Street with my father?'

Sophie's expression irritated me. New Yorkers prostrate themselves before money. When people worship wealth so blindly, the people who have it are treated like gods, no matter how they came by it. I hated the way people fawned over my father; he's a pig, and he likes being a pig, he's turned it into an art form, but no-one will tell him to his face because he's so damned rich. A sorry case of the Emperor's new clothes.

I stared out of the cab window, at this new New York. Advertising hoardings everywhere now, smoke Lucky Strike cigarettes, eat HO oatmeal, shop at Bloomingdale's. Everything was about money. 'I despise him,' I said.

'The way he looks at you. He adores you.'

'More fool him.'

'You don't mean that.'

'You don't know anything about my life, so just shut the hell up.'

I hadn't meant to snap at her. I guess the occasion of the prodigal son's return had affected me more deeply than I thought. She fell silent and from the corner of my eye I saw an astonishing thing. She was crying.

'I'm sorry,' I said.

I think it was then that I belatedly decided to treat her as a human being and not a pawn in the little mind game I was having with Anna. What did I hope to achieve? My affair with Sophie was just an ugly act of spite against a woman I loved. I should be ashamed to confess these things about myself, and I am. As for my father, what was I trying to prove?

'It's a long story,' I said, gently, trying to make the peace.

She shrugged her shoulders, as if she didn't care whether she heard it or not.

A deep breath. 'My father deals in stock issues and bonds and mortgages. I feel he has had a mortgage on me from the day I was born. I was always told that one day I would be a partner in the firm, as if it was preordained. I wanted the freedom to choose.'

'Is that the way it works?'

'For me it does. I wanted to be able to look at myself in the mirror, know I had made my own way in the world.' I didn't think Sophie would understand that. How could she? She had no ambition beyond finding the next good time.

'That's pretty hard on them, Michael.'

'I can't help that. Everything I have, I got myself. I have a career, a flat in London, and some money in my pocket, not much, but it's mine. I'm considered a good journalist in my own circles. I like that. But I'm not James Barrington Sheridan the second, that's for sure.'

'What's going to happen when he dies?'

'My brother gets all the money, I guess.'

'I mean I wonder if you'll feel this bitter when he's gone.'

'How you feel is how you feel.'

Perhaps that was what rankled with Anastasia. She wanted everything I had given up.

Too much champagne. Sophie sitting on my lap, her bobbed hair tickling my cheek, the room reeking of smoke and booze. A black jazz band whooping it up on stage, my own money gone, Sophie tucking a wad of bills in my shirt and saying, 'Tonight's on Felix,' and calling the waiter over for more drinks.

Good and drunk, floating through another wasted night, the promise of boozy sex later. Welcome to the life of Michael Sheridan, independent self-made man, paying for drinks with money from his lover's brother.

'Does she know you're with me?' I shouted in Sophie's ear over the noise of the band.

Sophie shrugged her shoulders by way of answer.

'Does she ever try to stop you?'

But Sophie did not want to talk about it, and another glass of shampoo disappeared.

'Is she happy?'

Sophie put her arms about my neck, her tongue explored my mouth.

I remembered how I had preached to her about living my own life, about freedom. The biggest hypocrite in the world reached for another glass of champagne, thinking of Anastasia, his hand around Sophie Rifkin's waist, her soft breast rubbing against his arm.

Anastasia took me by surprise, as I am sure she intended. Not exactly at my best at that hour of the morning, after a night at the speakeasies; threadbare dressing gown, bare feet, unshaven, just out of bed. Very little sleep. I opened the door and there she was, a vision in a filmy black dress, Perri gloves and black Milan straw turban from which a blonde curl had been teased to lie provocatively between her cheek and the collar of her coat. She wore an ermine wrap, and lipstick glistened on her mouth like fresh blood.

And those ice blue eyes, eyes that missed nothing. As she looked me up and down I had never felt so naked or so mean. Her lips gave the slightest twist downwards in verdict of me and my present circumstances.

'Are you going to ask me in?' she said.

I stood aside.

'Slumming it in the Village?'

'You need a mat on the inside of the door,' she said, 'so people can wipe their feet on the way out.'

'We can't all live on Fifth Avenue.'

'I'm surprised they let you drive on it.' She took off her gloves, a finger at a time, like a surgeon after a particularly messy operation. She held them in one manicured hand, and looked around for somewhere to sit. I watched her, hands in the pockets of my dressing gown. Damn her, I wasn't about to rush around after her like her butler.

'Haven't we got precious?' I said to her. 'You've lived in worse than this.'

'Only when I was sleeping on the street. Don't you ever clean up?'

'Doesn't seem much point.'

'Do you have coffee?'

'Think so.'

'May I have some?'

We regarded each other, as bitter enemies. I had never forgiven her for what she had done and her only defence before me was to pretend I was insufferable.

I went into the kitchen, put coffee in a grinder, a pot on

the stove. It was early, but there was a hum to the street already, New York waking up and going about its business. I had been in a speakeasy until two, had shamelessly allowed Sophie to pay again. At twenty-five dollars for apple juice, the dives Sophie liked were out of my league.

Anastasia stood by the window, looking down at the street. From there she also had a view of the bedroom through the half-open door. She was hoping to find Sophie there, embarrass us both, but she must have slipped out just after dawn.

'So you left Reuters?'

'The *Times* offered me more money, if you can believe it. Reuters had parcelled me off to Moscow. Most miserable God-damned city I've ever been in. But you didn't come here to talk about that.'

'No, I didn't. I came to talk about Sophie.'

'Is that any business of yours?'

'Are you trying to make me jealous, Michael?'

The answer was yes, but I feigned outrage, and I can do that very well. 'That's a little presumptuous, don't you think?'

'There are a lot of women in New York. Why Sophie?'

'You think this is about you? I see you've picked up a little Fifth Avenue arrogance along with the dead polecats you're wearing.'

'It's ermine.'

'Yes, how is life on the sunny side of the street?'

A hint, a suspicion, of tenderness on her face. 'Michael, you would have hated me if I'd stayed. There's never a day I don't think about you.'

'Really? Because I've never given you a thought in five years.'

'Then why are you doing this?'

'This has nothing to do with you, princess.'

'Don't call me that.'

She was right. Once I'd called her that out of affection. Now it sounded as if I was mocking her. Perhaps I was.

'How are things on that front? Sophie tells me your husband has a lawyer on the job now. You might have your day in court at last.'

She shrugged her shoulders as if, after everything that had happened, she didn't care.

'Does Felix think you can win?'

'It's not a question of winning. I'm claiming what is rightfully mine.'

'Which is what? What is there to claim? The throne of a country that no longer exists? The money and the jewels are gone.'

'It's not about money.'

'Did Felix tell you that?'

'He doesn't need money.'

'Never met a rich man who doesn't want more. That's the nature of it. I know from experience.'

'You've always been such a cynic.'

'And you've always been such a dreamer.'

'You started all this, Michael. Don't you regret it now?'

'It didn't have to be this way.'

She didn't say anything, which irritated me.

'Wasn't it enough for me to love you?' I asked her.

'I couldn't just be Mrs Sheridan.'

'Does it matter who you are as long as you love who you're with?'

They say a good lawyer never asks a question he doesn't already know the answer to. I thought I knew what she would say. But instead, she murmured: 'Yes, it does matter. Back then it mattered to me very much.'

'Well, I guess we have nothing more to say to each other then.'

She put on her gloves. 'I have to go.'

'You don't want your coffee?'

'I hoped I could talk to you, Michael. It's clear you're still angry with me, and I don't blame you. What I did was unforgivable. But I had my reasons.'

I didn't say anything.

'I'll let myself out,' she said.

After she left I stood there for a long time staring at the door. I hated myself for what I'd said to her and I was sorry she had gone. Being vicious to her face was better than standing here in the silence with fury burning in my gut like a cancer and nothing I could do about it, and nowhere for all that rage to go.

ANASTASIA

I shudder even now to think about what I did and the poisonous emotion that caused me to move in that direction. For one moment I truly was Anastasia again, the little girl who tripped servants and pulled her cousins' hair.

It was certainly one of the less honorable moments in a life founded mostly on unprincipled survival. I knew what Felix would do if he found out about Michael and Sophie; but he didn't know, would never know unless someone told him. That someone did not have to be me.

It wasn't something Felix forced out of me in the heat of the moment. I cannot lay claim to duress. I planned it for days, going broodily about the house, letting him know that I was upset. The trap was carefully laid.

He was usually too tired from work to notice my moods. But finally, one night, in our fashionable Art Deco bedroom with its yellow sconces and Egyptian statuettes, he tackled me about it. He emerged from the bathroom in silk pyjamas, hands thrust into the pockets of a crimson brocade dressing gown, and I knew he had got the message. I was combing out my hair in front of the dressing table mirror.

'What's wrong?' he asked.

'Wrong?'

'You've been sulking all evening.'

All evening? More like a week. But I pretended not to know what he was talking about, and let him force it out of me.

'It's Michael. He's back in New York.'

He turned a little pale, I believe. Michael was a subject we had chosen to avoid in the five years of our marriage, with good reason. I was sure Felix knew that Rachel was not his child, but we had an unspoken agreement to preserve the pretence of her paternity. 'You've seen him?'

I nodded.

'When?'

'He was at the polo match last month.'

A petulant expression; Felix, the little boy who did not like to be crossed. A man should not pout when he is in his pyjamas, he looks ridiculous. 'Why didn't you tell me this before?'

'I didn't want to upset you.'

'How considerate.'

'He means nothing to me any more,' I said and wondered at how easily the lie came to my lips. There had been so many convincing performances over the years.

'Has he been hounding you?'

'Not me,' I said.

There was a sudden colour to his cheeks. 'What do you mean?'

'Sophie,' I said, and let that one word state the case for me. I watched his face undergo a transformation as he made the necessary mental leaps, calculating Michael's intentions. Perhaps they were the motives I had ascribed to Michael, too. It never occurred to me then, and in fairness it may not have occurred to Michael either, that he actually felt any affection for Felix's sister.

'He's been seeing her?'

A nod.

'How do you know all this?'

'She tells me.'

'You don't think . . . that she's . . . that there's anything going on?'

A polite euphemism for the sensational sex Sophie had described to me.

'Well, you know Sophie,' I said.

'The bastard.'

'I'm sorry, Felix. I thought it best that you know,' I said, in a voice so cloyingly sweet I made myself sick. And that was it, really. It was all I had to do. Like every

298

good chess player I knew the moves several plays ahead. As I said, I despise myself sometimes. But there was nothing else to be done about it. It was unthinkable for Sophie to be happy with the man I loved.

Over the years Felix had gained a lot of weight, had become more fleshy than imposing. His sober Wall Street suits and diamond tie pins made him look soft rather than well-heeled. He towered over me, but even when he was angry as he was now, he never intimidated me the way Andrei had done.

He had come home early from the office to berate his sister. He could not have signalled the extent of his fury more clearly than by being home at six o'clock.

He patrolled the living room, martini in hand. The russet treetops of Central Park were visible through the open window. Sophie sat pigeon-toed on the Chesterfield, peremptorily summoned from her bedroom, where she had been preening herself for another night at the speakeasies. She looked unspeakably radiant.

'You've been seeing Michael Sheridan,' were Felix's first words.

Felix was accustomed to us all obeying him without question. He had an air of divine superiority that rankled with me. Now, even as he was firing the bullets I had made for him, I wanted Sophie to stand up to him.

I wasn't disappointed.

'What has it to do with you?' she said.

Felix stopped pacing and glared at her, further enraged by the tone she had taken with him. 'Do you know who that man is?'

'He's the son of one of the most influential share brokers in New York.'

'He's a drinker and a womaniser and a waster. I forbid you to see him any more.'

'I'll do exactly as I please,' Sophie said, and as much as I hated her I wanted to cheer for her, too. Perhaps

I was envious of her spirit; mine had been lost during the last five years, sold, or given away.

'On the contrary,' Felix replied. 'You'll do exactly as I please if you want to continue your present lavish lifestyle. You have it easy here, Sophie. I don't mind that, and I've given you a long leash. But you will not defy me in this.'

He stood over her, confident that she would buckle under. I thought his confidence was not misplaced. We all knew what Sophie wanted. She would scream and rage, but she would do as she was told if her line of credit was threatened.

Perhaps it was the part about the leash that antagonised her. She stood up and looked her brother in the eye. 'I love him,' she said.

'Love?' Felix sneered. 'How long have you known him? Two weeks?'

'So?'

'He'll use you like a dirty rag and go back to London when he's done.'

'Is that what you're worried about?'

'You know what this is about,' Felix said. There was a grim determination in his face. Neither of them could afford to back down. 'You spend your money on dresses and hats and shoes and champagne. You've had a good time, haven't you, and it's me who pays the bills.'

She was frightened now, I doubt she had ever considered a life outside the privileged circle. 'You don't own me, Felix,' she said, her voice choked.

'I pay for your upkeep. That's about the same thing in my book.'

Sophie spared me a look of such pure hatred I shall never forget it. Then she turned back to her brother. 'You can't tell me what to do.'

'I can and I will. I forbid you to see him. Defy me, and I'll throw you out on your ear. Have you got that?'

Poor Sophie; she'd never seen this side of Felix before. But you didn't get where he had in life without a streak of ruthlessness. 'Mother wouldn't allow it,' she said.

'Try me,' Felix said.

And that was all it took.

Felix often invited clients and business associates home for dinner parties. It was the crudest kind of social climbing, mixing business with what passed in some circles as pleasure. My function at these evenings was to look glamorous and talk pleasantly with the women about the latest fashion or charity fundraising and gossip about the social scene. It was stupefyingly tedious.

There were three couples that night; one of them was Felix's business partner, a man named Jacob Geller, and his dismal wife, Vivian. His lawyer, Martin Lachter, was also there with his wife, and a third couple I had never met before. This man's name was Peter Beard, and Felix had extended the invitation because Lachter hoped he might somehow help us with our claim in the German courts. It was not clear exactly how this was to be achieved.

Beard was not what any hostess might wish for as the ideal dinner guest. He and his wife were quiet, even restrained. He had deep, black eyes that I didn't trust and his hair was parted with a slide rule.

I now realise he must have been intensely curious to meet me. I was not the celebrity in New York that Anna Andersen was; I was regarded as a rather charming fraud, and less of a problem socially than Miss Andersen because Felix had his own standing among New York's inner circle. My looks, frankly, also helped me gain general acceptance. Felix's devotion to me and the court case in which he had invested so much of his money was seen as droll eccentricity. We were indulged by our friends, and my legal claim to be a grand duchess was treated with pleasant condescension. By then, of course, even I had begun to doubt the veracity of it. The passage of time and the world's indifference had eroded my belief.

I still wonder now how Beard felt about it.

I had no premonition when I met him. He was just another of my husband's tedious acquaintances. I had not the faintest idea just how rich he was, or how powerful.

He appeared to be another of those bland bankers that Felix cultivated through his work; urbane, impeccably groomed and as frigid as cold fat. When he spoke his words were clipped and precise as if he was making a statement to the police. And his accent; certainly not an Englishman, though he obviously wanted to be.

His wife reminded me of something Michael had said of an English baroness he had met in Shanghai: puckered at both ends. She would occasionally mouth some platitude in the singular way the English upper class has perfected.

I could feel Beard watching me through the evening, but I was accustomed to such behaviour. Despite the veneer of respectability that Felix had afforded me, I was just a glamorous pretender who had made a fortuitous marriage.

Inevitably, as we were drinking our coffees after the meal, Lachter turned the conversation, with little subtlety, to the real business of the evening: my claim to the Romanov titles.

'We have filed papers in Hanover,' Lachter said. 'But the date for hearing has been delayed many times. The Duke of Hesse is using all his resources to stall us. His actions are based on self-interest, of course. He has many friends in Germany.'

Beard seemed unwilling to get involved in this discussion. He must have known when he received his invitation that pressure would be brought to bear on him during the evening, but he did not look like a man easily intimidated by a little crude arm-twisting.

Lachter turned to him. 'We wondered if you might approach the Grand Duchess Olga. You have connections at Windsor and with the Russian Monarchist Council, I believe. Our Anastasia here has been ill treated, and it is time justice was done.'

Beard looked surprised only for a moment by Lachter's blatant appeal, but quickly recovered his poise. 'I shall talk to her, certainly,' he said, lying to Lachter's face, 'but I cannot promise you anything. Grand Duchess Olga is a lady of her own mind.'

'You know the Grand Duchess?' I asked him, surprised.

'I advised her on financial matters in my position as a governor at the Bank of England.'

I got a look from Felix: he would rather I remained purely decorous during such discussions. But that is not the way I was made. 'Excuse me, I did not realise you held such an exalted position,' I said, and he afforded us all a smile that was meant to appear modest. 'Still,' I went on, 'I would have thought she would have chosen an advisor from her own inner circle.'

Lachter blinked at me in surprise. 'You didn't know?' he said.

'Know what?'

'Mr Beard served on Nicholas's – your father's – cabinet for a time as finance minister.'

'So you're Russian,' I said to him.

'By birth. I anglicised my name, of course. In England, if you have a foreign name, people treat you like the most damnable fool.'

Everyone laughed politely at this.

'When did you leave Russia?'

'A year before the Revolution.'

'That was very clever of you,' I said. It was wicked of me to say it in such a way, it implied that he was a coward.

'The Czar sent me to London on business,' he said, stiffly. 'I was unable to return.'

More sympathetic nods. Why were they toadying to him? It was obvious why he left Russia, and it would not have been by royal command. He had run for his life.

'I have great sympathy for your cause, Your Highness, and I would certainly help you if I could.'

I smiled, as much in admiration for his cloying insincerity as anything else. He would not lift a finger, of course, but there was no sense in alienating me, if there was the smallest chance the suit might come to something.

'You said you anglicised your name,' I said, even though I felt Felix's eyes on me, willing me to be still.

'What was your Russian name?'

'Bardenov,' he said, with a tight smile and nod of the head, as if introducing himself once more. 'Petr Bardenov.'

'Otma.'

I looked around to see who had spoken, and then realised it was me. I had no idea what it meant or what had made me say it. Everyone was staring at me for explanation. The effect on Beard was sudden and dramatic. He turned pale and a sheen of sweat erupted on his forehead. He affected the most sickly smile I had ever seen on any man to disguise his discomfort.

'Are you all right?' Lachter said.

'Quite,' he said and gave the lawyer a withering stare.

'What was that you just said?' Felix asked me.

The strangest thing: it meant nothing to me. Otma. My Russian was not as fluent as it had once been but I knew it was not a Russian word.

I excused myself and went to the bathroom. My body was damp with perspiration. I felt light-headed, thought for a moment I was going to be sick. Otma. What did it mean?

I retired early, made some excuse about feeling unwell, hinted strongly enough that it might be woman's troubles so that our guests would not harp about it. The atmosphere in the dining room was tense as I left.

Apparently, Beard and his wife made their excuses early and went, followed soon after by the Gellers and the Lachters. When Felix came to bed I pretended to be asleep, but I lay awake for hours.

It finally occurred to me that Otma was not a word but an anagram. Olga, Tatiana, Marie, Anastasia: the first letters of the names of the Czar's four daughters. I must have heard it spoken somewhere. But why had I said it to Beard, and why had the word affected him like it had?

I had at last chanced upon a fragment of the past I

had lost. Beard's reaction had convinced me of that. But who could help me learn more?

No-one was in a position to take me seriously. Certainly not Felix, who courted Beard in business and wanted to use his influence to get us a fair hearing in Hanover. And not Lachter, who was clearly out of his depth and was really only the circus ringmaster; he knew company law better than anyone on the Street, but filing a suit in a foreign country involving a claim against the royal throne of Czarist Russia was a little rich for the blood of most New York lawyers, not just Lachter. Still, Felix had presented him with a cow, and like a good Harvard man, he was intent on milking it until it died.

But Michael might help me. He had to help me. There was a chance of a story and a smell of scandal in this; even if he had had enough Anastasias for one lifetime, and even though he hated me, I felt certain he would not turn his back on Peter Beard and Otma.

We arranged to meet in Central Park. A wild autumn day, the wind cold and strong and blowing from the north east, raising wavelets on the lake.

Michael arrived, head down into the wind, the collar of his overcoat pulled up around his face, and his hat down over his ears. He came and stood beside me, without saying a word. 'We should have met in a coffee shop,' he said, finally.

'I didn't know the weather was going to be like this.'

He leaned against the rail of the bridge. 'So what do you want?'

'Your help.'

He gave a short, barking laugh. 'You're rich.'

'I'm serious.'

'I should just walk away right now. This is crazy.'

'I wouldn't ask if this wasn't going to help you, as well.'

'You take my breath away.'

'The other night Felix brought a friend of his home,' I said, ignoring the face he made. 'The man's name was Beard. His real name is Petr Bardenov and he was my fath . . . he was the Czar's finance minister during the war. He changed his name to Beard, Peter Beard. As late as last year he was a governor of the Bank of England.'

'And?'

'He knows something, Michael. I want you to meet him, and I want you to say one word to him.'

He sighed. 'You have to forget about all this, Anna. It's been nearly ten years, for God's sake . . .'

'Say Otma.'

'What's Otma?'

'I don't know. It's just a word. I don't even know why I know it. But it frightened him. He knows something and I want you to find out what it is.'

'No.'

'Michael, I . . .'

'No. I won't do it.'

I had no right to ask for more favours. I am a madwoman, I thought. He must be relieved he does not have to put up with my moods and my rages any more.

'You know that woman on Long Island,' he said. 'What's her name? Andersen? They say she's crazy as a loon. That's where you're headed if you don't forget about all this. I told you, I was there, in Ekaterinburg, I met one of the men who did the shooting. She's dead, Anna, they are all dead.' He gave me a look of tenderness and not a little pity. 'Felix is wasting his money in Hanover. When are you going to tell him?'

'Michael, I know what you think of me. But this is your story, too. You were the one who found the first witness to the Czar's murder. If you won't do this for me, do it because you're a good newspaperman.'

He was quiet, watching a flurry of rain dimple the lake. I thought he was thinking over my proposition. Instead he startled me by saying: 'How old is your daughter?'

Oh, he knew. That much was obvious, from the way he said it, from the look on his face. Sophie must have told him. But I tried to lie, it was a habit with me now. 'She's almost four years old. Why?'

'Her birthday is on October 29. Sophie says she's almost five.'

What could I say to him? Another gust of wind threw the rain in our faces, it stung like a handful of sand.

'You were never going to tell me, were you?'

'No, I wasn't.'

'Why not? Didn't I have the right to know?'

I have done many things in my life that I am not proud of, but this, this was the one thing I could not forgive myself for. Yet until now I had argued with myself, successfully, that it had been the only way. Once I had made the decision to leave Michael and come with Felix to New York, how could I then tell him he was the father of my child? Felix and I had persevered with the fiction that Rachel was his, the same way we pretended there was a tooth fairy that left a nickel under her pillow for every time she lost a tooth.

I couldn't have told Michael then, I had not wanted him to find out now, or ever. I had thought it was best for Rachel that way, and that it was best for Felix, it was even best for Michael. Now I was not so sure.

'I'm so sorry.'

'If I had a dollar for every time you've been sorry, I could buy my father out.'

What could I say to him? There were no words.

He turned to go. 'You know, I found this little bookshop on the Lower East Side, it was like one of those shops in the Russian Quarter in Shanghai, remember? Little old man ran the place, only sold books about the Czar and the rest of the royal family. I went in and bought one, I started reading how Alexandra's pet name for Anastasia, when she was little, was *schwibsik*. It's German for "imp", because she was always getting into trouble, always playing tricks on people, always making mischief. The book also said she could be incredibly cruel.'

'What's your point?' I asked.

'I just made it,' he said and then he walked away.

MICHAEL

The old man sat there looking for all the world how I imagined God; silver, smooth, tanned and judgmental. The office walls were lined in walnut, and there was a blue and gold Persian carpet on the floor. There was a Hepplewhite desk between us, the green leather top worn with age, and there were gold-embossed leather bound volumes on the shelf behind his head. A small Dresden china teacup and saucer sat at his right hand.

'So, how are things with you, son?'

'Fine.'

I felt as if I had come to present myself in his study to explain my report card. So I just sat there, and let the silence hang.

'Got what you wanted?' he said. The muscles in his jaw rippled, and I realised we were going to have a real conversation, after nine years.

'Yes. Pretty much.'

'You enjoy living in that flea pit in the Village?'

'People do live without butlers, JB.'

He blinked at that. First time I'd called him by the name his friends used. He grunted. I don't know if it was a sign of respect or of disgust.

'So what brings you back here?'

'Work.'

'You call what you do work?' It was just his way of having a conversation. I let that one go. 'Nine years. You know what this has done to your mother?'

'I had a lot of growing up to do.'

'Still have.'

Like I said, it was just his way. He liked to challenge people, see how they would meet his charge, it let him get his measure of them. My way was to let him keep throwing punches, wear himself out.

'That girl you brought with you the other day. You're not serious about her?'

I thought I was going to get another anti-Semitic rant from the old man, so to stick a thorn up his ass I said: 'Maybe.'

He shook his head. 'You know her brother?'

I nodded. 'Worth a bit of money, I believe.'

'His father got out of Russia just before those damned communists took over. Used the money to set up a messenger service on the Street, now he's got almost two thousand boys up and down the district. I don't mind private enterprise but it doesn't mean I'm egalitarian, especially when it comes to family business.'

Two thousand boys. Was that what he had said? Most of those boys were grey-haired fossils who were too old to be clerks and tellers.

'Rifkin makes around twenty-five thou a week. Most of it he pours back into the market. He's done well for himself.'

'Good for him,' I said.

'Yes, good for him, but it doesn't make his sister Sheridan material.'

Well, here I was just off the boat and the old man was trying to run my life again. I wondered what he would say if he knew I was in love with Rifkin's wife and that Rachel Rifkin was his grand-daughter. There are some things it's better not to know.

'What's the problem with Rifkin? You don't like him because he's Jewish?'

'That's a part of it,' he said, with breath-taking candour, as if it was the most reasonable thing in the world to hate Jews. He held out his hands, as if he could hold the entire building in his perfectly manicured fingers. 'You could still be a part of this.'

And so for the next hour we talked about it; all the reasons I couldn't be a part of it, and all the reasons he thought I could. We came no closer to understanding each other, but he got off his chest everything he'd wanted to say to me the nine years I'd been away. When we'd finished I think he understood I really was lost to him. I hope it gave him some peace.

'So if you don't want a piece of Sheridan's, what do you want?' he growled.

'Your help,' I said.

'Finally.'

'It's a favour. You don't have to do it. I haven't exactly given you cause to want to help me out.'

'You're a sunnavabitch,' he muttered.

'Peter Beard,' I said.

'What about him?'

'Know him?'

'We do business occasionally. He's very well connected. No sense of humour.'

Well that was rich, coming from my old man. 'Do you know why he left England?'

'Is that why you're here? Digging up the dirt?'

'Is there dirt to dig?'

He thought about this. Everyone on the Street had something to hide, it was just a matter of degree. He was torn between the anathema of talking to a newspaperman and helping out his son, perhaps building a bridge. I was manipulating him for once.

'There's a whisper.'

I waited.

'He's a singularly well-connected man, Michael. He was on the board of the Bank of England for a time, but also, because of his connections to Nicholas, the Czar's mother asked him to manage her daughters' financial affairs after she died. He was also trustee for the old bird's estate. They say she kept a trunk under her bed during the whole ten years of her exile, with a fortune in jewellery inside it. When she died, the jewels were supposed to go to Olga and Xenia. Beard went to the funeral in Copenhagen and persuaded Olga to send the jewels in a diplomatic pouch to Buckingham Palace for safekeeping, to protect them from unscrupulous dealers. Instead, some of the most valuable pieces are said to have gone into Queen Mary's private collection for a fraction of what they were worth. Olga and Xenia are now utterly dependent on the King's good graces, living under his patronage in Windsor.'

'How do you know all this?'

'It's my business to know.'

It was a tantalising story. No newspaper in Britain would touch it, of course.

'Did Beard profit from this?'

'No, but it's why he got away with embezzlement at the Bank of England.'

I couldn't believe my ears. 'Go on.'

'You can't print this. It's unsubstantiated.'

'I know.'

He shrugged. 'The Romanovs were the richest family in the world, Michael. Their aggregate wealth was around one hundred and twenty million dollars. The Czar had investments in railroads, steamships and timber. On the death of Nicholas and his wife, the money should have gone to his children. But when it became clear that they were all dead, certain people may have decided to channel off some of the money for themselves. It simply disappeared.'

'Beard?'

He nodded.

'The government did nothing?'

'Beard knew what happened to the Dowager's jewellery collection. The Queen couldn't be implicated in a scandal like that. A few months later he offered his resignation to the board of the bank and decided to take an extended overseas vacation. He appeared on the Street about six months ago, with some very serious funds to invest. I'd say he's worth between ten and twenty.'

Million, thank you very much. Ten and twenty million dollars. A lot of money back then. Christ, the way my father said it, it was like these were low numbers.

'Who else could I talk to about this?'

'Tread carefully, Michael. No-one likes newspapermen on the Street. Beard's got dangerous friends.' He tossed the pen aside. 'Look, is this really what you want to do with your life?'

'Yes,' I said. 'It is.'

He shook his head, couldn't understand it. Not a lot of people do; not Sophie, and certainly not Anastasia. She would have been a perfect heiress. And I guess my old man would have made a much better Czar.

Beard kept a suite in the Duxton Building on Fifth Avenue. A security guard checked my name on a list and an elevator whisked me up to the eighteenth floor and his eyrie. I was searched by a burly Irishman when I got out of the lift and ushered through an unnumbered door.

Beard sat at a huge mahogany desk, in a studded leather chair, his hands behind his head. I was shown in by a secretary. He did not rise or offer to shake hands. Instead, he looked at me down the length of that patrician nose, and smiled. Not a warm smile, let me tell you, but the smile of a man secure in the knowledge that he was richer, quicker, stronger and faster than you and me.

He had set aside a few minutes from his busy schedule to throw peanuts to the public. He expected the usual litany of fawning questions: How did you make all your money? What's the secret of your success? Do you think the surge on Wall Street can continue? And – off the record – do you have any hot tips?

'Which newspaper are you with?' he asked, polishing his spectacles.

'The *New York Times*.'

He frowned, rechecked his diary. 'Haven't come across you before. Your usual beat?'

'I was with Reuters, headed up the Moscow bureau until a few months ago.'

'Moscow,' he said and the tiny lines at the corner of his eyes deepened a little. His eyes became wary. 'So what can I do for you?' He rechecked his fob watch. 'You have exactly ten minutes, I'm a busy man.'

And so we went at it, covering all the familiar ground; I asked him why he thought stock prices were falling, and he gave me a well-rehearsed lecture on the current state of the stock market, how some issues had been selling at ridiculously high prices a few months ago and the market was now going through a period of readjustment. He wanted, he said, to assure my readers that America had one of the greatest economies known to modern history and that the potential for growth was unlimited. He foresaw even greater profits for anyone bold enough to invest in the future of the nation's industries and mineral wealth.

'Anything else?' he said, when he had finished.

I kept my notebook open on my lap. 'One more question. You were once a governor of the Bank of England. Is that correct?'

He eased his hands out from behind his head and folded

312

them across the not-inconsiderable expanse of his waist. He didn't say anything.

'It's believed the Romanov family kept private accounts at the bank.'

Another smile, even colder than the first. 'What is this about?'

'It's about a rumour that you embezzled almost five million pounds sterling from the Romanov accounts. Do you have anything to say to that?'

A long silence. I think he meant to intimidate me, but it didn't really work. I just sat there and watched him trying to think what to do with me. 'Who are you?' he said, finally.

I knew I had him. He wouldn't be throwing me out until he found out exactly how much I knew and from whom.

'Nice office,' I said, looking around. 'They say you've made a fortune on the Street. I guess it helps to have good-start up capital. Would that be right?'

He leaned forward and whispered, 'Don't fuck with me.'

I didn't expect that sort of language from an Englishman. But then Beard wasn't an Englishman. The only quintessentially British thing about him was his fondness for stealing money from other governments.

'Does this mean our interview's over?' I said, reaching for my homburg. I saw the uncertainty on his face. He didn't want me to leave until he knew what I had.

'I hope you're not going to print anything,' he said. 'There are very strong libel laws on both sides of the Atlantic.'

'You deny it?'

'Deny what?'

'Embezzling money from the Bank of England.'

'If your ridiculous and insulting allegation were true, why isn't there a warrant for my arrest?'

'Because you helped Queen Mary get the Romanov jewels. Besides, who's going to miss the money? The beneficiaries are all dead. Or you hope they are.'

'Get out.'

'Do you know what Otma means?'

He just stared. His eyes frightened me, frankly. For all the blandness of my first impression, his expression now was the gaze of a predator, trapped and endangered. I remembered the old man's warning.

I was never good at staring matches so I picked up my hat and left. I hadn't a clue where I was going with this. Sometimes it's worth stirring the nest, see what happens. As it was, I made my own luck.

If you can call it luck.

She was the last person I expected to see.

When I heard the knock on the door I thought it was Sophie. Come crawling back, as the saying went. But I should have known better. Girls like Sophie don't crawl, and they don't ever come back.

Anastasia.

This time, at least, I wasn't in my dressing gown. It was four in the afternoon, and I was shaved, dressed – after my own scribbler's fashion, as my father would say – and the apartment looked rather better, with the sun flooding in through the west-facing window, and the smell of coffee percolating on the stove in the kitchen.

'You,' I said, not the brightest or wittiest of gambits, admittedly.

'May I come in?' she said.

She slipped off her fox fur coat and I was supposed to be there to catch it. She unhitched the silk scarf and it joined the coat and the stylish cloche on the hook behind the door, next to my shabby overcoat and homburg.

She crossed her arms and stood in the middle of the room, just begging to be hated. How do I hate thee, as the poet said, let me count the ways. The way you ran out on me in London; the way you didn't tell me I had a daughter; the way you're standing there right now, looking so achingly beautiful in that sleeveless Lanvin sheath and high black heels that I still want you as much as I did when I first saw you. This is not right, and this is not fair.

'What are you doing here?' I asked her.

'I wanted to know if you'd found out anything more about Beard.'

'Perhaps.'

'Don't I have a right to know?'

'The right to know? Forgive me, but I didn't know that was a concept you were familiar with.'

'This is different.'

'Is it? Do you want coffee? It's made.'

She gave an almost imperceptible shrug of the shoulders that I took as agreement and went through to the kitchen. She followed me. I felt her eyes on my back.

'Well?' she said, finally.

'What can I tell you? He's a crook. I can't prove it. If I ever do, it will be the biggest story of my career.'

'And you'll have me to thank for it.'

'Well, about time I had reason to thank you for something. You still take sugar?'

'Do you drink out of these?'

'Sorry, all the Dresden's in the sink.'

I brought the coffees out to the living room. She sat in that wonderfully regal way of hers, her spine straight, her skirt smoothed in one motion as she sat down, one foot carefully placed in front of the other.

'Who is he?'

'He's the man who stole the Czar's money. There was a lot of it to steal. They'll probably never find it all.'

'What about Otma?'

'I don't know. It sounds like a password to one of the accounts.' I told her everything I knew or had discovered about Beard or Bardenov. It wasn't much, and she listened to it all, her face impassive.

'You still don't think I'm her, do you?'

'Because you came up with Otma? It's a pretty obvious code, isn't it?'

'If you'd only seen his face when I said it.'

'It might have been indigestion.'

She looked away. I think she was hoping for vindication from me.

'Is that the only reason you came here?' I asked her.

'What other reason would there be?'

'Well, you know, a couple of nights ago Sophie told me she couldn't see me any more. Did you have anything to do with that?'

'Who you sleep with is not my business.'

'She told me Felix had given her an ultimatum. She seemed to think you were behind it.'

She sipped her coffee, and her eyes fixed on me over the rim of the cup.

'You're right, I didn't come here to talk about Beard. I don't know if I even care about Anastasia any more. I came here because I can't live without you. I've tried it, and it doesn't work. I love you, Michael, I think I always have and the last five years I've been trying to tell myself that I don't.'

It was a breath-taking declaration. It was what I had waited to hear from her, for almost a decade.

I stood up and held out my hand. She took it and I pulled her to her feet. I had kissed her many times, and I remembered those kisses not for what they were, but for what they were not. They were not without reserve; they were not lingering; they were not as passionate as mine.

This time she kissed me with a desperation that overwhelmed me. She bruised my lips, pressed herself to me so hard it was almost painful. Her hands went around my neck, her fingers entwined themselves in my hair; I felt one leg wrap itself around mine, felt her ankle at the back of my thigh, as if she were clinging to me for her life. She was throwing herself at me, at last. It was an act of surrender. I was not kissing a princess, or a taxi girl. Finally I had Anastasia.

She unzipped her dress and it fell around her ankles. She was wearing silk knickers, and a brassiere, a novelty I had not encountered before. I needed a little help taking it off. To compensate my bruised male pride I deliberately tore her knickers getting them off.

I still had all my clothes on, an emblem of my new-found power over her. A facet of my revenge.

I remembered her body but I did not remember making love with her this way, not in London and certainly not in Shanghai. Was it another performance? Not as far as I could tell, and you have to understand, I am only a man and incapable of subtlety. When we finished I had scratches on my back and a bruise on my neck and twice Anastasia had signalled a sexual climax with wild cries and displays of affection. Faked or real, I had no way to be certain, and through reticence or wisdom, I never asked the question.

Afterwards we lay on the floor. Someone was banging on the wall. We had disturbed the neighbours.

I put my hand on her breast, another act of possession.

The ravishing of a princess, I thought. Byron could have made something of this. Or perhaps Botticelli.

'I shouldn't have done that,' she said.

'Are you worried I won't respect you in the morning?'

She looked at her watch, the only thing she was wearing, apart from her shoes. 'It's only half past five. You won't even respect me by dinner time.' It was a weak joke and neither of us laughed. She sat up and got her clothes together. We'd made something of a mess. She ran into the bathroom.

When she emerged, she was a little dishevelled, but a lady once more. And she was changed in some indefinable way. I had dressed and was sitting on the windowsill, smoking a cigarette. I offered her one, but she shook her head.

'I'd better go.'

She seemed to be waiting for me to say something but I couldn't think of anything. I helped her with her coat. She checked her reflection in the hallway mirror and left. I watched her climb into a cab down in the street.

I had finally won the game. All I had to do now was collect my winnings and leave.

The Colony Club on Park Avenue, the ballroom glittering with silver. As I walked in, I was overwhelmed by the scent of hundreds of fresh-cut flowers, the golden glow of French champagne.

The cream of the social register was there, the women in their evening gowns, Chanels, Lanvins, Poirets and Schiaparellis, all of them shimmering with diamonds; the men were austere and immaculately groomed in black dinner suits, there were even a few wing collars.

I asked myself what I was doing there. For all my high-minded principles I didn't mind using my connections when it suited me. Perhaps I thought the old man owed me something, but you'd be forgiven for asking what. He had arranged the invitation for me, at my specific request; I wanted Beard to see me there among his own, perhaps shock him into doing something rash, which I believe he eventually did. Or perhaps it was just an excuse to see Anastasia again.

The talk around me, inevitably, was about the market. Prices had been tumbling all week. Just the day before, Westinghouse had dropped eleven dollars from its share price, General Electric another thirteen. But on the day of the ball the market had made a modest gain. I heard a broker telling someone that prices had bottomed out and now was the time to be smart, move in, make a killing. You never saw or heard such an optimistic group of people.

Of course, it's easy to be wise after the event. The fact of it was, madness had gripped America and none of us really saw the bloodbath coming or the extent of it, and by then it was just a month away.

I only knew a handful of people there, from the old days, but they all kept their distance, didn't want to be tainted. Even old school friends cut me. They knew about the war between the old man and me and they didn't want to get caught in the crossfire.

And then I saw Beard; he was with the Spanish Consul, talking to JP Morgan and an executive from General Motors. I would have liked a snapshot of his face when he saw me. He was a consummate performer, so the mask didn't slip for long; but for an instant he goggled at me like I was a naked chorus girl.

I stood there, drinking my French champagne, watching New York's rich and famous and pretending to have a good time. And then he was there, at my shoulder.

'What are you doing here?' he hissed.

'Don't you know who I am?' I had waited all my life to say that, hypocrite that I am. But once arrogance is bred in, it's like a stain, you don't ever get rid of it. For all that I had tried to deny it, I was still my father's son.

'Who the fuck are you?'

I nodded towards the old man, on the other side of the room, grey-haired and sublime, and surrounded by the preeners and hangers-on. 'JB is my father.'

'Crap.'

'You don't see the familial resemblance?'

He looked a little disappointed when he realised I was telling the truth. 'Why don't you get yourself a real job?'

'Can't, I was born honest.'

'Not if you're a Sheridan.'

'That's rich, coming from you.'

He stood closer, an unctuous smile on his face, we must have looked for all the world to the people around us as if we were old friends. 'I meant what I said. Don't meddle in my affairs.'

'Which affairs?'

'It's your last warning.'

Oh, Peter Beard was a real prince. Long, sleek, grey and smooth; a shark running hungry in the water.

I walked away and left him muttering threats to the silverware. I had seen my brother James on the other side of the room. Time to catch up on old times.

James was two years older than me and people often commented on how different we were, not only in looks, but in our personalities. It occurred to me, later in life, that this was not all due to chance. James was dutiful, I was rebellious; James had excelled at school, I was the one who caused the teachers headaches; James was diligent, hard-working and respectful, I had been lazy, careless and sullen. James had a plum up his ass; I, at least, had known how to enjoy myself.

My life had been sculpted to James's reflection; he's this, so I'll be that. I knew I could not compete with him academically, or for the good graces of my parents, so I tried to be whatever he wasn't. Apparently I had succeeded.

He was shorter than me, which must have irritated him. We had the same dark looks, but he never had the same success with women that I had. Women are drawn, in my opinion, not seduced. There is something they sense which attracts them to certain men, usually the ones that are no damn good for them. Like me.

In all the years we lived in the same house, I had no idea what he thought about me: I never asked him. We were never close after we reached our teenage years. I hadn't even written him all the time I had been away and he had returned the compliment.

He hadn't changed that much. A little stouter round the belly, perhaps, and, like me, he wasn't a fresh-faced boy any more. He looked as if he was going to be a man of some consequence. I think it gave him no small measure of satisfaction to see the way I'd turned out.

We exchanged a few pleasantries, as if I had been away for nine days instead of nine years. Small talk was fine with me. There was no unfinished business between us.

'How's life back in New York?' he said after a while.

'The old town's changed.'

'We're going to be the money capital of the world,' he said, as if this was the only thing that mattered.

There was a difficult silence, already we'd run out of things to say. 'How's the newspaper business?' he said, trying unsuccessfully to avoid condescension.

'Fine.'

'Dad was wondering, I think, if you could be persuaded to come back into the firm, now you've seen a bit of the world, sowed your oats.'

Sowed my oats. Prick. Or perhaps he was worried about it; I don't think he liked having me back. Like the prodigal son in the Bible; the dutiful son must have really hated his guts. James was the workhorse. He recognised me, correctly, as a show pony.

'I don't have a head for figures, you know that.'

He nodded, relieved, I think, but not convinced. And then we both stood there, desperately trying to think of something else to say.

And then I turned and looked across the room.

Anastasia looked as beautiful as I had ever seen her. It occurred to me that if she wasn't a princess, then it was a damned shame because she looked like one. She moved like mercury, and her skin had a radiance about it. Her eyes were like sapphire chips, catching the light, took my breath away.

I had caught her looking at me several times through the evening but neither of us made a move towards the other. Felix was watching, too, and his eyes had a different message.

But at last she detached herself from her husband and went out onto the balcony, alone. Felix looked like he was talking leverage and futures with some newly rich socialite in a monkey suit. I followed her outside.

A splash of light separated us. She stood in the shadows, facing away from me, her backless dress revealing a spine curved to perfect dimension. There was a glitter of gold at the nape of her neck, begging for a man's warm breath.

'So,' she said, without turning around, 'running with the hare and hunting with the hounds.'

'I learned it from you.'

She half turned towards me. She had a flute of champagne in her hand and held it to her lips.

'You look wonderful,' I said, after a moment.

'Thank you.' She said it so softly I almost missed it. I wanted to see her face, but it was hidden by shadow.

I crossed the bright divide between us, leaned on the stone balustrade, looked out over the park. Moonlight rippled on the lake.

'How's Rachel?'

'What do you want to know?'

'What is there to tell?'

'She's like every other five-year-old girl, Michael. She likes to play with dolls, she believes in the Easter Bunny, she hates the dark. She loves ponies.'

'Not every five-year-old girl has her own pony.'

'Every five-year-old girl would like one. She's lucky.'

'Yes, she's rich.'

'Michael,' she began, and I knew from her voice what was coming. 'Michael, what we did the other day. It mustn't ever happen again.'

'You told me you loved me, princess. You told me you couldn't live without me any more.'

'I do love you, Michael, and I don't know how I will live without you. But that's not the point.'

Strange how I knew she would say this. She had lost the power to astonish me.

'What do you want to do about Rachel?' she said.

'Do about her?'

'Do you want to come and see her?'

'No.'

'It could be arranged, without Felix knowing.'

'I don't give a damn about Felix.'

I suppose some people would think my reluctance unnatural. Yes, I was curious, I'd only seen her twice, both times from a distance. But why risk growing fond of something you can't have? That would be repeating an old mistake, it seemed to me.

Besides, there was healing implicit in such an act. Wanting to see this child of mine suggested forgiveness on my part, and I wasn't prepared to forgive her right then for that particular betrayal.

'Anyway, what would you tell her about me?'

'I hadn't thought about it.'

'Here's your real daddy, Rachel, go and play on the swings with him and then when you're done say goodbye, because you're never going to see him again.'

'It doesn't have to be like that.'

'She's not my daughter. She's belongs to Felix now. He's the one who tucks her in at night, he's the guy who takes her to the park on Sundays. I don't believe in biology, I believe in people being there for you.'

'I'm so sorry, Michael.'

A long silence. The band was playing the Black Bottom. I could hear whoops and yells from the younger members of the party. Decadence seeping in everywhere. My father blamed the Negroes.

'Do you remember that time in Shanghai, when I came home and found you playing the piano?'

'I remember.'

'Do you still play?'

She shook her head.

'I loved you once,' I said. I don't know why it was so hard for me to say that. It must have been obvious. I put out a hand to touch her, the skin on her bare arms was cold. I leaned towards her and kissed her on the cheek.

At the last moment she turned her head and offered me her mouth. A bittersweet moment for me, the shock of her tongue in my mouth for a brief but electric moment. I remember the taste of her lipstick, the scent of her perfume.

She was first to break the kiss and pull away. 'Help me stay away from you.'

'All right,' I said, and at that moment I believed I could.

'I have to get back inside,' she said. After she was gone I stood outside, smoking a cigarette. Her fragrance lingered for a while in the cool summer air and then was carried away on the high New York breeze.

And this was to be the moment of my revenge. A dish best served cold, as the saying goes, and I had let mine cool for some time. I had been her guardian and her saviour long enough, suffered enough rejection at her indifferent hand. Now she would see a different side to Michael Sheridan. I was about to go square with the house.

I had planned it from the moment she showed up at my apartment in the Village that afternoon. Even as I was sliding my hand along her thigh I knew where it would lead. My moment of satisfaction would not take place inside her. She had lacerated my soul, when she left me in London I had been speechless and heartsick. I had risked my career for her and twice I had saved her life.

There is nothing more bitter than rejection and nothing, I told myself, as sweet as vengeance. If I had cause for hesitation, she had just banished my reluctance.

It could be so simply and sweetly done: Oh, by the way Felix, I fucked your wife yesterday afternoon.

Did you enjoy dinner?

I went back inside, looked around for him. He was moving about the room with plumpish grace, started talking to my father. Everyone wanted to talk to my father. He conferred conversation like a duke holding court, handing out baubles and fiefdoms with equal grace.

I settled myself at his shoulder and pretended to listen to the conversation, welcome there, of course, because I was JB's son. Talk of the markets was followed by desultory conversation about the party and then my father moved away, his attention drawn to someone more important. There was an awkward moment as Felix and I found ourselves alone. He looked around the room for escape.

'We've never been formally introduced,' I said, and held out my hand.

To his credit, he didn't take it. 'Let's not pretend we want to be civil to each other,' he said.

I could have played the bewildered gentleman. I decided against it, and gave it to him straight back. 'There was a time I hated you so badly it made my teeth ache.'

'I understand that perfectly. But she's my wife now, and it's best for all of us if you bury the past, as I have.'

'Easy to say when you have nothing to bury.'

He was a big man, taller than me, and stoutly built. The softness about him was an illusion. You could see it in his eyes, he had the instincts of a street fighter, though probably not the stomach for it.

323

And this was my cue. He was waiting for me to do my worst. He knew, surely, that I hadn't cornered him this way just to trade in inconsequential unpleasantness. This was the moment I had waited for for five years. It would destroy the marriage, if I read him right. Anastasia would be out on the street again, her debt to me fully repaid.

He waited, and I waited, and the moment passed. I couldn't do it. Eventually he excused himself, and moved away. I had let the opportunity slip, if you could call it an opportunity. I was unavenged but relieved, and I felt better about myself than I had in a while. Making love to Anastasia had not been an act of revenge, though I had tried to persuade myself it was. It was just love and desire, as it had always been, and nothing would change that.

I smiled and drained my champagne glass, feeling curiously light-headed. I couldn't hurt her, no matter what she did, any more than I could tear off my own right hand with my teeth. Like the old man had always said, I was too soft to be a Sheridan, and I still take great pleasure in his summation of my character.

Two days later Beard declared himself.

There was a knock at the door of my apartment and I threw it open, thinking it might be Anastasia. Instead there was some rock ape in a dark suit. He pushed me back into the room and closed the door behind him.

'Michael Sheridan.'

I was scared out of my wits, I admit it, but I did my best impression of a man who knows how to look after himself. 'Who wants him?'

The act didn't fool anybody, least of all the rock ape, who really did know how to take care of himself. He pushed me down onto a chair. 'Just sit there and listen,' he said.

So I sat there and listened, as if I had any choice.

My visitor reached into his jacket and I thought for one crazy moment that he was going to take out a revolver and shoot me. But what he flourished in his right fist was a brown envelope, thick as a hamburger. 'Here,' he said, 'this is for you.'

'What is this?'

'Easiest money you'll ever make in your life, pal.' He was leaning right over me, one foot between my legs on the chair, I could smell the garlic on his breath from lunch.

'But what's it for?'

'I think you know.'

I tried to hand it back but he wouldn't take it. He looked tired and disappointed. 'He said you might not be sensible about this.'

'Who's he?'

'We both know what this is about.'

'I can't be bought.'

I wasn't expecting him to hit me, not without more preamble, which shows you how naive I was. There wasn't much I could have done about it anyway. He didn't intend any real damage, I figured later, or he would have broken my nose or my teeth. As it was he landed the punch on my cheekbone, snapping my head back and sending me arcing backwards off the chair. I hit the floor hard and lay there staring at the ceiling, stunned. The rock ape leaned over me with a look on his face that let me know he had enjoyed the experience a lot more than I had.

'You got to be smart about this,' he said. 'Save yourself a lot of pain. Take the money and run. Cause any more trouble, this is going to get much worse. Okay?'

He couldn't have been clearer than that. He straightened up, tossed the envelope at me and walked out.

I was convinced he'd fractured my cheekbone. There was a rhythm of pain drumming through my skull and when I finally sat up I thought I was going to be sick.

God alone knows why I didn't take the money and the message that went with it. Why did I think I could win? Sometimes it's good to be a little stubborn, but this wasn't one of those times.

It was a while before I could stand up, and when I surveyed the damage in the bathroom mirror I found that one side of my face was the size of a watermelon and my left eye was swollen shut. The guy had done that with one punch. Imagine if he had really wanted to work me over.

I got some ice, wrapped it in a cloth and laid down on the sofa. The perfect way to pass a warm Saturday afternoon in New York city, the fan clicking on the table, a faint breeze stirring the curtains, my head screaming like someone was drilling my skull with a jackhammer.

I stared at a fragment of blue sky and wondered what to do. My whole nature rebelled against backing off. Beard had made his move, now it was my turn to play ball.

There is a heart to every great city that gives it its pulse and its spirit. I had been to Rome, watched the faithful flock to the Piazza San Pietro on a Sunday, to make obeisance to the Pope; London has Trafalgar Square, where the British pay tribute in stone and marble to their own religion, their glorious, martial past; in New York's teeming heart is Wall Street, and it was there in the twenties that Americans created their own deity, the Almighty Dollar.

Wall Street was named after the wall that one of the city's governors, Peter Stuyvesant, erected on one side of a footpath known as Broadway to stop cattle straying onto it. It is just six blocks long and ends at the Hudson waterfront, bound at the other end by the spire of the Trinity Church and enclosed by the concrete castles the bankers and financiers erected in their own honour. It is short, narrow and gloomy, was even back then; the sun warms some sections of the pavement for less than twenty-hours every year.

The names of the streets around it are the only clues to the area's past: Maiden Lane, Old Slip, Liberty Street. Slave auctions had been held here in the eighteenth century, Negroes having the dubious honour of being the first commodities traded. It was here, too, that George Washington was sworn in as the nation's first president in 1789.

On to 1929, and the street had become a circus, the stock market was New York's Big Top, the Greatest Show on Earth. It had the buzz and clamour of a fairground. It was packed with people: lumberjacks from Montana, cowboys from Texas, shopkeepers from Milwaukee, housewives from Pennsylvania; they had come by bus or by subway, some had even bedded down for the night in the Trinity Church graveyard. They had come from all over America to ride the gravy train and get themselves a piece of the biggest bull market in history. Everywhere people talked animatedly about sure things and new stocks about to go sky high. Everyone wanted to invest their life savings in AOT – Any Old Thing. They all wanted to be somebody, and it was on Wall Street that their dreams would come true.

Clerks and stenographers and bankers and brokers shouldered their way through the crowds. A line of messengers shuffled along like a black snake, a human chain of twenty men, each carrying a locked metal box filled with securities and flanked front and rear by armed guards.

Over the din of the crowds was the jackhammer clatter of new construction work, the shouts of hawkers selling hot dogs and soft drinks, newsboys peddling the *Times*, the honk of car and truck horns, the boom of ships moving up and down the East River.

A self-appointed prophet, draped in the American flag, harangued the crowds from a podium on the sidewalk, preaching Sodom and Gomorrah and the end of the world, while organ music floated from the doors of the Trinity Church at the end of the street. A nice touch.

It was Tuesday, third of September, and the weather reports promised the hottest day of the year, the mercury would soon touch ninety-five degrees. By noon, when I arrived, the Street was breathless hot. I felt a grimy trickle of sweat down the back of my shirt. I checked the billboards; for once the newspapers were not headlined by the stock market. The Exchange had been closed for Labour Day weekend and Wall Street had been knocked out of the headlines by the Graf Zeppelin, which had completed its round the world flight and was on its way back to Germany from Lakewood.

I bought a copy of the *Times*. An economist called Babson had forecast a crash of sixty to eighty points on the Dow Jones. Already the papers were calling him the Prophet of Loss.

Prophet of Loss! Sometimes my profession embarrassed me.

I met the old man for lunch in the Stock Exchange Luncheon Club, a large and pleasant private dining room on the seventh floor of the building. A seat on the Exchange was a requirement for membership and so diners were assumed to be gentlemen. The old man had paid a hundred and fifty thousand dollars for his seat five years ago, and entry fees had risen so sharply since he now considered it a bargain.

We ate lamb noisettes Cussy, artichoke hearts with hollandaise sauce, and drank a bottle of Bollinger. Better than my usual corned beef on rye from the Jewish delicatessen on the corner.

I met him here to trade family loyalty once again for knowledge about Peter Beard. As I talked his fingers beat a tattoo on the table, a sign of his agitation. I was surprised. It was unlike him to give away his feelings. 'This is a dirty game you're playing,' he growled.

Well, that was rich, coming from him. 'You've never played dirty, I guess.'

'This is different,' he answered, without explaining how. He took another look at my face. 'What happened to you?'

'I got in a fight in a bar,' I said. 'You should see the other guy.' Yeah, you should see him. Not a mark on him.

'Have you seen a doctor?'

'I'm okay,' I said.

'Is this how you're going to spend the rest of your life then? Brawling in bars?'

'Did you find what I asked for?'

He was just starting to get in his stride, well into another sermon, and he didn't like to be deflected. But I think he knew it wouldn't do any good. He frowned, and lowered his voice. 'His name is Goldfinch, Leonard Goldfinch, he's thirty-eight years old, married with two daughters, twelve and ten. His wife's name is Margaret. He was born in Croydon in London in 1891. He started work at the Bank of England after leaving Guildford Grammar School in 1909, and when Beard became a director of the bank in 1926 he became his personal assistant. When Beard left last year Goldfinch accompanied him to New York, helped him set up an office on Nassau selling bonds and securities. These are not facts that are hard to come by. What is generally less well known is that since coming to New York he has taken to purchasing underage prostitutes, some of the girls I believe are as young as eleven or twelve years old.'

'Jesus. How do you come by this stuff?'

'Anything that happens on the Street is my business.'

'But how do you know?'

'I don't give away my sources. Do you give away yours?'

'You're supposed to be a stock trader, not the secret police.'

'You asked me to get you information, you must have been pretty sure I could get it. I don't expect any moral judgments from you.'

I backed down. I was shocked, that was all.

'Does Beard know about this?'

'I don't know. If he does, he's a fool, no man is indispensable.'

'But if you could get this sort of information, he must be able to.'

'It works this way. There's a certain person on the Street, provides specialised services to elite clients. Prostitutes, male or female, cocaine, liquor, girls, boys. He makes a lot of money out of it. He also makes a hell of a lot of money out of me. So occasionally I get favours from him. Like this one.'

'He makes money from you?'

He gave me a look of disgust when he realised what I was thinking. 'I make sure no-one in my office is doing anything I should know about, is all. I'm a careful man. Beard isn't careful enough.'

Now I understood why he was so agitated. He was breaking some sort of gentleman's code on the Street, taking its private business to a newspaperman; worse that the newspaperman was his son.

'How do I find him?'

He puffed out his cheeks. Never seen the old man upset, this was getting close. 'What if you don't get what you want? Are you going to destroy this man's life?'

'Not like you to have an attack of conscience.'

'I don't give a damn about Goldfinch. I want to know what kind of son I raised.'

I stayed silent.

He sighed. 'It's a hotel on the Lower East Side, on Clinton. It's called the Union. I don't know when he goes, or how often. That's all I can tell you. I don't even know why I've done this, this kind of information is worth more than you'll see in your crummy job in a year.'

'Thanks,' I said, the word sticking in my throat. So much for pride. I said I didn't need him, I'd gone out of my way to shove my independence in the old man's face but sooner or later he knew I would come back here sniffing for favours. This damned city.

'So what are you going to do?'

'I'm going to squeeze him,' I said, 'see how much juice runs out.'

A smile of triumph from the old man. 'It's funny, you know, all these years I haven't approved of what you were doing, as you well know, but I thought, well, he has his pride and he's trying to do things his way. I respected that. But you know, you're not much different from me.'

'I'm only after the truth.'

'There's no such thing.' He took out his fob. 'Well, that's it. I have money to make. You have to save the world from the Devil.'

He guided me to the stairs, two fingers lightly on my arm, just above the elbow. He leaned in close. 'You've got balls. James could learn a lot from you.'

He smiled at my look of complete astonishment and went back to work, a little table hopping before getting back to the market for the last hour before closing.

The Union Hotel was not the kind of establishment that competes for clients with the Ritz or the Waldorf-Astoria. It was a six-storey brownstone, elbowing for room among the crowded tenements of the Lower East Side. The streets outside were teeming with Hassids and Italians and Polish, the hotel frequented by sailors and down-at-heels come to the city with their last few bucks looking for work. And the hookers, of course, who rented rooms there by the hour.

The proprietor – I never caught his name – was a weedy Polack, with the sour smell of sweat about him, and eyes like a ferret. I took him aside and told him what I wanted, and although I don't think he objected in principle, he was worried it might give the place a bad reputation. His clients used the place because they could do what they wanted there without problems, and what I was suggesting was just such a problem.

He suggested a figure that might compensate him for any damage his business reputation might sustain, and although I beat him down by about half, it was still a little higher than my expenses allowed, and I still had to pay the freelance photographer. I hoped it would be worth it.

Not one of the proudest moments of my life.

From my proprietor friend, I got the number of the room and the time Goldfinch would be using it. I hired a photographer who had done some work for Hearst newspapers and was accustomed to this kind of stake-out. His name was Jimmy Collins, a chain-smoker with a soft Irish brogue, a wolfish smile and a sadistic pleasure in his work.

The streets of the Lower East Side were as hot and sticky as a steam bath. We got out of a taxi and went inside. The foyer was gloomy as a cave. The proprietor shuffled out, handed me a skeleton key, then went back into a little office behind the front desk and locked the door.

We went up three flights. There was threadbare carpet loose on the stair, and the wallpaper hung in strips like flayed skin. It smelled of damp, the combination of mould and unreliable New York plumbing. We heard screams from one of the rooms; rehearsed or real, I never found out.

He was in room 308. I put my ear to the door and listened. The action was already underway. I nodded at Collins, took a deep breath, put the key in the door and threw it open. Then I stood back.

I heard a girl scream, there were three flashes as Collins took his pictures. When he was done he ran off down the corridor without another word.

I took a moment to compose myself then went in and shut the door.

Women look great in their underwear, at least that's my opinion. Men just look ridiculous. As for girls as young as the one Goldfinch had in that room – well, for the sake of my soul, I preferred to look the other way.

I have no idea what they were doing when Collins took his pictures and I don't want to know. Goldfinch was in his underwear – vest, white shorts, socks and garters – and was fumbling on the floor for his trousers. His date looked as if she couldn't care less – she was sitting up in the bed in a white vest and not much else with a bored expression on her face as if this happened to her all the time.

Time to take charge.

I looked for somewhere to sit. The room contained a bed with greyish sheets, an old cupboard with one door loose on its hinge, a filthy net curtain that concealed a view of a fire escape, and a single chair, where Goldfinch had tossed the rest of his clothes.

I threw them on the floor and sat down.

'Who the hell are you?' he said, in a British accent.

'It doesn't matter who I am.'

I looked at the girl. She was chewing gum, didn't look the kind of girl who ever took it out. Couldn't have been any more than twelve, flat-chested and skinny, frightening. But paedophilia wasn't uncommon back then; just like today.

Goldfinch had stumbled into his trousers; no, wrong leg. He started hopping up and down trying to get himself sorted out. A man without trousers is a man without dignity. He is in no position to negotiate.

'You want your fiancée here while we discuss this, Mr Goldfinch?' I asked him.

'How the hell do you know who I am?'

He did a nice line in outrage, if nothing else. He was a tall man, didn't look at all like a predator with his thinning ginger hair and ginger moustache. Powerfully built, too, his body covered in a sort of russet fuzz that I personally found repellent, reminded me overly much of carrots.

At the third attempt, the trousers were secured. He glared at me, torn between finding his shirt and confronting me.

'I have the photographs, you have a wife and two young daughters. Put the two together and you have an explosive mix. Shall we talk about how to keep them apart?'

He found his shirt on the floor and now held it bunched in his right fist. His other hand clenched and unclenched at his side. He was considering violence as a way out of this.

'Anything happens to me, the photographs are printed and distributed to every newspaper in town. Your employer, Mr Beard, wouldn't appreciate that very much. So don't even think about it.'

His disintegration was as sudden as it was dramatic. His hands started to shake, his face crumpled. He sank to his knees, buried his face in his shirt. 'Oh, my God. My God, my God, my God.'

Men often find religion at a time like this.

I looked at the girl. She showed no sign of moving, or being moved, by what was happening.

Goldfinch's face was wet, he was using his shirt like a rag to wipe his face. 'I knew this was going to happen,' he said.

'You want the girl here?'

'It's all right, she doesn't speak English,' he said, and then our eyes met, and no-one has ever looked at me with such hatred. He wanted to kill me, no question.

I leaned forward, rested my elbows on my knees. 'I need you to help me out, Mr Goldfinch,' I said. 'If you do, let's see if we can't make this all go away.'

ANASTASIA

That first time I went to Michael's apartment in Greenwich Village, there were no promises made. I told myself I would not go back. I would punish myself rather than hurt Rachel and Felix. But I could not stay away. I was, I think, like an alcoholic who goes back and rewards themselves with that one small drink after years of temperance.

That one moment of weakness broke the dam holding back years of denial. Afterwards he was all I could think about.

It was not difficult to arrange our liaisons. I had already accomplished a secret life. I had practised years of deceit, spending hours every day at the women's brokerage suite at the Waldorf-Astoria, when Felix and Madam Rifkin thought I was at Bloomingdale's or an art showing or a charity committee meeting. To go to

Greenwich Village instead of a smart hotel on Fifth Avenue was as simple as giving different instructions to a taxi driver.

I had not intended to throw the scraps of my pride at him a second time, but there was no help for it. I remember riding up to his apartment in a creaking lift, walking down a dismal corridor, tapping gently on the door, feeling like an expensive prostitute. A taxi girl again. He opened the door and his face creased into a smile.

'I knew you'd come,' he said.

For all my bluster, a decision had been made, a wide river crossed. I could have left Felix a long time ago, I supposed. I had the money, enough for my own independence, if that was what I chose. I could live in the manner to which I had become accustomed. But that wasn't the point. Felix had been kind to me. And besides, there was Rachel; she wasn't baggage to be dragged along wherever I decided to go.

We lay on Michael's bed, as the shadows lengthened through the afternoon. My hand traced the band of hard muscle on his chest. So different from Felix's pale marble flesh. We were moulded into each other, Michael and I, like the pieces of a jigsaw, perfectly fitted together. Except the picture made no sense, no sense at all.

'Is this all there is?' he whispered.

I didn't answer him, didn't know what to say.

'I can't give you what you want,' he said.

'Which is what?'

'The apartment on Fifth Avenue, the Hispano-Suiza, the law suit in Hanover.' He turned on his back, closed his eyes so he did not have to look into mine. 'It wasn't enough in London, why is it enough in New York?'

'I'll keep coming here, as long as you keep opening the door. More than that, I can't promise you.'

And that was the way it was. Hunger and repletion, nothing else. It was love without consequence, and afterwards we had nothing to say to each other.

If this was the real Anastasia, I would be better off without her.

I had betrayed both the men in my life, each one for the other. Did my reasons really matter? Was my abandonment of Michael any worse than my betrayal of my husband? One sin is as bad as the other. I had broken a human trust: the first to my child's father, the second to my husband.

I knew I could not live with myself this way.

It would have been easier if I was that Anastasia, the spoiled little princess who never really cared for anyone beside herself. But she had not lived on the street, or been the recipient of the bewildering kindnesses of men like Michael and Felix. For Felix was kind; self-obsessed, perhaps, but always faithful, and he had only ever showered good things on me.

These days I watch him ever more carefully to see if he suspects. Perhaps the very act of watching will give me away. I have become so unmindful of him; in the evenings when he comes home from a long day at his office, his first duty is always to step softly into Rachel's bedroom, to bend down and kiss her gently on the forehead as she sleeps. He pulls up the covers to her chin, a gesture that owes more to affection than necessity. Then he slips away to eat alone in the dining room, to read the newspapers and drink a lonely glass of red wine with his supper.

I listen to a radio broadcast or flick listlessly through the pages of a fashion magazine while he sits in a leather wing-backed antique by the window, a glass of brandy in one hand, diligently working his way through the *Wall Street Journal*. Before Michael, I would pay him not the slightest attention, but now he catches me watching him, and wonders at my sidelong glances, while I wonder at his.

At ten o'clock each evening I sit at my dressing table and study his reflection as he emerges from the bathroom in a silk robe, hair carefully groomed for bed.

I wait until the bedside light is extinguished, before joining him in that massive and arctic edifice that dominates our bedroom. I dread the touch of his hand upon my shoulder.

But I do not think he knows.

Michael, in passion, bruised me one afternoon, but the small discolouration on the soft flesh of my throat has gone unnoticed, due, I suppose, to the scarves I wear on even the warmest days. I do not think he has noticed the flush to my skin that love lends a woman, though even Sophie has remarked on it and I think she has her suspicions now; but I do not think he knows, despite my growing repugnance to his touch, which I have tried to disguise. We were never very physical with each other and perhaps it is not something he thinks much about.

No, I do not think he knows. But I cannot be sure.

MICHAEL

One morning, about a week after Collins and I took the photographs at the Union Hotel, I got a call from Goldfinch saying he wanted to talk. We made a time to meet the next day, at a coffee shop in the Village. When I put down the telephone my heart was beating so hard it almost hurt. I knew the risks. But I was stubborn. I wasn't going to back down.

He was happy to meet me in the Village because he was afraid of being seen with me. Ironic really, because he stood out among the habitués of the coffee house like a poodle in a hog farm. In those days the Village was about as far from Wall Street as you could get, perhaps not geographically, but socially it might as well have been Paris. It was Bohemia then, full of Dadaists and communists and other fringe dwellers, the artists and the writers and the intellectuals; another name for people who like to drink coffee and talk a lot, but who don't actually have a job. Goldfinch showed up wearing a homburg and bow tie, all set for a day behind his desk on the Street. He was skittish, like a parson in a speakeasy. Worst white-collar crook I ever met in my life, and I've met a few, most of them friends of my father.

We sat down in a corner booth and it was straight to business. 'I don't think I can do what you're asking,' he said.

I ordered coffees and sat back and said nothing, a ploy I had learned from my old man when people tried to frustrate him.

'You don't understand the risk I'm running if I decide to help you,' he said.

I reached into my jacket pocket and tossed three black and white photographs on the table. He recognised them straightaway, and snatched them off the table as if they were his underwear. 'For God's sake,' he hissed at me.

'You don't understand the risk you're running if you don't.'

His face was beaded with perspiration, like sweating dough. You could smell the fear coming off him.

'I still don't know your name,' he said.

'Smith. John Smith.'

'If I help you, I'll want the negatives.'

'You'll do as I tell you to do and you'll get the negatives back when I say you can.'

I surprised myself. I was really very good at this. Goldfinch chewed on his lip so hard he drew blood. He pushed his coffee cup away from him. Poisoned chalice, I remember thinking.

'The Romanov accounts,' I prompted him.

'Five million sterling,' he said. 'One million for each of the five children. He stole everything.'

'Can you get me paper evidence?'

He ran a finger through his thinning hair. His Adam's apple bobbed in his throat like a cork. 'In Beard's safe. Carbon copies of letters relating to the release of Romanov funds, as well as copies of letters from the Home Secretary. They're his insurance policy, as he calls them. It would cause a scandal if they ever got out. Is that what it is? You're from the newspapers, aren't you? They're no good to you, you know. No newspaper will ever print it.'

'Not in England,' I said.

'Not anywhere.' He rubbed his forehead violently with both hands, his manner even drawing stares from many of the customers, who were accustomed to eccentric behaviour in this part of New York City.

'If anyone finds out I've been tampering with the files . . .' He left the sentence unfinished. I wonder that I didn't take him more seriously at the time. I still thought I could get away with it, as if being a Sheridan made me somehow immune.

'What about the sale of the Dowager's jewellery?'

'I think he burned everything.'

'Damned if he did, Goldfinch. They're his insurance against going to jail.'

'You don't know what you're asking.' We stared at each other. He was the first to look away; he looked away because he could still see Jimmy Collins standing in the doorway of the Union Hotel with a camera while he pawed at the knickers of a twelve-year-old girl. It wasn't an image any man is likely to risk getting disseminated, if I can put it that way.

'You should be careful, Mr Smith. You have no idea the kind of people you're dealing with.'

'Let me worry about that.'

'I'm not worried on your account, believe me.'

'I can look after myself.'

'Five words that would look very good on your gravestone.' He stood up so fast he spilled the coffees. The oily brown liquid spread across the table and dripped onto the floor. I called after him, 'Thursday, same time.' He raised a hand quickly to let me know he had heard and then he was gone.

When I got back to my apartment I pulled up the third floor-board in the right-hand corner of my bedroom. In the floor space was a small locked metal box about six inches square. I unlocked it and took out a roll of film, the negatives that Jimmy Collins had given me. I took them into the kitchen, took out a pot and threw them in. I set fire to them with a lighter and let them burn.

It was a bluff from the first. If Goldfinch had had the balls to call me out, it would have been over. I don't stand in judgment on any man, even though the Goldfinches of the world make me sick to my stomach. It was just leverage, as my father would have said; actually destroying a man and his family was not something I wished on my conscience.

The melted film left a sticky mess in the bottom of the saucepan that no amount of cleaning would ever get out. I tossed it in the trash and poured myself a stiff rye, feeling cleaner now that the damned things couldn't hurt anyone any more.

Goldfinch would either call my bluff or I would finally have in my hand the first solid evidence that my Anastasia might really be a princess after all. Did I really want to know? For now I had Anastasia and a few stolen afternoons. Would anything Golfdfinch could tell me change that, make a future for me, for her?

ANASTASIA

Every Saturday morning we went to the synagogue, a family ritual rather than religious observance, and afterwards we took Rachel to Central Park. It was a bright and windy day and Felix helped Rachel launch a new kite, while Jemmy, her new spaniel puppy, jumped and barked at their heels.

I sat on a bench to watch them, Madam Rifkin beside me. There was a heavy silence between us, I knew there was something she wanted to say to me.

Finally: 'I should hate to see my son hurt.'

I felt my cheeks burn, could hear the blood pulsing in my ears. We give ourselves away in so many ways, even accomplished deceivers like myself.

'Why would anything hurt him?'

'He moves in a dangerous world, only money keeps us from the wolves. But sometimes even money isn't enough.' She rearranged the blanket about her knees. 'He loves you desperately, you know.'

This apparent non sequitur was not unrelated to what had gone before. I wondered if the old lady knew about Michael.

'As I love him,' I said.

Madam Rifkin smiled. 'Love never counts for anything, my dear. It's something you put less store in as you grow older.'

The kite was airborne now and Rachel was laughing as it whipped in the wind. Felix was steadying the string with one hand, encouraging her to take control.

'Such an easy life we have here,' Madam Rifkin sighed. 'We so quickly grow accustomed to ease that we forget that it is a privilege.'

The kite came down and Felix came puffing across the grass, Rachel squealing as he held her high in the air. He pretended to drop her and she giggled even louder. He was a good man in many ways, I thought. He does not deserve me.

Watching them together, I knew I could not tear them apart. Even though he knew she was not his in blood, he had devoted himself to her without reserve. He could be a dry and conservative man, but Rachel redeemed him.

'Pony ride!' Rachel demanded as soon as he put her down. He was sweating, his face florid, there were two rivulets of sweat coursing down his cheeks.

'You've worn your father out,' I scolded her.

'Just to the gates then,' Felix said, ignoring me as he hoisted Rachel on his shoulders and set off. It was odd to see this fleshy, round man in an expensive three-piece suit and yarmulke running along the footpath with a child perched upon his shoulders, taking staccato strides to imitate the gallop of a horse. Here was a man to whom appearance was everything; yet now he was oblivious of the promenaders who stared at him.

Madam Rifkin gave me a look. You see what you are doing? How can you do this to us?

I offered her a bland and innocent smile and followed

my daughter and her dutiful horse from the park. The way ahead was clear: live with crushing guilt or live with everlasting regret. These were the choices I had made for myself.

I was never naked with Felix. If we made love at all, it was in the dark, an anonymous coupling, uncomfortably resonant of my days as a taxi girl. I thought of Shanghai often these days. Perhaps the separation of time had made it possible for me to reflect without anguish. I could tell myself that I had changed, justify shame with the fact of my own survival.

And it was true, I had changed; in Shanghai I never experienced shame and guilt, as I did now; in Shanghai I would not kneel naked on a man's bed and let him stare at me, the way Michael does. I enjoy the way he looks at me, and I love looking at him. I know his body as intimately as I know my own; the small white scar above his left knee, sliced on a tin train when he was a child, a favourite toy from when he was a child; the small mulberry birthmark at the base of his spine; the long white scar on his belly where a surgeon removed his appendix when he was eight years old.

For the first time I take pleasure in seeing how my body can arouse a man. I have found an intimacy with Michael that I have never felt with Felix, that I had never thought possible with any man.

That other Anastasia is never spoken of. Beard was the pretext for my first visit, but Michael does not mention him any more. Perhaps he is as tired of chasing the Romanov ghosts as I.

He lay beside me on the bed, watching me. 'How can you stay with him?' he murmured.

'Don't ask for more than this. You know I can't.'

'Why not? How can you live with a man you don't love?'

'I only have an hour, Michael, let's not do this now.'

I leaned forward to kiss him but he drew away. 'I've been offered another job,' he said.

I had known it would come to this. Life doesn't let you tread water, sooner or later it demands that you swim for the shore, or it sucks you under. Living is about change, not standing still.

'BUP. British United Press,' he said. 'They want me to take over as head of their Far East desk in Shanghai. Good money. Well, it will be when I'm in China. Nine hundred sterling. Three times what I was making in Moscow with Reuters.'

'You can buy a lot of taxi girls with that.'

'I don't want a taxi girl. I want you. I want you to come with me.'

Without Rachel, it would have been simple. She was the reason I counted these stolen afternoons enough, knowing they were all I could have. To go with Michael to Shanghai, I would have to take her away from Felix or leave her behind in New York. One avenue seemed impossibly cruel; the other was simply impossible.

'I can't.'

'Because of Rachel.'

'Yes.'

'She is mine, remember?'

'No, she's not. You said it yourself. You put life in her, as I did, but you're not her father. Felix is the only father she's ever known. He adores that little girl.'

He looked away. 'I can't live like this. I can't stay here in New York. And I can't do this, stealing an afternoon here and there with another man's wife.'

'I'm sure you've done it before,' I said, which was needlessly vicious, but right at that moment I hated him for bringing this to an end.

'You know I'll only ever love you, don't you?' he said.

What could I say? I felt as if someone were squeezing me by the throat, and for a moment I couldn't speak.

'Nine hundred sterling, we could live like kings over there. What? Why are you smiling?'

'It doesn't matter what you earn,' I said.

'That's not been my experience. You come with a heavy price tag, princess.'

'Don't call me that. Anyway, I have my own money. I've been playing the stock market,' she said.

'Hasn't everyone?'

'I've been in the market for the last four years. I've enough put aside to keep me in furs and lace for a very long time. Do you know what grangers are?'

He shook his head.

'It's a railroad that serves the wheat belt. Have you heard of Seaboard Airlines?'

'They fly planes?'

'It's a railroad. These are things you should know if you're going to buy and sell in stock issues. I'm not the only woman in America doing this, Michael. More than a third of US Steel's stockholders are women.'

'What sort of money have you been making?'

'If I sold out of the market now I'd have one hundred and seventy three thousand, nine hundred and forty three dollars of my own money, pure profit, that Felix knows nothing about.'

I watched his expression, his face changing from disbelief to complete astonishment. I tried not to smile. I had been waiting for so long to tell someone.

'You used his money as start-up capital?'

'It's called leverage. In this case, an interest-free loan.'

He thought this over. 'What about Anastasia?'

'She doesn't exist any more. There's nothing she has that I need. Let's not talk any more. I have to go home soon.'

As I came out of the bathroom I found Michael staring out of the window, lost to private thoughts. I imagined him thinking of the future, weighing possibilities; he had always had his pick of women, could he ever be happy with just one?

In the story books I read to Rachel at bedtime the prince married the princess and they lived happily ever after. But that was a fairy tale and in fairy tales there is only one beautiful princess, only one handsome prince.

I could still have everything I wanted. I had played the stock market at least as well as my husband and if I sold out now we could continue in a very comfortable style indeed in Shanghai. I imagined a Tudor villa in the French concession, dinners at the Cathay Hotel, long nights making love on a four-poster mahogany bed as the monsoon rain beat on the roof.

Just a daydream: it could never be real.

I finished dressing. I went to the mirror and studied my reflection but Anastasia, liar, deceiver, sham, harlot and adulteress, was well disguised. All I saw was a rather well-dressed young lady of means with an elegant cloche and red-rimmed eyes.

'Will you come with me?' he said.

'I have to think about this.'

'You have to come.'

'If I didn't, would you stay?'

He shook his head. 'This time you have to come after me.'

I left and rode the creaking elevator down to the lobby and the mean streets of the Village. I didn't know it then, but it would be the last time I made that treacherous journey. Our lives were about to change for ever.

We began to dine out at night when Felix returned from work, it had become the fashionable thing to do. We danced among the palms at Sherry's alongside the Four Hundred, who treated us with the refined condescension reserved for new-money Jews and misplaced princesses. Or we went to the Russian Eagle to watch the stars and starlets of Broadway mingle with high society at the midnight hours.

This change in Felix was alarming. I was accustomed to a husband who thought of little else but work through the week, whose conversation rarely strayed from the price of a Westinghouse or General Motors share issue. In the five years I had known him, he had never stayed up later than ten o'clock except on a Saturday night, in case it made him late for work.

Lately his attitudes towards me had transformed. He was almost diffident in his manner, and eager to please. He seemed distracted when talking about his work. I was almost convinced now that he knew about Michael.

One night, as we dined on vichyssoise and sole at a supper club on Broadway, he said, 'There is something I wish to talk with you about.'

I felt myself flush to the roots of my hair, but I tried to stay composed. I held my breath and waited.

'I had a telephone call today from Lachter,' he said and I almost laughed with relief.

Lachter was in Germany, at Felix's expense, of course, pursuing the court case. God alone knew how much he had paid that shylock so far, and he had nothing to show for it.

'He thinks we're close. He believes a date will be set down for trial in less than twelve months.'

Lachter had been saying that for years, ever since Felix hired him.

I was suddenly seized with the impulse to say: Finish with this, Felix. Enough. Why could he not give up this obsession? But of course I knew why: should I ever be acknowledged as the real Anastasia, be recognised as titular head of the Romanov family, it would instantly elevate him to the ranks of the Four Hundred, would be the sweetest vengeance on all those who laughed behind his back and regarded him as nothing more than a new-money upstart Jew.

Anastasia was also the bond that tied me to him. In the past, whenever he sensed that I was slipping away from him, he would entice me back with promises of recognition and birthright. He seduced me with the Romanov legacy as unscrupulously as a young man plying a virgin with drink. And I had allowed it.

345

But there would be no court case, I was sure of that now. Should I ever go back to Germany, the file on the death of my former husband would immediately be reopened. The Duke of Hesse had made sure of that. I would probably be arrested the moment I set foot across the border.

For years Felix had assured me that he could take care of it. He said that after all this time, the case would be thrown out of court, that the evidence against me was circumstantial at best. But I was no longer prepared to take the risk.

Not for Anastasia. Not any more.

Tonight Felix offered me this latest news, this ephemeral hope of vindication, as a bright and shining lie, tissue-wrapped, and the look on his face was of a new and hopeful lover. I could not hurt him. 'Thank you,' I said, and offered him a smile.

'I am going to make you a princess,' he said and held my hand and beamed at me.

And in that moment I was sure of it. He knew about Michael.

MICHAEL

I looked at my watch. Goldfinch was an hour late, he wouldn't be coming now. I pushed a spoon around my cup of coffee, the milk curdled on the surface like oil on the East River. I never wanted to drink it anyway.

So, that was it. He'd called my bluff. There was nowhere to go from here, since I had never intended to blackmail him. Once again, the mystery of Anastasia had eluded me. I paid the check and left.

Looking back on it now, I wonder what I was thinking.

I must have thought that truth and justice would protect me, make me invisible. I was proposing to bring down a scandal not only on the head of one of the big players on Wall Street, but on the whole British government and I thought I could walk through it unscathed. The truth was, I had no protection at all. Even my editor didn't know about Goldfinch, since I was unwilling to blacken my own soul by compromising Beard's assistant.

There had to be a reckoning.

Autumn in the air, the city cool and golden at last. The street vendors were selling hot pretzels and the ice carts were joined by coal wagons in the poorer neighbourhoods. It was also the start of the new social season and there were limousines queued outside the smart hotels up and down Fifth Avenue.

I was on my way home, people were out on the street, strolling, laughing, talking. I had no premonition. Crowds were already queuing for tickets for *The Singing Fool*, Al Jolson's next picture after the runaway success of *The Jazz Singer*. It was the first full-length talking picture to come out of Hollywood. Everywhere you went someone was whistling or singing 'Sonny Boy'.

I turned off Broadway, head down, my hands in my pockets. I was thinking about Anastasia, there was barely a minute of the day I didn't think about her. I couldn't stay in New York; I couldn't leave without her. BUP were pressing me for an answer on the Shanghai job. I had to make up my mind.

To this day I have no idea where they came from, if they were waiting in a car or in a doorway down the street. I can't admit to being scared; I think my first reaction was one of disbelief. I think perhaps I even laughed, it seemed just so unreal.

Two men, both holding baseball bats.

The shock of terrible pain takes your breath away. It's so bad you don't think you can breathe. You can't think, you can't do anything. Your body tries to escape it, which is why you see people writhe when they are in agony. It doesn't do any good but pain makes all reason and objectivity useless.

They didn't go for the head, which is a smaller and more difficult target to hit. Besides, they were professionals and whoever paid for this didn't want me dead. One hit me across the back, breaking ribs, the other went for my shin, breaking my leg instantly and incapacitating me, putting me down on the sidewalk.

The beating seemed to go on for ever, but it must have lasted less than a couple of minutes or I'd be dead. I remember trying to crawl away from them, which they enjoyed, because they stalked me, laughing. I heard a cry, it didn't sound much like a human being, but I guess it must have been me. Then they were standing over me and I knew they were going to hit me again and there was nothing I could do to stop it.

The next blow hit me across the back again, and my head was filled with an explosion of bright white light. The pain was so bad, so dramatic, that it was like an electric shock going through my body. I became an animal, clawing at the air. I remember hearing one of them laugh and I wondered what sort of man would take pleasure in something like this. Then I saw, or perhaps just imagined, the bat being raised again but I didn't feel it when it hit my head. Everything went black and it was all over.

ANASTASIA

When I got to the hospital the first person I saw was Sophie. She had always been elegant and flighty, a good-time girl, who would carelessly toss things aside, both men and empty glasses, and expect the servants or her brother to clear up after her. I never thought she gave a damn for anything beside Lanvin gowns and Manhattan cocktails. Now here she stood in the corridor, her face streaked with mascara, looking as if she had just emerged from a train wreck.

It didn't make sense to me then, it still doesn't. She didn't love him that much. I doubt if she loved him at all, except out of spite for me. But I could have been wrong.

'Well,' she said, when she saw me. 'I hope you're satisfied.'

There was nothing, conceivably nothing, I could say to that.

'Is he all right?'

'You won't even recognise him,' she said, and there was both triumph and horror in her voice. All that was left for her now was to see me crumple, and she could leave.

But I did not fall apart, it was too soon to feel anything. Instead I reached for Sophie, but she backed away from me.

When I heard what had happened I had rushed to the hospital, had needed to see for myself how badly he was hurt. Now, strangely, I wanted to delay that terrible moment for as long as I could.

'What happened, Sophie?' I said.

She wouldn't tell me.

Michael's father came out of one of the rooms further down the corridor, preceded by a phalanx of flunkeys and bodyguards. Even the two policemen waiting in the corridor saluted the silver-haired man in the Burberry overcoat.

I ran towards him. He knew Felix, of course; knew me, his wife. We'd mixed socially, as the saying goes. 'What are you doing here?' he said.

I think he knew, he was an intelligent man, had worked it out already. Another man's wife running white-faced down a hospital corridor to his son's bedside, you didn't have to be a Wall Street genius to figure it out.

I looked over his shoulder, a body lying on the bed, a nurse leaning over the mess of bandages, taking a pulse. Sophie was right, I didn't recognise him; his head looked like a pulped watermelon, twice its normal size, swathed in bandages, one leg in a plaster cast, the right arm as well.

That couldn't be Michael.

'What the hell are you doing here?' Sheridan repeated.

'Is he going to be all right?'

'Does he look all right to you?'

I went into the room. Michael turned towards me, one eye was swollen shut. He was awake, at least. I waited for him to say something. But there was not a sign of recognition. Nothing at all.

When I returned to our apartment later that evening, Felix was already waiting in the drawing room, reading the *Wall Street Journal*, his slippered feet propped comfortably on a stool, a glass of whisky on the table by his armchair. A table lamp threw a pool of yellow light over his newspaper. He seemed so calm. That was worse, much worse, than if he had ranted and screamed.

'How is he?' he said.

'You heard what happened?'

He returned to his newspaper. It was a performance; he must have learned a lot from me. I wondered what he was really feeling. 'I wonder what he got mixed up in?' he said.

I went to the icebox, chipped some ice from the top compartment, and dropped the shards in a crystal tumbler. I poured two fingers of whisky into the glass from the decanter. I drank it down quickly, like a draught of medicine. It burned going down, tasted vile, best single malt and it all tasted like drain water to me.

Felix raised an eyebrow.

'Is he all right?'

'He has a fractured skull, fractured jaw, and his right knee and shinbone are shattered. He also has a broken arm and he may lose the sight of his right eye. They broke ten of his ribs.'

Felix seemed unimpressed by this litany of trauma. 'I'm surprised you aren't still over there sitting vigil,' he said.

350

He was right, all I could think at that moment was: Please God, don't let Michael die. I'll do anything you want, but don't let him die.

'You still love him, don't you?'

'I love you, Felix.'

'If only that were true.'

I went out of the room thinking he would follow but he didn't. We were both lost to reflection, dazzled, I suppose, by the byzantine, bloody rewards of choice. No doubt he hoped Michael would die and that would solve all his problems. But he was wrong. His real problem was just a few days away and I don't think he ever saw it coming.

MICHAEL

Floating to the surface again from the warmth of a roseate and embracing gelatin world. It was like waking from a beautiful dream, and I struggled against it. There was no pain in that other place. The drugs they gave me, I suppose.

But now the spider web of dreams released me. I saw shapes in a white room. Someone leaned over me, I could smell the acrid taint of disinfectant on their clothes. They gave me a sip of water. I tried to remember where I was, how I had got here.

I must have drifted back to sleep again because the next thing I remember was the old man leaning over the bed. I recall the camel hair coat and immaculate grey hair and Sulka tie, and I thought I was dead, for he looked for all the world like God, or perhaps, as is more likely, the Devil.

I couldn't talk. I didn't know it but the doctors had wired my jaw together. My right eye was closed shut which was perhaps why everything was blurred. The morphine kept

351

the worst of the pain at bay, at least for now. That would change.

'Tell me who did this to you,' he whispered. 'Tell me who did this and I'll make them curse their mothers for giving them life.'

These were his first tender words. I thought: Did what to me? I couldn't remember anything. I didn't know who I was or where I lived. I don't remember Anastasia coming to visit me, or my brother and mother. I didn't recognise them. Unlike Anastasia, my memory came back after a couple of days, though it took much longer to finally piece together what happened that afternoon in that backstreet off Broadway.

As for the pain, morphine got me through, and still does some days, which is why I'm partial to a little opium. After a lifetime steeped in vice, bad habits get to become second nature rather than a choice.

The old man started in on me again several days later, when it was clear I wasn't going to take up an option in the family plot on Long Island. I was still eating lunch through a tube, but at least I could remember my own name, two times out of three.

'Tell me who did this thing to you,' he said.

What could I say to him? It could have been Beard. I thought about the big Irishman with fists like hams who had paid me a visit at my apartment in the Village. Now there was a boy who could swing a baseball bat.

But I couldn't be sure.

I remember Sophie coming to see me, just once. When she saw me, she had to be physically supported by one of the nurses. I could tell by the way she screamed and collapsed almost to her knees that I wasn't looking too good.

I didn't make much sense of anything she said. Perhaps she was distraught. But afterwards it seemed to me her reaction was out of proportion to her own feelings for me. Sometimes I still wonder if it was guilt rather than shock. Did she tell her brother about Anastasia and me, out of sheer spite? Was it Felix, not Beard, who paid for the beating?

I guess I'll never know.

I saw Anastasia just twice more. The first time was just before I was discharged from the hospital. I was sitting up in bed by then, managing solids providing it was pulped first, some ice-cream, stewed apple. Baby food.

Anastasia appeared like a vision, in ermine and pearls, bands of diamond bracelets around both wrists. She sniffed daintily at the hospital smells, disinfectant and the faintly perceptible aroma of old man's piss. She had brought me flowers and fruit. I didn't have use for either.

'You look just awful,' she said.

'There I was, thinking I was getting better.'

'Your face is the colour of prunes and custard. You look like a bashed lobster.'

'Thanks.'

She looked around with such disdain you'd think she had spent her whole life in supper clubs, that I had never had to pick her out of a Chinese river.

'A private room.'

'The old man paid for it.'

'I thought that was against your principles.'

'I had concussion, for Christ's sake.'

She sighed as if that was the sorriest excuse she had ever heard in her life. I watched her face, wondered what was going on behind those luminous blue eyes. There was no clue.

'Come with me to Shanghai.'

'I can't.'

'Why the hell not?'

'Perhaps before,' she said, and I realised that her refusal that afternoon in my apartment had not been as categorical as I had thought. 'But I can't, not now. Felix is in a lot of trouble, Michael. He needs me.'

'I need you.'

She smiled at that. 'No, you don't.'

I could not imagine losing her, not now. It made me

vicious. 'So what are you going to do, princess? I'm going to lose you again, aren't I?'

'What would you have me do?'

'I would have you say yes, I'll come with you to China and I'll bring your daughter with me.'

'I can't do that to him.'

'Why not?' he said. 'You did it to me.'

'Rachel didn't know you then.'

'What difference does that make?'

She reached out to take my hand but I snatched it away.

'I can't do it a second time, Michael. I can't do to him what I did to you.'

'Why? What's changed?'

'I have,' she said.

I stared at the ceiling, white flaking plaster, the clatter of a lunch trolley from down the corridor, someone crying softly in the waiting room. I could not believe that I would finally lose her.

'Michael, you'll get on with your life. You always do. Just think of all those taxi girls.'

'Just go.'

'You could always stay in New York.'

'And then what?'

'I can still be your mistress.'

'Better to make a fool of your husband than be honest with him?'

'Better he loses something he never had than the only thing he really loves.'

'I can't stay here, Anna. That's it.'

'You don't have to go to Shanghai. You're doing the same thing you accused me of in London. Putting ambition above the things you love.'

'If I stay here, how long before Felix finds out?'

'I think he already knows. But finding out is different from kicking me out. He won't do that.'

'You seem very sure about that.'

'He loves me, Michael. I can't hurt him, and I can't hurt Rachel.' She stood up. 'When you get to Shanghai you'll thank God for a lucky escape. One day you'll forget about me.'

'What about you? Will you forget me?'

She stopped at the door. 'Of course I will,' she said.

I stared at the empty, milk-white corridor. I thought about

what she had just said. She had always been an accomplished liar. I wanted to think she was lying again.

I spent the next few weeks in a wheelchair. The old man took me in, Mother just about begged me to let her nurse me back to health. For a while she would have her little boy back again, helpless and needy, just the way she wanted.

They couldn't give me my old room back because it was at the top of the stairs, so they emptied out one of the down-stairs parlours and put me in there. I had servants bring me my meals on trays, had someone to do my laundry, pay my bills, make my bed. All I had to do was get up in the morning and remember to breathe.

I was sitting in the drawing room, watching the day close on Fifth Avenue, thought I'd amuse myself by counting the horse-drawn carriages among the cars roaring and honking in the street. I had sat there for half an hour and I hadn't seen one horse, just the twentieth century bustling on here in old New York.

One of the maids brought me a lemonade, and set it down on the table next to my chair. The servants evidently had orders to make the prodigal son realise what he had been missing, and there was a constant flow of iced lemonades and turkey sandwiches and enquiries after my health and require-ments. I sat there, surfeit, reading the new Hemingway novel, wondering if this was what my dotage would be like. I was crazy to get out of that chair and out of that house. My leg itched under the plaster cast.

That afternoon my father came home early from work and appeared in the parlour, threw himself down in one of the wing-backed chairs. He was wearing a smoking jacket and a sour expression. I readied myself for a conversation of some weight, for he was no master of small talk. He didn't seem to know how to say whatever was on his mind – unlike him – so he picked up the *New York Times* and started to read.

I could feel the tension. Finally, he tossed the newspaper onto the floor. 'You remember Goldfinch?' he said.

'Of course I remember Goldfinch.'

'Well, I hope you're satisfied.'

'Satisfied?'

'While you were in the hospital, the police fished his body out of the East River. Suicide, or so the police say.'

A horse clattered by in the street outside, tossing its blinkered head, a black Ford tooting its horn in frustration behind it, voices raised, angry. The first one since I'd been sitting there. I thought about the horse because I didn't want to think about Goldfinch, about his widow and his two fatherless daughters.

'Well, say something,' the old man snapped.

'What would you like me to say?'

'Something, godammit. You're responsible, after a measure. And so am I.'

And I suppose, in a way, we were, though I was far more culpable than him. But that's not something you can work out straightaway. Guilt takes time to eat its way in, like rust.

'How do you know about this?'

'It was in the papers. They say he threw himself off the Brooklyn Bridge. Must have hit the girders on the way down. Face was a mess.'

'Christ.'

'I shouldn't have let you do this.'

'Do what?'

'Son, you were in deeper than you could handle. You really don't understand this town at all, do you?'

He didn't think it was suicide either. But I would never know the truth of that. It was possible to pulp your face by jumping off the bridge, but not very likely.

'I hope this has taught you a lesson,' he said and stalked out of the room.

I sat there, watching the golden afternoon fade to evening. Motes of dust floated on the air, illuminated by the rays of sun angled through the high windows. There were no more horses on the avenue.

Leonard Goldfinch showed up just on dusk, sat himself down in the same chair as the old man, and berated me for my role in his death. He had a young girl with him. It may have been his daughter, or perhaps my concussed brain had conjured a child prostitute as salve for my conscience. He told me that I was to blame, and that it had achieved nothing. The Czar's money was gone, back into the hands of the wealthy and the corrupt, where it belonged, so what had I hoped to achieve? He told me I was a fool, which I knew already, and he told me he was pushed off the bridge, that he did not jump. But he may have just been saying that to make me feel better.

For my part I told him I hadn't meant to hurt him, but he didn't seem to care about that and I suppose he was right. Good intentions don't mean a thing. Things either turn out right or they don't.

ANASTASIA

I remember it as if it was yesterday. It was Friday, the fourth of October, and the headline of the *New York Times* screamed:

> YEAR'S WORST BREAK
> HITS STOCK MARKET
> Trading of 1,500,000
> Shares in Final Hour
> Swamps the Whole List
> STEEL DROPS 10 POINTS

For over a month, all anyone wanted to talk about was the stock market. It kept falling and recovering. The city, the whole country held its breath.

It's easy to look back now and wonder why people behaved as they did; easy to judge when you already know how things are going to turn out.

357

Soon after Michael came out of hospital, US Steel declined to two hundred and nine. But if you'd had the money back then, you would still have put it on any major stock issue before you put it on him. They looked a better bet for a full recovery, I'm told.

But that's why historians always appear so smug. They already know the winners and losers.

It started on the Monday.

Felix didn't come home that night, had already rung me that morning to say it looked like being a bad day and he would be sleeping at the office. That afternoon I listened to the news broadcasts on the radio. Prices started to plummet just after noon; Otis Elevators dropped forty-three dollars a share, Westinghouse thirty-five. Radio Corporation fell from one hundred and fourteen to forty-five. Panic had set in.

Police riot squads assembled on Wall Street. I heard Thomas Lamont, JP Morgan's senior partner, over the crackle of the radio and the hum of the crowd around him: 'There has been a little distress selling on the Stock Exchange.' he said. He added that he thought the market was technically sound, that it was merely undergoing a period of adjustment.

The radio commentator was less restrained. He breathlessly reported long queues outside customer rooms in every brokerage house and bank on the Street. He shouted into his microphone that President Hoover was about to act, that Raskob and Miller had plans to salvage the situation, that the market was in pandemonium, the trading floor ankle-deep in ticker tape.

By evening the crisis was over. The big operators had kept their nerve and maintained their margins instead of selling out. The market had responded to the organised buying support from JP Morgan. It was going to be all right. The morning losses of six billion had been halved during the afternoon. The worst was over.

I thought about the Revolution that had taken place in my own country just twelve years before. The world, it seemed, was for ever a heartbeat away from chaos, all our lives held in such a fragile gossamer web.

I did not see Felix until Wednesday morning. He didn't get home from the office until after midnight. It wasn't yet six o'clock and he was already dressed to go back to work. I stood in the middle of the bedroom in my night-dress, while he manoeuvred around me, fetching his wristwatch from the bedside table, his tie from the dresser. There were dark pouches under his eyes. He looked exhausted.

'Is this something we should be worried about?' I asked him.

He gave me a tired smile. 'Of course not.'

'If the market keeps falling . . .'

'The market will recover.'

'But if we are caught . . .'

'Look, you don't know the first thing about the market! We're holding a lot of stock on margin and if I sell now I'm going to lose a fortune. We'll have nothing left! The market is all about nerve. That's how the big money's made. I don't intend to lose my nerve now.'

He went out. I tossed the morning newspaper on the bed. Then, in sudden rage, I threw it into the corner of the room. I couldn't stand to look at it.

For once, I wasn't worried for me. I was worried only for Rachel.

I wondered if it was better than being bored.

MICHAEL

My father didn't say anything to me as we drove down-town. He remained perennially remote, and now, with the experience of a few years, I understood why. Everything he had ever needed, respect, power, ease, a beautiful wife, he had obtained with money. It had never been necessary for him to ask for anything except the price. His had been a life lived by negotiation. It was why he didn't know how to deal with me.

We stopped outside a brownstone on 14th and Fifth. Davis parked the Packard behind a red Renault and hurried to open the door for us. The old man climbed out first and I followed him into the building. We rode the elevator in silence to the second floor. As we got out he took a set of keys from his pocket and opened the door to one of the apartments.

He waited as I looked around. He seemed uncharacteristi-cally nervous.

There was a bedroom, a large living room, a kitchen and dining room. There were fireplaces in the bedroom and the living room, Turkish carpets on all the floors. There was a cut-glass crystal chandelier in the dining room.

'What is this?' I asked him.

'It's yours, if you want it.'

'I have somewhere to live.'

'That shithole,' he said, and I blinked, for I only rarely heard my father say a word that could not be repeated in mixed company.

'You're trying to buy me out.'

A thunderous expression, the same bullying tactic he used everywhere. 'I am trying,' he said, between his teeth, 'to convince you that there is no need to live like a pauper the rest of your life.'

'Not like a pauper. I live like most other people. I don't live like you.'

'This is yours. No strings attached. I won't have you living like a Polack.'

I smiled, despite myself. His bigotry was so naked and unaffected, it was almost endearing.

'You don't have to work for the firm, like your brother, but I fail to see what is wrong with having money, respect and a place in modern America.'

When I didn't answer him, he said, 'Did you see the sports car downstairs, the Renault?'

I nodded. 'Is that mine, too?'

'It's a gift. Take it or leave it.'

'Thanks,' I said.

'You'll take it?'

'No, I'll leave it.'

'For God's sake, why? I'm making no demands on you, Michael, but for my sake, for your mother's sake, at least let us do something for you!'

It gave me no pleasure to hear him beg like this. I was astonished by it, but not pleased. Besides, it was not true, there were strings attached. Not right then, of course, but in time there would be. I didn't want anything I had not earned. And if my chosen profession did not pay as well as his, well, that was my problem, not his.

'Thanks, but I'm fine.'

'You're a sunnavabitch,' he said, and stormed out. I took one last look around. There was a moment's regret, I admit. But to me a birthright is something you get for what someone else has done. My self-respect was a small and humble thing, but I'd worked at it for years and it was a possession I was not about to throw carelessly away. I shut the door to the apartment, locked it, and went back downstairs to join my father, who waited fuming in his car.

The next day they took the cast off my leg, I handed back the crutches and emerged on the street with just a walking stick. The limp was bad, the doctors said it would improve, but I would always need the cane. The rest of my body had mended just fine, but not my knee. That would be my New York souvenir.

Davis drove me home in the Packard and the first thing I did was pack my bags and call a cab. My mother couldn't understand it, not that I was moving out but that I wouldn't let Davis drive me to the Village. I could feel the sticky webs of my family binding me in its prickly embrace. While I'd been sitting in my chair I'd done my thinking, made my decisions.

It was time to get on with my life. It was not a good time to start. While I was sitting in my wheelchair, America's runaway economy had derailed.

It was the first time I had been to Felix's apartment on the Upper East Side. A maid let me in and I waited in the foyer, looking around at the fashionable Egyptian statuary, the Syrie Maugham-inspired chrome and glass, the white and gold telephone on the hallstand. I could see through the arched doorway into the drawing room, copies of *Vanity Fair* and *Vogue* scattered around the couch like discarded underwear. Sophie and Madam Rifkin peered out at me, astonished, before Anastasia appeared and quickly drew the doors shut.

'Michael.'

'Anna.'

'What are you doing here?'

Here we are again, I thought, with so much to say and no words to bridge the gulf between us. How many times had we played this scene before?

Even now, I wasn't sure I was doing the right thing. I had lain awake all night, running through it in my mind, my own devil's advocate. I knew this would not be easy, and now I just wanted it done.

'You really shouldn't have come here.'

'I've come to say goodbye.'

She closed her eyes. 'Oh.' I watched, fascinated, as a single tear tracked a course down her cheek. Then her eyes blinked open again. 'You're okay?'

'Well, as you can see, I'm a scratching from the Olympic long-distance team. But I'll live.'

I watched her take inventory; the scar over my right eye, an angry pink cicatrice, and my nose, which had become even more, well, interesting, than it was before. And the cane, of course; people's attention was always drawn to the cane.

'A well lived-in body,' I said and smiled.

'What are you going to do?'

'I've taken that job in Shanghai. What about you?'

She looked towards the drawing room, where her in-laws no doubt had their ears pressed hard against the door. She gave a shrug that meant that she was staying.

'I'm sure you'll survive,' I said to her, wondering at the contempt in my voice and not liking myself for it.

'I love you.' She mouthed the words silently, so they could not hear her.

I didn't want to hear it either. What good is someone loving you from the other side of the world? No use to me whatsoever.

I had to be free of this.

She went to the hallway mirror, took out a handkerchief and tried to salvage her make-up, dabbing at the black smudges under her eyes. I stood behind her and our eyes met in the glass.

'Do you see Anastasia Romanov in there?' I said.

'Sometimes.'

'Tell me something, who was she anyway? Some spoiled little Russian princess that you recreated. Was she really worth bringing back to life? What if I'd kept you my secret in Shanghai? What if you'd never known all this?'

I was close enough to smell her perfume. Giving her up would be like cutting away part of my own body. She had been a part of my life for so long; even the five years we lived apart, she was always on my mind, had given every day its shape, its point of reference.

Just as I was leaving, she said, 'But what will I do without you?' She whispered it so softly I barely heard her.

I stopped at the door. 'I don't know,' I said.

ANASTASIA

I had always thought I would find a way to change his mind, or he would find a way to change mine. When I heard the door click shut behind him I had to fight down the urge to run after him and bring him back. I knew I had done the right thing, the hard thing. I could not say I wept; there were no tears left for all the mistakes I had made. If I would have wept at all, it was for the terrible decision I made five years ago, when I let him go. This was the postscript.

And so, this was the way it finished.

A week later, Felix came home early. It was the first time in our five years of marriage that Felix got home before six o'clock on a weekday.

I had been sitting alone all day, listening to the wireless reports. One of the foremost blue chip stocks, US Steel, had gone through the two hundred barrier. It was the largest drop in prices ever recorded on any day at the Exchange.

As the shadows lengthened in the room I listened to the latest bulletins from Wall Street. In a rising voice the reporter described the Street as an armed camp, four hundred policemen had been rushed in to keep order. He said he had just come from the Exchange and had seen brokers with sweat running in rivers down their faces and their shirts torn to shreds, looking, he said, as if they had been in a bar room brawl. The ticker tape and torn order pads once more littered the floor ankle-deep.

The market was collapsing again.

It was then that I looked up from the radio and saw Felix standing in the doorway, and the thing that frightened me was how normal he looked, except for his eyes which were focused not on the room, and not on me, but on something far in the distance; the future perhaps, black and unpromising as it now was.

He set his briefcase down by the door and shrugged off his coat before the maid could reach him. It fell in a heap on the carpet. He walked into the drawing room, went to the drinks cabinet and poured a large whisky. His hands were shaking and the glass clinked against the bottle as he poured.

I waited for him to say something. Instead he went to the window and stared at the shadows falling over the park.

'Felix?'

'We're finished,' he said. 'We've lost everything. We don't even have enough to pay off the leverage. There's absolutely nothing left.'

I felt nothing, nothing at all. For a time there had been a way out for me, and now it was gone.

Felix went on, relentlessly. 'The market has crashed. It's wiped us out and from this moment the only things I possess are mountainous debts. We'll have to sell the car and the apartment, and the servants will have to go, of course.'

'Is there no hope?'

'None.'

A curious thing: I remember thinking, well, we'll just have to start all over again. Ten years ago I was a taxi girl in Shanghai. I survived then, I'll survive again now. Perhaps this belief that I was her, that I was Anastasia, had made me strong. I was a survivor; and what survivors do is survive.

We stood there, twelve floors up, looking over Manhattan, at the darkening silhouettes of the trees in Central Park, at the lights winking on in the towers of this monstrous city. Our little drama was being played out everywhere in Manhattan that night.

It was different for Felix. It was his father who had spirited him and his mother out of Russia. This was his first trial and he did not have the strength for it. 'I lost two million dollars today,' he said. 'I owe close to three.'

It was time to tell him about my forays into the stock market. I guessed that he would be angry, for he considered money and business a male preserve. I had not told him before, it was a symbol of my independence, physical and emotional, my ace in the hole.

But I knew I must tell him now. I had calculated my profits in a little red book I kept in a secret drawer in my bureau. They would not be nearly enough to pay off the debts, but it might see us through this, after bankruptcy. I had taken some heavy losses, too, but I had sold out of the market two weeks before, so that I might still be free to go to Shanghai if I changed my mind. I had lost nearly one hundred thousand dollars on margin calls; my brokers had advised me to stay in the market, to keep my nerve, as Felix was always saying.

They did not understand that the game I was playing had nothing to do with leverage and margin calls.

It would hurt him, to know that I had succeeded where he had failed. But it would also prove something to Sophie and to his mother. I would finally have a place in this family. I would not be their grasping little refugee, the waif out for all she could get.

'Come inside, Felix. There's something I have to tell you.'

'I think I'll just stay out here for a while,' he said. 'You go in, if you like. I won't be a moment.'

It was cool and I went to fetch a jumper. When I came out again he was gone and a crowd was forming around his body in the street.

The funeral had been paid for. Felix was always careful in that way; it was why he had the courage to jump. It was the one thing he still had financial backing for.

There was a long line of black Hispano-Suizas outside the cemetery gates, Felix's friends. Most of the cars were for sale now; they had little tickets in their windows with a price.

It must seem a strange thing to say, but the funeral was a particularly grim affair. The atmosphere at Felix's burial was not one of loss, but of fear. His former friends and associates stood at the graveside in their long black overcoats, and what I read on their faces was: I'm next. Soon after, two of them took the same way out as Felix.

Afterwards I walked slowly with Madam Rifkin along the sad pathway between the graves. She looked frail and bent in black veil and gloves. Grief has a way of breaking the old, very quickly. Thinking that her son had left her not only bereft, but impoverished, only added to her despair.

Perhaps it was why she chose that moment to say the things she did. She had been left with nothing; she wanted me similarly bereft. I suppose it seemed only fair.

'What will you do now?'

'I don't know.'

'Life without money is no life at all. Is it?'

'I'll find a way to survive.'

'Of course you will,' she said, as if she had just bitten down on a lemon. 'But you'll have to drop the case in Germany, won't you?'

Anastasia, ephemeral creature that she was, would remain as elusive as ever. That was only right. It was Felix who had kept her flame alive, after all.

'I have something to tell you,' she said as we reached the gates.

I waited, and God forgive her, she said what she did as I was supporting her on my arm.

'Felix told you he was certain you were Anastasia.'

'It was the first thing he said to me.'

She looked up at me, the watery blue eyes glittered with triumph. She would get even with me for cuckolding her son. 'It was the first thing he said to the other three girls.'

'What other three girls?'

367

She sighed. 'I don't know if you're Anastasia or not. I never met her. But Felix did, when he was a boy. And there were three girls before you, one in Paris, and two right here in New York and he was sure each of them was her. He could never accept she was dead. She was the first girl he ever loved, but he never told her then, he wouldn't have dared. It was only her death that made her attainable. Do you see? You were a little lost princess and he was going to save you. Little Felix Rifkin.' She shook her head. 'He was my son and I loved him. But he was always such a sad little boy.'

I would have been less shocked if she had slapped my face. She had just read the eulogy for Anastasia Romanov.

I wanted to hit her. I have never felt such an intense hatred for anyone as I did for that old woman right then. But instead of striking out, I stood there, holding her upright, and said to her: 'Who were these other girls?'

'Just waifs like you with fair hair and blue eyes. The first one belonged in a lunatic asylum, which is where I think she ended up. The other two were just little Russian Jewesses with ideas above their station. But they all had families that could be traced or memories that proved them false and eventually I proved them liars, all three of them. But you were clever. You pretended to have no memory at all and so what could we do? Still, I suppose Felix got what he wanted in the end. He had his princess and he was happy. I'll give you that, you made him happy for a while.'

Rachel was crying, wanted to go home. Maggie, her nanny, had her by the hand; it was a kindness, she knew we couldn't pay her but she came to the funeral anyway to take care of little Rachel. A final service to us. An act of charity.

'Shush, Rachel!' I hissed and the sharpness in my voice, of course, just made her cry the more.

The fabric of my incarnation seared and burned. Michael had been right all along. Anastasia Romanov had died that night in a rain of bullets, her skull crushed by the rifle butts of her guards. I was just an invention of little Felix Rifkin as he reached to catch the hand of greatness.

'I'm sorry, but truth is best,' the spiteful old woman said. I helped her into the Hispano-Suiza and climbed in after her. I held Rachel on my lap as we drove slowly through the cemetery gates. It started to rain, a cold November day in 1929. I then possessed just ten years of memory and I was still no closer to discovering what had happened to the rest of my life.

My heels echo on the parquet timber floors of this vast drawing room. A bargain hunter can pick up an apartment like ours, on the Upper East Side with views to Central Park, for a fraction of what it would have cost a month ago. An Hispano-Suiza thrown in. Who has the money to pay for these things any more? Bootleggers and gangsters.

The furniture has been sold off to pay creditors, all that remains is a gilt mirror on the wall, an Egyptian-inspired lamp, a few packing crates. Madam Rifkin is gone, packed off to live with a cousin on the Lower East Side. Sophie, too. What will become of her? Her mother told her she might have to find work and she turned pale and almost fainted.

Even with sizeable losses, I had thirty-eight thousand dollars in cash, not a bad sum when you could pick up a Rolls Royce in the street for a little over one hundred. It would be enough to ensure Madam Rifkin was well cared for in her old age.

There are only ghosts left in the apartment and soon they will be gone, too. I believe ghosts live in people's memories, they have no affinity for places.

My ghosts will be with me always.

MICHAEL

My window looked out over the grey-tiled Chinese roofs with curlicued eaves. It was the start of the typhoon season, and the drumming of rain on the roof all but drowned out the sound of the abacus from the shop across the street. Grey sheets of water poured into the gutters. I heard the boom of horns from a Blue Funnel steamer as it docked near the Bund.

I watched the rain for a while and then moved listlessly about the rooms, the lonely curator of my memories. I alone could choose which objects were precious, which were for display, which were to be left to gather dust in the darkened storeroom below the stairs. I walked with the ghosts through my private museum; here, the curve of her breast; here, the twist of her smile; and see, over there, the time we walked in Hyde Park and watched the ducks troop across the path to the pond and laughed at them; here, the night we made love on the bed and reached the moment together.

On into the evening I walked those echoing halls alone, examining each small treasure, dissecting each particular nuance of misery, like a critic, a connoisseur of pain. Finally I reached my star exhibit; here, preserved under glass, the memory of the way she looked at me that night in the taxi club, when I invented her for myself that first time. Perfect symmetry, every woman in one, the sheath dress and mysterious smile and blood-red lipstick; I looked and wondered at the way she walked, from the hips, straight-armed and languorous, into my life.

What was there left? A few monochrome photographs of Piccadilly Circus and Belgravia Square pasted into an old album.

As for the others: I never found out what happened to Beard. He was hit hard by the stock market fall that year and then returned to Europe, they said. Or was it South America? I never heard of him again.

The old man took some heavy hits but he was still

standing, of course, like JP Morgan and the rest. They had had their wealth slashed overnight but they would keep the mansions and the cars and the servants. Old money would always triumph over new.

Felix was one of the unlucky ones, the Johnny-come-latelies hit hardest by the Crash, as they were calling it. I heard he did the concrete cha-cha a week after I left New York. The fire department had to hose down the sidewalk and more of Felix Rifkin ended up in the drains than in the cemetery. Poor bastard.

Mackie had laid his hands on some letters written by one of the Czar's cousins and had passed them on to me. How he got his hands on them I never knew.

> 'Oh, Anastasia! Olga and Tatiana, now, they were so serene, so responsible. Tall and stately, they would have made fine princesses. And Marie, a gentle and happy child, she was always smiling. And then there was Anastasia. What a wicked little child. And so unlike her sisters! She was always a little dumpy but she went completely to fat in her teenage years. And such an embarrassment to the rest of us!'

It didn't sound like my Anastasia at all.

> 'Anastasia was a little devil. No-one ever disciplined her. That mother of hers spent all her time praying and sitting with her "Baby", which is what she called Alexei, and closeted with that madman priest. The children just ran wild, did as they pleased. Anastasia was a bully, if she didn't get her own way she kicked and scratched and pulled your hair. There wasn't a kind bone in her body. In my opinion, the world's better off without her.'

My Anastasia wasn't the Czar's daughter, I'm sure of that. But it does not matter any more. I got free of her in the end, whoever she was. Except for thinking about her all the time, I am free.

Everyone wants a princess in their life, and I had mine. I don't know if that was a good thing or bad. It's for you to decide.

ANASTASIA

Junks with brown sails glide past on the current. Rain dimples the brown water, sampans drift in and out of the mist. I can smell Shanghai even before the Bund comes into view. My life has come around full circle.

I grip Rachel's hand and feel the answering pressure. She does not understand what has happened. Even now I do not know if I can ever really explain it to her.

I wonder what he will say when I find him. He is out there, somewhere in that grey, foreign city. Today, tomorrow, I will knock on some red-enamelled door and his Chinese servant will run to fetch him. He will see me standing in the rain with his daughter, our luggage piled beside us on the kerb. I wonder what he will do.

I have travelled a long journey and done things that do not make me proud. But I have survived and I think tomorrow will be better for me.

My name is Anastasia Romanov and I am coming home.

Aztec

Sold into slavery to the Spanish adventurer Cortés as a child, the life of the Aztec princess Malinali is one of the most enduring legends of Mexico. The daughter of a prophet, her role in history still divides opinion today. Reviled by some as a traitor responsible for the destruction of the native people and worshipped by others as a heroine and symbolic mother of the nation, her extraordinary and passionate story has never before been so evocatively told.

Colin Falconer brings all the glory and spectacle of the legendary Aztec empire to life in blazing colour as he traces the destiny of the enigmatic Malinali who rose from being the mere slave of the conquistador to his translator – and ultimately his lover. Contradictory, fiercely intelligent and sensuous, Malinali soon transcended her role as consort and found herself implicitly involved in Cortés' plans to overthrow the Aztecs and conquer Mexico.

This is the story of a beautiful, intelligent and intriguing woman who made her indelible mark in a world dominated by men – and inspired a legend.

When We Were Gods

He left her alone in the inky darkness of the future, and even from the moment of his final breath she could hear the slithering of cold bodies and the baring of fangs . . .

Arrestingly beautiful and fiercely intelligent, Cleopatra VII of Egypt was barely more than a teenager when she inherited the richest empire in the world – one that stretched from the scorching deserts of upper Egypt to the shining Mediterranean metropolis of Alexandria, with its famed libraries, storehouses and treasuries. Imperilled at every turn by court conspiracies and Roman treachery, Cleopatra brazenly sought a partnership with the only man who could secure Egypt's safety: Julius Caesar, a wily politician and battle-hardened general with a weakness for women. The result was a passionate love affair that scandalised Rome and thrust Cleopatra into the glittering but deadly world of imperial intrigue and warfare – a world that she mesmerised and manipulated even after Caesar was gone.

Colin Falconer's bold, sensuous prose takes the reader inside the walls of Alexandria's great palaces and into Cleopatra's very heart, creating a vivid portrait of an unforgettable woman who thrived and triumphed in a world ruled by men. This is the story of a legendary woman's most glorious time, a story that blazes through thousands of years of history to capture the imagination of readers today.